THERE'S NO
TURNING BACK

ALSO BY ALBA DE CÉSPEDES

Forbidden Notebook
(1952; 2023)

Her Side of the Story
(1949; 2023)

THERE'S NO TURNING BACK

A Novel

ALBA DE CÉSPEDES

TRANSLATED BY ANN GOLDSTEIN

**WASHINGTON
SQUARE PRESS**

ATRIA

New York   Amsterdam/Antwerp   London   Toronto   Sydney   New Delhi

WASHINGTON SQUARE PRESS

ATRIA

An Imprint of Simon & Schuster, LLC
1230 Avenue of the Americas
New York, NY 10020

This Washington Square Press/Atria Books hardcover edition February 2025

WASHINGTON SQUARE PRESS / ATRIA BOOKS and colophon are trademarks of Simon & Schuster, LLC

For information about special discounts for bulk purchases, please contact Simon & Schuster Special Sales at 1-866-506-1949 or business@simonandschuster.com.

The Simon & Schuster Speakers Bureau can bring authors to your live event. For more information, or to book an event, contact the Simon & Schuster Speakers Bureau at 1-866-248-3049 or visit our website at www.simonspeakers.com.

Interior design by Jill Putorti

Manufactured in the United States of America

1 3 5 7 9 10 8 6 4 2

Library of Congress Cataloging-in-Publication Data has been applied for.

ISBN 978-1-6680-8363-5
ISBN 978-1-6680-8365-9 (ebook)

TRANSLATOR'S NOTE

Alba de Céspedes's *There's No Turning Back* was published in 1938. She had previously published story collections, a book of poems, and a short novel, and had written for various newspapers and journals. Arnoldo Mondadori, the publisher of *There's No Turning Back*, had decided to launch the book with an extensive publicity campaign, directed at critics, often personally solicited; at foreign publishers, appealed to by a list of translations in progress; and, finally, at the public of readers, with posters and flyers, window displays, and other advertising initiatives, including a van carrying a billboard on its roof. In a letter to the critic Pietro Pancrazi, Mondadori wrote:

> *Recently I published* There's No Turning Back, *[a] novel by a very young writer, Alba de Céspedes, in whom I think I've found an exceptional artistic temperament. I launched this novel with means I've rarely used for young writers, and the welcome of public and critics so far has been what I hoped for. The first edition sold out in a week, and the first judgments have been passionately favorable.*

There's No Turning Back follows eight young women living in a convent–boarding house in Rome, most of whom are studying at the university. They come from different backgrounds, have different desires and goals, and make different choices, yet they are united in the task of finding their way in the world. "It's as if we're on a bridge," one of the girls says. "We've already departed from one side and haven't yet reached the other. What we've left behind we don't look back at. What awaits us is still enveloped in fog. We don't know what we'll find when the fog clears."

The story, which covers the period from the autumn of 1934 to the summer of 1936, is told in the third person from eight points of view, switching back and forth among the eight young women. De Céspedes is remarkably skillful at maintaining the consistency and individuality of the different voices as she keeps the narrative going. (Besides the eight young women, one of the nuns, in a briefer role, presents yet another version of a woman's choice.)

By the time the novel was published, the fascist dictator Benito Mussolini had been in power for more than a decade. His government promoted the idea that the proper place of women was to be at home and to bear children: *sposa e madre esemplare* (exemplary wife and mother). While there is no overt mention of Mussolini or Fascism in the novel (apart from a reference to "the Party" and to the war in Ethiopia), none of the young women conform to this female ideal. In fact, in their different ways they are challenging it, even if not intentionally or even consciously. In 1935 de Céspedes herself was arrested and briefly jailed for "antifascism."

The book was immediately and immensely popular, but, not surprisingly, the authorities found the novel's breaking of female stereotypes and suggestion of other possible pathways for women offensive. "Who can forget having been master of herself?" another of the young women says. "In our villages . . . those who remained, who passed from the father's authority to the husband's, can't forgive us for having had the key to our own room, going out and coming in when we want."

In 1939, the novel was to win the prestigious Viareggio Prize, but the honor was immediately canceled by an order to the jury from the government. In January of 1940, when *There's No Turning Back* was already in its twentieth printing, the Ministry of Popular Culture blocked further editions, claiming that it went against "fascist morality." (The publisher got around this ban by continuing to reprint the book and simply calling each reprinting the twentieth.) The ban also affected *Fuga* (Flight), a collection of stories de Céspedes published in 1940. The following year, the censors rejected a screenplay based on the novel, labeling it "depressing" and "immoral." Rewritten to focus on the more cheerful ("serene and optimistic") characters, it was accepted, and the film came out in 1945. (Ultimately, one character was eliminated entirely and another given a more conventional ending.)

De Céspedes revised the text of *There's No Turning Back* frequently, most heavily between 1948 and 1952, and again in 1966. The last version is the text on which this translation is based. An earlier published English translation, of 1941, was based on the original 1938 text, and, as the scholar Sandra Carletti points out in her 1996 dissertation on the novel, was marred by numerous mistakes and inaccuracies. De Céspedes's interventions were stylistic, linguistic, and structural; in all her revisions, she was, the Italian academic Marina Zancan notes in her commentary on the text in the Meridiani volume of de Céspedes's novels, aiming at an *alleggerimento*, lightening, or *snellimento*, streamlining, of the text.

In all her novels de Céspedes investigates women's attempts to both deconstruct and construct their lives and gain a sense of themselves, as she investigated her own life. In *Her Side of the Story* (1949), a woman who thinks her marriage to an antifascist professor will be a way out of the oppressive patriarchal system she has grown up in is violently disappointed; in *Forbidden Notebook* (1952), a woman who, in the aftermath of the war, and amid slowly changing conceptions of women's roles (and possibilities), decides to keep a diary grapples with her own self-awareness. *There's*

No Turning Back could be seen as a kind of laboratory for de Céspedes (though her women never become "types") as she explores the ways in which women go out into the world and the choices and hardships they face. And, even if the world has changed, her characters' struggles with becoming themselves continue to be familiar.

Ann Goldstein, New York, 2024

I

As the nun read the last words of the evening prayer, an indolent chorus of girls responded: "Amen." Silence followed, veined with impatience. Some of the girls stared, transfixed, at the lighted tapers on the altar, others turned toward the back of the chapel, waiting for a sign from the Mother Superior to release them. Eager to leave, they didn't even talk to one another. Soon afterward they filed out, two by two; in a compact column, they crossed the wide hall, where daylight lingered on the opaque glass of the front door.

They were grown-up girls, dressed in a variety of ways; near the stairs, as if at another signal, they threw off their veils and relaxed. Suddenly, the silence became a dense chatter; subdued laughter grew gradually more open and bold.

They talked about the university, the professors, some exchanged whispered confidences. One of the nuns, clapping her hands lightly, said: "That's enough, girls, enough, go to your rooms." She was the only sister the girls didn't dare talk back to. Besides, she wasn't a sister like the others; tall, slender, and still young, she had a melodious voice, slim white hands. When she spoke, the girls stopped to think, and, involuntarily, obeyed.

Right away they started up the stairs; only Vinca delayed, asking as she did every evening: "May I use the phone, Sister Lorenza?"

Her closest friends turned to hear what would happen; Valentina pulled her by the sleeve so hard she staggered.

"It's late tonight, Vinca; you'll call tomorrow morning."

"But I . . ."

"Tomorrow morning, I said. Now go to sleep or to study. Good night."

Gathering around, her friends snickered: "Bad luck, you failed."

"She does it because she's angry," Vinca replied, "because she's shut up in here. It doesn't matter: I'm sleepy, I'm going to bed."

"I'm tired, too," said Augusta. She was at least thirty, the oldest of the students at the Grimaldi: tall but heavy, her curly black hair cut like a mop. She said good night to the nuns, took Vinca by the arm, and they set off.

At the same time a plump blonde moved quickly among the girls, whispering to some of them: "We're meeting in 63."

These gave brief, wary nods. Then they faded into the shadows of the long corridors and disappeared into their rooms.

Room 63 smelled of stuffed dried figs; they were sent to Silvia from Calabria in large baskets that she put on top of the wardrobe: anyone who wanted some could climb up on a chair and fish around in the basket. Silvia, lying on the bed, seemed to be asleep. Ever since she arrived at the Grimaldi, three years ago now, she had worn mourning. She had dull black braids wrapped around her head, an olive complexion, and dark, slightly squinting eyes under heavy lids that shone as if they'd been oiled.

Because of the black garments hanging on the walls, mourning clothed the room as well; the girls often gathered there after dinner to study. Really they would have liked to go to bed, to sleep: overcoming that desire took an effort. Only Xenia was always awake. She decreed: "Let's go," and the others didn't dare refuse.

The lamp hung low over the table where Valentina was reading, numbed by the cold; it was mid-November, and the weather seemed to predict a frigid winter. Putting down the book, she turned toward the bed and asked: "Are you asleep, Silvia?"

"No. I'm thinking."

"You were sleeping . . ."

"No. I was thinking how tomorrow in my village there's a big celebration: my mother makes a raisin cake, a big log burns in the hearth, and the cousins come to our house to eat."

"Do you wish you were there?"

"No." Then she added, uncertain: "That is, I don't know. Tomorrow, yes. For a few days, maybe. But then I would feel remorseful about all of you and what I have to do. There's no time to waste."

"You're right," Xenia agreed. "Some nights a kind of yearning grips me: I can't close my eyes and I get worn out thinking how I'm caged in this cloister of nuns, while outside life is flowing, fortune passing by—who knows?—and I can't take advantage of it. You have to jump into life headlong, grab it by the throat. I won't ever go back to Veroli, anyway."

She was interrupted by Anna, who came in saying: "Did you see what a moon there is tonight, girls?" She went to the window and opened it. "Augusta's gone to bed, Vinca couldn't call. I don't know what I wouldn't give to know Spanish and understand what she says to Luis every night."

"What do you think she says?" replied Xenia. "The same things we all say."

"Or don't say to anyone," Valentina specified.

"Isn't Milly coming? And the new girl in 28?"

"I don't know," said Valentina. "I told them."

"Milly's tired, she says she's going to bed, then she'll read till late. The new girl said she'll come, but maybe she'll do what she did last night."

"I don't understand what she's doing here," Silvia observed from the bed. "She doesn't even have a book. She wants to study art history, she said—we'll see, she knows French, English . . . In other words the educa-

tion of people who know nothing. But she's not an ordinary girl. She an-
noys me because she forced herself on us."

"That's not true."

"It is true. She's the only one we invited to join our group as soon as
she arrived. When she sat at the table, in the refectory, it was you, Xenia,
who immediately said to her, 'Stay with us in literature.'"

"Are you sorry?"

"No, but . . ."

"That's enough," Anna concluded. "Let's enjoy the moon." And before
the others could respond she turned off the light.

Through the window, half covered by the shutter, a flood of light
poured onto the floor. Valentina, sitting at the table, was struck by it and
rose suddenly.

"With this moon," Silvia said, "everyone in my village will go out and
sing." Because of the shutter, they could see only a narrow rectangle of sky
beyond the thick brown treetops of Villa Borghese.

"There are people out walking at this hour," Valentina said softly.

"Yes, free people," Xenia added.

They were still in the dark when Emanuela entered, and at first she
didn't recognize them; in fact, thinking she'd gone to the wrong room, she
said, "Oh! . . . excuse me," and was about to leave.

But Xenia called her back: "Come in, come in, it's us. We were looking
at the moon—you can turn on the light if you want."

Emanuela stood, silent in the shadowy light. Walking through the
halls, she, too, had felt a desire to look out; but the big windows were
barred and locked.

"What did you come here for?" Silvia asked.

Emanuela was puzzled for a moment, not knowing if the words were
addressed to her, but the silence of the others made her certain. Resentfully she answered: "Xenia invited me, and Valentina said I should come
up to 63. I'll leave immediately."

"Silly! I meant what are you staying here at the residence for?"

"What about you?"

"I'm studying. But you can live without doing anything, so why didn't you stay home instead of coming here to eat cabbage soup?"

Emanuela, as if apologizing, said: "I couldn't." And, feeling that they were all waiting for further explanations, she added: "My parents are traveling. In America."

"In America?" Xenia observed. "They have a lot of money."

"Now I'm starting to understand," said Silvia.

"In America . . ." Valentina repeated, looking at the window, where the curtain was swelling in the night breeze.

Hearing the sister's voice, they all stirred. They turned on the light, closed the shutters. A voice made monotonous by habit was passing through the halls, crying, "Lights! . . . Lights! . . ." Prolonging the 'i' like a lament.

Anna moved the chairs, bringing them closer to the table. Valentina took an oil lamp from a shelf that held a little of everything.

"What are you doing?" Emanuela asked her.

"Didn't you hear? She said 'Lights.'"

"Why?"

"Well, you're on the first floor, like Milly; you pay more, but they don't turn off the electricity. After ten, if we want to study we have to arrange things like this. In a moment this floor will be dark."

"And the halls?"

"Those, too."

"Why in the world?"

"Because light costs money and the nuns are stingy."

"Misers," Xenia specified.

Emanuela asked: "How will I get downstairs?"

"You'll learn to walk like us: groping your way. Or we'll lend you a candle," Xenia answered. "Now we're going to study. You take a book, too; wait, I'll choose something suitable. Here, take this: poets of the dolce stil novo. Okay? But sit and pretend to be studying, otherwise she'll send you to your room."

"Who?"

Before Xenia could answer, the door flew open as if pushed by a gust of wind. A small nun appeared in the doorway; she was thin and pale, and wore thick lenses that magnified her lashless eyes. The girls began to laugh mockingly: "Sister Prudenzina! Sister Prudenzina!" She examined the room carefully, trying to discover something unusual, or guilty—she even looked under the bed—all without moving, her hand on the door-knob. Emanuela reminded herself that, days before, when she arrived at the residence, that same sister had said to her: "Take that stuff off your mouth," referring to her lipstick.

"What are you doing up here?" the sister asked her. "I'm turning off the lights here: go to your room."

"No, Emanuela's staying with us, she has to study. Go, go on, Sister Prudenzina, guardian of the night. You know what we call you? The light in the fist."

While the others laughed, Xenia went to the door to harass her. "Turn the lights off, go on: tonight we have the oil lamp, tomorrow, if we don't have enough money, we'll have candles. But we'll go out . . ."

Silvia interrupted her: "Quiet, Xenia, tonight we're rich, there's the moon."

"Yes, there's the moon. You can't turn that out, right, Sister Pruden-zina? Go on, try to turn off the moon, too."

The sister went on staring at them harshly. "You naughty girls," she said in a good-humored tone, and left.

Emanuela, astonished, turned to Xenia: "Are you crazy? You're not in prison! Why did you do that?"

"Because she's a witch. When I first arrived, I sometimes didn't have money for a candle. To you it may seem impossible, but I didn't have even that. And she never offered me so much as a stub."

Outside they could hear the cry: "Lights!" The "i" was longer than usual. Then darkness invaded the room, until the oil lamp shed its generous glow on the table, on the books.

Anna said to Xenia: "Calm down now, in a few days you'll be done: think about preparing, instead."

Emanuela found her book open to a sonnet by Guido Guinizelli. She had no desire to read. "I wonder why she gave me this particular book . . ." she thought. She observed Xenia, and the others, who were already studying, backs straight, and lowered her eyes to the book so they would think that she, too, was studying. She would like Silvia to believe her. From time to time she looked at her furtively: but Silvia was sleeping, her body a black patch on the white bedspread.

. . . .

Every night Emanuela resolved, "I won't go up," afraid of returning to her room alone. She had never dared ask for a candle: the others wandered like sleepwalkers in the darkness of the halls, the stairs. They avoided the corners out of habit, they knew by heart how many steps there were between one floor and the next, and they went up and down counting them: one, two, three, four . . .

And yet, when the time came, she joined her new friends, who gathered in one room or another: all the rooms the same, except for their smell. First they talked and smoked, although it was forbidden, then they studied. Now Emanuela, too, studied every night.

But when she left, after a tranquil "Good night," she was plunged into darkness. The blood burned her veins, causing a surge of damp heat to rise to her neck, her ears. She started walking only because she worried that her friends would open the door and find her still there, stunned by fear. She walked lightly, so that her footsteps wouldn't raise an echo between the high walls. "Hall to the right, hall to the left; and if a dead man should appear? Here are the stairs, one, two, three, four . . . and if, suddenly, a cold hand rested on my shoulder? Here's the landing, foot forward cautiously, here's the new flight of stairs, one, two, three, four . . ." She held her arm out in front of her to be sure that nothing was coming toward her, trapping her. Then, seized by the fear that her hand would meet a slimy, cold body, she immediately pulled it back. She stopped, eyes wide in the shadows. She felt a cry of horror rising from all her flesh, and her throat turned dry, suffocating her. Her heart seemed to be bursting in her chest. To help herself she tried persuasion: "I've done nothing wrong, nothing wrong." Then she remembered the lie, that terrible lie. She should have talked to the girls, said: "'I'm not what you think, I'm betraying your trust. Do you know who I really am? Do you know the story of Stefano? I've told you a pack of lies.' I'm part of their group, I know everything about them—and with the others they're so reticent—while they know nothing about me. On my birthday, there was a big bouquet of flowers in my room: they hid behind the door to witness my surprise. Then they came in with a big to-do, kissed me. They love me, but whom do they love? Who am I, really? Yet I'm not doing anything wrong, nothing wrong."

In this certainty she began walking again; but, entering the last hallway, she always seemed to hear a footstep or a creak. Flattened against the wall, she didn't dare go on to her room. "Certainly I'll find him there, white as a ghost, and he'll grab me, strangle me."

She calmed down only after closing the door of her room behind her and turning on the light: she saw the nightgown laid out on the bed, the books, the photographs. Her forehead still damp with sweat, she said to herself: "What an idiot. Spirits don't exist. Milly's sleeping on the other side of the wall."

Milly was studying music. She had a heart ailment, and she sat in a chair to study. Sometimes she didn't come down to the refectory. "She's not well," the nuns said, shaking their heads.

One day Emanuela heard the full, slow sound of the harmonium rising from the courtyard. The girls were all out: some at the university, some at the library. She had stayed in her room, lying on the bed thinking. It couldn't be a sister: it wasn't sacred music, it was a lied. Surprised, she looked out into the courtyard, red with Virginia creeper, and saw two windows open in the sacristy. Soon afterward she went down to the chapel. No one. Finally, venturing behind the altar, she saw Milly sitting at the organ: she recognized the long blond braids on her shoulders. They were neighbors but had never exchanged a word.

Hearing her, Milly turned suddenly, startled.

"Don't stop," Emanuela said.

The other, her face red, asked: "You're the one in 28, right?" And, to let her know that she, in turn, had overheard her, she added: "Last night you were crying." Then, signaling her to come closer, she resumed playing.

Now, waking, Emanuela would knock on the wall, and Milly, who had been studying for a while, was quick to knock in response. Milly had always kept to herself; but now she sought out Emanuela, inviting her in: she told her about herself and the reason she had left Milan, where she lived with her father.

"I was in love with the sound of the organ I could hear at the vespers service in San Babila. One night I got up, left the pew, as if I were going to confess: instead I went up a little wooden staircase and found myself in the organ loft. Have you ever been up there? The music is deafening. The organist was gray, all gray, and he wore black glasses. A blind man. But I had seen his hands! So every night I sat next to him while below the people sang. Then they left, the lights went out. Going down, he placed his hand on my shoulder."

She was staring into space, and, because her eyes were very light, she, too, appeared blind. "One morning in May we went to the Giardini Reali. Do you know Milan? The Giardini? You should go: there's a pond with a small temple and immense trees all around. They say that Foscolo went walking there. My companion saw nothing, but I told him: 'Now the sky is all pink' or 'It's dark now.' As soon as Papa found out about our meetings, he made me come to Rome. But I'm not unhappy here: I can play the harmonium and write to him with that device there, which is all holes, in the braille alphabet, made just for blind people. By now I can write well, and he reads my letters by running his fingers over them, like this, see?" She touched Emanuela's fingers lightly with her own.

That night Milly was in her chair, studying; and, seeing Emanuela enter panting, close the door, and lean against it, exhausted, she asked apprehensively:

"What's wrong?"

"I'm scared in these halls at night. I'm afraid there's someone waiting for me in my room and I don't have the courage to go in. Sorry, I'm a little unnerved." She sat down on the rug in front of Milly and looked at the open book she was holding. "What are you studying?"

"Harmony. Listen, Emanuela, give up going there at night."

"I can't," Emanuela answered.

She rested her head against Milly's knees and, letting her caress her forehead, her ears, her hair, she calmed down. In her own room she was gripped by memories: letters locked in the drawers, photographs, clothes reminded her of past days and events. Her recent friendships, instead, attributed to her another personality that she wore like a new dress.

"I can't do without it," she repeated. "I feel shut up, imprisoned, I don't know how to explain, I can't take it anymore."

"It's like that for everyone at first: there's no air. For me it was different: I was used to living submissively. You don't know my father and it would take too long to tell you. I breathe better here, even shut in. But you . . . You shouldn't spend so much time alone in your room. Go out, go with your friends to the university, go for a walk. I'd go with you, but I'm not well yet. You should go out with Xenia; or with Vinca, who takes everything easily. If instead of coming to me you went to Vinca's room, you wouldn't cry." But Emanuela shook her head: no one could help her, not even Vinca.

. . . .

Every night Vinca talked on the phone, while Sister Lorenza walked impatiently up and down in front of her, so that she would understand she mustn't linger. But Vinca, just to annoy her, sat serenely, smoothing her skirt over her knees. She talked in a leisurely manner, smiling, and staring at the sister with indifference: she challenged her, almost, protected by her foreign speech. Finally, when she saw her reach the peak of exasperation, her voice assumed a tone of farewell, and she stood up and said in Italian: "See you tomorrow." Hanging up the phone, she added contritely: "Thank you, Sister Lorenza," and left.

She spent the next day, until the hour of her date, getting ready. She went into her friends' rooms, her hair loose, wearing slippers and an old bathrobe, tweezers in one hand and mirror in the other. Every so often while she chatted, she'd twist her mouth, smoothing her forehead, and, *zing!*, pull out an eyebrow hair, then resume the conversation. She wasn't beautiful, but she had beautiful shiny, curly brown hair, a full mouth, and small sharp teeth.

As soon as she got out the door and past the entrance, she put on some lipstick and freshened the pink of her cheeks. Luis was waiting for her nearby; he took her arm and they set off.

They were both Andalusian, from Cordova, but they had met in Rome. Luis was studying architecture. They talked for hours about their country, and the very fact of speaking Spanish consoled them for being so far away.

Sometimes Luis proposed: "Shall we go to the movies?" He always chose a neighborhood cinema that wasn't crowded in the afternoon. Vinca followed him, annoyed; it seemed to her that everyone must know they went there to kiss. During the intermissions they'd separate conspicuously; she looked in the mirror, powdered her face. And, coming out, in a daze, she would resolve: "I'm not going anymore." They walked apart, as if they were strangers. He'd light a cigarette, sing softly under his breath.

In this way they would reach the neighborhood of the Grimaldi; the cars passed by them silently, people observed them. Finally, at the moment of parting, they'd stop in front of a store selling statues, cold and deserted as a museum. Vinca waited for something to reassure her, a word from Luis or a look, but he appeared lost in thought. She had to ask: "When will we see each other?" hoping he'd promise, "Tomorrow." His answer was invariable: "Call me." Then he'd go off, hands in his pockets, smoking. Vinca remained standing in front of the door, watching him go. Meanwhile she thought: "It was worth the trouble to be so late because of him!" And, imagining the harsh reproaches of the nuns, she felt an angry irritation with Luis. Yet she continued to follow him with her gaze until he had turned the corner into the square.

· · · ·

Meet in 40.

A room under the terrace, sweltering in summer, cold in these early days of November: through the window came the smell of the leaves fallen from the trees in Villa Borghese. But it was the only room that actually felt lived in: maybe because Augusta had been living there for three years already, and loved her home. She had brought from Sardinia a red and white striped rug. In her village in winter, she said, the servants made rugs with wool from the goats; they'd also made the bedspread and the doily on the nightstand. The table was in the middle of the room, under a lamp with a green shade. When Augusta sat down to study, her large bosom occupied the space that remained between the piles of books.

She, too, was studying literature, but she was six years late with her exams.

On the floor, a turtle Augusta had baptized Margherita moved clumsily. In winter, it hid under the night table and stayed there, in hibernation, as if dead, embalmed. Already its movements had become a little lazier. "It's sleepy," Augusta explained, as if she were speaking of a child. She polished the shell with a feather dipped in brilliantine, then, holding it out to her friends, said: "Smell it? It's perfumed now." But few could overcome their disgust and touch it. Augusta then put it back on the floor: "Go on, go, poor Margherita."

It was already late when the girls went up to her room; the lights were out. She was writing; but she rose ceremoniously to welcome them, and they dropped boisterously onto the bed as if it were a swing. Silvia sat cross-legged on the floor, on the rug.

"How nice it would be if this room were a big kitchen!" Silvia exclaimed. "Chestnuts on the fire and an old servant telling stories. Ours knows terrible tales of bandits. Really, it's a pity there are no more bandits: no more adventures. If I'd lived at that time, I would have wanted to marry one."

Augusta shook her head: "You talk about marriage too lightly."

Valentina started to say that they wasted all their evenings in amusement and gossip, without achieving anything.

"You're right."

And Augusta proposed: "Tomorrow night we could have a séance. We often did it, at home. You take a three-legged table, we all put our hands on it, the table knocks. Every knock is a letter."

"But it's forbidden by religion!" Anna broke in.

"A lot of things are forbidden," Vinca objected.

Augusta decided: "Tomorrow night, then."

But Valentina rebelled again. "I'm not coming. And you, Emanuela? You're not afraid?"

Emanuela, after a brief hesitation, answered: "No."

Now she, too, moved securely in the dark of the hallways and stairs; studying had given her the conviction that her life was similar to that of the others, that the past, buried in her, had vanished. And this conviction expressed itself in her appearance as well: like the others, she wore low heels, modest dresses, and, living as she had at eighteen, she appeared to be eighteen.

Silvia observed thoughtfully: "How much longer will we be together? A year, two years. At least if we all left here on the same day, if we didn't feel the void left by the one who departs as a death . . . We're together from morning to night now. And in a few years maybe you won't even remember my name."

"Not possible," said Emanuela.

"Very possible," Augusta replied. "We've chosen one another from among many, out of a certain sympathy. But it's only intimacy, daily habit, that binds us. Last year a girl left and got married. Someone who shared every hour with us: she didn't even send a postcard. And yet she'd promised that . . ."

"Getting married is something else," Valentina added. "It's crossing to another shore. What does she have in common with us anymore?"

Silvia said: "I'll never get married."

"And the bandit?"

"Precisely—there aren't any more bandits," she concluded, laughing.

The door opened softly, and Xenia entered. Valentina asked: "Where were you? I looked for you everywhere, your room was locked."

Xenia didn't answer: she was pale and her eyes were wide, red. It was clear she'd been crying.

"Xenia, what's wrong?" her friends asked. "Why don't you answer?"

Finally she explained in a lifeless voice: "I defended my thesis today. It didn't go well."

"Your thesis?!" Silvia said. "But weren't you supposed to defend it the day after tomorrow?"

"I lied to you. I didn't want you to come, I was afraid; I didn't want to go back to the classroom with you to find out the result. A disaster. You won't forgive me, right, Silvia?"

"It's not that. We would have wanted to be with you," Silvia said. "What we can't forgive is the lie."

Impulsively Emanuela rushed to hug Xenia.

"Forgive you! With what right? Under what guise? But what did your parents say?"

"What do you think they said? I have to go home," Xenia answered, and added, crying: "I'll never go back, never, I'd rather kill myself!"

"Xenia!" Anna exclaimed.

The others said: "Sit down, calm down, there must be some recourse, they'll let you stay till March."

Xenia shook her head: "It's impossible, they don't have any money, not a cent. In order for me to study my father mortgaged the vineyard. 'Well worth it!' they'll say in the village, and laugh. But I'm not going back, I won't give them the satisfaction." She started crying again. "I did as much as I could. In the morning when you were sleeping I got up at the nuns' first bell . . . You should have seen Trecca today, caressing his mustache: 'We'll expect you back in March, Signorina Costantini.' I didn't make it: I wouldn't at the next sessions, either." Sobs choked her. "I have to go. I can't stay even one more day: my parents have eaten potatoes all year to support me here. It's my own fault," and she hit her forehead with the palm of her hand: "My own, mine . . ." Then, recovering herself, she murmured: "Forgive me. I've disturbed you. What were you doing? Studying, right?"

In that question there was so much regret that Augusta answered: "No, we were chatting. Take my chair, sit here with us."

Xenia refused politely: "No, I'm sorry, I don't want to chat; I just came up to give you this great news. I'm better now, I'm going back to my room."

"Alone?" Emanuela observed. "I'll come with you."

"No, please, Emanuela: I need to be alone." And she added: "Don't worry, I'm not going to jump out the window. I thought about it: I'm a coward. I'm going to sleep. But maybe now that I can sleep till noon I won't sleep."

With a wave she said goodbye to all: her face was barely visible outside the circle of lamplight. They all felt they ought to go with her, comfort her, and yet they didn't know what to say. They sat there thinking, "I'll go, I won't go," each waiting for another to move. During that uncertainty, Xenia had opened the door and disappeared.

· · · ·

Until then, none of them had thought their thesis could fail. The next day they were all depressed; in Belluzzi's class they didn't even sit together; they met on the way out. Emanuela, seeing them, exclaimed cheerfully, "Look what I got!" and held out a note. They all read it: some on the steps of the university, others at the gate, and they advised her: "You should go."

Silvia said: "Don't torture her. She should do what she wants."

And Anna: "You're right; I'm just saying that Lanziani is an intelligent person, serious, who's never fooled around with anyone."

Walking, Emanuela was almost pushed by the others, who pressed close around her. She was unsure. "I don't know what I'll do," she said. "Why should I go?"

"But you want to, confess you want to."

"What's the harm?" Vinca insisted. "He's not a stranger. He's our friend, he's a colleague—whenever you came to class the two of you talked."

The appointment was for the following evening, at six, at the fountain of Moses, on the Pincio: Emanuela would have liked to go, arriving late to make the young man worry a little, let him fear she wouldn't come. Then she'd appear, fresh in the gray dress, the new one. Augusta always said: "The essential thing in life is to expect something."

They returned to the Grimaldi chatting and laughing; their entrance animated the gray refectory, where, through the large windows, a bleak courtyard was visible, decorated with stiff bamboo and dusty palms. Many were already at the table: the subdued sound of voices could be heard, the clatter of silverware: at the back of the refectory Sister Lorenza waited to serve.

The friends sat down laughing, not at all intimidated by being late or by the sister's severe gaze. They unfolded their napkins, poured the water, the wine, talking loudly.

At Emanuela's place a letter was leaning against the glass: she immediately recognized her father's crabbed handwriting. She looked around to see if her friends had noticed the postmark, but they were distracted, telling Augusta about the note from Lanziani:

"Emanuela doesn't want to go, what do you think . . ."

Meanwhile, she opened the letter and, after glancing at it, quickly closed it again. Her friends mustn't know that her father was in Florence: Papa's in America, he'll be back in the spring.

Valentina asked her: "Well, did you decide, Emanuela?"

"Yes: I'm not going."

Augusta asked her: "Let me read the letter."

"Which one?"

"What do you mean which one? The one from Lanziani, no?"

Emanuela handed it to her and afterward, unobserved, reopened the one from her father and reread it. It said: "Sunday, if you want, you can go and see the child."

. . . .

On Sundays the girls awakened early, as always, and instinctively started to jump out of bed. Then they thought: "It's a holiday." But the very day when they could have lingered, idled, habit took over, compelling them to get up.

One by one the windows opened, the girls looked out, called to one another, coming up with a plan for the day even before washing their faces.

Augusta, instead, on Sunday mornings went out early and bought flowers for her room and lettuce for Margherita, then changed the doilies on the furniture and dusted the books. A sensible girl, said the nuns; her friends thought that by now—she was no longer very young, she wasn't going to succeed in her studies—she could become a nun herself. When they said that, in fun, Augusta responded: "I have other things in mind."

Emanuela was lazy: she ignored the voices calling her insistently. Then she went sleepily to the window. "What are you doing today?" they asked.

"Whatever you are. What shall we do?"

Bewildered by that day of obligatory vacation, they didn't know how to enjoy themselves in a city where all they were acquainted with was study. Emanuela decided: "Let's go to the zoo." Or: "Let's go to the movies. I'll pay."

But that Sunday she said: "Today I'm busy."

"Did you get another note from Lanziani?"

"Oh! No, a relative."

Xenia, filing her nails, said: "If you wanted to, you should have gone."

Emanuela talked purposely about other things; but the day before she had followed in her mind the young man waiting at the fountain of Moses: at first he'd be distracted watching the children play with their boats in the pond; then he would have started looking at his watch, frequently, ever more frequently; finally he would have gone home—wherever he lived— and that evening he probably turned unhappily to his studies.

"It's always Sunday for me now," Xenia observed. She was calm: on awakening they'd heard her singing.

The first bell sounded: they all withdrew with quick waves of farewell and from the rooms came the sound of water and pitchers.

Soon afterward, hair combed, fresh-scented, they came blithely down the stairs, drawn by the smell of *caffellatte* and fresh bread: an irresistible morning fragrance, particular to residences and schools, that, once those years had passed, they would never again know. They poured into the refectory, sat before the white bowls, broke the crusty bread.

All except Anna. On Sunday mornings she left early, caught the tram, and went to the old neighborhoods where there were markets. That was her vacation. Tired of books, she listened to the simple street conversations, but was humiliated by feeling she was a foreigner. She bought chestnuts roasted on the coals and lingered, talking to the seller. Then she slipped the chestnuts into her coat pocket and went to eat them looking over the parapet of the Tiber.

The river flowed, slow as yellow mud, between bare, narrow shores. Anna nibbled on the chestnuts, absorbed in her thoughts. One more year, then she would return to her village; she would deliver her degree to her parents and at last resume the life she preferred: going around the farm, talking to the farmers, cultivating the vegetable garden, the flowers.

Thus dreaming, she didn't notice the passing of time. At noon a great clangor of bells roused her: the market was winding down, the city enveloped in Sunday boredom. Anna rummaged in her coat pocket—not a single chestnut left, too bad—and slowly, along the old narrow streets, she returned to the residence.

That Sunday, coming in, she found her friends plotting. Silvia was saying: "Tonight. In Vinca's room." But Vinca was opposed: "I don't have a three-legged table anyway. And then if the spirit is in my room, how do I get him out? When the spirit possesses the table, he takes refuge in the house and you have to call those women who know the magic words to persuade him to leave."

"That's in Spain," said Augusta. "But here . . . Anyway, tonight we'll have the séance. No matter what."

Xenia repeated, "Tonight," thoughtful. Then she turned to Emanuela and asked her: "You're going out today, right?"

"Yes. Why?"

"Oh, nothing, I was just wondering."

Anna offered, conciliatory: "You could come to my room." And the girls parted ways, saying: "In 58, then, at Anna's."

As they went up to their rooms, Milly took Emanuela by the arm: "Why are you going to that séance? Those girls are silly. Afterward you'll be even more afraid to come down."

Emanuela reassured her: "I'm not scared anymore, you know? It was the first days, as you said." In her room, she found the window open. Shivering, she went to close it, then began to dress carefully, as she hadn't done for a while: she chose a black dress and a fur coat, also black, that she hadn't worn since coming to the Grimaldi. The purse, the money in the purse . . . She wondered if she should wear the emerald. She looked at it, turned it over: no, better not, it would rouse the curiosity of her friends, the distrust of the nuns. From a packet of papers locked in her suitcase she took a photograph, put it in her purse, and left.

As soon as she was outside, all the lightness of her new life vanished, as if just at that moment she were getting off the train that had brought her to Rome. She had tried many times to imagine the institution that housed Stefania; she feared it would be cold and dark. Instead it was a white villa on Monte Mario, in the countryside. The door opened into a large lobby where there were some sacred statues; at the far end the green of the garden was visible.

"I'd like . . ." she said, ". . . could I see the Andori girl?" The reception area was a porch warmed by the sun and brightened by geraniums and begonias. There was no one else; Emanuela was relieved. Then she heard a bell ring and soon afterward an old nun entered and said, with a respectful aloofness: "Hello, signora: you wish to see Stefania?"

Emanuela nodded and her throat was dry, constricted.

"You are?"

Emanuela murmured: "Yes, the mother."

"We received the letter from your father; the child is happy at the idea of seeing you. She's grown. She's clever," said the nun. And added: "Here she is."

Stefania appeared in the doorway and stopped, staring at her mother. She was a slender child, with blond braids knotted over her ears, a scowl on her face. When the sister disappeared, Emanuela hugged her daughter, picked her up. The child asked her, serious: "Did you bring me any candy?"

"Oh! No, no candy, Stefania . . ." Emanuela answered, disconcerted.

"Chocolate, then?"

"No."

"I know, a doll," she concluded looking around.

"Nothing, I didn't bring anything today, but next time, you'll see."

"The nuns said you'd bring me candy when you came back from America. They told a lie. Even they tell lies. Isn't there candy in America?"

"Yes, there is . . ."

"Then why didn't you bring some? I've been good. *Très sage.*"

"Wonderful, Stefania . . . Now, do you love me?" The child nodded yes. "You were expecting me, right?" Stefania kept saying yes, touching her mother's fur coat.

"You're glad I came?"

"Of course. You'll come on Sunday?"

"Every Sunday, always."

"So next Sunday bring me some candy."

Emanuela promised, and then she didn't know what else to say. "Are you eating? You feel fine? Are your companions nice?" And so on. Then she opened her purse, took out a photograph and handed it to her, saying: "Stefania, this is a photo for you, of your father."

"Give it to me."

She looked at it for a moment and then, stamping one foot on the floor, said harshly: "I want Papa to come here, I want him to come right now."

Dismayed, Emanuela looked at her daughter. "You love him, right? You love Papa very much?"

"Yes," Stefania answered distracted. "But my friends don't believe my father is a pilot: I want him to come, so they'll see," and, without giving her mother time to respond, said impatiently: "The girls are playing. I'm going back."

The conversation was over, Emanuela thought, over. For this, then, she had fought for months, years. I should have brought some candy, she said to herself: certainly everything depends on candy, it's my fault. But she felt like crying. She picked up her daughter and sat her on her lap, caressed her hair, looked in her eyes, which were hard, scarcely childlike.

But Stefania, hearing the voices and laughter of her companions, was anxious to join them. Emanuela let her slide off her lap. "I'll be back on Sunday," she said, as her daughter escaped.

Outside the school gates was open country; Emanuela walked slowly in the sun. She thought about her parents, about the villa in Maiano: her room, the bed with the flowered coverlet, the dining room, dinners under the broad lampshade that spread a circle of brightness over the table. Silent, hostile meals: ever since Stefania had been taken from the wet nurse in Switzerland and sent to boarding school in Rome, and she had been unable to see her, Emanuela hardly spoke at all. Good night, Papa, good night, Mamma. And every few days the usual scene. She entered her father's study around twilight; he sat at the window, a blanket on his knees, contemplating Florence, the hills, the red roofs of the houses sticking out amid the green.

"Papa . . ."

"Emanuela . . ."

"You know, Papa . . ."

"What is it?"

"I want to go to Rome, to Stefania."

"It's been decided that you'll stay here."

"But Papa, understand me, it's inhuman, I can't live without my child . . ."

"The decision has been made."

The old man resumed reading or looking out; she left in tears, and her mother didn't even dare ask how it had gone. Emanuela went up to her room, threw herself on the bed, in the dark. There was no recourse; what could she do? Leaving Florence, without any money, was impossible: all she had was Stefano's ring. Her mother said: "Your father's right,

now, he doesn't want to struggle and risk dying, how could he die leaving the two of them to confront this problem alone? "No, don't apologize, you were a victim, too, I won't say anything else now, I won't reproach you anymore; but there is the fact, the fact exists, and one has to bear the consequences, including the child, poor thing . . . Come, don't cry now . . . But it was a tremendous blow. Therefore, to Rome by yourself, no; because up to now you haven't shown that you have any judgment about men, and this misfortune you'll have to carry for your whole life is enough . . . But in Rome there's a kind of boarding house . . . yes, for young women, what's it called now? A residence, you go out during the day when you want, to study, at a given time you return . . . What time? I don't know, seven, eight . . . Yes, nuns . . . And how could they know that you're going to see the child? You go out and no one asks where you're going. You'll say to the nuns you're there to study until we return from a journey, a long journey, a sojourn in America. And to our friends here we'll say you're going to Rome to study, I don't know, art history, let's say . . . I know, it's painful to lie, but one can't do otherwise, for me, for my position, one can't let everyone know there's a child and a child without a father . . . Unfortunate, yes, him, too, but he was thirty, a man who flies and is always exposed to danger, may he rest in peace, but he could have considered it."

It was Sunday then, too. Emanuela, walking back, pondered all that again. She breathed a mild air, families strolled, the women with languid steps, the children stopping at every café, in the hope of going in. It didn't seem to her that she had been to see her daughter; she recalled only a few words—"Did you bring me any candy?" She had a snapshot of Stefania beside her bed. "Who's that child?" Milly had asked. She had answered absently: "A niece." And had intended to hide the picture, so that her friends wouldn't get any ideas.

She took off the fur coat: what a mild day, really a Sunday warmth. Surely Papa and Mamma had gone out for a walk. She took their name and their money. She didn't send many letters, and they were short: "Papa,

I'm well; Mamma, I'm well." At home, at the Grimaldi, with Stefania—
everywhere she played a different role, had a different life, another character. But which was truly her? She needed the strength to summon her
friends and say: "Listen, I've told you a lot of lies …" But maybe they would
all go away if they knew that she was "on the other shore." They always said:
"This is the shore where you wait." And after that disheartening visit with
her daughter, Emanuela feared she had nothing more to wait for.

· · · ·

In the Mother Superior's room the bed was all white and stood in a corner, behind a white curtain. The walls were white, and the prie-dieu; the
cushion on the prie-dieu was plumped, untouched. It was clear that no
one ever prayed there. The chairs were covered in red, the cloth on the
table was red. The room was saturated with the odor of incense and wax,
as if she brought a little up from the chapel every day, in the folds of her
skirt. The Abbess was old, very old; she had fat, buttery hands, like her
face. Her only task now was to come down, supported, into the chapel;
her only sacrifice climbing back up the stairs. For the rest of the day she
stayed in her room, sitting in an armchair, her feet on a footstool. You
didn't see her when you entered; you heard the rosary jingling, the voice
asking, "Who is it?" Guided by the voice, you could see two stony gray eyes
in the shadowy light.

When she entered the chapel the girls bowed their heads, as if a dead
person hoping for sainthood were passing. Two young nuns supported
her, depositing her cautiously in the chair at the back of the chapel, where
she dismissed them with a wave of the hand that indicated both condescension and blessing. They fled quickly, swishing their skirts to right and
left with gentle curtsies; the Superior crossed her hands on her lap and
looked at the altar, as if waiting for a show to begin. When the service
was over the two nuns delicately braced her as she struggled up the stairs,
panting, but without complaint. They sighed in her stead: at every step,

while she stopped to rest, one of them rapidly blinked her eyelids over the white of eyes raised to heaven.

In reality, Sister Lorenza was the one in charge. You had only to see her ladling out the soup: she ran her eyes around the room, counting the heads of the girls like a herd of cattle: "All, they're all here." And she deeply enjoyed feeling them shut up with her behind the big windows that imprisoned their youth, their nights, their awakenings.

It was she who opened the mail in the morning. Girls wrote from all over Italy, and from abroad as well. She answered in a clear, inviting handwriting, with maternal tenderness; and when she learned that they had accepted, that they would come, she repeated their name many times to herself, caressed it almost, then abruptly transformed it into a number, and repeated name, surname, number. Whenever a new girl arrived and the bell summoned Sister Lorenza to the reception room, she adjusted her veil, looking at her reflection in a windowpane, wondered anxiously "What will she be like?," went to meet her smiling, welcomed her affectionately. But she never spoke in the first person: it was always "the Mother Superior who . . . the Mother Superior wants . . . I'll tell the Mother Superior that . . ." letting her imagine that the person in charge here was the Abbess. She was pleased, however, that the new arrival, listening to her, admired her fine hands, her tall, slender figure.

In summer, when the girls went home, Sister Lorenza grew pale, was often unwell. "She's tired," said her companions. But when the evenings began to get shorter, she went at sunset to say her office on the terrace: a high terrace over the city, over Villa Borghese. "It's autumn now," she thought, huddling in her light shawl. In autumn the girls returned. "Did you have a nice vacation, my child?" But she didn't want to know anything about their home; in fact she avoided talking about that. At night, she fell asleep happy.

In the Mother Superior's room a lamp swathed in white was lit. That light endowed things with a fantastic aspect: the Superior's hands looked like ivory. Sister Prudenzina was motionless near the prie-dieu; suddenly she began pacing nervously until, hearing the rosary jingle, she remembered the Mother's presence and went back to the wall, her hands under her apron. It was already late: she had heard the girls go up to their rooms, talking loudly; worried, she drew from her pocket the watch hanging on a black cord. "I'll have to go up soon and turn off the lights," she said. She would have liked to talk to the Mother, but she didn't respond: she continued to jiggle the rosary in silence, perhaps dozing.

Finally the door opened slowly and Sister Lorenza appeared: Sister Prudenzina stared at her questioningly, and the Mother's sleepy eyes turned to her as well.

"Nothing," Sister Lorenza murmured disconsolately. "You were right, Sister Prudenzina. The porter nun says she saw her go out with a bundle under her arm. Maybe she should have asked her . . ."

"But, Sister, any girl can go out with a bundle!"

The other spread her arms. "It's true."

The clucking voice of the Superior concluded: "We can only say: she ran away."

All three were silent, imagining the fugitive: they saw her go out the entrance, cross Piazza di Spagna, looking around warily. At noon, in the refectory, she had passed by Sister Lorenza, greeting her with a slight nod, as always. She had already made her decision, at that hour: they had let her get out of their hands without noticing.

"We'll have to inform her parents," said the Mother Superior. "You write, Sister Lorenza—who knows, maybe she went home."

"But to her friends?"

"You'll say she's gone home."

"They won't believe it."

"No, of course not. And then they'll all run away, one by one," Sister Prudenzina interjected with a malicious smile.

Without saying so, all three thought she had fled with a man. Sister

Lorenza wouldn't be able to sleep at night, that empty bed in Room 33 would prevent it. They'll all run away. No, she would be at the door herself, she would stop them: where are you going, my child? She would lead them back to their rooms.

"Sister Lorenza, you'll say to the girls that she went home because her mother's sick. It shouldn't be known that here, at the Grimaldi, a girl ran away."

"They'll all know it," Sister Prudenzina said coldly. "These are things that can't be hidden."

Sister Lorenza nodded. "Yes. And of course we know it."

The rosary in the Mother Superior's hands jingled. Her voice replied, irritated: "We *don't* know it. A girl has gone home, that's all. We don't know anything else, do you understand, Sister Lorenza?"

They heard knocking at the door of the adjacent study; the two nuns looked at each other. The Abbess closed her eyes again; she wasn't used to being awake so late. The knocking grew louder. Sister Prudenzina went to open it.

From the next room came Silvia's voice:

"I want to talk to the Mother."

"The Mother's sleeping."

"Sister Lorenza, then."

"She's in her room, I'm going to turn off the lights now."

"No, Sister Lorenza is in there, I want to talk to her."

Then Sister Lorenza appeared. "What do you want, Silvia?" she asked in her usual tone, which seemed hostile.

"I want to know where Xenia is."

"Xenia left," the other announced calmly, pulling the curtain that separated the study from the Mother's bedroom. "She went to Veroli."

"No. Her things are here. And she wouldn't have left without saying goodbye to us."

"A strange character."

"No, she wouldn't do this to us. She said she'd stay here. Where did she go, Sister Lorenza?"

"I repeat that she's in Veroli. And now go to sleep, go study. Really, Silvia, that's enough."

But Silvia turned pale. "Sister Lorenza, tell us." And she whispered: "Did she kill herself?"

Then, terrified by her own words, she burst into sobs. The sister remained icy. Silvia insisted: "We're her friends, we have to know: tell me, that's it, right?"

Sister Lorenza shook her head. "I don't know, my child, we don't know anything. She left today with a bundle and hasn't returned. Did you see her room? Everything is in order. She ran away. She didn't say anything. She left."

"Did she bring things with her?"

"Something, it seems."

"It's our fault: we should have helped her, offered her everything we had. Where could she be now?"

Sister Prudenzina began: "Silvia, you'll tell the girls . . ."

"The truth, I'll tell the truth, because they think she's done something crazy . . ."

The nun smiled bitterly and said: "It seems to me that . . ."

"Yes, leaving like that is also crazy . . . but after all it's her life, she can do with it what she likes." She paused, then: "I'm going upstairs," she added. "I'm going upstairs. Good night, Sister Lorenza, good night, Sister Prudenzina. Oh yes, you're going up for the lights, go ahead, it will be terrible to sit in the candlelight tonight, go ahead, Sister Prudenzina."

Sister Lorenza stayed in the study: the register of the girls' names was open on the desk. She glanced at the pages, went to the letter "C": Coppola, Corsi, Costantini, Costantini, Xenia. She wrote the date: December 2, 1934. Then she canceled name and surname with two straight lines, her pen dipped in red ink.

. . . .

Emanuela, tired from the visit to Stefania and her long walk, had stretched out on her bed before going down to dinner, and in a short while had fallen asleep. She woke with a start at Silvia's energetic knocking: "Is Xenia with you?"

"Xenia? No, why? I was sleeping."

But Silvia was already knocking on Milly's door, repeating the question: "Is Xenia with you?"

"Why would she look for her at Milly's," Emanuela wondered. "She never goes there: Milly's baffled when she listens to Xenia talk, as if she were speaking a foreign language. It's late, I haven't even eaten. Silvia's coming to call us for the séance." It seemed to her she'd awakened in the middle of the night, but it was only nine thirty: the fur, the purse, were all where she'd tossed them when she came in. She opened the drawer to put the money back in the box, along with the emerald. "Where's the emerald?" She searched everywhere: she rummaged, picked up hand-kerchiefs, unfolded them, opened the box again, shook it, as if Stefano's ring would fall out of a false bottom: nothing. "It must be on the table, I have to search calmly: in the purse? No, impossible, maybe on the floor, under the night table." She lighted a match to see better: dust, lint, nothing.

She rang the bell twice, and when the maid appeared Emanuela examined her distrustfully: "Did you come into my room?"

"Yes, I made the bed."

"And afterward?"

"No, afterward no."

"You didn't see an emerald?"

"An emerald?"

"Yes, a ring with a big green stone."

The other shook her head.

Emanuela was full of suspicions. "Who did you see come in here today, anyone?"

"Signorina Milly, with you . . . Signorina Xenia knocked to see if you were there, then she went in. She was looking for you, obviously."

"No, not the girls. No one else came by?"

"The sisters."

"Oh no! I meant strangers, I don't know, workers . . ."

"Workers? What would workers be doing? Everything's in order. No one came."

"All right, thank you."

The woman left: she was lame, she seemed dazed. "She's playing her part well; but I'm going to see Sister Lorenza right away," Emanuela thought, and she started to go out. As she closed the door she saw Silvia.

"Silvia . . ." she began. Silvia interrupted her.

"Did you hear, Emanuela? Did you already hear? Xenia ran away."

"Where?"

"Gone. No one knows where. She was carrying a bundle, a package, her room is all in order. The nuns wanted to deny it. We thought she'd killed herself—she's gone, she had no money at all."

"Xenia!"

"Yes, Xenia."

("Signorina Xenia knocked . . . she went in.")

"Oh!" said Emanuela.

"There's something you're not saying? Do you know something?"

"Me? No. I don't know anything."

"Where are you going? Are you coming up?"

"Yes, I'm coming up for the séance."

"What séance are you talking about? What's wrong with you, Emanuela? Don't you understand yet that Xenia's run away?"

"Of course I understand, that's why I'm muddled. I'm coming up with you, let's go."

They joined the others in Augusta's room; she was sitting with the turtle on her lap, caressing it like a cat. Anna was cracking nuts with her teeth.

Silvia said: "Emanuela doesn't know anything."

"It still doesn't seem real," the latter added.

And Augusta: "It doesn't seem real to any of us: we were afraid, you know? that she'd killed herself."

"No," said Emanuela, "she didn't kill herself."

"What do you know about it?" Vinca asked.

"But ... didn't you hear? She left with a bundle. And then, when someone kills herself, she leaves a note—you think she wouldn't have written us a note?"

"Yes. But why run away? If she'd asked us for something, we would have helped her."

"No," said Augusta harshly. "We say that now. No one would have helped her. She knew it, so she left like that."

The nun's voice could be heard shouting "Lights!" Augusta got up, lighted the lamp, and set it on the table, where Silvia had sat down, distressed.

"It's night now: she won't come back, she won't come back tomorrow, either. For us, in spite of that, everything continues: Sister Prudenzina shouts 'Lights!,' our other companions don't know anything: they study and we don't even go and look for her."

"It would be pointless."

"Yes, but at least we'd be doing something for her. Instead we're doing nothing, nothing at all. Who knows where she is tonight."

"She must be with a man," said Anna with conviction. "What would she do alone?"

"No," said Emanuela, "you're wrong: if she had gone away with a man she would have told us."

"If she were with a man she'd be happy."

"What do you know about it?" said Augusta.

As soon as the lights went out, Valentina began to cry: "I'm scared . . . maybe Xenia threw herself in the Tiber, and she's dead." Then she whispered: "Maybe she's sleeping next to a man and this is her first night of love."

"If that's the case," Anna said, "Xenia is in mortal sin."

Silvia broke in: "Who knows if God exists! I doubt it, you know? I have to confess to you: when we're in chapel and we kneel and pray, I think that we do all that in vain. That God doesn't exist. He's only a phenomenon of collective suggestion; rather, a fable invented to leave us a little hope. To enable us to endure this absurd life. So I don't want to hear talk of mortal sin. What does it mean?"

"Yours is a comfortable morality," Vinca replied. "I, on the other hand, am a believer, and I think Xenia did wrong to act like that."

"She did wrong, maybe," Silvia said, "but not because it's a sin. Because, maybe, outside of here there's nothing. Xenia believed there was something, she always said 'I'll never go back to Veroli.' She's gone beyond what we know. Like those who die."

"But they don't come back," Emanuela observed.

"Xenia won't return, either, to tell us what's on the other side."

They were silent. Valentina suddenly started: "Shhh . . ." she went. "A footstep."

They all turned toward the door.

"No," said Anna. "Nothing."

· · · ·

When the old man finished reading the letter from Sister Lorenza he folded it carefully, put it in his pocket. "Maybe now the door will open and Xenia will walk in saying 'I'm tired,' the way she always did. Maybe she's already here, in her room, and hasn't dared appear."

In Xenia's room the light of dusk entered through the half-closed shutters: soon night would descend, soft and thick. The day before, tidying the room, the father and mother had said: "We'll leave the desk clear, she'll put her books there." She would shut herself in her room. "I don't want to see anyone," she had written. But for now she wasn't in her room. And yet the letter from Sister Lorenza said clearly: "Xenia left here Sunday at four." Sunday at four he was playing cards at the café. At that time he hadn't yet heard that his daughter had left, "with a bundle under her arm."

He opened the door of the house and looked out. In the big meadow opposite, at the foot of the hill, a clump of poplars was stirring; in summer Xenia would sit there to study. She'd come home excitedly: "You'll see, this winter," she said, "when I have my degree . . ." Now, though, her slim figure was nowhere in sight: the road was deserted. "It's impossible that she won't come, maybe she'll come tomorrow: she'll be nervous the way she was when, during vacations, she got home late: 'It doesn't matter, I won't eat: why do we always have to eat at eight?' She would return saying: 'I didn't say goodbye to anyone, I have a horror of goodbyes.' It must be that," thought the old man; and, reassured, he lighted his pipe. But the smoke caught in his throat, as when you swallow a big mouthful of bread.

Already the shadows of people passing by the house on bicycles could no longer be distinguished. "It's night now," the old man considered. Soon afterward his wife returned from the station and together they went in.

"She's not here, right?" she asked. "I met the last train: nothing. And yet she said: 'I'll arrive the day after tomorrow.' Maybe she'll be here tomorrow. 'Don't come and get me, I don't want people to talk about my return.' Who knows why she wrote that . . . I went just the same, keeping my distance so she wouldn't see me."

"You mustn't worry," said the old man. "I received a letter from the nun, Sister Lorenza, you know? She says that Xenia will be a few days late."

"And the money?"

"She also says she won't have to pay anything, so don't worry."

"Where's the letter?"

"The letter? Here's the letter," said the old man, searching in his pockets. "It's not there, I can't find it, I must have left it in the café, I'll go get it later, if they haven't thrown it away. But it said just what I told you."

The woman looked around: "I was used to the idea that she would be here tonight."

"Yes, me too . . ."

"I think I was right not to make pizza. There's the broth, the meat we'll leave for tomorrow, what do you say? She might arrive tomorrow."

"Eh, yes, maybe tomorrow. Let's leave the meat."

Darkness outside, an impenetrable darkness. The father was dismayed: "It's night." An increasingly insistent anxiety made his hands and lips tremble. Yet he wished to appear serene in order not to worry his wife. He repeated in his mind the words of the letter, tried to convince himself that Xenia would come home: tomorrow, or in an hour. He would have liked to go out, go to the station, wait for every train.

His wife was sitting in the kitchen. "It seems to me that she's here," she said. "That she went out into the village and should return at any moment."

"Odd, right?" he said. "I have the same impression." And taking a chair he sat down beside his wife, who repeated placidly: "I'm really glad I didn't make pizza."

. . . .

Xenia was uneasy entering the trattoria alone. Besides, she had to choose from the menu, and she couldn't decide: she read it, reread it, and ended up ordering something she didn't like at all. Waiting, she glanced through the newspaper. She was afraid of finding a notice in it: "Her parents beg their Xenia to come home, everything will be fine." In fact, she didn't realize what she'd done. The day of her flight, she was about to head back to the Grimaldi at the usual time; it seemed to her that fleeing had to be much more arduous.

She had left a little after four: she went first to a movie, but because of her agitation she couldn't focus on what she saw on the screen; and then she was bothered by a man near her who looked at her through the darkness and every so often whispered some words in her ear. To get rid of him, she left, and wandered through the streets, with the bundle growing heavy under her arm; finally, toward evening, she entered a modest hotel near the station. The porter, preceding her up a narrow, dimly lit stairway, asked, "You're alone?" and at her affirmative answer requested her documents. At that moment she was afraid of being discovered: but the man, taking her identity card, left calmly. Xenia sat on the bed, as if waiting for the police or the nuns to come and get her. "Now my friends have realized it." But already the Grimaldi was like a landscape seen in a dream: her friends' faces appeared blurry, imprecise. She recalled clearly only Emanuela's room, the night table, the drawer that resisted. There was no money. She had searched everywhere, even among the underwear. She had opened the jewelry case. What a beautiful ring! She put it on her finger. She hesitated a moment, then slipped it into her pocket, closed the drawer, and went casually out into the hall.

She spent the evening in the cold hotel room, going over all this. She wished morning would come, but the hours passed with discouraging slowness; finally she undressed and got in bed, lying motionless and breathing softly, as if the least movement, the least sound would be enough to ruin her.

She left the hotel early in the morning and headed to a doorway that she had often seen men and women enter circumspectly. Inside were a lot of people already familiar with the place. She preferred to wait till last, missing her turn many times. An asthmatic face looked out of the little window, calling: "Signorina . . ."

Xenia presented the ring in silence. Then she waited, anxious, fearing the stone was fake. In the night that doubt had kept her awake: Emanuela never wore it.

The man, his eye encapsulated in a lens that magnified it out of all proportion, examined the stone at length: then, turning to Xenia—one eye squinting, the other enormous behind the glass—had asked:

"How much do you want? Is a thousand all right?"

"All right."

He examined the emerald again, then asked her name, surname, address. Xenia gave a false name, a false address. "You never know, he could report me." The man counted out the bills one by one, making them crackle.

At the station Xenia discovered that the train for Milan wouldn't leave for two hours: at noon. She sat in the waiting room, beside a child with a bandaged head and a sailor. She was afraid of hearing footsteps approach, feeling a hand on her shoulder: "Police." Her heart was pounding, her temples burning. Then, calming down, she waited patiently. She could have bought a book, but her agitation would have kept her from reading.

Not even on the train was she able to reassure herself: she sat without moving, straining to listen. She looked out the window at trees, houses, unknown streets. Again she saw evening fall, lights go on.

The hotel in Milan was like the one in Rome. Xenia went to bed and fell asleep, repeating, exhausted: "I have to give the ring back to Emanuela immediately."

· · · ·

Instead, three weeks later, she was sorry she hadn't asked more for that ring. She was at a restaurant; but soon, if she didn't find work, she would be reduced to *caffellatte*. She had had to pay an entire month in advance for the room; and the money went somehow, she counted it every night. "It's impossible that I've spent so much, I must have lost some," and again she added up the expenses.

"The bill please."

"No fruit?"

"Fruit? Oh yes, fruit."

The soup one and eight: filet with potatoes four fifty, that's six thirty, then fruit, service, cover, tip. Expensive: tomorrow I have to spend less. As she did these calculations in her head, Xenia had eaten the tasteless orange. She was supposed to appear immediately at the bank. The ad said: at two precisely.

There were already other girls in the waiting room, and at the sound of the door they turned to look at her. After two, they began to show signs of impatience. A voluptuous blonde declared, "I'm leaving," as if she were there to please the management. They all jumped up when the head of personnel appeared in the doorway: a large man in a vest festooned with gold chains. With a gesture he beckoned to the closest girl, saying: "Come in . . ." and the door closed. The blonde sat down again, sighing, and uncovered her legs up to the knees. Xenia was among the last.

"University? Good. Degree?"

"No, but . . ."

"Oh! High school diploma at least?"

"Oh yes, I had already presented my thesis and . . ."

"What faculty?"

"Literature."

"Literature . . . How can anyone choose literature today? Your name?"

"Xenia Costantini."

"From Milan?"

"No."

"Tell me, tell me. Father, mother, tell me." He waved the pen bombastically as he wrote. "You're enrolled in the Party?"

"In the student union."

"Do you have the card from the employment office?"

Here we go again, same thing. Nothing today, either.

"No."

"We can't, then; we state-controlled organizations can't. You have to go to the office, first of all . . . In any case, your references?"

"I don't have any. I've never been employed. As I said: I presented my thesis ten days ago."

"Family, friends, relatives to whom . . . ?"

Xenia answered, getting up: "No one."

He looked at her without putting down the pen: he took off his glasses to examine her.

"Why are you leaving, signorina?"

"I'm leaving before you tell me to. I'm not enrolled in the Party or the employment office, I have no references. I know, it's not your fault, it's the rules. And in the meantime I'm going to die of hunger." Her voice was fraught, her distress threatened to break through in tears. "And yet I'd be an excellent employee: I know French, English, a little German. Let me tell you the truth: I ran away from a university residence so I wouldn't have to go back to my village. Now that I've told you this, you'll hire me? Say it, you'll hire me?" Supporting herself on the desk she leaned toward that man on whom everything depended; then she drew back, serious. "I knew it. I told you all that because I needed to vent. You are very kind. But there are the rules: and at the employment office they want references. It's fair. I could just as easily be a thief, right?" she added, smiling bitterly. "Those other girls all came with their piece of paper in their pocket, they live at home with Mamma and Papa, and they work so they can buy stockings."

The man listened to her with curiosity.

"I'm sorry," Xenia continued, "it's desperation. Yes, I'll return if I have the references, thank you. Oh, thanks!" She took the card the man handed her, bowed her head slightly, and left. Another girl was ready outside the door; the blonde asked her, as she'd asked each one coming out:

"Did it go well?"

"No."

The other repeated: "If they make me wait any longer I'm leaving."

Xenia read the card as she left: a pretentious card with the honorific titles in italics, abbreviated but magnified. At the foot of the stairs, Xenia lingered in the entrance, looking at the people passing: unknown people hurrying to get to a job or an appointment. She alone had nothing to do in that city, knew no one.

. . . .

It was only three days until Christmas. Not many of the girls had gone home. Sister Lorenza had convinced them: "The Grimaldi at Christmas is lovely." But at night they all talked about their families, home, sisters and brothers. Some could have gone to the houses of relatives or friends for dinner. They didn't: better to be here all together, all alone. After dinner, instead of going up to their rooms they gathered in a large parlor where, because of the severity of the cold, two braziers were lighted; and every so often, breaking off their writing, they went to warm their hands at the fire.

They all sat around a big oval table in that large, high-ceilinged half-empty room: the girls from literature, from law, and from the sciences, and even those from music, who always formed a group apart. But each girl was isolated in a world that the others didn't know, where they couldn't reach her. One by one, they pushed away the books, tired, and crossed their arms on the table, or started talking.

Only Augusta was always missing: studying with the others, at her age, seemed ridiculous to her, inappropriate. Maybe that was why she hardly ever went to the university. But the light filtered out from under her door until late at night. On holidays Augusta was even less sociable. Sometimes she summoned Valentina and they talked.

One night Emanuela didn't come down to join her friends in the parlor. "She's with Milly, who's ill," said Anna. "If Milly doesn't get better we'll have to give up having some nice Christmas music."

In Milly's room the lamp, shaded with blue paper, gave off a pale glow. Milly was sitting on the bed, her hair loose over a soft wool jacket. She started, hearing someone enter, but when she saw Emanuela she said: "Come on in. I was just reading."

She wasn't holding a book and, besides, she couldn't have read in that light. Then, approaching, Emanuela saw that she had a sheet of paper in her hand.

"He wrote to me," Milly said, and showed her the white page, covered by small holes with raised edges, over which she kept running her fingers, delicately. Her face was alight. "It's much more beautiful like this," she explained, stopping. "The words enter into your skin, your blood. Are you aware that you're breathing? And yet life enters into you. That's how it happens with his words. He says we should play the same oratorio at the Christmas Mass. I have to be well, I have to go down, you see? Otherwise it would be a betrayal."

"Do you feel better?"

"Now, yes. But last night was terrible. People who are well don't even realize they have a heart. Whereas I feel mine: it opens, closes, the blood pulses, fills me, so it seems that it has to gush out of my nostrils, my mouth. Then my heart starts racing faster and faster, gallops, and finally an iron hand grabs me by the throat, squeezes, suffocates me. I fight to find the smallest breath still in me. But tomorrow I'll be fine, I have to go down and rehearse the oratorio on the harmonium, and you'll see, I will."

She went back to running her fingers over the sheet of paper, staring into space. The doctor had said: "It could be now or two years from now." Her friends entered on tiptoe.

"Why are you walking so softly?" she asked, embarrassing them. In the last crisis her pulse had been so weak that Sister Prudenzina had felt it fail. "Enough of this responsibility," she had said to the Mother Superior. "We have to send her back to Milan right away." Instead Sister Lorenza had written to her father: "The healthy and happy life of the convent is very beneficial to your daughter." That night Emanuela dreamed that Milly had died and gone to heaven transformed into a comet: her hair, luminous, incandescent, formed the long trail of the star on its course through the firmament.

Milly continued: "Listen to what he writes. 'I, too, will play the oratorio, I wait eagerly for that moment, my light.' My light . . ." she repeated.
"Can a blind man say more?"

During the day, Emanuela wandered around the streets decorated
for the holidays. She went into stores, paused for a long time, uncertain,
before the display cases. She had bought a lot of toys for Stefania; her
Christmas consisted in searching for things the child would like. She already knew that once she gave her the presents the celebration would be
over. Stefania was quickly bored with everything.

In the store the doll looked alive; as soon as she was in her room
Emanuela took it out of the box, held it in her arms, hugged it, pushed it
away, embraced it again, hoping she'd arouse some tenderness in herself.
In vain. As a child the same thing had often happened to her. She would
get excited in front of a window, fascinated by a doll: she wanted it, got it,
carried it home proudly in her arms; but when she was alone with it she
didn't know what to do. Dolls at the time had fixed eyes and a cold por-
celain smile. "Stupid!" Emanuela said to her softly. "Stupid, why don't you
say something?" She undressed her and dressed her again without pleasure; finally she abandoned her. Disappointed, she went to the window:
there she sat for hours, following the flight of the swallows, the changing
shape of the clouds as they drifted across the sky. It was her favorite game.

· · · ·

Now that Christmas was approaching, Vinca no longer complained about
the nuns; in fact one night she asked humbly:

"Give us a nice Christmas, Sister Lorenza."

Luis, too, was melancholy. "This isn't a real Christmas," he told her.
"You can't even eat roast suckling pig. I talked about it with the landlady,
who stared at me and said: 'At Christmas we eat capon.'"

The day before, Luis had suggested: "Let's take the tram." It was a long
ride. The line skirted the river, beneath the still leafy plane trees of the

Lungotevere, to the Lungara. Finally they got out, and he led her through narrow streets of houses whose windows were half-hidden behind clothes hanging to dry: the old city, where he liked living. "I breathe better here," he said. "The people are similar in every latitude. See the geraniums in the windows? Like Spain."

Stopping in a small square, before a doorway with a beautiful Renaissance frieze, Luis asked her, "Do you like it?," indicating the façade with his gaze. Above, a large window flamed, reflecting the light of sunset. Luis said: "That's my new studio. I'm living here with another student from Spain. I'm freer and I like it better, even though it's far from the Academy. Why don't you come up for a moment?"

"What about your friend?"

"He knew I was coming, he's gone."

"No, thanks."

"Come up . . . From there you can see some old terraces."

"Keep them for yourself," she replied harshly.

"You're an idiot. What are you afraid of?"

"I'm not afraid. But you can stop calling me if you're hoping that eventually I'll come up."

She set off at a rapid pace, eager to leave the neighborhood, to be free of Luis, who followed her in silence. She thought that Xenia might have gone off with someone like this, everything ends this way, sooner or later. Or maybe Valentina was right: Xenia had thrown herself in the river. Sometimes you can't see any other means of resolving life. "Why are you running away? What's wrong?" Luis asked. She herself didn't know why she was running. Now the house was far away, and, besides, once she'd said no it was pointless to hurry. And yet she couldn't wait to get home, as if she feared she'd change her mind.

"Don't run like that, Vinca. If you want, I'll go."

"Yes, go on, go," she said bitterly. "What are you waiting for? Because I'm not going there or even to the movies, ever again. You're wasting your time."

The young man continued to walk quietly beside her, taking her arm, and she waited for him to speak, to say "I'm sorry," maybe protest: so that she could respond to him and let go. But Luis said nothing, and, as a way of spiting him, she resolved: "Tomorrow I'll start studying day and night." In Piazza di Spagna they stopped in front of a florist who was already putting the flowers back in the baskets. "Bye," Vinca said, arming herself against his possible objection or revolt. But he repeated "Bye" and went off.

Vinca didn't move, hoping he would turn; she would have liked to call him back, go and look for him in the trattoria where he ate: "Yes, I'll come, I will: as long as you don't leave me like this." But she didn't even know where that trattoria was: Luis hid everything from her, he had moved without telling her. "I'm going with friends," he'd say. What friends?

When they first met he'd asked her:

"Do you have a boyfriend?"

"No, and you?"

"Me, neither. There's a girl in Spain . . . at home they'd like it. But I like being free."

"What's her name?"

After a moment's hesitation Luis had answered: "Her name is Sol."

Now that name came back to torment her. Maybe he wouldn't have invited Sol to go up. She had to study, study, not think of anything else.

"Always late," the sister reproached her, seeing her come in.

"Tomorrow I'll be back early."

"Tomorrow is Christmas Eve."

Fine Christmas! She barely greeted her friends, sitting down at the table; then she pushed the plate away, saying: "I'm not hungry. I'm not eating."

· · · ·

When Xenia no longer knew how she would go on, she found a job as a salesgirl in a glove store. She owed it to an acquaintance she'd made sitting in office reception rooms: a girl her age but smart and experienced, who'd already had a lot of practice with waiting in vain. Her name was Vandina, and she had finally got a job at a mining company, because she knew shorthand. They had left together and Vandina invited her for lunch to celebrate.

"You don't know how to manage, how to get by," she said to Xenia. "Why do you insist on wanting an office job? Did you read that at the Grandi Magazzini, the department store, they're looking for salesgirls? Don't turn up your nose! What will you do tomorrow? You can't eat the books you studied!" As she spoke she polished her nails with the napkin.

"You'll get something else later, you're not going to grow old at the department store. It's easier to satisfy them: for the information direct them to me, say I'm your cousin, say whatever you like. They won't pay you much, you'll see, but it will be enough for stockings, lipstick, and to eat a meal instead of *caffellatte*. We'll go together, you want to?"

Nothing at the department store. She was hired by the glove store because she knew French and it was in an area frequented by tourists. Xenia had a refined appearance; she was well brought up. So when the owners saw her, and heard her speak, they didn't even ask for references.

Vandina said: "There, that's how you do it, and at least you get a start. One of these nights I'll introduce you to some friends, people in business, big companies: they'll find you something better."

That uncertain promise helped Xenia endure the discomfort she felt at the glove store. She was disgusted by the constant contact with hands whose fingers and joints she had to caress, smiling. At night she went home tired, ate a sandwich, and read to keep herself company. Sometimes at night she dreamed that the store was full of customers and she was the only one there to wait on them: so many hands reaching out toward her that she was exhausted caressing them; there was no more talcum powder in the jar; every pair took her a very long time, and the other customers got impatient, until the owners, unhappy, threw her out and she had to return to Veroli.

She had written home that she was working in an office and at the same time studying to defend her thesis again. Mamma sent her a wool sweater because Milan is a cold city. Sometimes Vandina came to pick her up at the end of the day, saying that the office wasn't bad, the boss had taken her under his wing, but the secretary—who was supposedly the "friend" of the boss—was at war with her. She would leave soon, the salary was meager, and, now that winter was coming, she needed a coat.

Xenia disliked many things about this young woman: certain vulgar expressions, her insistent ogling of men who passed, her dull, untidy blond hair; but, seeing her, she felt encouraged by her round face and her rouged cheeks, and by the word "arrive," which Vandina repeated constantly. Besides, she feared the bleak solitude of her room. She was tired of reading, the books she was studying repulsed her, but she couldn't buy others; so when her friend was about to leave, she'd say, "Wait just a moment." Vandina always had something to do: "Friends," she said; or, more often, "my boyfriend."

One night Vandina called her: "I don't want you to be alone tomorrow night: it's Christmas. You'll have dinner with us. Oh, I don't know where, we'll decide, they're coming with the car—wait'll you see what a car! Who are they? Friends. Really smart people. You have to dress nicely. Do your eyes, okay? I said you're a beauty. True! True! On the street everybody looks at you."

Xenia had only one dress, and her friend offered to lend her one. "You're taller, but I'm fatter, one makes up for the other—it should fit you."

The following night Xenia went to Vandina's to get dressed. The dress fit; in fact it fit very well. Vandina looked at her in admiration: "What a nice figure you have! And then, goes without saying: you have a high-class look."

At the front door, a big car was waiting for them. Vandina whispered: "What did I tell you? Look at this!"

Two young men, dressed with exaggerated elegance, got out of the car and went toward the girls. Vandina introduced Xenia, then they all got in and the car drove off.

There was a reserved table at the restaurant, and the younger of the two men—whose name was Dino—seemed to be well known there. Two orchestras alternated, the tablecloth was shiny as silk, the glasses light as air.

When it came to choosing the wine, Dino ordered champagne. Another poke from Vandina, who wanted her to appreciate the generosity, the luxury of the place.

But the men didn't say a word to her: they discussed with Vandina things and people she didn't know. "Sole or lobster?" Dino asked, menu in hand, gazing at her spellbound, and, turning to Vandina, said, as if she weren't present: "You were right: she's really a looker." Xenia was dismayed for a moment, then she laughed. They started talking about the glove store. No, they all said, she couldn't stay there, given the vulgarity of those people. Talking, she drank a lot: she didn't like champagne, but she liked the act of drinking, the undulation of the wine in the fine glasses. Meanwhile she looked around. Yes, this is really festive, really Christmas. She didn't even mind wearing Vandina's dress. What mattered was being here. In Veroli the streets are dark and steep, the families gather around the panettone, the same faces, a narrow world: if they could see her here, they would die of rage. And at the Grimaldi? Apart from Emanuela, who was a lady—and it was absolutely necessary to give her back the money—the others, at most, would teach in a provincial high school: cold classrooms, chilblains.

They danced until late into the night. Vandina, who had drunk too much, told off-color jokes. Dino had moved his chair close to Xenia's and mechanically threw small colored cotton balls at people passing by. They were among the last to leave; but they had no desire to sleep. "Let's go somewhere else," Dino proposed. They drove aimlessly through the streets, went into any place that was still open, but each was sadder than the one before, they said, and ended up drinking hot chocolate in a *latteria* where the tram drivers were already having coffee.

At Xenia's door they said goodbye effusively, resolved to see each other soon, very soon: tomorrow. Vandina walked Xenia inside, embraced her, said "Merry Christmas," and added, in a whisper: "What gentlemen, eh? Dinner, champagne, and then, you noticed? Nothing. Not even a kiss."

. . . .

After Guido Belluzzi's lecture, the students got up from the desks and headed for the door; only those who were doing their thesis with him, if they had something to discuss, approached him. Silvia, still seated, gathered up her lecture notes and put them in her bag. Every so often she raised her eyes to look at the professor. She was on her way out when he called her: "Custo ..."

Silvia turned: "Me?" She was doing her thesis with Belluzzi, but she had spoken to him only a few times. Immediately she turned and went over to him.

"You have no questions for me this evening?"

"Thank you, no, none, professor."

"I, however, have a question for you. Could you come and see me tomorrow, tomorrow at ... let's say four?"

"Oh! Of course."

"You're not busy at that time, you're not studying?"

"No, really, professor."

"Good. Then till tomorrow."

Belluzzi lived in old Rome: the entrance hall of the apartment was vast, crowded with statues, with fragments of archeological finds. Silvia was intimidated as she crossed it, following the maid and trying to make as little noise as possible. She entered a large library with a painted ceiling and walls lined with shelves overflowing with books. The afternoon light grazed their spines, brightened the gilded lettering.

"The professor will be here in a moment," said the maid, indicating a closed door.

She had no idea what he wanted from her. Maybe he would tell her: "Custo, listen to me, go back to your village." Besides, what could she say, in the face of all that had been said in those books? What new word? Uplift humanity! When Xenia heard that phrase, she laughed: "It's too heavy, no one will ever lift it up."

"Custo . . ."

From the doorway Belluzzi beckoned her into his study; but he didn't sit down behind the desk, as he had when Silvia came to talk to him about her thesis: they sat together on the sofa.

"Coffee?"

"No, thank you, professor."

"Have some: it's good at my house." He spoke affectionately, and Silvia was surprised, seeing him shift from the cold austerity of the professor's desk to a friendly welcome.

"I asked you to come because I'd like to propose something. I've had my eye on you for some time, Signorina Custo. You're very intelligent, attentive, determined."

"Thank you, oh, thank you."

"I'm sure you'll go far."

Silvia's face became radiant, lighting up her eyes, which were always burdened by dark circles, and brightening her skin, her hair, the mourning she wore.

"And I'd like to propose that you work with me . . . secretary isn't the right word: rather, collaborator. I always have new research to do, to . . . In other words I need a person who can help me, who understands me . . . Rather, who understands." After a pause he added: "For many years I had a smart young lady here. Now she's married, this young lady, and I didn't think I'd find anyone to replace her. Then I saw you, I've seen you work . . . Would you accept, Signorina Custo?"

"Oh yes, of course. I don't know how to thank you, professor."

"Don't thank me, then. I'll expect you after the holidays. I hope you'll have a good Christmas, a happy Christmas."

"Now yes, absolutely, professor."

"January 7, all right? Come at three. I'll introduce you to my wife."
And, smiling, he stood up. "I'll walk you out, signorina. As for your compensation . . ."

"Don't mention it, professor, please."

"As you wish, we'll talk about it later."

They passed through the library, the great entrance hall. Silvia said
goodbye quickly, went down a few steps, and when the door closed behind
her leaned against the wall, exhausted.

She had no precise thought: she let the joy spread through her, flow
with her blood. After a moment, she started down again, slowly. She walked
along the street intoxicated, dazed: the cold wind penetrated her nostrils,
stung her ears, pushed her happily along, and she gave into it with a
sensation of lightness, of flight. On January 7 she would go to work with
Belluzzi, in fact "collaborate," he had said; and that filled her with pride.
Sometimes when she went out with her friends she noticed that men,
passing by, always looked at Vinca or Emanuela, and she felt humiliated,
disheartened, by her unattractive appearance. But Belluzzi had chosen
her from among so many. "Custo . . ." he had called. Me? Really me, yes.
"I've seen you work . . . You'll go far." To compensate him for those words
she would do something great, extraordinary.

She couldn't wait to tell her friends: she would call them right away,
all of them. Xenia was missing. She saw her big restless eyes again. "You
won't forgive me, Silvia, right, for failing?" She had been too harsh, and
maybe it was precisely for fear of her, of her opinion, that Xenia had left.
She seemed now to hear her voice again, the sarcastic tone she used with
the nuns: "Easy for you to speak, you're Belluzzi's favorite!" How could
she make her believe that she hadn't asked for anything, that it was he
who'd summoned her? No one would believe it. She had to write to her
parents: "I'm going to work with Belluzzi." But they don't know who Belluzzi is, they don't read the papers, they don't understand a thing. Her
mother shook her head when Silvia talked about her aspirations: "That's

not a life for girls." Who knows, maybe she was right, but how to give it up now? Perhaps they had all thought, seeing her leave: "She'll be back." And until now she had been afraid she would be forced to return: today no more.

. . . .

Her friends, excited by the preparations for the séance, welcomed the news distractedly. Vinca asked: "How much will you earn?" Only Augusta understood.

In the meantime the others pushed the table to the middle of the room and darkness surprised them before they had time to get the lamp ready. Valentina asked, dismayed: "Where are you?" And she reached a hand out to find her neighbor.

Vinca lighted the lamp, lifted it up to widen the circle of light and look at her friends: "Why do you want to do this?" she insisted.

"Stop it!" said Augusta. "Let's sit down."

Vinca placed the lamp on the shelf: the light fell on the girls' bent heads. Hesitant at first, they all placed their open hands on the dark table, one beside the other.

Valentina asked: "And now?"

"We have to wait, like this, without thinking of anything."

But no one could stop the chaotic and tumultuous thoughts that rose from the depths of their apprehension. It was Augusta who whispered: "It's moving."

The table jerked. Suddenly they all took away their hands, then put them back, timidly.

"What's it doing?" Valentina stammered.

"And now?"

"You speak, Augusta."

Augusta questioned: "Who are you?" in a frightened voice. The others held their breath.

A light knocking could be heard at the window. Emanuela said, merely moving her lips: "It's the rain."

"It's true, it's moving," Vinca exclaimed and, taking her hands off the table, crossed them on her chest. "I'm scared, oh my God, I'm scared."

Valentina, carried away, also lifted her hands. The others remained intent; in the weak glow of the lamp their heads projected disproportionate shadows on the wall. The table shook, bumping the knees of Vinca and Valentina, who were motionless, as though the blood had frozen in their veins.

"Who are you?" Augusta asked again. The two girls looked at her in admiration: it was terrible, to speak as you waited for a dead man to answer from the beyond.

On the other side of the walls their companions were sleeping: in the silence they heard the water spattering the trees on the Pincio. The oil lamp emitted a black line that rose toward the ceiling. Valentina wondered, "Why did we do this?" While, in a pressing voice, Augusta repeated: "Who are you? Are you a woman?" A pause. "Are you a man?"

The table rose on one side and then fell heavily: yes.

A man. The room was invaded by that hidden presence. A dead man, thought Emanuela.

"A man," Augusta confirmed, while her hand touched the table lightly.

Emanuela had the impression of sitting with her friends around a coffin in which a live man was imprisoned, who responded by knocking against the lid. A coffin as long as Stefano's. She hadn't been alone then: the four airmen in their uniforms seemed made of lead, rigid, eyes distant, bayonets flashing in the tremulous candlelight.

"What's your name?" Augusta asked.

Anna begged: "Enough, that's enough." If a name was said, a man's ghost with that name for a face would sneak into her room: every night when she returned, she would find him waiting for her.

Augusta, inexorable, counted the knocks that the table tapped on the floor. Valentina and Vinca, close together, recited the alphabet with her, but soundlessly: "A, B, C, D . . ."

Emanuela had read the name engraved on the brass plate on the coffin. Commander Stefano Mirovich. It was Stefano's name, but it wasn't possible that Stefano was lying in that polished coffin with the brass studs—in a piece of furniture.

"E, F, G, H . . ."

She didn't know the face of Stefano dead. Stefano dead: words that at first seemed to her without sense. They could all be dead, except Stefano—such misfortunes happen to others, not to one of us.

". . . Q, R, S . . . It's not going farther." In the silence Augusta's voice, hoarse now, confirmed it: "S." After an interruption the table began to tap the floor again and Augusta resumed:

"A, B, C, D . . ."

The dead don't respond, thought Emanuela. They're crazy if they delude themselves that they can communicate with the dead by telegraphy. Again she felt on her knees the cold of the hospital floor. Again she saw the soldiers, immobile, the laurel wreath, the flowers, the big flag spread on the wall. Kneeling at the coffin she whispered: "Stefano, let me feel that it's really you in there, or I'll never believe it. A sign, give me a sign, and then, only then, I'll believe it." Suddenly she noticed that the words were forming in her mind like a prayer: then she understood that Stefano really was dead. She shivered, her bones trembled.

"S, T . . . A name that begins with ST." Still addressing the table, Augusta said: "I ask and you confirm: Stanislao? Steno? Stefano?"

At that name Emanuela jumped to her feet, shook the table as if to drive something out of it, then pushed her friends away, one by one, placing a hand on their chest and saying: "That's enough! Enough! I won't allow it! It's a joke, you should be ashamed, if he didn't respond to me he can't respond to anyone! The light," she said, "turn on the light right away!" And before the girls' astonished eyes she kept twisting the switch, in vain.

Then she went to the window and opened it, seeking air: a damp, penetrating cold entered; the sky beyond the frame was all white. Emanuela
leaned on the windowsill, sobbing: "Why did you do this to me?"

The friends stared at her, bewildered. Silvia moved first, and went over
to her. When Emanuela looked up, she saw her, ahead of the group, mutely
asking the reason for her sudden fury. In a whisper she explained: "I lost
someone named Stefano."

Silvia said sadly: "We didn't know. It wasn't a joke, Emanuela, we would
never have had the poor taste to organize such a thing."

"Was he your fiancé?" Vinca asked.

"Yes. An affair of many years ago."

"I understand," said Silvia. "I was agitated tonight, too. We were wrong."

She began to put the chairs back, and Augusta placed the books on
the table again, so that the room would regain its usual appearance, and
the event was over. Still Valentina wanted to know: "Were you supposed
to get married?"

Emanuela bent her head, assenting.

All night long, in the darkness of her room, Emanuela heard the dull
tapping of the table. Augusta's voice as she pronounced the letters echoed
in her ears. And, finally, with her face in the pillow, she gave in to tears. At
the time she hadn't been able to cry. Events hadn't left her time; she had
wept for what was happening in her and around her. Her father blamed
her, her mother blamed her: Stefano's death, rather than a tragedy, had
seemed to them a bad deed.

The rain started falling again monotonously, with the sound of a
water course flowing under her window. Lightning flashes illuminated the
iron sky, then the room was dark again. Emanuela thought of Stefano, of
Stefano alive; she had met him at a friend's house and didn't imagine that
her whole life would be changed because of him. He had arrived in Florence recently, from Portorose, but everyone was talking about him, prais-
ing his skill in the riskiest test flights. So she had been flattered when he

asked her: "Shall we dance?" They had stayed together all evening, and, seeing her get up to leave, Stefano had said regretfully: "Already? So early?"

The following week she had run into him on the Lungarno. It was dusk, and Emanuela should have turned onto the Ponte Vecchio, taking the way home, but the hour was so beautiful she had decided to keep going to the next bridge. A few steps later, there he was. He apologized for his unshaven beard: he was coming from the airfield. "It's not visible," Emanuela said, fearing that, because of it, he would leave her immediately. Instead they started walking together, on the almost deserted Lungarno. Every so often they stopped and looked over the parapet, gazing at the houses on the opposite shore that seemed to rise out of the water, as in Venice. It was easy to talk, like that, eyes wandering over the river: in the distance you could see the green of the hills, and the banks of the Arno were grassy and cool.

"I don't know Florence well," Stefano confessed. "Only the roofs, the cupolas: I always see it from above." Emanuela said that each of us knows a city in our own way, each of us preserves a different image.

"And for you, what's Florence like?" he asked.

They saw each other again the next day, and then every day. Sometimes they met people they knew: Emanuela was happy to be seen with Mirovich, she was gratified by it. She intended to please him and succeeded: in a short time he had begun to love her graceful gestures, her walk, her eyes. Instinctively, Emanuela chose for their meetings a frame that made her stand out. She led him to ancient churches to show him a holy-water stoup, an altar cloth, a pulpit.

Once, they had descended into a subterranean chapel, a crypt, where there was a chill, sepulchral dampness and an oil lamp shed a reddish light: on the cross that hung over the altar a large Byzantine Christ opened his fleshless arms. Emanuela stopped in the middle of the chapel, looking at her shadow extending along the floor, infinite. Stefano took hold of her shoulders and kissed her neck, where the stray curls just formed a down.

Then, close together, they climbed the steep stairs leading to the upper church. And, saying goodbye, they switched to the familiar form of "you."

On the old tram that brought her back to Maiano, she was unaware of anything around her—stops, jolts, bells. A joyful ardor flowed to her cheeks, suffusing them with pink. At home, her parents were already at the table. She embraced them excitedly. "What a lovely evening," she said, as the rain slid over the windowpanes.

"I'm in love," Emanuela thought when she woke the next morning, anxious about her meeting with Stefano. The days already had the urgency of early autumn; the branches of the plane trees along the avenue were bare. Every day Emanuela chose a different dress, to go to Florence. They walked arm in arm, and the smell of his cigarettes lingered on her sleeve. At home no one noticed anything: her mother worked interminably at her knitting, sitting in the garden, her father read and often commissioned Emanuela to buy him a book. Coming home, she would say, "Here's the book," afraid he would ask: "Where have you been?"

When winter came, Emanuela and Stefano had tea in the covered courtyard of an ancient palazzo, in Via Tornabuoni, frequented by old English ladies. You had to speak in a whisper, otherwise threatening looks appeared behind the eyeglasses.

One day, as soon as she arrived at the appointment, Stefano said: "Let's take a taxi." She agreed, smiling, with a trace of uncertainty in her mind. A narrow, rocky street that descended from Viale dei Colli; the taxi bumped along and finally stopped in front of a small entrance. Emanuela got out, pretending to be relaxed, but she didn't understand what it all meant or where they were. He unlocked the door with a key, awkwardly, then pushed it open, letting her enter. Inside there was an odor of paint and of staleness. There wasn't much furniture: a wide sofa, a large mirror in a gilded frame. It was almost dark, only a little light filtered through the shutters. Stefano opened them: below you could see the swollen Arno flowing, the red houses, the bridges that crossed it. Emanuela looked out with an exclamation of wonder: she was still uneasy, but, intimidated, she didn't dare say, "Let's go, what are we doing here?" They contemplated Florence for a long time, quiet, close, both disturbed by this new solitude. Meanwhile it grew dark. Emanuela shivered with cold, but she didn't move from the windowsill. Finally Stefano closed the window.

. . . .

Returning to Maiano, Emanuela clutched the key Stefano had given her when he left. "Tomorrow's Sunday: we could eat here, a cold lunch, it would be good, fun . . . A day all for us. Will you be free?" She nodded, still mute. She got home late, exhausted; at the table she didn't have the strength to speak. Papa asked her: "My book, Emanuela?" and, looking attentively at the soup bowl, in order not to meet his eyes, she answered: "I forgot." She was afraid he would ask: What did you do, where were you? But he said only: "Then tomorrow."

It was a cold winter; Emanuela and Stefano often took refuge in the house in Viale dei Colli. When she entered, she would find Stefano reading the newspapers or waiting for her, impatient at the window, and she rushed to embrace him, just as if she were entering her own house. She was happy to recognize the scent of his hair, to recover every day their habits, their intimacy: she knew how many buttons there are on the uniform and how to loosen the knot of the tie; she helped him fasten the cufflinks at his wrists, while he kissed her bent neck, her hair.

Lying beside each other on the couch they talked, smoking. That was the sweetest time. But when Stefano mentioned his job, his flights, Emanuela always said, "I'm afraid," while he asserted: "I haven't been afraid since you've been here waiting for me."

Once he had said: "As long as they don't promote me. If they do promote me," he added, "they'll certainly change my posting."

Emanuela hadn't found the strength to respond right away. "Far?" she asked later.

"I don't know, but near or far has no importance: I can't think of living in a city without you in it," he answered. "Nothing would have purpose for me anymore." She thought: "He's leaving: that's why he's saying he loves me. He's saying it to console me: maybe he's already been transferred, and tomorrow he's leaving." The voices, the footsteps that rose from the street echoed in her like circles of sound. Stefano was smoking, staring at the beam of a headlight projected on the ceiling. Then he said: "Before that happens, we should get married. If, naturally, you, too, feel you can't do without . . . without all this."

"No, I can't, either," Emanuela answered in a whisper.

The next day Stefano brought her the ring with the emerald, and, returning home, she announced: "I'm engaged."

. . . .

Not a week had passed; Emanuela, entering the house on Viale dei Colli, found it dark. A gray crepuscular light came in through the windows. "Stefano, please, don't scare me!" He was hiding, she thought, and would jump out. "Don't be an idiot!" she said, laughing. Then she turned on the lamp, looked everywhere: he really wasn't there. Besides, it wasn't even five. Without taking off her fur coat, she went over to the radiator to warm up. Then she heard footsteps in the street. "There he is," she thought. "What will he say when he sees my new coat?" But the footsteps kept going past the door, without stopping.

Five. She had read the whole paper that Stefano had left there two days earlier. Now and then, absorbed by reading, she didn't even remember that she was waiting for him. "Might he have gone elsewhere, to the Cortile? No, he said here, right here. He must have been detained at work, he'll be here soon." She made an effort to think of other things, so that the time would pass more quickly. Instead she kept listening for street noises; the room was on the mezzanine floor, you could hear the conversations of people passing. From the apartment above came the sound of a piano. "There are still people who take piano lessons." How many years she'd wasted at the piano, as a child: in winter the teacher would hit her numb hands with a rod, and she had to smother the impulse to rebel. She was almost terrified as she waited for the lesson; if the teacher was five minutes late she thought, "How nice, today she won't come," and suddenly, instead, the doorbell rang. How much time had passed, how long since she had heard someone studying the piano. "It's the *Valse Triste* of Sibelius. As soon as I get home I'll open the piano, start playing." The room grew dark, then the piano ceased. Finally she decided to go out to telephone the airfield.

The street was deserted; Emanuela waited another moment in front of the door, before setting out. No one. The piano playing resumed.

She went to telephone in a smoky, noisy bar in Porta Romana.

"Hello . . . airfield?"

"Yes."

"I'd like to speak with Commander Mirovich."

"Who?"

"Commander Mirovich."

"Commander Mirovich?" Not hearing anything more she insisted: "Hello, hello . . ." Finally at the other end of the line the voice said: "Wait."

She waited a long time; the cashier at the bar looked at her every so often, and the men sitting at the little tables looked at her, too. The air was dense with smoke; you could hear the billiards colliding, the players laughing. In the receiver, silence. "Maybe the line's been disconnected." A comment of Stefano's came to mind: "These damn new devices . . ." Uneasy, she kept saying: "Hello . . . hello."

Finally a different person, certainly an officer, came on and asked: "Who is this?"

"Is Commander Mirovich there?"

"Who is this?"

For the first time, hoping to get news more easily, Emanuela said: "His fiancée."

The officer, too, like the airman, was silent. After a moment he said: "The commander is out."

"Flying?"

"Yes."

"But where?"

"We don't know; he's flying."

"Has there been an accident? Tell me!"

"No, no, signorina . . . calm down. Leave me your name, rather, and also your address. We'll keep you informed." But she had already hung up the phone. She left the bar, saw that it was raining. There were no taxis available, what a nightmare, still she signaled every one that went by, while the passengers looked at her in surprise: don't you see the lowered flag? The cold bit her ankles. "What shall I do?" she thought. "I have to get to the airfield, absolutely." Finally an empty taxi passed: "To the airfield, right away, as fast as you can." The driver grumbled, "It's slippery," and drove at a snail's pace.

When she found herself in the officer's presence, she understood immediately what was going on. She remembered him clearly: he was tall and blond, and his normal complexion must have been pink, but he was pale, livid, while he explained to her incoherently that it was a long flight, that because of poor weather conditions the radio on the plane had failed. Staring at him, she shook her head continuously, thinking that if it had been a minor accident, they would already have told her; whereas the officer no longer knew what to say, and, fearing her silence, continued to provide details. Until, interrupting him, she asked decisively: "Where did it come down?"

As if he hadn't spoken at all until then, in fact denying everything he had said, the officer said softly, "Near Bologna."

"Dead?!"

"No, but it's serious."

"Where is he?"

"In the hospital at . . ."

She arrived there after midnight. There were no taxis at the station, in the deserted square outside.

"Where's the hospital?" she asked a railroad worker.

"Go straight, turn right, then left up to the big avenue."

She had started walking, in darkness and silence. Her steps echoed loudly on the pavement. She was afraid that someone would appear and she would have to justify her presence, give explanations. Right, then left. From half-closed doors came a strong odor of straw, and along the avenue the trees assumed frightening shapes. After she'd been so afraid for Stefano she was afraid for herself: that someone was following her, would approach and attack her, kill her. She was covered with cold sweat when, finally, she saw the red light of the hospital.

Once she got there, she stopped thinking that Stefano could be dead; she thought that this nighttime adventure was over, that she would enter a warm room and throw herself on Stefano's neck, then sit cautiously on his bed, that together they would forget the horror of the day, and all they had had to go through before they could be reunited.

She waited for a long time; finally someone appeared and opened the door. She said in a humble voice:

"I came to see Commander Mirovich."

"You can't until he's in the coffin."

She remained calm, just a harder pounding of the heart, a painful shudder on her skin. Dead, over: the coffin. And she was there, talking to the nurse. She would never speak to Stefano again: she couldn't even tell him she had rushed to get there right away. Now I'm going to faint, I'm going to crumple onto the floor, but no, nothing. She remained standing there, without losing consciousness.

She asked: "I'd like to see him now, close his eyes . . ."

"Oh, the eyes, my dear girl . . . he has no eyes."

The nurse whispered these words with cruel sweetness. At six she could go in, not before six, she should wait here, in the waiting room.

She sat for long hours in a cold room that smelled of disinfectant. Tears were locked in her throat, but she couldn't let go. In her mind she heard only the nurse's words: "He has no eyes." She saw them again in every detail: that yellow pinwheel in the green of the iris, the thick black lashes, a small star at the corner of his left eye. "It's not a glorious wound," he had said. "A fall at the academy." They aren't there anymore. She couldn't forget Stefano's look when he said: "These damn new devices . . ." Where are Stefano's eyes? She wore herself out with that anguished question; and even when she knelt beside the coffin she looked at the eyes of the airmen and, shuddering, imagined Stefano, trim in his blue uniform, clean-shaven, hair neatly combed, with two horrendous voids in his eye sockets, two red caverns.

On her knees, fingers intertwined in a gesture of prayer, but without praying, without weeping, she, too, was unmoving in the icy silence. So she had spent the early hours of the morning: until, suddenly, outside the door, she heard a tortured weeping, and the nurse came over and whispered, "The mother's here." Emanuela withdrew toward the wall, near the laurel wreath. The door opened and a figure enveloped in black veils collapsed on the coffin. The girl didn't see the face, but she heard the cry, saw the hands touching the wood. She went out slowly, retraced her steps along the big avenue, departed.

For a few days she stayed in bed with a fever: a nervous fever, they said. She had read in the newspaper that "during a training flight, for reasons unexplained, a plane from the Luigi Gori Airport crashed; the pilot, Commander Stefano Mirovich, unable to use the parachute, is deceased." A few lines. Beside it the latest prices of wheat, below it an announcement of the arrival in Italy of Jeannette MacDonald.

She was struck by the word "deceased." Stefano was deceased: biographical information. The mother had carried him off, home, to Fiume, maybe without even knowing that he no longer had eyes. All over: the hours of watching the placid flow of the Arno, the house in Viale dei Colli.

No one knew anything, it was as if nothing had ever been. She knew little about Stefano's life: their true intimacy was about to begin. And now Stefano was "deceased." She felt a bitter pleasure in wounding herself with that word, she called the airfield to hear the response: "Commander Mirovich is deceased," then she hung up the phone. But she covered her ears when the hum of a plane passed over the house.

It was a dull, profound pain that resembled a great weariness. Her limbs weighed on her; she sat in the garden idly, hands in her lap, cold as stone; other times she gripped the bars of the gate and watched the people passing by outside, on their way to Florence. She followed their footsteps as long as she could, restrained, imprisoned by a mute apathy.

When she began to fear that the terrible thing might be true, her energy returned. No, it was impossible. Stefano was dead, he couldn't keep her bound to him. She wasn't supposed to continue their story, otherwise he wouldn't have left, abandoning her like this. She had started going out again, to convince herself that everything around—and therefore her life, too—was as before. But she couldn't think of anything else; that fear was an obsession. "Stefano," she whispered on the street, "no, no, you know it's impossible, how could I manage?" She was repulsed by the idea of carrying inside herself a creature that was taking her blood, that was growing inside her in spite of herself, was master of her life even before it was born. How could it be born without a father, without a name? She had to wait, and not despair. "If it's really so," she concluded serenely, "there's always one recourse: I'll throw myself in the Arno." She calmed herself by thinking that at worst she could jump off the bridge one day and everything would be resolved. But she didn't really imagine herself dead, only that her anguish would die with that act, if, in the attempt to punish herself, she found the courage to jump in. Then she would climb back onto the shore and resume her life, free of that nightmare, the terror of expecting a child; and the suffering at Stefano's death, everything, would remain at the bottom of the river while she,

Emanuela Andori, would again go out on the streets of Florence smiling at the new season.

"It's certain by now, I'll have to jump, there's no other solution," she concluded one night, sitting in the dining room, while her mother was knitting. She hoped that making the decision would give her some peace. But then she had thought that dying meant being closed in a long, narrow box, like the one where Stefano was, not to have eyes, not to see, not to touch and feel oneself alive and warm: to disappear, in other words, to be forgotten even by those who have loved us. Then, hearing the regular click of the knitting needles in the silence, she turned toward her mother and started sobbing. And when her mother came over to her, asking what was wrong—Mamma so old, so far from reality—she had hidden her face in her lap and, in the warmth of her wool skirt, confessed everything.

Six years, six years had already gone by. Stefano was now a white skeleton in his grave. Emanuela didn't dare look around: maybe now he'll appear and speak to me? What voice do the dead have? Maybe he came to the table tonight to tell us what the end was like: there's a deafening sound in Emanuela's ears, the din of the airplane that flounders, drops, spins, then rears up and climbs, trailing a wake of fire, red as the hospital light. Jump, Stefano! Jump with the parachute! But it's hard to hurl yourself into the black sky, as hard as jumping off the bridge over the Arno, the engine's hum fills her ears, along with her mother's soft voice, Stefania's harsh voice asking: "Where's Papa?" He crashed, burned, he's in pieces, he has no eyes, nothing is left of him, not even the emerald, Xenia took it, but the plane continues to circle the earth like a meteor, everyone's looking at it, shouting, fleeing, thinking it's the end of the world, but it's only her end: she alone can't be saved, something restrains her, heavy, like Stefania in her womb. Stefania flees, her friends flee, abandon her, but she remains, she is condemned, the hum approaches, the plane is crashing, hits her, she feels herself falling, she falls.

. . . .

On Christmas Day it snowed in Rome; and that was the only cause of joy for the girls of the Grimaldi. They all looked out through the windows at the white courtyard, at the heavy snow falling on the palms, the bamboo, like the cotton wool on their childhood Christmas trees. Because of that unhoped-for novelty, they were expecting a happy surprise, as when, in the past, they'd waited impatiently outside the living room door, while Papa was fooling with the lights on the tree and Mamma was wrapping presents in tissue paper.

But their joy was an effervescence that quickly vanished. Soon they all returned to their problems. Vinca had received a letter from her father, saying that Spain was peaceful again, so there was no longer any reason for her to study in Rome: "I was terrified at the idea of leaving. I blamed my stepmother. You can't understand, but it's terrible to see a girl of my age sleeping with him, where my mother slept. But then I realized it's not because of her, it's because of Luis. Yesterday when I told him 'I'm leaving' he said: 'Lucky you! I didn't think you'd abandon me so soon. But you're right to leave.' While he was speaking, I decided to go home: 'It doesn't matter to him at all,' I thought. Instead, coming back here, I wrote to Papa that I'd prefer to stay in Rome, and I felt a profound rage, a violent rebellion at the fact that I was unable to act as I want. I don't recognize myself, I'm not me anymore."

When lunch was over, they lingered, talking, in order to put off the approach of an empty afternoon. What can those who are alone in a city on Christmas Day do? Sister Lorenza came over and proposed: "Let's sing."

After Xenia's flight she had stopped feeling that she possessed them; she understood that all of them, at heart, wished only to leave. Every evening she came down to be sure that the gate was carefully locked; and at night she stayed awake for a long time, ears straining. Once it had seemed to her that footsteps were cautiously descending the stairs, reaching the front hall: she had dressed in a hurry and gone down, wrapped in her shawl, without even the coif on her head. But the halls were deserted, behind the doors of the rooms she heard not a breath.

They sang sitting down: Sister Lorenza, standing in the middle, beat time. They sang religious songs that reminded many of processions in their own villages. Suddenly Anna said, "That's enough! It's making me homesick."

Emanuela suggested: "What about going out?" But it was a pale day; the snow was already melting and the streets were dirty.

They ended up in Augusta's room. At five they ate dried figs from Silvia's basket, drank wine from Anna's farm, sent out for roasted chestnuts. Animated by the wine, they talked, made plans for the future, gave each other advice.

Vinca described her house in Cordova, its big patio overflowing with jasmine, and the sadness that in those days both she and Luis, far from Spain, were feeling. "I'm used to it, it's the third year, but he . . ."

Valentina interrupted to ask her: "And how will it end, for the two of you—will you get married?"

"How should I know? Sometimes I'm convinced that Luis adores me, other times that he's amusing himself with me and is in love with that other woman."

"What other woman?"

"Sol, someone who's in Spain."

"What lovely names you have there. Sol . . . Have you ever heard a more beautiful name?" Vinca was silent, annoyed. Valentina resumed: "I would know if he loves me."

"How?"

"If he loves you, he marries you."

"Really? And if he loved me and married the one his parents want? I have nothing and, if I go on studying like this, I don't promise to earn much."

"And is Sol rich?"

"How should I know? Who knows her? Of course she must be. When do parents ever like a poor girl?"

Milly said: "What does the future matter? The important thing is to love. I don't understand you."

Silvia observed: "How could you understand?"

Valentina was surprised that Vinca, on a day like this, hadn't gone out with Luis.

"There, good for you, try to figure out if he loves me! He said that today he had to go out with the architecture people."

"Each of us has a different way of thinking about love," said Milly.

"Some of us," Augusta said, to be precise, "don't think about it at all."

"That's not true," Vinca replied. "Only there are some who admit it and some who don't."

"Why? You think one can't do without it?" Silvia interrupted. "Augusta's right."

But Vinca insisted, shaking her head: "Hypocrisy! You were complaining, until yesterday, that no man ever looked at you, and now you're trying to convince yourself that it's you who despise love and, naturally, the instinct, the senses. But work for you is a substitute. When you came to tell us that Belluzzi had chosen you to work with him, you had an expression . . ."

"It's true, very true!" Valentina laughed.

"And when you come out of your room, after working on your thesis, you look exhausted, with dark circles around your eyes, like me when I come out of the movies with Luis!"

"Vinca!"

"Why are you offended? As children we were always in love: with our teacher, with a friend, with a tree, maybe. I wrote the name of one classmate, Bellita, with a pin on the skin of one arm. I never told her."

"We've all done something similar," Augusta admitted.

And Valentina made an effort to laugh: "There's the stink of the confessional in here!"

Anna exclaimed: "But it's nice to talk like this, among ourselves, all women. If there were a man here, we wouldn't dare to be sincere. I wouldn't know how to be even with my father—in fact with him less than with others. Women are sincere only among themselves. Isn't it true? When my father leaves the house, my mother and I take another tone. I have no idea why, but there's always a certain hostility toward men."

"The hostility of not being able to do without them, if only to be born," Augusta murmured.

Silvia was playing with a pencil, slowly sipping her wine, and finally she said: "You know, Vinca? At first I was offended by what you said. I would have liked to hit you, or at least get up and leave. But no: you're right. The only thing for me is work. Besides," she added, "I consider that what's essential in life is to choose a path and follow it to the end, provided you have faith that it's the right one."

And then Emanuela realized that she wasn't following any path: she went here and there, indecisively. It seemed to her that she was a spy everywhere, but camouflaged so well that the others have no suspicions, in fact they welcome her into their tent, to their table, they reveal their secrets, they tell her they're afraid of the battle. To live with such companions, you have to be similar to them: girls from the provinces, still pure, inexperienced, coming to Rome to study. That morning, on the pretext of bringing holiday greetings to a relative, she had gone to see Stefania. The child grabbed the toys and ran away, scarcely saying *"Au revoir, Maman."* Emanuela was disappointed: "You're not even giving me a hug? You won't say thank you?"

But Stefania looked at her in surprise: "Didn't you tell me that Baby Jesus sends them?"

So, thanks to lies, she had disappeared, she no longer existed.

In her place, two characters played each her own part: the girl who lived in a residence for students, the mother who visited her daughter's boarding school. Was Stefania really her daughter? "In reality," she thought, "what belongs to us is only what life, and people, recognize in us. If we have a million under the mattress and we don't spend it and no one knows about it, it's like being poor."

"You're not saying anything?" Anna asked her.

"I'm listening."

"It's a strange Christmas."

"No," Silvia said. "It's the only one appropriate for us. A Christmas without traditions, without precedents or future. This isn't our home and we won't all be here next year. It's as if we're on a bridge. We've already departed from one side and haven't yet reached the other. What we've left behind we don't look back at. What awaits us is still enveloped in fog. We don't know what we'll find when the fog clears. Some lean too far out, for a better view of the river, and they fall in and drown. Some, tired, sit down on the bridge and stay there. The others, for good or ill, go on to the other shore."

"Excellent!" Emanuela said, laughing. "Top marks in literature."

II

Milly died in the spring.

She had been getting worse for some time, but no one noticed: driven by the desire for new, light air, she got up from her bed and sat beside the window: "I'm studying harmony." Few knew precisely what that word "harmony" signified, but it seemed right for Milly. Now that the days were getting longer, the girls wandered through the streets after classes, chasing the light; a mimosa tree in the nuns' garden emanated a dusty scent of perfumed fabric that rose toward the windows; the younger girls, dazed by that perfume, ran a hand over their forehead while they studied. They all took tonics for the lethargy caused by the season.

Augusta announced solemnly: "Margherita has awakened. This morning I found that she'd come out from under the night table and moved to the middle of the room. Now it's really spring." Milly said to Emanuela: "I'm worse." Her friend reassured her: "I feel sick, too: my legs are like rubber, my heart's racing, irregular: it's the season."

Milly insisted: "It may be, but yesterday the sister said she wants to write to my father. If she writes, Papa will come and get me right away; and if I go back to Milan with him I'll certainly die. There are a lot of things, it's hard to explain: you'd have to know my father. But the main thing is that there I wouldn't be able to get his letters or see him. Now I say to myself: 'He's far away,' and I'm resigned; there I live around the corner from San Babila and at night, when he plays, I couldn't stand it. Why do they want to make me leave? I don't give much trouble or, at least, I won't for much longer. . . . You have to help me, Emanuela. The sisters listen to you: talk to Sister Lorenza, please."

Emanuela had promised: "All right, I'll talk to her."

Anna, who often stayed in to study for her thesis defense, came down toward evening to keep her company. She alone had realized that Milly really was getting worse.

She informed the others, at the table. Swallowing spoonfuls of soup, they said: "After dinner we'll go see her." But, gripped by the euphoria of the season, they laughed, talked in loud voices—they had no desire to be sad. Besides, no one thought that Milly could actually die; her normal condition of life was illness: she'd been among them for fifteen months, always with death on her. One might have said that she was glad of it, like a habit. Why didn't she go out, rather, why not go and sit in Villa Borghese, in the sun's warmth, she who needn't be shut up in the cold classrooms of the Sapienza? Even Emanuela avoided her, annoyed by her habit of taking her hands and stroking them slowly while they talked.

The doctor had stopped coming. He had filled the night table with bottles that Milly didn't touch and which the lay sisters dusted every morning. Years, the doctor had said, or a day.

Now Milly was happy: her father, who often was traveling, said nothing more about making her return to Milan. The organist had sent her a photograph, and she showed it warily to Emanuela.

He was already an old man, gray, heavy: his mouth feminine, his eyes hidden behind dark lenses. Emanuela was unable to say anything. But Milly didn't expect comments: she caressed the photograph with the gestures of a blind person; the paper was already a little creased.

One night, Emanuela woke to the sound of footsteps hurrying up and down the hall. She strained to listen: she heard the door of the next room open and close. She jumped out of bed and rushed in, in her bathrobe: Milly had been very ill, she was struggling to breathe and the light was swathed in blue again. Seeing Emanuela she smiled and said: "Why did you get up? Thanks. But I just needed someone to come and put a pillow behind my back." She was sitting on the bed like a child forced to go to sleep. "Go," she kept saying. But Sister Lorenza stayed all night in the chair, watching over her; Emanuela, when she saw that Milly was asleep, went back to her room.

The next day, Milly was better. Emanuela, going down to dinner, left her sitting in the chair copying some music into braille.

"Want me to stay?" she offered.

"No, why? I'm fine. I'll finish copying this Bach for him, then I'll re-read his letter that arrived this evening. He says maybe he'll come; if he does we'll go out together, it will be like the Giardini Reali."

When Emanuela returned with Silvia, she opened the door slowly and saw that Milly's head had fallen back, her hands open on the piece of paper, eyes wide. "Milly," she called softly. And suddenly, upset, she clutched Silvia's arm. "Milly!" she called again, her voice choking. Then they ran to get the nuns.

The news spread in an instant: "Milly ... Milly ..." Only the name: no one dared say, "She's dead."

The girls gathered in the hall, outside her room. Sister Prudenzina gripped the arm of the person closest, so hard she hurt her, insisting: "Order. First of all, order. It's pointless to fuss now." Sister Lorenza had entered with Emanuela and Silvia, and closed the door. Milly was motionless, eyes staring into space. "She still seems alive!" Emanuela murmured, but thought that, in reality, she had never been alive. A nun hurried in with vinegar—when by now it was too late—and the basin gave off a sharp smell. Sister Lorenza touched Milly's forehead: "We have to hurry," she said. "She's already cold."

"Sister, let her friends see her first."

"It's impossible, Silvia."

"Us from literature, Sister, just us."

In the meantime, Anna, Augusta, and Vinca had entered. Valentina, in the hall, resisted Silvia, who wanted to make her go in. "No, no, it's too distressing, I don't want to."

"You don't want to see our friend?"

"No, believe me, I can't."

Two or three more girls came in: one from music who was in the same course, and Loretta, who was studying medicine. But they didn't dare approach, restrained by a physical horror: already Milly was no longer their companion but only a dead person. They stared compulsively at that waxlike immobility, to hold on to the image; but, deep inside, they were anxious to leave.

The lay sisters arrived with white cloths, basins, water; Sister Prudenzina opened the closet, looking for a white dress, stockings. Milly's possessions were already the dominion of all, possessions that no longer had a possessor. When everything was ready, Sister Lorenza said: "Now go, girls." And without protest they withdrew, looking into the room: they saw two lay sisters approach Milly, raise her arms, then the door was closed.

In the hall the girls were whispering, in groups along the wall or at the windows; the nuns passed by with a great rustling of skirts and disappeared into Milly's room. Silvia and Emanuela had to keep repeating the story of how they'd found her.

" 'Milly,' we called, 'Milly.' She didn't answer, and we knew immediately that she was dead."

"But how was she?"

"Like this, her head fallen back on the pillow, and her gaze . . ."

"Her gaze?"

"Wide-eyed, staring, glassy."

"How was she, I didn't hear, how was she?"

"I went in, with Silvia, we called 'Milly . . .'"

"But hadn't you just left her, a little before?"

"Yes, in fact she said to me: 'Go, Emanuela, go on.'"

On the other side of the door you could hear the bed being shifted, people moving, hurried and careful steps, as in a mortuary. When a lay sister passed by with two candles, there was a reverent silence in the hall. Then the girls began questioning Emanuela again.

Loretta recounted: "The other morning, at the hospital, the nurse enters the ward to wake everyone up and finds a girl who doesn't respond, calls her, shakes her . . . Same thing: heart. A girl of twenty-three."

Augusta thought: "Now Milly knows what's on the other side. She didn't know she was dying, luckily. It must be terrible to say to yourself: I'm dying, it's over, and soon I will be in the beyond. Does the soul struggle to free itself from the body, as if from a tight sheath, or does it suddenly rise up, like a balloon when you've cut the string? And finding yourself suddenly before God. What's he like, God? Maybe he's sitting on a throne in a dazzling whiteness of clouds; and, seeing Milly arrive, with that blond hair, so white, surely he must have said: 'Come in, you're an angel.' It's true that God knows everything about her, even the thoughts we couldn't know. And maybe he's a terrible God, armed with lightning bolts, who will enumerate her sins without pity, then point her to a downward path. Milly would start walking, feeling heat that was mild at first, then became intolerable, and finally her cries would be lost amid the cries of a multitude of sinners. Silvia claims that there's nothing beyond, that the soul is extinguished in a breath of air, like a candle, and darkness falls where it was burning." Dismayed, she said to herself, "It's not possible, it's not possible that everything we do to refine our spirit, to improve it— our suffering, our effort, study, money, ambition, everything—dissolves in darkness." Milly now knew the truth. A little earlier, what? Two hours? She had gone in to say hello: Milly was well, smiling. And now everything was over for her, even music.

The door opened: the nuns stood aside and let the girls enter. Milly was lying on the bed: her hair, loose, already looked fake, made of straw. The room smelled of alcohol. The dim, tremulous light simulated a fluttering of eyelashes over Milly's face. Valentina, sobbing into her handkerchief, looked at her friends as if asking for help, and fainted. Loretta and Anna picked her up. "Out," the others murmured, "carry her out."

In her room she revived, with smelling salts. The nuns were furious. What did this scene have to do with anything?

"Sister, I can't sleep alone, don't leave me alone," she begged desperately.

Emanuela, Silvia, Augusta, and Vinca stayed all night beside Milly, watching over her, rosaries in hand, without praying.

. . . .

The entire Grimaldi was at the funeral, along with Milly's classmates at the conservatory and many students from the university, who didn't know her but whom the sudden tragedy had moved to pity.

Her father had arrived the morning after Milly's death, in a dark suit. He was young, he couldn't be more than forty, but already his hair, just slightly darker than his daughter's, was thinning. He had sat in Milly's room, alone with her, for an hour, and emerged pale and serene. He didn't regret that he hadn't been there the night before, that he hadn't seen his daughter until she was already marble. He inspired uneasiness, and you could understand why Milly preferred to stay away from him; but he was pleasant and very polite, shaking hands and saying, "Thank you, thank you." Leaving the church, he turned to the girls, who would have liked to follow the carriage to the station, and took his leave with a cold bow. The horses were stamping impatiently. Emanuela still had her friend's gentle voice in her ears: "I don't want to go back to Milan." A blaze of heat rose from her legs to her waist: "You have to help me, help me, Emanuela." Her hands were bathed in a cold sweat, and she seemed to have a piece of ice on her neck and, inside, a spreading chill. Someone took her by the arm, led her into a bar. "A Fernet," he said in a loud voice. It was Lanziani. "Are you better now?" he asked.

Surprised, she responded: "Yes, but I nearly collapsed when I saw Milly leaving."

"Don't think about it, don't speak about it anymore. It must have been terrible for you at the Grimaldi."

"Did you know her?"

"I'd seen her once with Costantini."

"With Costantini? It seems impossible. They were so different!"

"What was Milly like?"

What was she like? Her wide-eyed gaze into nothingness, her voice saying, "Help me, you have to help me": these would remain forever in Emanuela's memory.

"She was blond, she had a soft voice . . . She was studying music, harmony."

Coming out of the bar they walked side by side; when they had to cross a street, Andrea guided her by the elbow, resolutely, and let go as soon as they were on the sidewalk again. At the same time, she was examining him: he was tall, dark, with black eyes, a strong chin.

In Piazza di Spagna Emanuela stopped, saying: "I don't have the heart to go into the Grimaldi."

"Then don't. Call and say you're staying out for lunch: we'll go to a little trattoria I know, nearby."

"Lunch together?"

Andrea lighted a cigarette and, turning to Emanuela, said: "Let's go."

The trattoria had a big window that looked onto a courtyard spotted here and there with restless sun: six or seven tables, empty. An old man was eating at a corner table, absorbed in a newspaper.

"Here, you can call from here," said Andrea, going over to the phone: "Tell me the number . . . 66438? Go on, it's free."

Emanuela explained to the nun that she was going to lunch at the house of an aunt; then, hanging up, she stared at Lanziani, who was waiting.

"Let's sit down," he said, and, indicating the room, asked: "All right?"

Emanuela assented. She was happy, she looked around while Andrea chose from the menu.

"Risotto?" he proposed.

"Risotto."

"And afterward turkey breast?"

"Very good."

"White wine, cold," he said to the waiter. Then he turned to Emanuela, smiling: "You don't study much, right? I never see you in the department."

"But I'm not studying literature, I'm studying . . . Really I'm not studying anything," she confessed. "I wander around the galleries with an art history book under my arm."

"Have you seen the pulpit at Santa Maria in Cosmedin?"

"No."

"The mosaics at Santa Prassede?"

"Not those, either."

"Better: we'll go together."

She didn't say yes or no. She smiled, looking at him, and listened to him talk. Andrea said he would get his degree next year, he'd missed one course because of an accident, a fall while skiing. What he would do with a degree in literature he didn't know, but he had chosen that department because of Belluzzi's lectures, and because he didn't know, exactly, if two and two makes four or five.

"You go for Belluzzi, too? He's all the rage."

"Why?"

"Even I go to the department to listen to him. Silvia Custo, you know? The girl from Calabria . . . she's been working with him for two months, she's really enthusiastic . . . But you write, they say."

"Oh, nothing serious. They made me an instructor two years ago, because the others were worse writers than me. Since then I haven't written anything. But three newspapers have published my photo and I've been asked by a movie company to play in a sports film."

They laughed. Then, pouring some wine for her, Andrea said: "You know, I waited for two hours that evening on the Pincio?"

"Two hours?"

"Two hours, yes. I learned by heart a nursery rhyme some children were singing nearby. You want me to say it to you? It's the one with the countless beautiful daughters of Madama Doré."

Emanuela asked him: "Why did you wait so long?"

Andrea answered simply: "You know very well, why." Later, while they were having coffee, Andrea drew the layout of his room on the back of an empty cigarette pack: "Here's the bed, it's a sofa bed, one of those uncomfortable contraptions that are neither one thing nor the other, here's the desk, but so loaded with books that I can't write there and end up working on the dining table. Here's the cat's chair, he's a very old cat, half blind, my friend since I was a child ... Here," and he turned the pack over, "here's space to draw your room."

He had a way of speaking that was both affectionate and brusque; he moved unpredictably from one subject to another, forcing Emanuela to follow him, to tell him what he wanted to know. They ended up talking about her friends. Emanuela insisted: "I'm telling you, Silvia is a genius."

"She may be, but she's ugly, she's not a woman."

"Don't talk like that, I'm sorry: Silvia is a superior person."

"And the Spanish girl, what's she like? She must be crazy; the other day she nearly hit a classmate who paid her a compliment in passing that was, let's say, a little bold. She went after him with an umbrella. Vinca Ortiz ... Now, she is a woman: she's more than beautiful."

Emanuela didn't answer. It was time to go; the trattoria was now deserted.

At the door of the Grimaldi, Andrea asked her: "What time shall we meet tomorrow?"

She repeated, surprised: "Tomorrow?"

Andrea nodded, lighting another cigarette. Emanuela was thinking: "I shouldn't accept, it's not a good idea, but he's an unusual young man, I could see him tomorrow, tomorrow only, then that's the end," and she answered: "Here, at five."

· · · ·

Milly's death weighed on the institution; but Emanuela, returning, didn't notice. She went up to her room happily, murmuring Andrea, Andrea. Her contentment seemed to be reflected everywhere in the room, making it hospitable. For the first time since arriving at the Grimaldi, she forgot her friends; she was even sorry she was in Rome to occupy herself with the child.

"Papa's right. I should free myself of Stefania: she'll go to a boarding school abroad. No one knows anything: no one will ever know anything. So, if I want, I can remake a life for myself. I can't give up everything at the age of twenty-four because of this business of Stefania. Andrea is so congenial, with his old cat and his arrogance. Amusing. As long as no one knows anything, there's always some recourse. There are wonderful board-ing schools in Switzerland, she was born in Switzerland: she'll be very comfortable. Those schools where they do sports, learn languages, and a lot of other things. Anyway, children are ungrateful, selfish, they go their own way, as I did; they don't remember the sacrifices made for them."

Someone knocked at the door. "Is that you, Silvia? Come in."

"It's locked."

"Here I am."

Silvia was ready to go to Belluzzi's: she was wearing a black hat pulled down over her forehead. Andrea's right: she's not a woman.

"Silvia . . ."

"I was thinking it would be good to ask the nuns for the letters from him, the organist. All her things are still here."

"What things?"

"What's wrong with you? Milly's things, no? Her father gave orders to send them tomorrow."

"Oh . . . right. You want me to ask Sister Lorenza?"

"Yes. I have to go out."

"Silvia: you're not even asking me where I was."

"When?"

"Today, at lunch."

"Oh, yes. In fact, at the table, we were wondering."

"I was with Lanziani."

"With Lanziani?"

"Yes. And I'm afraid I'm in love."

Silvia looked at her: she had an unusual expression, more passionate.

"Great, without saying anything to us."

"But it's only since this morning!"

Milly's funeral had taken place that morning.

The girls had returned to the Grimaldi disconsolate. Silvia couldn't understand how Emanuela had chosen just that day to fall in love: the others couldn't escape the nightmare of the tragedy that had unfolded within these walls. At the table Vinca had questioned them: "Do you think I offended her, poor Milly, on Christmas night? That thought won't let me rest." And then they heard her in her room reciting the rosary, rapidly, in Spanish. In their ears they still had the grim stamping of the hooves of the horses pulling the carriage, saw again the indifferent gaze of Milly's father, and would have liked to know what there was between him and his daughter.

"You'll tell me tonight, it's late now," said Silvia, and left her.

Emanuela saw that there was a letter on the dresser. It came from Milan. When she opened it a hundred lire bill fell out and a green receipt.

It was from Xenia. Emanuela jumped as if she had seen a letter signed by Milly. None of them had heard a word about Costantini. Valentina said she dreamed that she was writhing in the flames of Hell and that she shouted to her. When Sister Prudenzina named her, she said: "That unfortunate girl."

It was a strange letter.

Dear Emanuela, I know that you are intelligent enough not to show this letter to the sisters or to our friends. I played a dirty trick on you, but I was feeling pressured, and I was sure you wouldn't report me. You know I'm not a thief. The ring is pawned for a thousand lire at Monte di Via Piè di Marmo, the narrow street we passed going to the university. It will be unpleasant for a person like you to go and get it, but you must believe that I suffered more in taking it there: and not so much because the ring didn't belong to me as for the way in which my new life began. I was hungry for two months, then I worked in a store selling gloves, and now I have a job in an agency for American gas for cars. One of the countless X&X companies. I earn pretty well, but it costs to live; because of that I can only send you a hundred lire a month until I pay off this debt, which torments me. I'm not giving you my address: we wouldn't have much to say to each other now. You may think badly of me, but I still love you, Emanuela; you were the only one I really liked there. I intend to arrive. Arrive is a little vague, right? But I will arrive. Hugs, Xenia.

Below she added:

Does Sister Prudenzina still turn off the lights at ten?

. . . .

The X&X Company ran a rather disorganized office. People came in, people went out, slamming the door. A dozen employees. For what Xenia had to do, six hundred lire a month was a gold mine: and yet when she left at night she was very tired and couldn't free herself from the world of the office right away, as Vandina did. It wasn't a job that required intelligence, but she tried to perform it with intelligence, to be noticed: she sat at the typewriter, one telephone on this side, one telephone on that, the first communicating with the outside, the second with the director. She copied letters that were always the same: "In response to your valuable . . ." But she had to interrupt at every moment: "Hello . . . yes, X&X . . . who is it, please? . . . I'll see right away if the director is here . . . I'm sorry, he just went out" or "Hello . . . I'll give you the director." In a few days Xenia had understood to whom she was supposed to give the one answer and to whom the other: generally when it was a female voice she was to say that he was there. "Everything lies in understanding how the system functions," Dino said. The director was a likable man, and when Xenia brought him the letters to sign he always asked: "How are things going, Signorina Costantini?" He had promised to increase her salary in July. But July was far away.

Dino came to the office frequently; Xenia owed the job to him. At first he had seemed very polite, and now, instead, she saw him push open the office door with his shoulder, hat on, jacket unbuttoned.

"Is the director there, Xenia?"

If the director wasn't there, Dino sat down next to the typewriter, smoking, while Xenia continued writing or answering the phone. "I need a secretary like you," he said to her. In general they saw each other when she left; Dino addressed her informally and Xenia expected that one day or another he would make her some proposal. Instead he treated her like a friend, as he treated Vandina. From the start Vandina had said to Xenia: "Listen, to avoid misunderstandings, I'm telling you right away that Dino for me is like a brother."

"I thought Dino was the one you call your boyfriend."

"Oh no! My boyfriend's poor. But Dino's practically thirty-eight and he's twenty-four. He's refined, like you, you know? He's a student. I'd intro-

duce you, but he's a bear; then he never has money and I don't want him
to make a bad impression."

After these explanations, Xenia went out with Dino every night when
she left the office: he came to get her in a car—"a spectacular car," he
said—and they went to dinner in elegant spots where often other friends
were waiting for them. At first, it happened that Dino forgot to introduce
them to Xenia: she was uncomfortable and said to herself, "In a moment
I'll leave," until finally he seemed to remember her: "Oh, sorry, what an
idiot!" He made the introductions and went on talking about business.

Now all day Xenia heard talk only of cars. In the office, less consump-
tion, greater yield, and at night the conversations of Dino and his friends:
"Did you sell? What did you sell? Did you see that new model?" Dino
had told her patronizingly: "I'll explain how it works. It's a large-scale
business, buying and selling cars, money comes, money goes, big deals.
Private citizens, naturally, you twist their arms. But you have to do it in a
way that the customer always says thank you, thinking he's made a good
deal. You have to flatter him so that he believes it: but, impossible as it
seems, despite being swindled so many times, he always does believe it.
'I've kept this car aside for you . . . You alone, in Milan, can have a car like
this . . .' You talk, you offer cigarettes . . . But it's quite a vast business and,
of course, sometimes you take a risk. Many, many times you take a risk."

Among Dino's friends there were three regulars: Tom Barchi, a young
man who had lived in America for two years; his girlfriend, a thin blonde
whose name was Maria but whom he called Mary; and Raimondo Horsch,
an older man, of German origin, who was tall, almost bald, and gray. It
was he who held the reins of the business, although he seemed not to be
involved in it. In general he would join them in a bar, where they'd spent
hours waiting for him. If he came for dinner, he ate only boiled vegetables
and drank only orange juice. His conversation was pleasant and intelligent. Talking to Horsch Xenia had a break from Dino's cars, Tom's America, the X&X Company's telephone. Mary listened and coughed. They all

knew she was consumptive and the life she led wasn't the best for getting
better. "I'd like to get better," she said, "but how can I? We're used to this
routine; we don't have the courage to break it off." Xenia, too, had grown
used to a new style of life; but in the morning her knees were heavy, her
eyelids puffy. "Tonight I'll go to bed early," she'd say to herself. Then, leaving the office, she'd find Dino waiting for her.

"Where shall we go tonight, little one?"

"I'm going home."

"Home?! What a sad idea! Why would you want to go home, my little
chick?"

"I'm sleepy, I'm tired."

"Okay. Then listen: we'll go have dinner at Icaro's, it's a quiet spot, and
afterward not even a small whiskey: I'll take you right home. You won't
make me dine alone!" As soon as she saw him at the entrance she knew
she'd be home at three. When Dino left, he gave her a peck on the cheek
and said: "Good night, little girl," nothing else. And yet he treated her with
a disconcerting familiarity, as if she were his girlfriend. Xenia looked at
herself in the mirror: "He doesn't like me." And while they were together
she tried to intuit the reason for that indifference.

"How's it going in the office, Xenia? Does the old owl treat you well?"

"Very well."

"But he exploits you, you earn a pittance. Six hundred, we said. It can't
go on. We'll find something better, but it's a bad moment, companies are
shrinking. Even us, with this iron shortage, we'll soon end up selling toy
cars."

At the X&X Company, Dino entered the director's office like a gust of
wind, without being announced. "You, my girl, have not yet understood
who Dino Ricci is. When I wait it's only to look at your beautiful eyes!"

On her birthday, Dino gave her a silver fox stole: "You can't go out
like that, with nothing around your neck." He also gave her a purse and a
dress. When she had these things, Xenia thought again of the Grimaldi.

They were all living the same life as then. They washed with cold water. It seemed ridiculous to her to have studied so much, to have been on the point of killing herself after the failure of her thesis, and all that in order to teach the declension of *rosa rosae*, earning a few lire a month. She had sent the second hundred-lire note to Emanuela, this time without a letter, only a piece of paper with her signature, not at all curious to know what her friends of those years were doing. Now that she was sure of not going back to her village, she often thought about it. Her parents wrote that there was a lot to do in the garden, the sowing, that her poplars were covered with new leaves, stirring nostalgia for the days when she walked alone in the countryside, or went to the fountain to see the women fill the brass jugs with water, balance them on their heads, speaking to one another in the rough accent of the dialect; or for certain country foods that her mother would prepare for her during vacations.

Sometimes she imagined returning to the village with Dino, the silver fox over her shoulders, to demonstrate to her mother how comfortable she was in the big car, listening to the radio while it sped along the highways: returning to make her old friends envious, see the poplars, eat pizza rustica, and leave again.

Her father regretted having mortgaged the vineyard. And one night Xenia wrote to him emphatically: "You'll see, one day, that, too, will be resolved. Pray God that I'll always have a job." And she was sincere as she wrote it, although by now she knew that with work alone she couldn't do much. Yet if Dino had asked her to marry him she would have said no.

She would happily have married Raimondo Horsch; but Horsch had a wife and a grown daughter, whom she didn't know. Raimondo Horsch was an important man: when he came to the office the director walked him out, saying to her: "Signorina, the door." She asked Dino what Raimondo Horsch did, and he said, "Business," and changed the subject.

In May Dino said to her: "There should be a secretary's position in a cement company. I talked to the managing director. You'd start at nine hundred, but net, without deductions. I said you speak French fluently and that you can manage in English. You won't let me make a bad impression, right?"

"No, of course not."

It was Sunday, a light-filled morning. Dino proposed going out of the city for lunch. "Do you know Pavia? There's that thing there, the Certosa, which is a national monument, and I know a trattoria where you eat very well." He turned on the radio, but there was a harp audition. After cursing the stupidity of the programs, he began talking about his deals again.

"You know what, Xenia? I've hit the jackpot. A shipment of trailer trucks to send to Libya. Naturally Horsch is also involved, he has the lion's share. But there's a good slice left for me. So I thought: you leave the job at the end of the month—yes, yes, a week's notice is enough . . . and you take a week off before starting at the cement company. Tom will look after my affairs—he's not a genius, Tom, but for a few days he'll do very well—and the two of us will go to the Riviera, to San Remo, maybe Nice and Cannes. Do you have a passport?"

"No."

"Too bad. Then Nice and Cannes we'll leave for another time. San Remo is amusing enough, there's the casino, roulette. It'll be a nice trip. Because, after all, it's time you and I went to bed together, no?"

Xenia didn't answer; she would have liked Dino to stop the car, at least kiss her; Dino, instead, had turned on the radio and was saying: "Oh! Finally some cheerful music!"

. . . .

At night now, all the windows on the façade facing the courtyard at the Grimaldi were lighted. After dinner the girls no longer gathered to talk: each shut herself in her own room, seriously preparing for exams or thesis. In the courtyard you could hear the monotonous flow of water in the fountain. Outside the thick gray walls it was summer.

Emanuela remained alone: luckily, there was Andrea. At first the news of their meetings had made the girls curious: they had asked endless details, they wanted to know about him, his character, his preferences. At the table they'd say, "Would Andrea like this dish?," as if he were everyone's boyfriend. Then those meetings became habitual, like Vinca's phone conversations.

Sometimes in the evening Vinca and Emanuela went down to the courtyard for a little cool air. They listened to the hours striking in the bell tower of Trinità dei Monti.

"Ten," Vinca said, "and we're shut up in here. We couldn't go out if we wanted to: the gate is locked, the sister sleeps with the key under her pillow. You know, when I arrived that half-closed gate in the entrance hall—unnecessary after the glass door and the outer door—frightened me? In fact it's a symbol . . . What's Andrea doing tonight?"

"Studying. And Luis?"

"How should I know? I think he goes to a café to talk politics. Have you heard? In our country, they're starting again. Papa wrote that, just as a precaution, he and his wife are leaving the city, going to the countryside. We have a house near Cordova: if I go back you have to come see me. It's a cottage, you know?, but sweet, because my grandparents lived there, and it has beautiful furniture from when we were rich. Everyone was wealthy once, even us. In the garden there are only orange trees."

"It must be lovely."

"Yes. The orange blossoms have a perfume that stuns you, makes you sleepy: a perfume that becomes the very air of the village. That's why we Andalusians are so lazy. Luis says things are going badly, and if this continues there will be civil war. Now, instead of studying, he and the other students, including the son of the ambassador, go and write 'Long Live Spain!' on the café tables. They drink and talk until late; then in the morning Luis is sleepy and misses his date with me."

Anna and Silvia, who were defending their theses in October, spent the morning in the library, suffocated by the heat and oppressed by the silence, by the mute round between catalogues, cards, dusty old books.

In the afternoon, Silvia went to Belluzzi's house. There, they barely seemed to notice her presence, maybe because she always walked on tiptoe, placed the papers on the professor's desk, and left immediately, closing the door softly behind her. Belluzzi was so absorbed and aloof she didn't dare disturb him. Protected by his thick gold-framed glasses, he went back and forth to the university without even seeing the streets he walked on; he found the entrance to his building by habit, went up the broad gray stone steps in a dignified hurry, and moved around his own house with the same distant air that he had in the street.

For some time Silvia's work went unobserved. One evening she entered the professor's study with a gray folder, full of papers.

"What's all that?" he asked.

"It's the material for the talk," said Silvia. (And meanwhile she thought: It won't be of any use at all to him. How much wasted effort!) She added: "Maybe it's not sufficient, or not useful, tell me what else I should do."

"We'll see. I'll review it tonight and tomorrow we'll talk about it," he answered, without looking up. "Thank you, signorina."

Silvia left discouraged, thinking: "It takes something else to succeed . . ." All she had was diligence, willingness, modest intelligence—no more. The next day she waited impatiently until it was time to go to the professor's; he called her in right away and was standing beside the desk.

"My dear Custo," he said, "what you've done is excellent. Where did you find such information? I wouldn't have been able to do it. And I wonder if, honestly, I can appropriate all this work, passing it off as my own. I'm pleased to have discovered you in the department in the back of the room. Why do you always sit in the last row? I've already told you: you'll go far. Perhaps I'll be gone by then. Don't forget me."

Silvia had on her face the expression of servile gratitude typical of those who are accustomed to submission from birth. Who were her parents, after all? Scarcely more than peasants. Someone had always taken possession of their work without even saying "Thank you, well done." Confused by that praise, Silvia would have liked to promise: "I won't take my eyes off the books, professor, I'll even work at night"; but at that moment Belluzzi's wife came in, carrying a cup of tea.

She was a plump, dark-haired woman no longer young, in a light-colored dress, arms spilling out of sleeves that were too short. She always looked at Silvia with amazement because she worked amid her husband's papers, which to her were incomprehensible.

Once Silvia had heard her say on the phone: "It's like having an animal in the house. I won't say anything about her intelligence, but she's so black and sad, I don't know how Guido can stand to have her around." She had no doubt that she was talking about her.

The professor, seeing his wife, emerged from his tranquil detachment, took off his glasses, and went toward her: "Oh, thanks, Dora, you're always thinking of me."

He had only to see her enter to light up; everything Silvia had done was dwarfed beside that cup of tea. She had spent nights and nights at her desk, rubbing her eyes over work that wasn't hers. Vinca was sleeping in the next room; she seemed to hear her regular breathing, inviting her to sleep. Then, to keep herself awake, she tugged on her earrings, two little clusters, black for mourning, and the next day her lobes were inflamed. "But I will never know how to enter his study dressed like that: enter on a wave of perfume, face powdered, carrying a cup of tea. She enters like a woman, while I work beside him like a comrade. He doesn't even notice that he's no longer alone when I enter: I'm with him, on the men's side."

Silvia was surprised, listening to Signora Dora speak to her husband as if she really loved him: she knew that as soon as she left the study she would put on her hat and go out. The professor didn't ask: "Where are you going?" She was going to her lover. She often talked with him at length on the phone, and Silvia, without intending to, through the thin wall heard gurgling laughs, childish endearments, blandishments. In those conversations the professor was only a pronoun: "he." He's gone out, he's back, as soon as he goes out. Third person singular. No more than that. Before going out Signora Dora brought "him" a cup of tea. And all day he tasted its sweetness.

Many times Silvia had thought of leaving, abandoning her work, not wishing to be a witness to what was happening in that household. Dora could leave her husband, if she wanted, but not betray him. You don't betray a man like Belluzzi. She could say to him: "I'm bored here, I'm leaving." But she didn't want to give up her nice house, her maid with the white apron, the gilded living room.

She considered, however, that the lovers lacked the pleasure of deception. For that reason, perhaps, they would soon get tired of it. "He" didn't notice anything. It was like cutting the throat of a sleeping calf. Outraged, Silvia would have liked to tell her friends, to relieve herself.

But she forced herself to be quiet; she didn't want her friends to imagine the lovers talking on the phone, saying foolish words of love while Belluzzi was serenely commenting on thirteenth-century sonnets.

· · · ·

One night Augusta said to Emanuela: "Come up to my room, I have to talk to you."

Augusta's room felt like summer: the turtle was making its way among the lettuce leaves, the Sardinian rugs were in mothballs, and a hydrangea plant adorned the night table.

"Want a coffee?"

"I'd love one."

While Augusta was busy with the spirit lamp, Emanuela observed the framed photographs. All were portraits of Sardinian people, faces carved into the old stone of the nuraghi and marked by powerful cheekbones; under the mass of black hair, as strong and wild as horses' manes, the features, pervaded by an age-old melancholy, were not illuminated but pierced by the grim intensity of the eyes, which seemed to reflect the desolation of rocky fields grazed by woolly flocks and swept by a feverish shivering.

"It's comfortable in this room."

"The rest of you, all you think about is leaving: so yours are like hotel rooms. You hesitate to unpack your suitcases, afraid of binding yourselves to these walls." Augusta was already old: there were many silver threads in her hair; maybe she was lying about her age, and was close to forty. One day she had asked Anna: "How old do you think I am?" Anna had answered, "Thirty," and she had smiled, saying, "You're kind."

"I asked you here because I can't go on like this—take the coffee, there's the sugar—and I thought you would understand me."

Emanuela was everyone's friend: it seemed impossible that the same person Xenia liked could also have been so loved by Milly, and called on for help by Augusta. Maybe because Emanuela had a quick, active, constantly vigilant intuitive faculty: which revealed and illuminated, in those who approached her, only the aspect of the self capable of inspiring a mutual sympathy. So each saw her own image reflected, as in a mirror; and although the mirror had many faces, it projected only the one that it animated. And this game of reflections was a continuous revelation for Emanuela, too, who saw rising from the depths of herself, and appearing on the surface, constantly new and until then unknown aspects of her personality. Illuminated from the outside, exposed by the contact with others, her true physiognomy emerged gradually, and in a surprising way, from the shadows.

"Do you like my coffee?" Augusta continued. "It's good, isn't it? Would you like a cookie?" Without waiting for an answer she resumed: "Have you never wondered what I'm doing here at the Grimaldi? I've wondered about you . . ."

"But you know perfectly well, Augusta, that I'm here to study art history and because my parents are traveling . . ."

"But they write to you from Florence. Anyway, it doesn't interest me. I'm not taking any exams. But since I'm enrolled in the department you all think I'm studying. I don't study. Not even when you see the light on until late."

"Then what are you doing?"

She hesitated before responding; she wanted to confide in her friend but it cost her a great effort. Finally she murmured: "I'm writing."

"Writing? What are you writing?"

"Novels, stories. Here," she said, taking a bundle of pages out of a drawer, all lined with her precise handwriting.

"This is tonight's work."

"Really?"

"Yes, but I have to confess everything. I work, I wear myself out, and no one wants to know about my stuff. You need to have help, know people . . ."

"What do you write about?"

"Love, always love." From the drawer she took a roll of papers tied with a ribbon. "I want to read you this story. And you have to tell me if you like it or not. I sent it to a literary journal, waited a month, then wrote, and wrote again, always including the stamps for the response. Nothing, not even a word. Finally after the third letter they rejected it, saying it lacks backbone, as if to say it doesn't stand up. You're an intelligent girl, you've read, you've traveled. The others live in their little world, they don't have a sense of the universal. They wouldn't understand."

She untied the ribbon and, as she unrolled the pages, resumed: "You must have thought: 'Augusta has to be really stupid if she doesn't even try to take the exams.' I always say I'm going to take them. Anyway, these girls leave, go back to their villages, get married."

"But how long will you stay here?"

"Until I've done something. I go back to Sardinia only for a month or two, in summer. By now, one can't go home anymore. Our parents shouldn't send us to the city; afterward, even if we return, we're bad daughters, bad wives. Who can forget having been master of herself? And in our villages a woman who's lived alone in the city is a fallen woman. Those who remained, who passed from the father's authority to the husband's, can't forgive us for having had the key to our own room, going out and coming in when we want. And men can't forgive us for having studied, for knowing as much as they do. That's for young women. I'm now already . . . already mature. As a girl I was engaged and it was said that Loris did it out of opportunism. Now, since they can't say that my behavior is immoral, they say that I'm a failure in literature."

"And why do you care what they say?"

"I shouldn't worry about it, really. But when we reach the point of being indifferent to the approval of others, it's a sign that many things for us have faded. When we're no longer afflicted by defeats, it's a sign that we no longer believe in victories: that life runs over us without doing us good or ill."

Out in the hall the sister cried, "Lights! . . . Lights! . . ." and opened the doors, violating all intimacy. She opened the door of 40 and found them talking quietly, while Augusta got the lamp ready: disappointed, she said, "Good night," and fell on the door of the next room, from which came voices and laughter. Augusta waited for the abrupt cutting off of the current; then, as soon as her eyes became used to the weak glow of the oil lamp, she cleared her throat like a singer and began to read.

It really was the work of an unmarried woman, like filet lace, Emanuela thought, struggling to resist sleep. And yet when, at the end, Augusta asked, "Do you like it?" she said, "It's good, very good." What would be the point of telling the truth?

"Tell me what you like best."

"When she talks about the river."

"And yet to me it doesn't seem lyrical enough. Anyway, thank you. A secret you carry alone is much heavier. Now go down and I'll start working."

"So late?"

"It's barely eleven. At this hour, in the silence, I work very well. Besides, I have no choice. I have to work quickly. I don't have much time ahead of me." She spoke haltingly, as if she were speaking to herself, aloud.

. . . .

Right after the exam, Andrea called Emanuela to tell her the result: "Splendid—top marks." And she went to knock on her friends' doors, giving them the news. Then she went out, impatient to join him nearby, on the San Sebastianello pathway up to Villa Medici. "Bravo," she said breathlessly. "Bravo. My friends are happy, too, you know—it's really great." They set off at the slow pace of a stroll. On the broad path other couples were walking arm in arm, in front of them, behind them, like a procession. "I'm happy because I'll be finished soon," said Andrea. "That's my next-to-last exam before the degree; but you always feel some disappointment after exams, even when they go well. You study, and then you leave the classroom at the same point as before." The path that led up to the square on the Pincio was swarming with black shadows, but every couple was enclosed in its own solitude, as if the Villa were its domain; words were barely whispered, or even silent. The only sound was the crunching underfoot of the leaves that had fallen from the plane trees. It was sunset: the city was turning red, bristling with bell towers and dense with cupolas, and from the windows flashes of purple sprayed like fireworks.

Emanuela and Andrea sat down near a fountain surrounded by a semicircle of myrtle. The water gurgled up from a spring amid the green with a soft, subdued sound.

"It's comfortable here," he said. "It's as if we're in the garden of our own house. Today, thanks to this exam, our house seems very close. And yet the day of my degree I'll feel as I do now: content but useless. I certainly won't be able to appear in an office, saying: 'Here I am, I'm the one who got his degree this morning.' And find someone there who will lead me to a room in a fake-Renaissance style, pointing, and saying: 'Here, sit down, that's your chair, I was waiting for you.' And so? Go teach somewhere or other with a miserable salary. How will I feed you, wife?"

They laughed, but he resumed, serious: "Let's add it up. Five hundred for the house ..." and he continued to calculate until he concluded: "Even if you give up the living room and I soccer games and cigarettes, we can't manage without two thousand lire. And we can't deprive ourselves of these things: so twenty-five hundred."

"Between you and me."

"All right. And then if I have a toothache and have to have the tooth pulled: and if you go and get a perm? Please, Emanuela, don't tell me again that you have your money—for that very reason I have to have mine."

"So the problem is insoluble."

"It has to be soluble, because I won't give up the joy of knocking on the door of a house that has my name on the door and seeing you come to meet me smiling, of smelling as I enter the good smell of a roast, and seeing the table set for two, Professor Lanziani and his wife, one on this side, one on that. But, in contrast, I think of so many of my married friends, who have sad eyes, their wives have sad eyes, the children are pale, and they, too, have sad eyes. No, believe me, it's terrible. We've been spoiled up to now, you and I."

"And so?"

"So imagine Papa's face today at the table when he congratulated me on the exam and I said to him: 'Yes, good, I'm very pleased, but after the degree I'm coming to work with you.'"

"You said that?"

"Yes, and you don't know what a fight we had when I enrolled at the university. 'Three generations of jewelers, the royal crown in the window, and you now ...' Papa was in despair: but I was immovable: 'I don't love your work, I don't want to be behind a counter ...' In short you can't imagine what happened in those days; Papa didn't speak to me, Mamma rushed from one to the other. So today he was shocked, but I continued:

'I'm coming to the shop, and you give me that two thousand lire a month you promised if I didn't go to the university.' 'And the degree?' he said. 'I'll put it in a frame.' I went on in this tone and suddenly he explodes, throws down the napkin, shouting: 'Tell me, Andrea, what does all this mean?' Wild, Papa when he's angry, you know ... I said: 'It means I need to earn money because I'm getting married.'"

"You said that?"

"Exactly that. You see the scene, no? Mamma's crying, the maid arrives with the plates, Papa gets up, shouts: 'I'm not eating anymore.' But I know what he's like. Tomorrow I'll put your photo on the night table and in a month I'll bring you home."

Andrea had always talked with horror about the life of the shop: he disliked everything about it, from the yanking of the shutters to the velvets of the display windows and the servile and frustrating wait for the customer. "I hate the life that my parents have led for years: Papa shows off the stones as if he were handling precision instruments, the salesmen go around with catlike steps, Mamma sits in the back room of the shop. It's a cozy little room, furnished like a room at home, and she goes there every afternoon and knits; but if a customer comes in, she puts the work down on her knees, strains her ears, then resumes. When the store is empty, Papa takes the newspaper and joins her." And now Andrea had accepted all this, for her. It was the moment to speak to him: "Andrea, I have to tell you something, it's something past, over, he's dead, you understand, but the child remains; she'll go to Switzerland, you're an intelligent man, you'll understand." She had to speak, otherwise all these conversations, these plans for the future were pointless, morbid, like getting the clothes ready for a baby you know will be stillborn.

"Listen to me, Andrea ..."

"No, I'm not listening to anything. All right, there will be your money, but along with mine. Or are you ashamed to be the wife of a shopkeeper rather than a professor of philosophy?"

It was impossible to speak. He had started talking about the house again. "You women can't understand, for you your parents' house is your home, but we are strangers in any house that is not ours: I mean the one where our woman is, where our children are born. And I want to have a shelf where I can arrange my books without Papa sticking his mysteries next to them, I want to find, when I return, someone who's waiting for me, waiting just for me. But maybe you'll come to the store sometimes, like Mamma. When I'm wearing glasses," he added, pinching her cheek affectionately.

How to say suddenly: "Andrea, I have a child"? A selfish child who lives in a world of her own that others enter only to attend to her comforts. When Emanuela visited, Stefania was bored. They had nothing to talk about, except meaningless matters. What should I bring you? What are you bringing me? As soon as Stefania had taken the package the purpose of the visit was over: Emanuela would have liked to hug her, hear her talk about so many things, but the child broke away from her, wriggled free, seeking her own autonomy: "Having children's not worth the trouble if they won't even let you hold them." Her maternity existed only behind the door of that school: as soon as she left she was free of it. And yet when Andrea mentioned their future she felt torn, thinking: "It's impossible." Tears rose to her eyes and, imagining that she was moved, he treated her like a silly girl, took her hands, kissed them, calling her jokingly "Dear wife," unaware that she was weeping precisely because all that would never be. So she decided: "It's better to go on like this, Papa will help me, he'll talk to him, on the eve of the wedding; Andrea adores me, he wouldn't be able to live without me."

· · · ·

A few days later, Emanuela and Andrea went with Vinca to see Luis's new studio. At first Andrea resisted: "I don't much like that girl. What's their relationship? They're not even engaged. It doesn't seem proper for you."

Then Emanuela accused him of being bourgeois, and, saying, "No, really, no," he agreed to go.

There was nothing remarkable about the studio except the old front door with that Renaissance frieze; the stairs were narrow and poorly lit. As they went up, a door opened and an odor of frying escaped, along with a child's crying. After the last, steep flight, they found themselves in a large, bare room, with a drawing table in one corner, walls covered with architectural plans, two sofa beds, a tea service. But everything was ennobled by the light that came from the huge window, which framed a picturesque view of roofs and domes crowned by the green Janiculum.

Luis was waiting for them with Pepe and other students. "It's best that we Spaniards all stick together now," he said; so he had wanted Vinca to meet his colleagues. But she was annoyed, seeing that Luis treated her like an ordinary friend: if he didn't want the others to know, why had he made her come up here? The young men talked about politics; the Spaniards in loud voices, Andrea in his determined, calm tone. Vinca and Emanuela sat on one of the sofa beds, but they didn't know what to say to each other. They got up to look at the plans pinned to the wall: many bore Luis's signature, others were signed by friends, also Spanish. Vinca was enthusiastic, admiring them, and turned her gaze to Luis, who was speaking excitedly: he was talking about Red Spain, about Falangist Spain, about churches gutted by bombs, women thrown into the sea in sacks, children with no hands, the dead disinterred. "And we, here, can do nothing: we have to witness, indifferent, the destruction of our country!"

At this point a fat older woman with reddish hair and heavily powdered face, wearing a flowered dress, burst into the studio followed by a pale young woman and a young man with glasses. They, too, were Spanish: the young woman was engaged to Pepe, and her brother, Ignacio, was studying architecture. Vinca had heard about them.

The mother sat down heavily on the sofa, out of breath from the long climb and the heat that was starting to become oppressive. Luis made the introductions, and she held out her hand absentmindedly, because of her weariness. She spoke a mixture of Spanish and Italian in a loud, strident voice.

"We had to walk," she complained, "no carriages in the square, and Pilar said 'It's *aquí* nearby.' *Y* the stairs . . . the stairs . . . But beautiful up here, why *no abrir* the window a little?"

The sweat dripped down her made-up face. Pilar approached Vinca, they smiled at each other without speaking, displaying a timid sympathy such as happens between children. The older woman observed Emanuela and Vinca with her lorgnette and then exclaimed:

"*Dios!* How charming! *Que bellezas!* What beauties! Which of these two is Luis's girlfriend?"

It was the first time Vinca had heard herself called that and she didn't dare respond; but, with Emanuela pushing her by the arm, she answered, blushing: "Me."

"Come, let me look at you! Let's see, how old are you? Twenty-one? *Como mi Pilar*—the same as Pilar! Have you seen *mi* Pilar?"

Then, detaching herself easily from Vinca, she said she was agitated because of a visit she had received and was eager to recount. "*Esta* morning there comes into my room the *criada*, how do you say?, the maid, and she goes: 'There's a young lady from Spain.' Imagine! I *estavo* still undressed, in my bathrobe, but 'from Spain,' she had said, I'm coming right away, I say, tell her to wait. I go and I find a lovely creature, beautiful, slender, a platinum blonde, just like a film star. A friend of mine sent her to me, an old friend, whose son was killed with a bullet in the back, *bang*, right there, at the age of twenty-two. So the girl was pale, like wax, *pobrecita*, poor thing: she's saved by a miracle, they wanted to shoot her. She was imprisoned for a month, with other women, people from the aristocracy, two nuns and a pregnant woman. They arrested her in the middle of the street, come with us, and she immediately thought: they'll kill me."

Pilar interrupted her: "First you have to say she's not Spanish, that at the consulate . . ."

"Oh yes, true . . . so she's North American, but she likes Spain, her mother is Spanish and that's why she was living in Spain. At the American consulate they tell her: 'Don't worry, you're an American citizen, they can't do anything to you, they won't touch you.' But those devils don't care about papers. So imprisoned in a *sotano*, how do you say?, a cellar, with many other women: two of them came out to be shot. They call them saying '*Vamos de paseo*,' we're going for a walk, and they don't come back. She arrived here exhausted, dying of hunger, she told me all that while she's eating. So the nuns prayed, the pregnant woman wept, until one day she begins to groan, then she starts shouting, it's the labor pains. Twenty-four hours of labor, and shouts, shouts, and they knocked at the door, nothing, alone there, like dogs, in the dark, the nuns helping that poor woman, who, the next day, is finally freed."

"The child was dead," Pilar interrupted. Donna Inés gave her a dirty look, because she had taken the words, and their effect, out of her mouth. Then she continued: "Dead . . . and the mother half-dead, there, in the filth, weeping, desperate, warming it with her breath so it would come back to life. After two days they take away the corpse, the mother had a high fever, infection, it was serious. The nuns had gone back to praying: that muttering, says the *muchacha*, drove her mad. The next day someone opens the door, says '*Es domingo*, Sunday, we eat a roast, roast rabbit.' They all devour it, starving, even the nuns, even the woman who's just given birth. And, afterward, those men, two or three standing in the doorway laughing, roaring with laughter. '*Bueno*, right?' they asked, laughing like drunks. 'You know what the rabbit was? It was the baby!'"

The girls gave an exclamation of horror; the men, uncertain, stared at Donna Inés, who, exhausted by her long speech, had gone back to fanning herself, raising her dress slightly off her sweaty chest.

"And what about her?" Luis asked. "How in the world was she saved?"

"She was saved like this. The next day, those men returned and took away the nuns. *Las pobrecitas* go *como* to martyrdom. Then they come back, but they aren't praying anymore: they're thrown in a corner, without coifs, their short hair a mess. And soon after that they call the girl, the *muchacha*: 'A pasear.' A walk. She told me she wasn't afraid, she knows she's cold-blooded, better to die than this nightmare, she thought, the others were weeping, and she goes out with the men. She says she'd decided: before they shoot I cry 'Long live Spain!' At least her fiancé would know. And then, you know what? Like in a film, at the last moment the United States consul arrives and takes her away, unconscious. She was ten days in the consul's house, very ill. She was delirious, shouting, 'Long live Spain! Long live Spain!' and she was spitting because she couldn't get out of her mouth the taste of that dead baby."

Donna Inés stopped, choked by emotion, and resumed, sighing: "She's leaving tomorrow, the consul's sending her back to the United States, I gave her what I could, she's desperate because she's afraid they've murdered her fiancé—a beauty, that *muchacha*." Then, seeing that the others were stunned by her story, she concluded: "That's what it's like in our country."

Vinca thought: "Luis will leave soon." Pilar was holding Pepe's arm tight. Donna Inés continued talking, fanning herself with a large Sevillian fan on which a small square circled by blue majolica tiles was painted, along with a house with geraniums on the balconies, and the soaring bell tower of the Giralda. Vinca's eyes were staring at the fan, and Donna Inés noticed.

"What are you looking at, *chica*? The Giralda? *Ay!*" she said, pressing the fan to her heart. "Who knows if *la veremos* again, the Giralda! Will we ever see it again? Isn't there some water, Luis? I'm thirsty. Thanks, *hijo*, my child. *Ay*, the Giralda! Pilar, you drink, too. They say there will be war, in our country: it's a matter of days."

Pilar said in a choked voice: "I want to get married if Pepe leaves." And she burst into tears. Donna Inés screamed: "*Hija*, no, good God!

Who said Pepe's leaving? The boys are staying. What would they do, the three of them, against so many of those cynical barbarians? What would they do?"

"No, Donna Inés," Luis interrupted her. "I'm leaving. And you?" he asked, turning to the other two. "You'd rather stay?" Donna Inés, bewildered, looked at her son, but Ignacio shook his head. Pepe asked Pilar: "Would you really want me to stay?"

Donna Inés intervened: "*Vamos vamos*, kids, let's go, this is chatter, talking just to talk, no one's leaving, Pepe's not leaving, Pilar, *alma mia*, my heart, Pepe *no se mueve*, he's not moving, *vamos, vamos.*" And she changed the subject: "Luis, weren't you supposed to show us your projects?"

Luis, rousing himself, took a bundle of drawings from the drawing frame and showed them around: "Here, this is the project that was entered in the competition for the summer colony: it failed. We're foreigners. This is a plan for working-class housing. The three of us worked together, Pepe, Ignacio, and I. Got nowhere."

Pilar repeated: "You, *también*, Pepe, you, too?"

Pepe nodded, smiling at her, while Luis continued: "This is the plan for a villa, a Rational villa: terrace, solarium, garden, tennis, pool . . ." But before displaying the drawing, he said, puzzled: "Will they ever again build villas and pools in our country?"

Donna Inés said: "*Hijos*, you're young. You have time to build villas, many villas. But *nosotros*, we others . . . will we ever return to walk in the Retiro again, we old ones?"

. . . .

Belluzzi's lecture was a great success: to help him Silvia had neglected her studies, doing her own work only at night; she went to sleep at four, got up at six thirty. She sat at the desk again in the pure morning silence and with an effort opened the folders, tormented by a dull pain in her back that forced her to straighten her chest every little while.

The night before, the professor had read it to her, standing behind his desk, while she sat in a chair; at the end he had said, "You'll come to hear me just the same, right?" and had given her an invitation. "Afterward come here, to my house."

She went and sat in the back row. There were already a lot of people in the large hall; it was adorned with mirrors, and on the ceiling plump little angels danced, holding wreaths of roses.

Among the guests, who all seemed to know one another, Silvia felt isolated. She had the impression that her neighbors were examining her, looking her up and down. Signora Dora had taken a seat in the first row, where there were gilt chairs, but she kept getting up, to greet this one and that one, as if she were the mistress of the house. She wore a green dress and a large black hat with a green feather that waved gently when she bent her head in greeting. On a raised platform stood a red chair and a low table with a bottle of water.

Silvia knew that the professor got agitated before speaking in public, so she would have liked to be with him in the small room where he was waiting with people who, surely, annoyed him. In the hall, Signora Dora welcomed two tall, white-haired gentlemen, dressed in black, who must be important, since people moved aside to let them pass and, afterward, commented in low voices.

The two important gentlemen sat in the most visible chairs, elbows on the armrests, hands supporting their chins, waiting. Signora Dora also sat down, every so often turning to direct a glance of understanding and satisfaction at the audience behind her. Then a small door opened, Belluzzi appeared, hurrying, head bent, and stepped onto the platform without even greeting the audience, who applauded. Even the two important gentlemen clapped their hands lightly. After one of his dry coughs, Belluzzi began to speak.

Silvia followed the nervous motion of the professor's hand as he turned the pages that she herself had typed. In the eyes of the listeners you could perceive interest, agreement; the two important gentlemen listened intently.

When Belluzzi finished speaking, the crowd gathered around the dais, like students after a class.

Silvia lingered a few minutes at the back of the room, watched him smile, nod. No one knew that that small woman in black had worked with Belluzzi; but she did, she knew. Slowly she left the room and descended the grand staircase between valets who looked at her disdainfully, but she felt intoxicated, happy.

The day after the lecture was a holiday, so she went to Belluzzi's two days later. The professor wasn't at home, but on the table were congratulatory cards, telegrams. She read them with pleasure, standing near the window. Summer didn't enter the professor's house: it announced itself only with white slipcovers on the chairs. When he arrived he moved toward her with hands outstretched.

"You know that Saturday I immediately came home, for you? You didn't come to the lecture, and so I could even tell you it went badly, right?"

"No, professor, you couldn't, because I was there."

"You were there and didn't come to greet me?"

"You had so many people around you, professor."

"But you aren't like the others, for me, dear Custo. I will be in a bad way when you leave, after your degree."

"I'll stay, professor."

"You can't. You have to make your way. What could staying with me offer you? You'll waste a few years, nothing more. And in life there are no years to waste."

"There's time to think about it, professor."

"Yes, there's time." After a pause he said, looking at the sky: "Summer has arrived suddenly this year. I only realized it today, going with Dora to the station. She left. And I'll be leaving soon."

"You'll join the signora at Abbazia?"

"No. I'm going to my cottage in the country, in the Veneto, it's old and run-down. It was my father's house; and it does me good to go there once a year. I would almost say I feel rejuvenated, maybe because I lived there as a boy. And then one needs a little respite before resuming work."

"And the signora will join you there, naturally."

"Oh, no! She came one year, to please me. But she's so bored, poor Dora, she nearly made herself ill over it." He smiled at the memory. "Dora is very different from us. She likes people, action. She's so full of life, Dora, she's really a woman ... a real woman, that's it. What more can one say? With her I can never talk about my work and that's restful for me. We who are always busy thinking, we need a person beside us who doesn't think at all, otherwise we'd suffocate. For me, when I see Dora at dinner, in the evening, it's like opening the window and taking a breath of fresh air. That marvelous ignorance of the things that for us are vital proves to me that every art is essential only for those who make it."

"I don't think so, professor."

"You're still young: you'll realize it."

The professor had said: "Really a woman ... a real woman." And Silvia didn't understand if he intended those words to express admiration or benevolent indulgence. For several days Signora Dora hadn't been making calls: she was shut in her room writing, on the delicate Maggiolini writing desk, lengthy letters that she enclosed in elongated violet envelopes. She was writing to Abbazia, she had left for Abbazia. Really a woman ... a real woman.

When Silvia was a child she'd liked racing with the boys of her age, while her sisters wove garlands, embroidered, listened to fairy tales beside the hearth. At most, she sewed ruffles on the mule's saddle while the servants told stories about bandits. In the morning she wore her older brother's pants and went horseback riding along the canal; then, tying up the horse, she lay down on the grass to read or think. Suddenly, at thirteen, she had asked her mother: "Tell me, Mamma, I'm really ugly, right?"

"Who says that?"

"Some girls playing with my sisters. They were laughing, my sisters were laughing, too, and they even added: 'Haven't you seen her in our brother's pants? She's a boy, too.'"

"Why do you listen to that nonsense, Silvia?"

"Then tell me, am I ugly or not?"

Her mother caressed her hair, saying: "No creature is ugly who is born in the image of God."

Then they sent her to the city to study: her sisters stayed in the big kitchen waiting for husbands. Immacolata was already engaged.

"They did the right thing," she said to herself. "I wouldn't be a good wife. I'm not a breath of fresh air. I could only marry the bandit who would carry off even me on his saddle. But I think I would prefer to have my own horse and gallop beside him."

She found her friends after prayers; the chapel was fragrant with lilies. On the first warm days the Mother Superior would be overcome by sleep during the service. Augusta, who received the confidences of Sister Lorenza, said there was talk of sending her back to Genoa, to her mother-house, where the old nuns go and wait to die. "They sit on the terrace in the sun, pray, doze . . ."

"It must be terrible," said Emanuela, "to see one's companions die, one by one."

"I don't think so," Augusta replied. "When one dies, the others are happy they're still alive, holding out. They shudder at the danger that's just grazed them and passed them by."

Now, in the evening, the girls went out to the courtyard to talk for a while. There was a new girl who was studying the cello and from above came the affectionate notes of Offenbach's barcarolle, when Vinca entered the courtyard, distraught, and showed her friends the newspaper she was holding: Spain was at war.

"I want to go out," she said. "I want to go to Luis."

"Oh, Vinca, it's late now."

"What do I care? Donna Inés told me I can come to her house when-ever I want, with Pilar. I have to go." She ran to the entrance and found herself facing the porter nun, who was turning out the light: "Sister, I have to go out!"

"At this hour? Are you mad?"

"I want to go out. There's war in my country, you understand? I can't stay here, open it right away."

"It's almost ten. Go to sleep, Vinca: you'll go tomorrow morning."

"Who could sleep? Open it, I'm telling you."

She hit the door angrily. The old sister rang the bell and Sister Lo-renza came running.

"What is it, Vinca?"

"I have to go out, it's urgent. There's war at home, I want to join the others. After this news they'll all be together."

"What others?"

"My other friends. Why are you looking at me like that? Yes, also Luis, why are you making that face? What, haven't you always known about Luis? Let me go out, I said!"

Sister Lorenza tried to calm her: "Don't you want to telephone in-stead? Come, you'll go tomorrow morning."

But Vinca went on pounding with her fists on the door: "Open it, Sister, open it for me, have pity. What if they leave? Luis said he'll leave at the first announcement."

"No, come on, he can't leave right away, like that."

"What do you know? What do you know about men, Sister Lorenza?"

Anna and Emanuela had arrived to persuade her, but Vinca insisted:

"No, no . . . You, at least, Emanuela, you should understand me. What if they leave? If he leaves, what will I do, tell me?" They brought her to her room, raving: "The war . . . there's war . . . and I'm shut up in here, buried alive. I've always said I felt like a prisoner. What if Luis leaves?"

"It's impossible for him to leave tonight."

"Everything is possible for him. He leaves me a note, departs, and I'll never see him again! Tell me: What if he's killed?"

She was sobbing. The others, silenced, felt for the first time that Vinca was a foreigner: what happened in her country didn't touch them. As if she were sick, they undressed her, put her to bed. Sister Prudenzina brought another candle, a cup of chamomile. Seeing the nun, Vinca yelled at her: "You could let me go out instead!" Then she said to her friends: "We're suffocating here in the midst of these holy old maids and their selfishness!"

Her sobs faded into a long, muffled bout of crying. Her friends stayed with her, Silvia read the paper. "A bad business," she thought, twisting her mouth. When they were about to go, Vinca opened her eyes, grabbed Emanuela's hands, and said in a faint voice: "Don't leave me alone. I'm afraid that from now on I'll be alone forever."

. . . .

Luis decided to depart immediately. He gave Vinca a map of Spain so she could follow events. Pepe, too, departed, and so did Ignacio. Those who were going to graduate in October decided to join them. Luis said: "But at that point we'll already be returning. We'll return to be offered a drink the day of your graduation. And you won't get away with something cheap. But now that we're going, the war will be over in a week."

They were joking, and Vinca, too, tried to joke, but she kept asking Luis: "Will you write to me? Will you write to me forever? You'll leave me the plans?" And when Luis threw away his old slippers, she picked them up to save with other garments of his.

She had decided to leave the Grimaldi. Donna Inés had invited her to her house. "That way my Pilar won't be alone," she had said, and Vinca had explained to her friends: "I wouldn't be able to study now, anyway." Excited by the change, she wasn't even sorry to leave them. Sister Lorenza found her some Spanish lessons, and, grateful, she kissed her hands. Her father had taken refuge with his wife in Portugal and from there had telegraphed the nuns that Vinca could go and live with Donna Inés. Once her suitcases were closed, Vinca went around the rooms, saying goodbye to her friends: "I don't seem to be leaving you, since I'm staying in Rome," she said. "We'll see each other every day. Maybe after the summer I'll even come back to the Grimaldi."

Distracted by so many changes, she had almost forgotten Luis's departure. One day he called: "Come to the studio today, Pilar's coming, too, with Donna Inés." Vinca, entering the studio, found him packing. He was alone. Pepe had taken Pilar home because she couldn't bear the preparations.

"Already?" she asked, turning pale.

"We're leaving tomorrow. At the border we'll find out our destination."

He was really leaving. That very morning, in the paper, Vinca had read: a hundred and nineteen dead in a clash. Spain was far away: three days for a letter.

"You'll write to me?"

"Yes, when I can."

When I can . . . Maybe one day he wouldn't be able to. No letters. Maybe Pilar would have no news of Pepe nor Donna Inés of Ignacio. The newspaper would cite the number of dead. And no letters. For the others, life would be nice and peaceful even if mail didn't arrive from Luis.

"Listen to me, Luis."

"What?"

"I love you."

It was the first time she'd said it to him. Luis stopped folding a jacket and turned; and seeing her trembling he came over and put his arms around her. Holding her close, Luis caressed her back with hands different from the greedy ones she had known in the dark of the movie theater. Tomorrow he would no longer be with her, his hands would no longer caress her, in any way.

"Luis, you'll take my picture with you?"

"Of course, the one I took on the Janiculum that day we had a fight."

"What else can I give you? Here: take my fountain pen. Otherwise how will you manage to write to me from the front? You remember Donna Inés's address?"

"Yes, of course."

Luis spoke to her sweetly, to reassure her. The last light of the sun had reached the window and ignited it as it had the day he had asked her: "Why don't you come up?" And now he was leaving for war.

"Luis . . ."

"Vinca . . ."

"You remember that day we came to see the studio from the street?"

"When?"

"When I didn't want to come up."

"Yes, I remember."

Vinca, staring at him, said: "Well . . ." Her voice was unlike her usual one, firmer. "You want to, now?" she offered with desperate eyes. "Do you want to?" He hesitated at first, without understanding. Then he hugged her tight, kissed her hands.

"No," he said.

"Why not? Then . . ."

Luis shook his head: "It was something else, then. Tomorrow I'm leaving."

"I want to now. I love you, you don't know how much I love you, Luis . . ."

"I do know." He nodded, serious. "I'll be back soon. Or you'll return to our country. Don't you remember the conversations we had about Andalusia? If you wait for me, if you have the strength to wait for me . . . I'll be back, you'll see."

The sun had left the window. The big bare room was gray, full of shadowy corners.

"I'm afraid," Vinca confessed. "Don't leave me."

. . . .

Xenia and Dino left on Saturday afternoon. The night before they'd had dinner with Vandina and, afterward, Horsch and Tom joined them. The men had gone to the bar to talk business; the girls remained alone and Vandina took advantage of that to say in a low voice: "Good for you! I'm really happy about your good fortune."

"What good fortune?"

"Well, this trip, the clothes, the purses, shoes . . . and you'll see, it won't end there. You're not at all in love with Dino?"

"No, but . . . I like him."

"Better. You see what tricks fate sometimes plays? You go for a job interview, you meet another girl looking for a job, you chat, you become friends, and then, one thing leads to another. I knew right away that you were a refined type and people would like you. Someone else, in my place, would have left you to manage on your own. But I'm pleased when I see people happy," Vandina had said to her. "At San Remo put a louis on twenty-two for me. It's my number. I was born on April twenty-second, then on another twenty-second . . . yes, well, you understand me, I mean that afterward I was no longer a virgin and martyr. And on one twenty-second I met my friend, when I was twenty-two. What do you think? Wait, another twenty-two . . ." She broke off because the men had returned.

Horsch was in a bad mood and didn't open his mouth; he became livelier after two whiskeys and in fact drank to their trip. Everyone knew that Dino and Xenia were leaving together. She had written home that she was going on a trip, for the office, of course, so she would be able to send some postcards and the postmistress would tell the entire village.

They reached San Remo at lunchtime. During the trip Xenia looked eagerly this way and that. She couldn't help thinking: "I always get where I want to be."

Dino entered the hotel as if he owned it: he asked for two communicating rooms, each with its own bathroom. Soon afterward they were at a table in the hotel dining room, where the orchestra was playing chamber music. "Drink," Dino insisted. And Xenia was pleased by the thought that the typewriter she wrote on for hours, until she had a piercing pain in her back, was far away, in Milan; and she was in San Remo. Now she would ask Dino if she could go to the cement company: a month off would be good for her.

After coffee, Dino threw down his napkin and they went out. It was so many years since Xenia had seen the sea! The last time, she was twelve: a Sunday outing in a burning-hot third-class carriage. On the beach the cool wind, smelling of rock, had dissipated her tiredness. But her father wanted to go right away to a trattoria famous for its fried fish.

"Will you take me to see the sea, Dino?"

"The sea? What, you don't see it from here? You need to walk down there? Let's go make some bets at the casino instead."

The casino: a kind of large office where people were crowded around tables under green shades. No one spoke: only, from time to time you heard the ball jumping around in the roulette wheel, the voice of the croupier. The players lost and won, impassive. Xenia and Dino approached a table, and at the sound of their footsteps the people sitting there looked around suspiciously.

"Is it very difficult?" she asked.

"Very easy. You put one of these tokens on a number. Let's see, what number do you want?"

"Twenty-two, because Vandina ..."

"Okay, twenty-two. Now wait." After a moment he informed her: "You lost."

They stayed for three hours: Xenia stood behind Dino, who, every so often, changed position. Finally he hit the jackpot and went to the cashier to exchange the tokens for a large number of bills.

"Did you see? I was reduced to zero. But I know how to seize the right moment. For me it's always like that: in life, too." Then, taking a five thousand lire note from his pocket he said:

"Here, you brought me luck."

"But I didn't do anything!"

"Take it, I'm telling you!"

Xenia looked around, embarrassed, and slipped the money into her purse, laughing. She had a great desire to laugh, to be happy, to hug Dino. When they left, he walked with his hands in his pockets, cocky, and told her about a famous night in Monte Carlo when, if he'd had the courage, he would have won fabulous sums.

"Everything depends on courage. What do you think is the secret of Raimondo Horsch? Courage."

She thought of her flight from the Grimaldi, of the ring stolen from Emanuela's drawer. And now she was in San Remo with five thousand lire in her purse. Basically, courage consists of very simple gestures. The flight had been nothing more than going out and not returning that night.

"Horsch looks at you, eh? He likes you."

"He's an amusing man."

"Yeeees . . . and then he always has the upper hand. You know he has a wife and daughter in Menaggio, in a very modest house, so they think he's in Milan struggling to earn a living? A man with twenty million!"

They walked wearily up toward the hotel. Dino wasn't even close to her, and she wondered: "What sort of man is he? He still hasn't kissed me. Maybe that day in the car he was joking. He's always joking, Dino!" He was talking about other famous places he'd seen, and no longer seemed to appreciate where they were. The road climbed steeply between the walls of wealthy villas with gravel drives that looked blue in the moonlight, and a dusty scent of geraniums, sugary scent of wisteria. "I'm in San Remo. A year ago I was at the Grimaldi weeping in Silvia's arms. Silvia what? . . . oh! Silvia Custo."

Suddenly, at a turning in the road, they saw the sea. It sparkled in the moonlight, driving a foam of diamonds along the shore. Xenia thought: "Surely now Dino will stop and kiss me." Instead, dragging her by the arm, he kept walking.

So they reached the door of her room. "Take your time," he said. "I always have a shower at night. I'll call down for a bottle of champagne: I smoked too much. Come and have a sip." Entering the room Xenia was thoughtful: all their friends, talking about her, said, "Xenia, Dino's friend." "Friend," in that case, had a precise meaning. But in fact, no. Not even Vandina believed that their relations were really that. "Maybe . . ." she said, but it was clear that she stuck to her opinion. Xenia, thinking of Dino, concluded: "He doesn't like me."

Now she had put on her nightgown, gone to the mirror. A pretty nightgown of pink voile, transparent: it was worth the trouble to become a man's lover if only to be seen in that nightgown. "It's my bride's nightgown, but it's not white. And yet white means purity: I'm pure. But is a woman who's decided to have a lover pure? Or is she impure even if untouched? Either way, this is my wedding night." She thought of her mother, who for years had been embroidering coarse linen sheets for her trousseau. Then she went to put on her bathrobe, returned to the mirror. She had to go now, enter Dino's room in a natural way. And yet she couldn't overcome an emotion similar to the physical sensation of feeling slightly unwell. Basically, if she wanted, she could pack her suitcase and leave immediately, go away, without even saying goodbye, she had five thousand lire in her purse, but she had quit X&X and she didn't know anything precise about the cement company where she was supposed to work. Five thousand lire is soon gone. She would have to return to the village. At noon lunch, at eight dinner, a few words and to bed, gossip, poverty, Mamma who suffers from rheumatism, Papa who complains about taxes. Old parents are boring; if a sense of duty didn't replace the emotional ties that time wears down, what relation would there be between our life and theirs? Who would choose them, so different from us? We wouldn't want them even as friends.

Freedom. A great thing, freedom. She tried to convince herself that, these days, family and marriage don't have much importance; she even tried to laugh at them. "The truth is that not many women have the courage to confess: I'd like to have a lover, yes, I'll take one."

Vandina always said: "These respectable girls make me laugh! Papa and Mamma take care of everything, while they eat, drink, have a car, don't know what it means to earn your living. In summer the beach, in winter they ski, alone in the mountains with the men; anyway, they always find a husband, thanks to the money from the business. A white veil as long as from here to there, and afterward they have a lover, when it doesn't even take much courage, because the husband, if he knows, keeps quiet so as not to lose money." Xenia preferred to play her life like this.

She knocked on the door of the adjoining room. Dino answered: "Come in," and she opened the door.

He was wearing a blue striped bathrobe, rustling like a female garment, blue pajamas, a blue scarf at his neck.

"Sit down, I'll open the bottle, just a minute, okay? I'm very orderly, even fanatical. Maybe," he added regretfully, "I could have risked another round at the casino." He was arranging brushes, combs, nail file, in the same order in which they'd been in the suitcase. Then he began folding his pants: he took the money out of the pockets, put it on the night table, in order, all the coins in a pile, and placed the pants carefully on the chair. "Otherwise I couldn't sleep," he said. "Even when I get home at four in the morning I put everything in order, like this."

"Dino . . ." Xenia murmured, looking at him.

"Here I am, I'm done. We needed this bottle, no? I smoked too much." He took the bottle off the ice, uncorked it.

"You have a sad expression tonight. Come here, drink, it will do you good."

They drank, then Xenia, exasperated, called again: "Dino . . ." He kissed her and afterward lifted her face by the chin, saying with a smile: "You see? I knew the champagne would do you good." Meanwhile, his hands were lightly taking off her bathrobe. "Sweet, this nightgown." And he pushed her toward the bed, laid her down. Xenia was trembling, with a sudden cold that froze her blood. He, too, took off his bathrobe, the scarf, and lay down beside her. Xenia's teeth were chattering: "Cold?" Dino asked, and she nodded without looking at him, then asked: "Turn out that light."

"Whatever you like," he agreed after a moment.

In the darkness Xenia no longer saw Dino's face, but she felt the panting warmth of his breath, she felt eager, unknown hands. If she'd had the courage she would have said: "Turn the light on again, I want to see you." Was Dino that body that smelled of new silk? Were his those unknown hands? The voice no longer seemed to be his that, soon afterward, murmured: "What a magnificent bosom you have, my girl."

. . . .

Xenia woke early in the morning, her head hurting, her mouth bitter, her eyes burning, as when she got home late in Milan and hadn't had much sleep. I wonder what time it is? The hotel was silent; in the bathroom there was a sporadic drip. "It's that drip that woke me." Then she startled at the memory of the night just passed and, without turning, felt someone breathing behind her. Dino was sleeping on his back, his mouth half open, his nostrils shiny as if he were sweating. Xenia would have liked to call him, shake him gently, say, "Dino, I'm here" but, in truth, she was afraid of his awakening: the empty bottle was lying on the floor, beside the heap of bathrobes: everything recalled crudely what had happened during the night. Slowly she rose and went to open the window.

White, the sea was barely breathing; waves moved slowly under the surface like a vein under the skin of a hand. The town was silent; the windows of the houses were shuttered, the street deserted. Until, somewhere or other, a chilly robin began to sing, announcing the morning. Soon afterward a woman opened her shutters, yawned, and looked at the sky, screening her eyes with her hand. Xenia went back to bed, and its warmth was a comfort. "I'll go to sleep," she thought. Instead, as soon as she closed her eyes she saw the calm gesture of Sister Lorenza pouring the *caffellatte*, smelled the enticing fragrance of fresh bread spreading through the re-fectory. "I'll send Emanuela a card. Well, no, better not: what would it say, knowing that I'm Dino's lover?" Dino's lover. That, too, had been easy as the escape from the residence; only her limbs felt weary. Everything had happened in the dark, then they had fallen asleep, without even looking at each other. "Ten days together, ten nights like that. But then I won't go back to the office. Oh no, absolutely not. Dino himself wouldn't want it. Work, to what purpose? If they told me the degree is here, ready, on the night table, I wouldn't even reach out my hand to take it: I'm too tired."

. . . .

The first day, Dino took her around the streets of San Remo and touring in the car in the nearby towns; the second he began saying that he found San Remo less fun than in other years; the third he looked around hoping to meet some friends; and the fourth, luckily, he met some. Friends who lived in Paris and "were in cars," too. One was very important, Dino said, because many "deals" depended on him. A French girl was traveling with them, named Yvette. They liked Xenia. "Very refined, your friend," they said to Dino, and he was flattered. "A student," he explained. Later Xenia wanted to know: "Why didn't you tell the truth?"

"What truth?"

"That I'm a secretary."

"Why should I say it?"

"Are you ashamed?"

"No, of course not."

"Yes, you are; besides, I'm sick of being one. You don't know what a relief it is to let my nails grow without worrying about breaking them on the typewriter keys. It's a hard job: at night, when I leave, my back is breaking and my shoulder hurts."

He agreed: "I understand," but distractedly.

The trip, which should have been their honeymoon, had become a business meeting. Dino discussed with his friends during the day, and at night they went to the casino, all together, as if to the office. "I'm keeping at it because I have a hot hand, these days," he said; the last night, in fact, he won seventy thousand lire.

"I'm happy for you," he said to Xenia. "I have a little plan in mind, now I'll tell you. You're a smart girl, and you've brought me luck: with these French people I've set up a major deal. Provided Horsch is also part of the arrangement."

"What's it about?"

"That's my business. Women in these affairs . . . Although you're an intelligent girl, everybody says so: you have a reasonable mind."

"I don't like not knowing everything about your work," she objected.

"Well, I can't explain it now. And not so much on my account as on Horsch's: if he knew I talked to anyone, he'd pull out. But if the deal goes through, once the business is over I'll take you to America. What would you say to a nice trip to America? You see how I do things? Like a gentleman. My goodness! You didn't dream of it, eh? Besides, not even I dreamed of certain things about you." Then he sat her on his lap, saying, "Hold on, the surprise is coming. You're right: I can't have a secretary for a friend—it takes away from my prestige. Here's twenty thousand: you can rent a place, three rooms are enough. Buy what you need for now: the rest we'll get on installments. And if I make this deal we'll go to America."

Xenia was uncertain: "And you, Dino?"

"For me this is enough," he said, slapping his forehead with his hand. "Who managed the business with the tractors? And the tractor trailers?

Me, always me. What would Horsch do without me? I arrange everything, I do the talking, I sign. But if this Paris business works out, I won't need him any longer."

Xenia, instead of listening to him, repeated: "The house would really be mine? For me?" "Of course, for you," Dino nodded, smiling. Then he added teasingly: "Good Lord, if it's raining some night and I don't have a place to stay, I hope you won't send me to sleep under the porticoes of Piazza del Duomo."

In Milan, Vandina, hearing about the house, was dismayed; but she recovered quickly and said: "What can you do? That's a stroke of luck! Besides, I couldn't accept anything like that, because of my friend; and then you are educated."

Xenia gave her the present of a purse and they went together to look for an apartment. The rents were all too high: finally they found something that would do. Dino let her choose everything she wanted. One night, she asked him hesitantly: "Can I put my name on the door?" He couldn't stop laughing: "Of course, what name would you put? It's your house." And Xenia repeated often to herself: it's my house. When Dino saw the apartment, with the furniture in place, he said: "It's not a palace, but you've done things with judgment and taste." On the door was a shiny brass nameplate: Xenia Costantini.

They were at dinner together one night and Dino said: "It's taken off, you know? The big deal with the French: it's starting."

"What's it about? Cars?"

"Yes and no; but this time it's more complex—export. Horsch dropped out: the job is up to me. He washes his hands of the risk. Today we almost had words because of you."

"Me?!"

"Yes, you. We happened to talk about San Remo: you understand, right, babe? Men's talk. I was saying that I was really fond of you. In fact, it came down to details and he acted incredulous. I insisted: 'Hey, I'm not an idiot!

Virgin, she was a virgin!' He thought I was boasting. 'Why,' I said, 'if even I didn't know it?'" He smiled again, shaking his head. "I let it go because otherwise it would have ended badly, and I can't make an enemy of him."

Xenia was silent, eating hard, frozen cherries that almost made her teeth hurt. What a fool Dino had been to tell that story. As if responding to her thought, he added:

"You know? It was important to me."

She proposed distractedly: "Let's go out, it's hot." And as soon as they were outside: "I'll drive."

Dino had taught her to drive, and she liked feeling a car obey her will. She drove fast, changing gears abruptly. She was irritated by Horsch's sarcastic distrust. It seemed to her that Dino had let him into a room where she was naked. "Horsch up to now judged me like Vandina or Mary; and he's right, basically." In a rage, she drove out of the city.

"Where are you going?" Dino asked her uncertainly. He knew he had said something that wounded her; but he didn't know what. "Where would I go?" she answered harshly. "I want to get a little air."

· · · ·

On a Sunday in mid-July the Superior left.

It was a very hot, sunny day. At the Grimaldi there had been a solemn lunch, with the bishop present. But a farewell ceremony can never be cheerful: it seemed like a deposit on the funeral of the Abbess, in whom—now that she had become harmless—shining virtues were acknowledged. In fact, her funeral would have been less sad. Everyone would have said, simply: "She was old."

The Superior already felt like a guest: she no longer had a rancorous look in her glassy eyes; she kindly planted a kiss on the forehead of the youngest girl as she handed her a bouquet of flowers, and smiled like a sick person who has taken final communion. She even seemed energized, now that her inactivity no longer had to be justified by old age.

After dessert, white as a funeral monument, the bishop fell asleep with his chin on his napkin; the heat was like a weight around the windows, the flowers wilted. The Superior, sated and somnolent, had stopped respond-ing to compliments. In the meantime, alert, fresh, not at all burdened by the food or the hour, Sister Lorenza got the old woman ready to go. The nomination wasn't official yet, but everyone knew that the new superior would be her. The bishop, taking his leave, enveloped her in a blessing and a long look of understanding.

Shortly afterward, girls, nuns, lay sisters, and servants crowded at the door to say goodbye to the Superior, whom, until then, they had con-sidered an old piece of furniture. In front of the door, in the sun-struck square, a carriage was waiting: the horse mutely beat one hoof on the cobblestones. The Superior got in, sat down, and spread her violet skirt around her. A young nun settled herself in the little remaining space. A moment of embarrassed silence: then, to the large hand raised in fare-well, many young hands responded, waving. In the deserted square, the carriage left, the clatter of the wheels echoing loudly. They all lingered, watching it grow distant, until Sister Lorenza went back inside and or-dered them to follow.

In reality, she had already taken possession of the Superior's apart-ment. She wasn't sleeping there yet, since she was waiting for the letter from the Mother General, but she already considered what was there to be hers. The study had belonged to her for some time now: the re-cord books were filled with her writing, the Mother's shaky signature appeared only here and there. She would find it difficult to get used to the room where the chair still bore the imprint of the old woman and the drawers preserved the odor of an old person. Until then she had been accustomed to enter that room on tiptoe. When the Mother was in bed, or sick, she spoke from behind the white curtains; and in that way, too, the room was full of her. Sister Lorenza pushed aside the curtains, to be sure she was no longer there. "She'll be on the train now." Yet she still didn't feel in full possession of her powers: and the sisters, her companions, made sure she knew it. Although they were aware that the position would be hers, they made a show of ignoring it in order to begrudge her even the slightest bow.

Sister Lorenza feared that the others would take the reins of everything, and reject her, isolate her; now Sister Luisa would keep the record books and the correspondence, and in a short time they would force her to spend her days in the red armchair, pretending to say the rosary. Impossible, impossible! But wasn't it she herself who had created that halo of respect around the figure of the Mother? Little by little, she had taken the entire house out of her hands, gently, hypocritically, not allowing the important information to reach her. She had accustomed her companions to fearing the Superior, since it was in her name that she conveyed the harshest orders. When a French girl she didn't like was sent away, she said to her: "It's by order of the Mother, my dear." And the old woman knew nothing about it; she thought the French girl was leaving for health reasons. When Costantini came to ask for a discount on her board, she had said: "The Mother won't agree." The Mother, always the Mother; at the sound of that name the girls felt an instinctive hostility. And now the Mother was her.

She looked out the window into the courtyard; the other nuns were sitting in a circle, talking. It was the hour for recreation: Sister Luisa was reading a sacred story from a book. They hadn't called her. But who would dare disturb her now? Sister Luisa stopped reading and began talking, softly, with the others. Of course they're talking about me. It's Sister Luisa, that scheming Venetian. She's always chatting with the girls; now that they're leaving for vacation maybe she'll be writing to them. They're all leaving this year: even Emanuela, because her parents have returned. I wonder if she'll come back in October. Some won't return: Fanti is getting married, Ortiz has gone to live with the Spaniards. Augusta stays, and little Bongiovanni who's repeating an exam. Augusta knows everything about the girls, she'll be able to report on what they say about me. I'll go talk to her later, casually.

Quickly she went down the stairs and into the courtyard; the nuns were all sitting there; three of the youngest were playing ring-around-the-rosy, singing softly. Seeing her, they were silent and some rose, dutifully. She gave her face an expression of surprise.

"Why are you getting up, Sisters?"

Without explaining, her companions stood looking at her.

"What were you talking about?" she asked, approaching. "Let's sit down again."

They had left a chair free, but she pretended not to notice and took her usual place on the bench, between Sister Luisa and Sister Prudenzina. Since the others were silent, she crossed her hands on her lap and waited. But they didn't start talking again: after a few moments of uncertain silence, Sister Luisa again opened the book and began to read: "This was, therefore, the first appearance of the Virgin to the shepherdess Bernadette . . ."

III

The journey to Puglia was tiring. In the early hours of the afternoon, the train slowed down, as if overcome by the heat; the houses dozed on the desolate plain, amid the strident panting of the cicadas. Anna and Valentina, their faces shiny with sweat, had looked out the window in search of some relief: but the wind was a hot breath. Below the station platform drooping campanulas looked like dead butterflies.

Anna's parents had come to get her in the carriage; her father immediately smothered her with news, her mother was sweating in a gaudy summer dress. The two girls separated, embracing. Valentina set off toward home with her mother; but as soon as she arrived, she felt the slight melancholy of satisfied desires. The vacation, the longed-for meeting with her mother: that was it. This was her first year at the university. During the winter, from Rome, she had always written: "Imagine, Mamma, when I come home . . ." And now she had come home.

Anna, entering the house, stopped in astonishment: in the dining room there was new furniture, in a modern, angular style, and, instead of the old chandelier, diffuse lighting that cast a gloom on the walls, which had been painted a pale green.

"Nice, isn't it?" her father said proudly.

"You didn't write me anything . . ."

"No. We wanted to surprise you. The furniture comes from Bari; I brought the lights from Milan."

"We're renovating the whole house," her mother added quickly. "Unless . . . We'll talk about it at the table."

But Don Alfonso insisted: "You haven't said yet if you like it. Maybe it seems rather paltry to you?"

"Oh no, really . . . Only I didn't expect it." Then, seeing that her parents were waiting for more comments, she observed: "It must have cost a lot."

"A lot, yes. But as you see: it's not money thrown away."

The servants who came to greet Anna stayed on the threshold, not daring to set foot in the new dining room. It seemed like a room from another house, even though it was so close to the old hall, where guns and saddles were still hanging. Finally Anna withdrew, to straighten up from the journey, and the servants disappeared into the farmyard.

Anna's room was on the second floor. She entered apprehensively, fearing that it, too, had been modernized; but it was the same, with the big iron bedstead, the window dripping with jasmine. Anna took a breath, relieved, and turned to embrace her mother: she smelled the new scent that came from her skin, a heavy amber perfume, different from the fresh talcum powder she had always used. Suddenly, moving away, she asked in a worried tone:

"And Nonna?"

"Yes. Go say hello to her right away. Your grandmother can't be controlled, she doesn't come down to eat in the dining room. She'd rather eat in the kitchen, can you believe it! We kept her from doing that, so she eats in her room, but she puts the leftovers in her drawers, and they smell of mold; and she steals—it's a mania—steals food and hides it. Yesterday she stole all the sugar she could, and emptied the sugar bowl into her pocket. Imagine: a few days ago, Alfonso received those people from Milan, yes, you don't know yet about the company . . . we'll tell you later. In short, strangers, important people, and your grandmother comes down with the shawl over her head. We pretend not to see her, hoping the others will take her for a peasant, but she introduces herself and says: 'Alfonso, stand up when your mother enters.' Embarrassed, they stand and greet her, but she doesn't respond, instead she says to her son: 'Who gave you permission to touch the old wine?' My God! What a scene! All day she goes around through the fields, gives orders to the farmers, shouts from the window: 'I am still the mistress!'" Donna Matilde sighed: "Go and say hello to her, but be quick: dinner's ready."

Anna knocked on the old woman's door. No one answered. Then she pushed the door, calling: "Nonna Antonia..." It was dark inside: from the open window came a faint glow. The old woman, leaning on the sill, was eating.

"Is it you, Anna? Come in. I couldn't wait for you to get here: I have to talk to you urgently. Everything's ruined here."

"Why are you in the dark, Grandma?"

"I can still see: it's a pity to waste the light. There's enough waste in this house. Have you seen what I'm reduced to? Poor me, they wish I were underground. Every day your mother asks: 'Are you well?' 'Very well,' I say; and I touch wood. I have a strong constitution, I can hold out. The land is mine; but they're throwing away money by the fistful, like seed. Have you seen the dining room?"

"I don't like it, either. But what can you do? Papa . . ."

"Oh, it's not him: it's your mother. Trouble came to our house the day Alfonso disobeyed me and married her. But I'm still alive: I see everything, I keep an eye out as much as I can. I collect things in the drawers: for you, my Anna. They've turned the servants against me, and everyone pushes me back up here, they lock me in . . ." Donna Antonia started crying. Her granddaughter caressed her wrinkled hands, the thin shoulders wrapped in the shawl, but absently: she was looking at the sky and the first stars. The moon was high above the house; the fields extended into infinity. Then the old woman stopped whining, got up, and went to open the big chest, taking the key from under her skirt: "I have to keep every-thing locked: otherwise, when I'm out, they come and steal. Here," she said, holding out to her granddaughter some moldy almond cookies: "Eat these but don't let them see you. I took them for you, one night when your father was having an orgy."

"It must have been business associates . . ."

"Business! What business! Where does the money he's wasting come from? From the land; and yet he doesn't take care of it. The farmer steals the olives and no one stops him. In the kitchen, the wine flows in rivers. Your mother wants a car, they've ordered a radio."

She spoke in a hurry, as if all that was in her heart and she felt relief in getting rid of it.

"I have to go downstairs now, Nonna. We'll talk tomorrow. Are you coming?"

"No," said the old woman. "I'm going to bed. I'll come to the door with you because I want to lock it. If you need me knock three times, or rather four. Otherwise I don't open to anyone. At night, I hang a chair on the handle because, that way, if someone touches it . . . Besides, I never sleep. Many times I've heard them trying to enter."

Anna went out, leaving her muttering to herself, while she locked the door. She found her father and mother sitting at the table.

"Sorry," she said, "Nonna . . ."

"Don't apologize. We know her," Don Alfonso answered, filling her glass. Amid the new furniture, Anna sat stiffly, as if she were eating in someone else's house. On the walls there had been photographs of her as a child, of her grandfather, of her mother in unfashionable clothes; on the windowsill, in terracotta pots, grew roses supported by reeds, white geraniums, and petunias. All gone. And her parents, surrounded by that furniture, weren't the same. Papa talked about his mother mercilessly:

"Of course, when old age makes us like beasts, it's better to die. She'll only dress like a farmhand, as if purposely, to embarrass us."

"I understand," said Anna, "but why force her to change? She's old, the old can't emerge from their age, from the time when they lived."

"But when you're here with important people and she appears and ..."

"She's your mother, you shouldn't be ashamed of her."

"Easy, in theory!"

"Alfonso, please," Donna Matilde interrupted. "Don't discuss this subject with Anna. Tomorrow she'll put on cloth shoes, too, she'll go through the fields and come home taking bites of a tomato, like the farmers."

"Why should I behave differently if that's how I want to live and that's how the life of my family has always been lived?"

"Always until yesterday. Today it's different. You study in the city and we're tired of living out of the world. The papers don't even get here," said her father.

"There's not a dressmaker who knows how to make a dress," sighed Donna Matilde.

"And today the money we have will yield more, in better investments."

"Tell her about the company."

"Yes," the father nodded, and settled into his chair, as if about to begin a lecture. "I've joined a Milanese company with branches in Rome and Bari, interesting work, appropriate for our social position. We've made new acquaintances and ..." With a gesture he invited his wife to continue.

"What, you're afraid to say it? Anyway, next year we'll move to the city."

Anna was silent for a moment, then she said calmly: "You can't. What about the land?"

"There are the farmers, for the land. We'll hire a manager, a reliable person, I thought of Peppe Conti, who's been the manager for the De Angelis family for years. And then we'll return in the summer, a couple of months in the summer."

"You're used to the city by now, too," said her mother.

"Oh, Mamma, I'm dying to finish my degree so I can come back!"

"No, Anna, you have to continue, get your teaching certification, we've talked about it in the village—I'm not concerned about the money for printing your publications."

Anna was thinking she would never again see autumn come to her village. On the train she had been saying to Valentina: "In October, when I leave, it will be for the last time." Yet she wanted to prepare well for her thesis, close the city chapter, say goodbye to her friends, return to her fields—to hear not the clatter of the tram on its tracks but, every so often, in the distance, the train crossing the plain.

"I don't want to study anymore," she said. "And what would I do with a teaching certification? If it weren't to make you happy, I wouldn't even get my degree. I don't need to earn a living, you always say we're very wealthy—isn't the degree enough? I hope to get it with top marks, I've done everything I could . . ."

"But Valentina will also get to that point, and she's socially your inferior."

"And so what? Papa, listen: I would come up against disappointments. What I possess is only a fair amount of patience, of willpower, I don't have talent, and it's cost me a lot to get this far. You don't know, you don't realize; I did it to please you, but I'm tired, all I've thought about is this house. And now . . ."

She was nearly weeping: her broad face sagging in an expression of discouragement. Her father said: "Nothing's decided yet, don't upset your-self like that."

"But I have decided," Anna said with firm sweetness. "I'm not going."

Some friends of Don Alfonso, with their wives, came in noisily from the farmyard. They were there to welcome Anna, whom they'd known since she was a child, and immediately asked with smiles of admiration what she thought of the new furniture. "It really seems as if you're in the city," they said, sitting down in the springy, fake-leather-and-chrome armchairs. Coffee, wine, *ciambellone* were served; then the men gathered around the table to play cards. Four played, and the fifth, sitting beside Don Alfonso, advised him, silently indicating with his finger the card to play. Anna said good night shortly afterward.

"We heard you want to go on studying," one of the women said to her as she was leaving. "Congratulations!"

Instead of going to her room, Anna stopped in the hall: beyond the porch you could see the fields, illuminated by the moon, and the scattered shadows of the trees. A lamp was burning at the edge of the vineyard, on the road that led to the village. Everything was untouched: as it had been last year, as when she was a child. Behind her she heard the women's laughter, the exclamations of the players. "What more are they looking for?" she wondered. She thought of the cold walls of the residence, those lifeless rooms, the distrustful nuns. And all the books she had consulted in the library, studied by candlelight, without ever possessing them completely. "I'll stay," she thought. She went up the wooden staircase and passed by her grandmother's room. Who would remove Grandmother from her land?

At daybreak, when the house was still sunk in sleep and the lamp at the entrance to the farm still burning, the stairs creaked under the old woman's heavy tread. Through the windows the first light entered like a cold blade. Donna Antonia, as soon as she reached the kitchen, took the copper bowl from the wall, filled it with water, and drank, to wake herself fully: then she tried to enter the pantry. It was always locked. She knew it, but every morning she hoped someone might have left the key in the lock. Through the little window that opened to the kitchen came the smell of apples, of *lardo*. Donna Antonia lingered a moment, then went to wake the servants. The women were sleeping half-dressed, arms flung in all directions. But they got up immediately, ran a wet hand over their face, and, still sleepy, went around barefoot with brooms and buckets, opened windows. The old woman wandered among them, giving orders that no one carried out, as if she were commanding a herd of deaf-mutes.

Soon she went to wake her granddaughter; and when she heard her respond, returned to the kitchen to prepare the *caffellatte* for her. Anna liked to drink it in the farmyard, in the morning coolness. The farmers going to work took off their caps to greet her.

"This is the only time when we still seem to be in the old days," said her grandmother. "But at ten your mother comes down."

As soon as she heard her daughter-in-law's voice, Donna Antonia glanced rapidly this way and that and left. Then, afraid she would be forced to go up to her room, she went out into the fields.

She visited the farmers. She entered their kitchens, sat down to talk to them: as an equal, not a mistress. The farmers knew that her words shouldn't be heeded: yet she was still the old mistress and the only one who knew the land as they did. Sometimes she treated them harshly, but at least she knew what she was talking about.

Anna stayed in her room for a long time. She sat at the window studying: beyond the garden, beyond the green rustling of the ilexes, she saw the fields burned by the sun. The air appeared to shift with the rapid breathing of the cicadas. From there, she could see the Apontes' red house: the glass of the closed windows shone, dazzling, the fields around were desolate.

"They left the son in poverty," Don Alfonso said. "The father was a gambler, the mother was with someone else for years." Anna, out walking, had passed by the garden that surrounded the red house: the flower beds were thick with weeds, the earth furrowed by cracks.

In the afternoon she went into the village, where everything—the iron color of the church steps, the patina of the fountain—everything bore the imprint of a faithful continuity, of customs handed down. Donna Matilde didn't like the village; she rarely went there, and when she did, she would look around disdainfully. Walking through the alleys she wrinkled her nose and asked her daughter: "You like this nice smell?" Anna answered: "I don't know if it's nice, maybe not, but I like it." Some loved Anna, others judged her a little too placid. Donna Matilde told everyone that her daughter's attitude was a pose assumed to spite her.

But Anna shunned the village gossip, the people who spent their time in idle conversation; she took her bicycle and rode off on the paths through the fields or on the shady avenue that led to the station. Often, at dusk, she went to see Valentina.

When Anna came in, Valentina always said: "I'm sorry, really . . . Sorry." At the Grimaldi the two girls were equals; here, instead, she felt humiliated, living as she did in a modest house surrounded by a weedy vegetable patch, rather than a beautiful garden like the Bortones'. Yet her friendship with the daughter of the wealthy landowner gave her a certain prestige in the village and she hoped it would help her find a husband more easily.

Anna preferred to go and talk on the terrace. Among old things thrown out in a jumble and rotted logs, there were big platters of tomato paste set to dry in the sun and basil and mint in chipped enamel pots. And you had a view of the entire plain.

Every so often, Valentina, interrupting the conversation, glanced into the house, then said, reassured, "It's nothing, nothing." When, inside, the rooms were dark, the girls lingered, looking at the stars crowding the vault of the sky. Anna said: "In the city you never see a star appear. Suddenly it's shining and you didn't see it come out."

"There are so many other things in the city."

"What things? For me none of them have the value of these."

"And your parents are still talking about moving?"

"I don't know. Yes, I think so: when I'm not there. But it seems to me," she continued, "that emerging from one's own class and forcing one's way into another is a mistake. Many problems seem to arise precisely from the fact that, today, everyone wants to lead a life superior to his origins or his own capabilities. Nevertheless a descendant will eventually appear who has in his blood the aspirations of his forebears. Like me. I'm staying. I'm twenty-two: no one can make me go."

"And your degree?"

"I'll get it: I'll leave with you, but when I've finished I'll come right back. Unless I fail like Xenia." And she added: "I wonder where Xenia ended up . . ."

"No one can convince me she's not dead."

"We would know. But Xenia wasn't the type who kill themselves. I still don't understand why she didn't make it: she had a sharp intelligence."

Valentina interrupted her: "Shhh! Quiet!" and again strained her ears toward the house.

"Who are you afraid of?"

"Afraid? No . . . It's because of the brothers."

Once, hearing a carriage stop in front of the door she had said: "Listen, it's better if you go now. I'm sorry, really, sorry."

In the doorway Anna had run into two men of a certain age: one short, with a malicious look, the other tall and strong. The next day Valentina explained: "They're my father's brothers. Since he died they've supported us: out of pity. They pay for everything, including my studies. They're not bad, at heart."

"And so?"

"So . . . well: they constantly remind us of what they've done, what they do—every mouthful of bread we eat. Have you seen Mamma? In just a few years she's aged, because she barely touches food. I'm young and overlook a lot of things. But she . . . The land belonged to all three brothers, my father's part should be ours now. But they say: 'Our land, our money.' I didn't want them to find me chatting idly with you. When I teach I'll be able to support my mother, and it will be over. But I wasn't born to work; I'd like to get married, get married right away: I think about it night and day."

"Why the hurry? You're not even twenty."

"It's not age that matters. I'm poor and I'll have the burden of my mother. I can't leave her. And who will take me like this? No one. My childhood friends are getting married, others are engaged. They come to visit and they say it with a triumphant expression. And then they look at me, smiling, as if to say: 'So you're still home?' And when it's not about them they come and tell me about friends in common, relatives, to wound me. 'You know what? she's marrying So-and-So. A big wedding!' Maybe it's not true. And me, I'm still here. If you only knew what life is like in my house! The brothers smoke cigars that poison the air, we cook, we serve them at the table, we wash the dishes. In the morning, when they get up, they leave behind in the bedroom the stench of the wine they drank the night before at the tavern. Then they go out: and we're left with the beds to make, the underwear to wash, the chores . . . Did you know that even Linda's getting married?"

"Yes, but to Toma's son, a halfwit."

"Still, she's getting married."

"Oh yes, still . . ."

"Also at the Grimaldi," Valentina continued, "a lot of them have 'found.' Vinca, for example, Emanuela. Emanuela met Andrea through us, at the lectures."

"She's very pretty, Emanuela."

"Yes, and very rich. And Barbara in political science?"

Anna observed: "There are more than a hundred of us at the Grimaldi."

"But couldn't I have been among those?" Then, seeing Donna Antonia in the window, she asked: "Your grandmother's crazy, right?"

"Who told you that? No. She's old, a little obsessive . . ."

Donna Antonia called to the girls, so they hurried over; and when they were below her window, she began whining: "They've locked me in here. They hope to find me dead: come up, for goodness' sake, let me out."

"Who was it?" Anna asked.

"How should I know? Your mother, it must have been. They've locked me in because there are people downstairs and they don't want to let me see the wine they're drinking."

She began complaining again, and the girls, who no longer wanted to listen to her, decided to go in. Crossing the hall they noticed, in the dining room, a young man in mourning talking to Don Alfonso. Seeing them, he invited them in. Valentina smoothed her hair, whispering to her friend: "It's Mario Aponte."

The guest stood up and greeted the girls. Donna Matilde introduced Valentina with a patronizing smile and Don Alfonso was surprised that Anna didn't remember Mario. They had played together as children, my goodness, how many races they'd run.

"I was there, too," said Valentina, decisively. "I remember everything, every detail."

In the intervals of silence, the old woman could be heard crying at the window. Anna excused herself: "I'm going up to my grandmother for a moment." Valentina, instead of following her, stayed to listen to the young man: he had had to abandon his studies and return to get the farm, and the house, back in working order. "Not all the window frames have glass; the manager stole as long as he could, and now we don't even know where he is."

Grandmother wasn't locked in her room. "I was wrong," she said, "but they're always doing it." And she continued to feel sorry for herself, speaking of herself in the third person: "Poor Antonia, shut up like a pig, but one day, finally, she'll die."

Anna resolved to overcome the revulsion she felt for her grandmother's hands, which she used in place of a handkerchief, and to endure the unpleasant smell of the room and spend more time with her.

In fact, the next day she went with her on her rounds through the fields and her visits to the farmers. In the white courtyards of the farmhouses, the children were completely naked, heads shaved, gray as mice. If Anna questioned them they didn't respond: they stared at her open-mouthed and then laughed behind her back. They chewed leaves and berries, made dolls and balls with the mules' dung. At five or six the girls were already carrying bundles of wood and pitchers of water on their heads.

Anna was hot, she drank cool water at every house. Her grandmother walked quickly, the black kerchief tied under her chin.

"Your mother is trying to poison me," she said. "Yesterday the poison was in the meatballs, the way it's done with dogs. I'm going to play a nasty trick. You know they want my signature for some business of your father's in Milan? I say 'Yes, I'll sign.' And then, when the moment arrives, no! For now I'm stirring up the farmers against him, and one day they'll come and shout under the balcony: 'We want the old mistress!' That day your mother will be taken by one of her usual fainting fits."

She didn't even calm down when she returned to the house and found Mario Aponte, saying, rather: "I wonder where she'll put the powder today."

Mario often had dinner at the Bortones': Anna admired him for his calm, for his reflective way of speaking, for the love he had for his land. But he regretted his interrupted studies.

"Then sell the land and return to the city," Don Alfonso advised him.

"You can't sell land. It brings bad luck."

"Nonsense. Sell it, if you want to."

"There: maybe I don't want to."

Anna would have liked to support him, but she held back in order not to contradict her father in front of a stranger. But she smiled at him while Don Alfonso declared:

"The land yields almost nothing, a pitiful amount. It rains, the harvest rots. Or it's too hot, or too cold: there's always something that goes wrong."

"It's stubborn work, work that requires tenacity. That's why it attracts me," said Mario.

The sound of a barrel organ rose from outside; Anna stifled the impulse to get up and run to the window. Donna Matilda exclaimed: "What torture, that music! Luckily in a few days we'll have the radio."

. . . .

Letters arrived from Vinca, from Emanuela. Even Augusta wrote, though she'd stayed at the Grimaldi: she talked about Sister Lorenza and Sister Luisa, who, from a distance, seemed like characters in one of her stories: and yet the girls had lived with them for months and months. But—in that white, chalky village, lost in a desolate plain, under the high sun— how to imagine the gray walls of the college, the shadowy hallways where the windows were perpetually closed?

In rambling letters, written in bad Italian, Vinca talked only about Luis. She said she was going to church to pray for Luis, that she was waiting for Luis, that Luis was very brave, in fact heroic. She described life in Donna Inés's house: three women waiting for the mail, exhausted by the heat. "I was at the Grimaldi: Sister Lorenza hugged me and wanted to know if I would return in October. 'No, truthfully,' I answered. She was disappointed. 'Why?' she asked. 'Weren't you happy here?' and I burst into tears, thinking of Luis."

Emanuela had left Florence on a car trip with her parents. She sent a postcard from every little village where they stopped: "The weather is fine. Tomorrow we'll be at the Lago di Braies." In the midst of this news that had no importance she announced: "I'm getting married soon."

Valentina was upset by these letters that were always about love. At night, in the moonlit silence, she heard the young people of the village singing and laughing as they passed by under her windows. She and her mother were now confined to the kitchen. The brothers didn't even call them to the table anymore: they ate and drank, threw pieces of meat and liver to the dog. But if they surprised Valentina doing nothing they said: "Why don't you get your friend Bortone's daughter to support you?"

One night, they began speaking in a vulgar way about Anna, about her shapely figure: "Come here, Valentina, tell us: have you seen her undressed, at the residence?" She took refuge on the terrace, slamming the windowed door; her mother came out, to soothe her: "Calm down, be patient: it's just a short time. When you've got your degree . . ."

Valentina rebelled: "Two years, that's what it will take! And then what do you hope from the degree? If it goes well, I'll get a job as a substitute teacher!"

She knew what awaited her, after that longed-for goal: the precious days, months, years of youth that she would spend correcting homework, alone, amid mountains of shiny black notebooks, like cockroaches: a thankless task, a struggle that no one knows, no one appreciates, sailing in the dark without ever seeing the lighthouse of a port.

She went to bed early. The nights were swarming with stars: when the swallows were silent, the crickets' song began and the frogs croaked in the swamp. Awake, motionless in the dark, she waited for her usual dream, the faithful image of the Indian prince. Instead, the glow that reached her window through the trees drew more precise figures and faces: Andrea, Luis, and now also Mario.

She went to Anna's, hoping to see him; if he wasn't there, she urged her friend to stop studying. "Come for a walk," she'd say: she took her by the arm and, as if by chance, headed toward the Apontes' farm. Mario was always around, with the workers who were fixing the house, with the new farmers from the Veneto. He always seemed happy to see them, talk to them; then he walked them part of the way back.

"He's looking at me," Valentina thought. "Maybe he's in love." At night she imagined him somehow or other showing up in her room. "Here I am," he said to her, leaning over the bed to kiss her. A sweet languor seized her at that thought, her breath quickened. So the hours passed, measured by the tolling of the bell. Sometimes the sky was already getting light when, recalling the thoughts she'd given in to, she whispered: "God, forgive me," and invoked in her defense the summer night.

. . . .

Anna's parents didn't take part in the patron saint's celebration: they stayed away from these popular festivals. But Donna Antonia wanted desperately to light oil lamps in the windows, even though the procession would pass at a distance. At night, the lights quavered in the wind.

Anna went to the celebration with Valentina and Mario.

On the main street and in the square you could still smell the fragrance of burned incense. The Saint—a big wood statue clothed in red and gold—had passed through the village, swaying threateningly on the shoulders of his bearers as his glass eyes flashed. Then, as if after a cautionary inspection, he returned to the church, where a sweetish scent wafted from the flowers. The people, who had been contrite and imploring, now began celebrating on the paving stones still beaded with wax. The cry of the prickly pear vendor rose above the din of the crowd.

Behind the church, fireworks exploded. Valentina and Anna laughed at every bang and plugged their ears with their fingers. They had eaten pralines, drunk sweet wine; without objecting they let boys jostle them as they rushed past, blowing into papier-mâché trumpets. Valentina leaned on Mario as they headed toward the square.

In the tavern yard the villagers were dancing. During the breaks, the dancers sat on benches, men on one side, women on the other, and a red-haired girl went around with glasses of wine; when the accordion started up again, the young men rose, adjusting their pants at the belt, and approached the girls, who waited silently, hands in their laps. They followed the boys immediately onto the dance floor, and danced without changing expression, earrings swinging beside their austere faces.

The music ended suddenly; in the same way, the dancers separated, resuming their position on the benches; men here, women there, not even exchanging a smile.

Anna and Valentina would have liked to dance; but they didn't dare mix in with the peasants, fearing they might stop, out of respect. Besides, Mario was already leading them to the carousel.

Anna sat on a horse with dilated nostrils, painted red. On the barrel organ a small wooden man in a mask beat time to a faint barcarole. The lively, bright-colored world of the fair reawakened in her a childish, unrestrainable joy. Valentina looked at her: "She's posing," she thought. "Her mother's right, she's posing."

Around the carousel a dense circle of people had gathered to watch the others enjoying themselves. The movement of the carousel made Anna slightly dizzy. She felt all eyes on her, even those of Valentina, who was studying her, surprised. Mario's gaze never left her for a moment. "He knows I drank too much and he's afraid I'll fall. How embarrassing . . ." But she couldn't really be embarrassed. She was having fun—she had never had so much fun. Tomorrow she would go back to studying, too bad: it would be a whole year before the celebration returned.

Getting down from the carousel, they made their way through the crowd that was thronging around the balcony of the town hall for the raffle. Anna murmured, "I have a headache."

"Let's stop here," said Mario. "There's more air."

Emerging from the crowd, they sat on a low wall just outside the square, looking at the lights that garlanded the balconies. Below them was the precipice known as the Thief's, because a bandit had jumped off it in the early years of the century. Valentina felt drawn to it: the jump, the crash, and she would roll to the bottom, among the rocks, and remain there, eyes wide, seeing nothing, like Milly.

The faint sadness of a good time that is over descended on them. "It's late," said Anna. "We should go home." She never turned to Mario; but from the start of the evening he had had his eyes on her. After walking Valentina home, they would have to go back together, alone. To avoid it, Anna proposed to her friend: "Come sleep at my house?"

The other, after hesitating, refused: "No, Mamma would worry. I can't." And, leaving them alone, she said sincerely: "I'm sorry."

Anna and Mario went back through the village without exchanging a word; from the taverns came the voices of men playing cards or, if they were drunk, singing. Every so often a street lamp cast a circle of yellow light, then the street slid back into darkness. But stars filled the sky, the Milky Way was hurled like a scarf across that bright swarm. Reaching Anna's house they stopped at the gate: it was difficult to part with only a goodbye, as on other nights. Yet to act differently would have seemed un-justified. Anna, to overcome her uneasiness, said: "So many stars tonight! I'll look out my window at them."

"Which is your window? That one?" Mario pointed. "I'll look out of mine, too."

Anna laughed. "It's far!"

"It doesn't matter," said Mario. "I'll see you just the same."

• • • •

In the days that followed, Anna studied for hours and hours: in Rome she would have to have the thesis copied and get ready to defend it, that was all: whatever might happen, it was now finished.

Mario had stopped coming to see her, and she was gradually persuad-ing herself that his looks the night of the fair, his words at the gate, were not proposals of love. A week later, walking with Valentina, she had gone purposely up to the iron fence that separated her farm from the Apontes'. The grain had been cut some time ago; the land around the haystacks was all burned stubble.

Mario wasn't there, but they heard him. Valentina began speaking in a loud voice, laughing, to get his attention. Then they called and he came and sat on the other side of the fence.

"I've done a lot," he said, "but there's still a lot to do. The house is a mess." Abruptly he said: "Hey, Anna: would you help me choose the furni-ture and organize the garden?" Anna answered, blushing: "I'd be glad to, but I'm leaving soon."

"Then," said Mario, "I'll wait for you to get back."

Valentina looked from one to the other, suspicious. "They've tricked me," she thought, and getting up suddenly, said, "I'm going." "Me, too," said Anna, and Mario went off placidly whistling.

Donna Antonia was at the window. "Quick," she cried, seeing the girls arrive. Her granddaughter hadn't seen her all day: she knew she had gone to the Mattia farm, where the wife was giving birth, bringing with her a piece of bread and a tomato.

"Listen to me, Anna," she said when she saw her. "I can't even eat the bread anymore. Your mother is poisoning me: I've had pains in my stomach all day. Yesterday I saw Our Lady of Sorrows coming in with her— the one from the cards. They must have cast the evil eye on me. Since yesterday my eyelid's been twitching: that's a sign of misfortune. In fact your father today asked for my signature to free up the certificates: 'The company in Milan needs them. They'll come back doubled, but it will take your signature. You promised.' 'I don't remember, I promised nothing,' I said. Company, nonsense; business, nonsense . . . They're needed for the orgies and your mother's clothes. 'No signature,' I declared. 'Donna Antonia Bortone will not sign.' The house was exploding with cries, you didn't hear it?"

"I was out with Valentina."

"Better. You know what my own flesh and blood said to me? The fruit of my womb?" she sobbed desperately. "He said he'll have me locked up in a mental institution."

"That's not possible, Nonna."

"Yes, it is, and you'll see, they'll manage it. They say I steal. But what did I take? A little sugar, for you, if war comes and you can't get it anymore, the way it happened in 1918. The Court will remove my signature because I'm crazy. Poor Antonia! Crazy!" she repeated. Then she said threateningly: "You'll see, it'll happen."

That night, Anna talked to her father for a long time and had to agree with him. The next day Don Alfonso was leaving on a trip: Milan,

Biella. On his return he would pass through Bari and would put the practical details in the hands of the lawyer: persecution mania, kleptomania, irresponsible—there was enough.

The next morning, after her son left, Donna Antonia went out and was gone for hours; she returned smiling. The sky was cloudy, lacerated by lightning flashes. Toward evening some farmers appeared, followed by their wives holding children by the hand, and one of them asked to speak to the master.

"He's not here," said the maid. "He's left."

"Oh! He's left!" Nicola repeated. Then, exchanging a glance with the others, he said: "The young mistress, then."

Donna Matilde came down with her daughter: in front of the farmers she stopped, upset, and pulled her housedress tight around her as if to protect herself. "What is it?" she asked, examining them anxiously.

The farmers remained silent, each waiting for the other to make up his mind. Finally, after a nudge from his wife, Nicola stepped forward: he said they had learned that Don Alfonso was selling the land to outsiders and was going to throw them out, regardless of agreements or duty.

Donna Matilde tried to protest, but Nicola insisted with stubborn tenacity: no, no, it was pointless for the mistress to deny it. They knew everything: she and her husband in the city with the car, the daughter professor, and the old mistress in the insane asylum. Why the insane asylum? She was the only one who came to see if they were still alive and how their children were doing. So it was better to make the terms clear: they would not leave the land, they would not put their children out on the street. And Don Alfonso should remember that his parents had been farmers.

Matilde repeated that none of that was true, whoever had said it must be crazy. Nicola suggested, "Crazy as in the insane asylum?" The others sneered maliciously, and Nicola threatened: "But he won't drive us out: otherwise, we'll drive him out."

Then Anna made her way among them: "You have to believe me, I grew up with you, in your houses. No one intends to sell the land. Don Alfonso left on business, but business that has nothing in common with this, nothing to do with all this. It's not true that he's going to send Nonna to the insane asylum. The land that has given food to you and to us can't be sold. Don Alfonso will come and talk to you himself, when he gets back. No one will drive you out of here."

The farmers loved Anna, so they were puzzled; some started off home. "We're leaving, but we're ready to return," said Nicola, and followed the others along the road to the farmhouses.

Anna wasn't in time to keep her mother from rushing into her mother-in-law's room. Donna Antonia was at the window, pretending to recite the rosary, but she had followed what happened in the farmyard.

"You did this to your son, so that maybe they'll kill him when he gets back! Then you say the rosary, right? But there's God, up there . . ."

While the old woman mumbled that she didn't know anything, what had happened? who did they want to kill?, Anna dragged her mother away, and she collapsed, fainting, on her bed.

. . . .

The night brought pale white clouds that hid the sky; low rumblings moved through the air, the storm hovered but didn't break. Exhausted by what had happened, Anna went to the window to close the shutters: her mother had had some chamomile tea and now was sleeping; in her grandmother's room, after footsteps and sounds of searching, there was silence.

Suddenly, in the shadows, she saw a flash of light on the closest haystack. Impossible, she said to herself, straightening up to see better: a serpent of fire, lightning-like, was attacking the haystack.

Stunned, Anna cried: "Fire! Fire!" She ran down the stairs, opened the servants' rooms, and called them: "Hurry! The haystacks are on fire!

Quick!" She went to the kitchen and grabbed a bucket, while the servants, right behind her, did the same. Outside, she saw that the flames were invading the right side of the haystack. "Fire!" she shouted again. But already people were dashing out of the farmers' houses, crossing the stream. In an instant, a double chain of men and women had formed between the stream and the haystacks; they passed the buckets from hand to hand, threw water on the fire, rapidly sent them back. Driven out of the base of the haystack, the flames reached the top and from there licked the sky: a dense, acrid smoke tinted the night yellow.

Anna ran toward the dividing fence calling: "Mario! Mario!" He arrived with his people, carrying buckets. He freed himself from Anna, who was holding on to him, begging, "Help me!," and went to the head of the chain.

Fields, farmhouses, trees were illuminated by a sinister light. A tuft of burning straw fell off the haystack, like an incandescent tail, and the flames began to creep into the nearest field, planted with castor beans.

Anna, passing buckets, asked: "How did it start?" No one knew. Those who were dipping water, bent over, had their feet in the mud forming along the stream. Sparks falling on a cherry tree ignited it. "How did it start?" Anna repeated, when, in the red light of the fire, she saw, opposite her, her grandmother.

Donna Antonia gazed at the flames in astonishment as, bowed by the wind, they threatened another haystack. Nervously she groped at her skirts, lifting them to her knees.

"Nonna!" Anna cried, horrified. "Nonna, what have you done?" The old woman, dazed, stared at the fire with satisfaction. Anna, having passed the bucket to her neighbor, ran to her grandmother. "It was you, right?" she said, breaking into sobs. "What have you done, Nonna? Now all the haystacks will burn and then the fields, the trees . . . all of it. All of it will burn, the land is finished!"

As if only at that moment she understood the gravity of what was happening, Donna Antonia started crying, beating her chest, tearing her hair. "The land . . ." she sobbed. "The land . . ." Then she turned her back on the fire and staggered off.

The slender branches of the cherry tree were pierced by arrows of flame. Anna went up to Mario, who was bending over, his hands aching from the rapid passing of the buckets.

"It was my grandmother!" she said to him. "Think of it, Nonna! It will all burn, won't it?" Mario answered breathlessly: "I don't know, I hope we can stop it. We'll stop it." The smoke caught in their throats; some, with choking coughs, straightened their backs and looked at the haystacks, discouraged.

Then, in the silence, a voice cried: "It's raining!"

The farmers, without slowing down, interrogated the sky, the air dense with a smoky fog. "No way," they said, shaking their heads. But another confident voice confirmed it: "Yes, it's raining!" and voices rose here and there, along the chain: "It's raining!"

On their faces, on their necks, they all felt the drops, hard and heavy, like coins. Anna held out her hands to catch the water: "San Nicola, grant this favor! . . . San Nicola!" The rain fell harder. The fire, slapped by the angry gusts, waned, then rose again boldly and dwindled, defeated. But they continued to heave buckets of water, in the superstitious fear that, if their efforts ceased, the rain, too, would cease. Anna said to Mario: "Look! It's going out!"

The snake of fire retreated from the cherry tree, but the branches were outlined against the sky, sketched in coals. The rain, whipped by the wind, poured over the countryside, along with an odor of burned wood. Her face dripping, her clothes and hair soaked, Anna repeated: "Safe, the harvest is safe!" Once the fire was extinguished, the darkness of night again spread over the land. The farmers, distrustful, waited, as if the fire might suddenly blaze up again. Then they went back to their cottages, grumbling about the rain that would rot the grapes.

Mario put an arm around Anna's shoulders as she leaned against him, wearily, murmuring, "Thank you . . . thank you."

It was still raining when they got home.

In the dining room Donna Matilde was weeping, saying that, one of these days, the old woman would set fire to the house. Donna Antonia wasn't there.

Anna asked: "Where did she go?"

They took the lanterns and went out to look for her; they called to her in the farmyard, in the vegetable garden, straining their ears. The fields were a swamp. And it was still raining. They pushed through the thickets as water crashed suddenly from the leaves. The servants shouted: "Donna Antonia! Donna Antonia!" Anna called "Nonna!" The lanterns passed like eyes along the paths. "Maybe she found shelter with the farmers." They weren't received kindly. "What is it? What else is burning?" Donna Antonia wasn't there.

They found her at dawn, facedown in the ditch, at the far edge of the farm. Her black skirt was sticking out, a white hand. The torn-up bushes showed where she had clutched them, trying not to fall. In the muddy meadow, her tracks were still visible. Between her teeth she had some blades of grass, and mud.

• • • •

September was beautiful. The villagers sang as they passed by the Bortones' farm. Behind the windows, closed in sign of mourning, Anna, wearing black, studied diligently for the entire month, and left with Valentina, as she had arrived. Those who came to say goodbye said she was a good granddaughter because it was clear that she was suffering and had lost weight. Even at the station, the horror still weighed on her. "What a tragedy!" groaned Donna Matilde. "What a scandal!" Then she felt ill and people crowded around her.

Anna and Mario were left alone, as on that night at the gate. It was her first moment of peace after so many sad hours. When the whistle blew, signaling the train's arrival, Anna said: "We'll see each other in a month. At the end of October." Mario asked her quickly: "We'll get married immediately, right?" She nodded. "Anna," he said, but his first words of love were lost in the rumble of the locomotive.

IV

Sister Lorenza's new rank prevented her from going down to meet the girls as they arrived; from her room she heard the sound of the bell calling Sister Luisa into the parlor, and she seemed to perceive a hurried rustling of skirts on the stairs. No one came to summon her anymore: yet she hoped for it every time. "Why didn't you call me?" she asked, looking into the hall. The answer was always the same: "We didn't want to disturb you, Mother."

Later, preceded by Sister Luisa, the new arrivals were introduced in her study: in the Mother's presence, the girls assumed a dutiful expression, and some even tried to kiss her hand, but she pulled it away, in irritation; after some polite conversation, Sister Luisa led them out.

The only one who upon returning went immediately to see her was Silvia Custo. It was a few days before her thesis was to be defended.

"And afterward?"

"Who knows?" Silvia answered. "As long as I can continue working with Belluzzi." She looked out into the courtyard; she saw the sad green plants, the fountain, the benches where the nuns sat. "Everything's always the same," she said.

Sister Lorenza replied bitterly: "Does it really seem always the same to you?"

"You know, at home I forgot what my room was like here. And the other rooms and the halls: they were all vague, in a fog. Even the faces of my friends escaped me; and yours, too, Sister Lorenza. Oh, excuse me, Mother. The Grimaldi seemed very far away; now, though, it seems I've never left."

Then Anna and Valentina returned; the last was Emanuela. They embraced smiling, with loud, effusive greetings, but at first they found nothing to say to one another. Anna, pointing to her mourning, explained: "I lost my grandmother."

Augusta never came down to greet anyone. Emanuela entered her room joyfully, to surprise her, and found her at the desk, as always. At her feet, Margherita was dozing. Even before welcoming her Augusta said:

"See how thin I got? I worked day and night, worn out by the heat; I didn't even have the energy to eat. I've almost finished a new novel. You'll see, this one won't be rejected."

"Set in Sardinia, like the other one?" Emanuela asked.

"Yes, but this time it's about a universal problem: the conflict between man and woman. It will provoke a lot of argument, because I assert that we can do very well without men; that we support them out of an age-old tradition of slavery, not out of true physical attraction. I talk, in fact, about the instinctive repugnance that woman feels for man. A revolutionary book, in short. Want me to show it to you? Wait."

With a sigh she shifted her large bosom to take out of the desk drawer a manuscript that she held out to her friend like a delicate, fragile object.

It was almost three hundred pages. Augusta really had got thin; there was a livid furrow under her eyes. In summer, the residence was deserted: even the nuns went to play in the courtyard. Augusta looked out, letting her eyes be dazzled by the metallic gray of the sky. I'll go, I won't go. Finally, triumphing over herself, she decided: I'll stay. The hours weighed on her like days, the weeks like years. From her town everyone wrote, asking: "And so, this novel? When will it come out?" And she had done nothing. In fact she was led to linger in that parenthesis of waiting, which detained her in a fictitious youth. At the Grimaldi, despite her age, she was still a student: outside, she would be a woman.

With a gesture, Emanuela indicated that, if nothing else, she admired the heft of the manuscript, and Augusta took it back. Then, realizing she'd talked only about herself, asked:

"What about you, what did you do?"

"I traveled a little, but Papa isn't well."

"When will you be married?"

"In a year: after Andrea gets his degree."

Augusta, without even expressing the customary congratulations, stood up to get two glasses and a bottle that appeared to contain medicine: "It's a homemade liqueur—it's good, it has a flavor of aromatics. You should taste it." While they drank she lighted yet another cigarette. She had assumed masculine gestures and attitudes.

"You're smoking a lot now," Emanuela observed.

"Yes, especially when I work: to keep myself awake."

It was twilight, and slow shadows invaded the room. An awkward silence fell between the two friends. Emanuela realized that Augusta was preparing to tell her something; and instinctively she would have liked to avoid it. But she was constrained by something indefinable: maybe by Augusta's life, different from the lives of the rest of them. "Wasted," she thought, "and yet she always seems to be sustained by an illusion."

"Listen," Augusta said finally, in an affectionate tone. "You're happy to be getting married. You're getting married. But have you considered that, from that day on, you will no longer be master of yourself? Even when you're alone, a presence, a will, a power alien to you will dominate. You won't keep anything of yourself, not even your name, you'll be only the wife of Signor Lanziani, who will have the right to know everything about you: what you do, what you think, and if you hide anything from him it will be a betrayal. Your children will also be his. You'll bring them into the world, and he, by law, will dispose of them as he likes."

"No," Emanuela interrupted, "what does the law have to do with it? We'll do everything in agreement, Andrea is a civilized person, he trusts me, he leaves me free."

"For now," Augusta said maliciously. "But once you're married, you won't be free ever again, not even within yourself. I know about it . . ." She sighed, shaking her head. "Women are either devastated, and they become smiling and empty as dolls, or resist the devastation and, in order to resist, have to acquire a monstrous strength. It's the worst case: they become blocks of stone, rocks, against which anyone is wounded. Tell me: have you thought that a man will have the right to enter your room even at night, put his hands on you when he likes? And you will have *the duty* to satisfy him. The duty! How can one speak of duty or right, when it comes to a human body? Dispose of something that is animated by a soul as if it were an inanimate object?"

"You're judging it all in theory," Emanuela objected. "Don't you take love into account? Physical attraction?"

Augusta leaned toward her, staring into her eyes. "But are you sure you'll always feel it? Are you sure you won't feel that right as a sordid abuse, when you've already sworn, signed, when you're already bound? Forever! Until your young, fresh body becomes only a mass of sagging flesh like the Abbess's. Do you really like the way men kiss? I, too, was engaged, years ago: I wanted to be alone with him—Loris, his name was—I was overwhelmed thinking of a kiss from him. We were in the garden: he kissed me and his face was different from usual, different eyes . . . So many years have passed, but if I think about it I spit. I'll never be able to forget that intrusion, that violence . . ." She broke off, overcome by the unpleasantness of the memory. "Have you thought of that, too, Emanuela?"

Emanuela nodded: she thought she would know hours like the ones she'd spent with Stefano in the house in Viale dei Colli. She would have liked to answer: "All right, I want to tell you the truth, Augusta. I already know it all and I like it." But she had to continue to play the role of the innocent; and, in a way, it amused her.

Augusta took one last drag of her cigarette and, putting it out, observed: "I understand more and more clearly how urgent it is for me to finish my book, so that all women can read it." After a pause, she added: "And your father? What does he say about it?"

Emanuela repeated, uncertain, "My father?"

. . . .

She had talked to him a few hours before they left for Alto Adige. She had gone into his room while he, in shirtsleeves, was packing his suitcase: it was a task he liked to perform with calm and attention, so she hadn't chosen the moment well; but now she had made up her mind, and if she put it off again she wouldn't speak to him. She knew that the news would upset him, yet she hadn't taken that into account, since it seemed to her that the very fact of being the father implied that one's children's lives took precedence over one's own. In the same way, years earlier, she had told him that she was engaged to Stefano; then that Stefano was dead, that she was pregnant, and that she wanted to acknowledge the child, and she had tormented him about Stefania, to be with Stefania. And now she was going to tell him that she intended to marry Andrea Lanziani.

Papa was wearing a white shirt, white pants; his head, completely bald, looked like old wax. Hearing the news, he continued to arrange his underwear in the suitcase without even turning toward his daughter.

"Are you already the lover of this one?" he asked.

"No," she answered, adding, resentfully: "Besides, what would it matter?"

"And Stefania?"

"She could go to a boarding school abroad for the moment. Later we'll see. You've always said that Stefania shouldn't influence my life."

"Yes, but then you convinced me of the opposite."

"I made a mistake."

"How many mistakes have you made, my dear?" her father replied. "It seems to me that it would be difficult now to remove Stefania from your life, and you persuaded me that it wouldn't be right. He, well ... this young man ... what does he say about it?"

"Andrea? He doesn't know, he doesn't know anything about it."

"He doesn't know?!" the old man repeated, irritated. "But then why discuss the subject now? Or are you thinking of keeping him in the dark forever?" Emanuela didn't respond, because, in fact, she had no plan. "Tell him everything and then we'll talk about it again, we'll see."

He ran his hand over his wrinkled brow, as if to chase away those thoughts; with a sigh, he turned back to the suitcase. Emanuela was vexed as she left the room. Stefania was in Amalfi, in a beautiful villa where the school took up residence during the summer. The sisters had written that she was well, eating, swimming, having fun. "It's not enough to have secured all this for her? By the sole fact of being alive, can she, in turn, prevent me from living?"

She should have listened to her father in the beginning, when, to persuade her not to acknowledge the child, he asserted that—thanks to the modern mind-set, devoid of outdated social prejudices—foundlings today do very well. She had said that the fear of that illegitimate granddaughter was, rather, the proof that such prejudices endured. But her father insisted: the first to be damaged by the acknowledgment was Stefania herself, who would not have either the freedom of those with no family or the advantages granted to natural children, since she would always desire what she didn't possess.

For her, on the other hand, acknowledging the child had been the only alternative. She wanted to make Andrea understand that; but since she hadn't told him right away, it was better to wait. "If Stefania's father were still alive, I would have confessed everything to you immediately: otherwise, you might have been jealous, supposing that I was still attached to him. But since he's dead . . ."

Did Stefania really have a father? She couldn't connect in any way what had happened in the Viale dei Colli house and the child. The conception of Stefania seemed due to her alone: a daughter growing in her like a tumor. And yet the child didn't resemble her: she didn't possess her capacity to inspire liking. According to the nuns, she was rather hard, capricious: selfish, they concluded. Maybe her father had also been like that: Emanuela didn't know much about him; they hadn't met that long before. It occurred to her to tell Andrea that she had been the victim of an attack. A stranger on the way from Florence to Maiano, and then the child: a misfortune. "That's why we hid her." Then she discarded the idea of that absurd stratagem. In yielding to Stefano, she said to herself, she knew what she was doing.

Although, to tell the truth, she knew only vaguely. "You never know anything, before; a girl is always inexperienced, always alone faced with these things. She doesn't have the courage to mention it to her parents because they talk about it as of something dirty, or scientific. Described by them, the act of love becomes a sort of surgical operation, not at all appealing. Of what you feel beside a man, the instincts, the senses—parents never talk about that, they don't take it into account." . . . "A stranger who appeared before me on the street one day and compelled me by force." Ultimately it really was a stranger who appeared before her on the Lungarno: and had compelled her with the force of the curiosity a girl feels toward every aspect of love. But Papa would never go along with such a pretense. There was no escape: the invisible presence of Stefania in her life forced her, chained her, took away her freedom. She would never be able to dispose of her own future; in the face of any dream, any plan, that obstacle would arise, inexorable.

During the journey to the Dolomites, it had been an effort to play the part of the daughter; by now she was used to independence, to arranging her day, her schedule, and here it was her father who decided everything. Augusta was right: it's impossible to go home after experiencing freedom, even if it was simply the innocent freedom of going out with her friends, attending the university, living the chaste and carefree life of the Grimaldi. Also to be young, to laugh, one needs to be free: they all thought so and were all intelligent girls. Xenia had done well to leave: the poor can start their own life by stealing an object or the trust of a soul. Besides, by stealing the ring, Xenia had shown she loved her, since she had chosen her to ask for help and sympathy, even if in a guilty way.

Risking everything—Emanuela was considering—is the privilege of those who have no social position. The others, despite freedom and even a flaunted open-mindedness, are constrained by vague but invincible fears, by traditions that everything around them evokes. Absurd as it may seem, freedom is denied to those who exist not only in themselves but also as an expression of a precise value, like social class or wealth. Her father, by forcing her to conceal the child, had defended those values, even though he had always refused to define himself by the goods he possessed. When he traveled he stayed at modest hotels. In restaurants he was frugal. "But today is different," Emanuela said to herself. "Today money counts more than anything and can replace everything: even the father's name missing on the birth certificate." In those months, she had talked a lot about her future. Papa listened, bewildered, mechanically cleaning his eyeglasses with his handkerchief. Her mother always added a kind word: "Yes, really, Bepi . . . Emanuela has the right to go back to the point of departure." ("What departure," she thought. "For where?") Now she promised: "At the first good moment, I'll talk, I'll tell him everything."

Returning to Maiano, Papa had found a letter from Andrea: tired from the journey, moved by an instinctive sympathy for the young man, he had answered that, for his part, he saw nothing against their marriage. He made no allusion to Stefania.

. . . .

"What should my father say?" she answered Augusta. "He's pleased."

Then they went down to dinner. In the hall they met other girls going down; the new ones had a lost expression. One of them, Cloe, passing by Emanuela and Augusta, said in a friendly way, "Good evening." She was studying singing, and it was said that she would become a great contralto.

Now it was she who played the harmonium in chapel; for that reason, Milly's friends felt a kind of rancor toward her. Yet the first time she sang at the evening service, they had been shaken by her dramatic voice, which seemed to reproach the Lord for all the misery of the human condition. Emanuela had thought back to Milly, who caressed her hands, who read the letters from the organist with her fingertips. In the last days of her life she had neglected her because of Andrea; and that singing awakened in her the memory and the remorse. Cloe came over to the two girls asking: "What are you doing tonight?" It was clear that she would have liked to join their group. At the table Emanuela and Augusta talked about it with the others, but Silvia was intransigent. "No," she said, "we shouldn't let any of the new girls join us. We'll die out, little by little, like a noble line. Xenia fled, Milly is dead, Vinca . . ."

"What's Vinca doing?" Emanuela interrupted.

"Oh yes, you didn't see her. She came to visit when you were still in Florence. She works now, she gives a lot of lessons. She lives with that Spanish woman, a fanatic about the monarchy. You should go, it's nearby, in Via Sistina 87."

An old house, a long, dark entranceway, uneven stairs of peperino stone; on the door of the apartment a creaking bell you had to twist to ring.

There were three rooms crowded with the things that Donna Inés had brought with her into exile and that bore witness to her past wealth: damasks, old china, silver, all displayed on the furniture and on the shelves intended for books.

On the walls were portraits of the royal princes, of Pilar and Ignacio as children, postcards with scenes of Andalusia—which the women stuck in the frames of the paintings to recreate the familiar landscape—open fans; on the floor sumptuous *mantones* with knotted fringe. On the grand piano, in a great silver frame, the Bourbon profile of the dethroned king.

Donna Inés and Pilar stayed in bed until midday. Vinca, accustomed to the schedule of the Grimaldi, woke early and immediately called Pilar.

"What's wrong?" the other said, opening her eyes wide.

"Get up. It's nine."

"Nine? At that hour I sleep."

"It's a shame, let's go, Pilar!"

"Let's go, where? I have nothing to do."

Vinca went to her students and, returning, found the two women still in their bathrobes. Donna Inés wrote interminable letters, sitting at the dining table; when they set the table, she pushed aside a plate and continued. She wrote to all her friends, in order not to be forgotten. She was afraid they were talking about her as if she were dead. "Remember Inés? Poor Inés." She read a lot of newspapers and kept them piled on the chairs. She had bought a map of Spain and pinned onto it a nationalist flag, which she moved after every battle, with a geographic skill acquired for the occasion. "On one side the Spain *de Dios y del Rey*, on the other the Spain of the devil," she said.

Pilar waited for dinnertime sitting at her vanity and brushing her long black hair, which, divided in the middle by a wide part, fell along the sides of her face as shiny and polished as onyx. She brushed it diligently, from the roots to the tips, then ran her hand over it and, eager for perfection, started over again.

Vinca sat beside her and they talked, helping one another endure the anxiety of waiting. Letters from Spain usually arrived in the evening mail. In the afternoon, following the Spanish custom, the three women sat at the window: Donna Inés on the right, Pilar on the left, and Vinca in the middle, as in a box at the theater.

It was the only moment when they allowed themselves some distraction: they sat there, carefully groomed, lips and eyes a little too heavily made-up—but wearing slippers on their feet, without stockings. Via Sistina was a fashionable street, with an abundance of expensive stores. People lingered in front of the windows. Those heading toward Piazza Trinità dei Monti for a date had an expression at once bold and wary. Vinca, who was the most imaginative, reconstructed their stories as if they were in a novel. "There are the ones from Thursday," she'd say; or "Today the girl in the red coat must have had a fight: look at that face!" and, not seeing a couple pass by for several days, she'd say, regretfully, "Maybe it's over."

Suddenly one of them would cry, "There he is!" With a single look they followed the mailman as he entered the doorways and came out again, weighed down by the large bag on his belly as if by a deformity. When they saw him disappear into the entrance of their building, all three, quietly, hearts in a tumult, pretended they were still looking out in order to endure the anguish of uncertainty. Meanwhile the time passed ("The porter's slow, there are a lot of steps, maybe she stopped to chat"), and finally one said, her throat dry, "There's nothing."

If, instead, they heard the rasping twist of the doorbell the girls jumped up, Donna Inés urged "Calm down, calm!" and Pilar ran to open the door. Most often, the mail was for her: Luis and Ignacio were lazy. Pilar grabbed the letter, went to her room, and closed the door.

Donna Inés and Vinca, although respecting the lovers' intimacy, paced impatiently outside the door; when Pilar delayed too long, they shook their heads as if she were behaving badly. Then she returned to the living room and read the letter aloud. Luis hardly ever wrote, but Pepe spoke at length about him as well; he said he was brave, really brave, that he encouraged his younger comrades, who were still practically adolescents. In other words, he was an example for everyone and Vinca should be proud of him.

Vinca was. Yet Emanuela, visiting, noticed that she had a kind of constant feverish shiver.

She was wearing the same housedress she'd had at the Grimaldi, now threadbare.

"Are you back? You're all there?" she asked Emanuela; and it was clear that she would regret not being with them if Luis's absence had left space for other regrets. "Last year, remember?, you were new and Xenia invited you to join us. You've heard nothing about Xenia?" Emanuela shook her head. "We were so happy!" Vinca sighed: "Too bad we realize we've known happiness only when it's over. How many things have happened in a year ... Remember how lively I was at school? I didn't know then that I was in love; gradually you realize that a worm is eating away at your soul and your health, that someone has become more necessary than the air you breathe ..."

Emanuela wondered if she felt the same about Andrea.

"Now I live for the arrival of the mail. Often it brings me nothing, but I've waited for that hour with hope; and when, for good or ill, it's passed, I start waiting with equal hope for the next day. If one day the mailman arrived and I weren't waiting for him, it would be the first sign of decline. Isn't that true?"

"I don't know if it's true: each of us has our own idea of love."

"No. There are many ways of loving, but love is unique, like art. A thousand forms, but art is there or it's not."

You had only to look at her to understand that in her there was love.

Emanuela stared at her in admiration, and couldn't help observing also her mended stockings, her dirty housedress.

"In this situation it doesn't even matter to me that I'm shabby," Vinca said as if responding to her friend's gaze. "A lot of money goes for the mail, I write every day, by air mail. Luis isn't here now anyway. When he comes back I'll buy a new dress."

"When will that be?"

"Doesn't matter. The point is for him to return. When there's no mail, I think maybe he won't ever write again, and Pilar thinks the same about Pepe."

Emanuela reproached her, to comfort her: "Why do you say that, Vinca? You shouldn't even say it."

"I never do say it, in fact none of us do, it's the only possibility we don't talk about. Every day, the newspapers publish photos of the ones who've gotten medals, but they don't write more. I don't speak, Pilar doesn't speak. If Pepe comes back on leave, they'll get married right away."

"And you?"

"Us? We've never talked about it. But Luis has to think about studying. Have you seen how interesting his projects are?"

Emanuela responded evasively. Then she left because she had an appointment with Andrea in Piazza di Spagna. He was waiting at the foot of the stairs and watched her coming down with a look of satisfaction. "You know?" he said. "What most struck me about you the first time was your way of walking. It's very important, for a woman: some arrive by force of will, of control; you must have walked like that even when you took your first steps," he said, laughing, and holding her tenderly by the arm. "Now, there's something very important today: Papa has agreed to our marriage. In fact, if I want, he's willing to give me a monthly check, without my working at the store, to help me make my way in literature or journalism. I said I'd think about it. He was very frank. So we have to think about it seriously. I'm afraid that literature can't be a career. In the time of Lorenzo the Magnificent, maybe I would have been named court poet and had a beautiful apartment with frescoed walls. For a literature graduate today, there's only teaching. A position at the high school in Bitonto, for

example. You want to be the wife of a professor in Bitonto? It seems un-
likely, not with that way of walking you have."

"Why do you say that, Andrea? It's distressing to me."

"On the contrary, silly, that's exactly what I like. Thus the teaching,
no. I'm afraid that weighing diamonds is still the best solution. No one
can prevent me from writing at night. But doesn't it seem ridiculous to
you, a jeweler poet?" he asked, smiling. As he spoke he guided her quickly
through the crowd, as if he had a precise goal.

"Where are we going, Andrea?"

"To the store. We'll surprise them."

"Now? Like this? No, no!"

She had decided that she wouldn't get to this point before she had
told him everything; but now, in the middle of the Corso, how could she?
On the narrow sidewalk people bumped them, divided them. Also that
hat didn't look so well on her, her hair was untidy, and she would have
liked to bring flowers to Andrea's mother: men don't understand these
things. "Andrea," she said, determined to tell him everything.

They were already in front of the store: he made a sign to be quiet and
looked through the window.

"Andrea," she insisted. And in her mind she continued: "Listen to me,
Andrea, I have a child." Just like that, in the middle of the Corso: it was a
place like any other, and that moment had to come. But Andrea said, "No
one's there," and made her go in.

Their footsteps were muffled by the brown carpet of the elegant, sober
shop, where jewels shone in a small lighted window; the salesman rose, seeing Andrea, who headed for a door hidden by a curtain. There, in a small
warm room, sat the two old people, just as Andrea had described them: she
was working, he was reading the newspaper. Hearing the door open, the father peered over his glasses. Andrea said with a smile: "Here's Emanuela."

Although Emanuela had imagined this meeting many times, she was
ill at ease. It was the two old people, kind and good-humored, who broke

the ice: the mother came up to her, they kissed each other, the father kissed her, too. Emanuela couldn't seem unpleasant, she could never seem unpleasant to anyone. Besides, she was pretty and her way of dressing, her manners made it clear that she was also well-off. All parents are pleased when the future wife of their son is pretty and well-off.

In the end they invited her to lunch at their house, the following Sunday. Andrea was happy, with an expansive, almost boyish happiness.

"Sunday?" Emanuela repeated, bewildered. (Every Sunday, at two, she went to see Stefania; maybe, for once, she wouldn't go; or she would go in the morning.) "Sunday, all right," she confirmed with a smile.

· · · ·

The following Sunday at eleven, Emanuela arrived in a taxi at the boarding school in Monte Mario—so out of the way!—asked the driver to wait, and, as she rang the bell, peered here and there, as if afraid of seeing Andrea emerge from behind the hedge that bordered the street and ask: "What are you doing here?"

She asked the maid who opened the door about the child in an anxious tone, intimating that the odd hour was due to circumstances beyond her control. She heard the bell ringing in the courtyard, but in place of Stefania a nun appeared. "Now she'll tell me that the girls can't come down to the parlor at this hour. Nuns, always stubborn . . . anyway, I came." Instead the sister told her that Stefania was ill.

"I wanted to let you know yesterday, signora, but we didn't have a way of getting in touch, in fact it would be useful for . . ."

"Ill? Nothing serious, right?"

"Scarlet fever."

"Scarlet fever?!" Emanuela repeated, frightened.

"Yesterday she had a very high fever, this morning it went down a little. She was delirious all night, it was pitiful . . . she didn't fall asleep until dawn," the nun explained. "I'll take you to the infirmary."

They went through cloisters and courtyards; everything was white and clean, white chrysanthemums filled the flower beds of the enclosed gardens. They're comfortable, thought Emanuela, they're better off than at home. And so they reached the infirmary ward set aside for infectious diseases. Stefania was in a small white room.

As soon as she saw Emanuela in the doorway, the child murmured, relieved, "Mamma . . ." Her face was pinched, her voice murky, veiled: her braids, no longer coiled pertly over her ears, fell on her chest. "Why didn't you come before, Mamma?"

"I didn't know, sweetheart, I didn't know."

"If you were here, Simonetta wouldn't come."

The nurse said in a whisper that the child was delirious again; the fever had risen.

"I can hear everything, I understand everything," Stefania said. "It's really true that Simonetta comes to do my braids. That's why my head hurts." Her eyes were closed, her cheeks flushed with fever. "You won't leave, right, Mamma?"

"No, no."

"Look . . . My whole body is covered with red dots, like strawberries."

The sister whispered to Emanuela that the doctor was coming at one ("We'll expect you at one," Andrea's mother had said to her). "It will be better if you speak to him yourself," the sister continued. "Naturally if you wish to spend the night with the child, the rules don't prohibit it."

Emanuela repeated: "Oh, they don't?"

"No. In fact, in certain cases, to avoid responsibility, we prefer that . . ."

"Stop it, Simonetta, you're hurting me!" Stefania began raving in a voice different from her usual commanding tone: a blurry, distant voice. "It wasn't me, I told you: your sandwich is there, on the window, forget my braids." Then she widened her eyes, looking around: "Did Papa come?"

Emanuela didn't answer: the nurse was facing her, the sister behind her. Perhaps only the sister knew the child's biographical information: Stefania Andori of unknown father and Emanuela Andori. Stefania called out for that unknown father. How to answer? Emanuela didn't answer, hoping the child would be distracted by that thought. But Stefania, after two or three incoherent phrases, repeated: "Did Papa come?"

Emanuela, trying not to feel the sister's presence behind her, whispered: "Papa's working."

"Still the airplanes?"

"Still."

"Tell him the one he sent me was a toy, not a real airplane."

Emanuela placed her hand on her forehead. "She's burning!" she murmured to the nurse, who, looking at the clock, said:

"It's twelve fifteen. The doctor's coming at one."

A quarter of an hour passed in a flash. Stefania seemed to be sleeping, saliva bubbled on her lips, as if she were playing. Emanuela, looking around in search of some compassion, announced: "I have to go."

The sister turned in surprise. "You're not waiting for the doctor?"

"At one precisely I have to be in the city."

"If you like you can telephone," the other suggested, moving to precede her.

"Telephone? No, the appointment is in the street."

The sister was silent, gazing at the floor, then she looked up to ask: "And tonight?"

"Tonight?" Emanuela repeated.

It was a torture, a torture: she wanted to beg them not to torment her anymore: she couldn't stay now or return later to watch over her daughter. No girl resident at the Grimaldi could spend the night outside the institution: it was a strict rule. If she went out, she would never return. She could have pointed to the pretext of a sudden departure for Florence, but

Andrea? What would she say to Andrea? He would insist on going with her to the station, he would telephone her in Florence, that same evening. "What can I do?" she moaned to herself. The nun was waiting. "No," she said, swallowing a bitter pill. "I can't stay here tonight."

The sister nodded coldly. "As you wish," and the nurse added, "I'm here."

"I'll be back later," Emanuela promised. But the sister was no longer paying attention to her. When she got up to leave the chair scraped the floor and the child opened her eyes.

"Where are you going, Mamma?"

"To the office, to telephone," the nurse answered quickly.

"You're not leaving me, right?" Stefania insisted.

"No, I'm just going to telephone, didn't you hear?" Emanuela said and bent over her daughter's burning forehead, to hide the blush caused by that lie.

Stefania stared at her, eyes alight with fever. "Take off your hat, then!" she ordered in the commanding tone Emanuela was used to. Then, seeing her mother obey, she closed her eyes and made a gesture that was both "bye" and "come back."

Emanuela waited another moment before cautiously picking up her hat from the nightstand and tiptoeing out of the room. She passed through the school behind the muffled swishing of the sister's skirts; at the door, putting her hat on as gracefully as she could, she said, "Thank you, Sister": as if she had received alms.

Outside, Stefania's illness was a vanished nightmare; it no longer existed, or, rather, Stefania no longer existed. In the speeding taxi, jolting and tilting her as it rounded the corners, Emanuela tasted the joy of being free: she had feared even that they wouldn't let her leave, as the porter nun at the Grimaldi had refused to open the door for Vinca when she wanted to go to Luis.

It was two minutes to one when Emanuela, smoothing her jacket, rang at the door of the Lanziani house: a tall dark door with dazzling brass fixtures. While she waited, standing straight on the doormat, she thought: Stefania will cry when she sees I've left, not finding my hat on the night table. She felt a sharp pang, an acute remorse, but it was short-lived, because the door opened suddenly, the maid smiled, she smiled, and she entered.

. . . .

Anxiety about Stefania seized her again that night at the Grimaldi. During the day, every time the thought of the little girl surfaced she had driven it out harshly.

It had been a really lovely Sunday: in the Lanziani dining room a faint ray of sun entered through the window and struck the polished, heavy old furniture. There was an air of family peace, a little cloying, but in it she had forgotten the anguish that gripped her in the school infirmary, under the nun's accusing eye. After lunch Andrea wanted to show her his room, his books; beside the bed was a picture of Emanuela. "But it's old," he said. "I'd like a more recent one, one that shows you as you are now." That one had been taken by Stefano in the Boboli Gardens. In her life now, everything was mixed up: past and present, lies and truth.

In chapel during the evening prayer, she was assailed by the fear that she would be unable to hurry to Stefania if it was necessary. She hadn't intended to call; but she couldn't resist, and, before going up to her room, she called the school.

"Hello," she said. "I'd like to know how the Andori child is."

"Are you the mother?"

"Yes," she said in a whisper, as if to be that a little less.

She waited a long time, on burning coals: she feared that one of her friends would join her, preventing her from speaking openly. Finally the usual sister came to the phone. "Complications have occurred. Stefania's condition is very serious," she said bluntly. "And the doctor hasn't disguised his worries. The fever is very high, the child is delirious. She's calling you, signora."

"Oh. I understand, thank you, good night," Emanuela said, breaking off because people had come into the room.

She returned to the front hall. The door was already barred and Sister Prudenzina was making sure that the girls returned to their rooms, meek as sheep. Soon the hall gate would close, squeaking; then, at the cry of "Lights!," everything would disappear into darkness. If Emanuela begged her, "Open it!," she would not let her go out.

"Very serious," she repeated to herself, going up to her room. Again she saw Stefania delirious in her bed, flushed with fever, again heard the voice, until then unknown, ask: "You're not leaving, right?" She had betrayed her, abandoning her with a smile on her lips, hat in hand. She had been false with her, as with everyone. Her life was merely an airy architecture of deceptions, a cathedral of glass that, because of this illness, would collapse: the various characters that lodged in her would find themselves face-to-face, unmasking one another. She would lose everything: Andrea, her friends, even her daughter. "It's very serious," she thought, and I'm not there.

She paced up and down the room, in a frenzy. What can I do? What can I do? This imploring question escaped her like a sob. She would feel her way down the stairs, down to the door on which a cartouche bore the word "Cloister," and appear in the nuns' dormitory. Augusta had been sick one night and had gone in there. An oil lamp burned perpetually before a sacred image: and in that glow, near the beds enclosed in white curtains, she had seen the black caps placed on stakes, like severed heads impaled on spears. Give me the key, quick, she would say: "My daughter is ill, she could die tonight." At that idea she stopped, stunned.

"And if she died?" she thought. As if tempted, she repeated in a whisper: "If she died?"

She was afraid the door would open to let in a scowling, implacable God, dressed in white and armed with lightning bolts. She waited, frozen: nothing.

If she died, no more conversation with Andrea. She would go to the funeral alone, her face veiled, with the shadow of that unknown father who built airplanes. A sharp pain bit her in the womb that had borne her child. Yet that thought made its way into her, tenacious as hope. If she died, some playacting on the wedding night would suffice. Andrea was young, trusting, he wouldn't suspect anything. A traditional marriage, white dress, long train, bouquet of gardenias, and the organ echoing loudly. Where? San Marco in Florence? Or in Rome, amid the mosaics of the Navicella? Everything in place, everything normal, as if Stefania had never been born. Besides, who knew of her existence? No one.

She would be able to fly back over the years, lightly, lightly, to the day she had met Stefano on the Lungarno. It all hung on a few moments: if she hadn't kept walking past the Ponte Vecchio, enticed by the season. "If she died, it would be as if I'd turned onto the Ponte Vecchio that day, taking the road home." A girl sets off over the bridge, a man walks along the Lungarno. Matter of a few steps, of moments. And they will never meet.

"She'll die, certainly. And free me."

How many children die at the age of five? Her sister had died of scarlet fever at that age. A wave of pity invaded her as she heard Stefania's voice again: ". . . red dots like strawberries." She suffered as if she had been forced to offer her daughter in sacrifice. "It's for her good," she said to herself. Everywhere Stefania would have to reveal that original shame: father unknown. Maybe one day she would reproach her: "Mamma, why didn't you kill me as a child?"

Standing in the middle of the room, she stared at the door, as if someone were supposed to enter with the news. But all was silent in the house, the lights were extinguished: she alone was awake. Besides, she thought, at five one doesn't yet appreciate life, one doesn't suffer by dying. And she trembled and wrung her hands, until, exhausted, she dropped onto the bed, waiting for that certainty to become solid in her: Stefania will die.

She fell asleep in her clothes, without noticing. At dawn the light coming through the window woke her with a shiver of cold. Stefania . . . she thought immediately, in the tremendous certainty that at that hour her child no longer existed, was dead. "And I killed her," she said to herself. "Murderer." Finally the nuns' bell chimed three times. Emanuela, distraught, left, hurried to the school, entered the infirmary. "I couldn't, Sister," she said, weeping, "I really couldn't last night . . ." and was so distressed that the sister placed a hand on her shoulder to comfort her. She spent the whole day at her daughter's bedside, every so often calling her timidly: "Stefania . . ." And it was as if she wanted to say: "Forgive me." She didn't move, even to eat, shook her head when the nurse asked her to rest. At four Stefania, without opening her eyes, murmured: "Mamma, I'm hungry." So she had heard her, she knew that she had been there, beside her. At six the child began to sweat. The fever had fallen when, at seven, Emanuela left.

At the table, her friends greeted her with glances of understanding; she sat down, exhausted, and began eating with her head down. Silvia said to her in a low voice: "Things seem to be going badly for you."

"For me?"

"Well, yes! Yesterday out at lunch, today out at lunch . . . Sister Prudenzina talked to the Superior."

"Oh!"

"You're not saying anything?"

"What should I say?"

Later they gathered in Anna's room. Silvia, hearing the sister approach, was quick to put a book in front of Emanuela. Sister Prudenzina couldn't object to anything; but before retreating she observed, "You're studying a lot, Andori, too much."

Valentina, Silvia, and Anna, looking up from their books, interrogated Emanuela, who explained: "Well, I didn't do anything extraordinary: yesterday and today I had lunch at Andrea's parents' house."

"Did they give you a ring?" Valentina asked.

"No, not yet."

"The fact is," said Silvia, "for two days you've been looking upset. The sister noticed your empty place at the table, and there was a lot of talk among the major skirts. I think they're wondering what you're doing here in Rome. I must tell you that I wonder the same thing."

"I'm studying: do I need to be enrolled in the university to study?"

"No," Silvia said, "no, of course not. But do you like studying? Maybe you prefer doing nothing."

"Or taking walks with Andrea," Valentina said, laughing.

"Not even," Silvia insisted. "Doing nothing. And I'd like to convince you that in life you can't do nothing."

"Emanuela will have her house, her children," Anna pointed out.

"I don't think that interests her very much: Emanuela is nothing but a consumer of money."

"Why are you angry with me, Silvia, what's wrong?"

"Nothing. I'm telling you what I think. What's the use of being friends except to tell each other what we think?"

"You think friendship has to be useful for something?" asked Anna.

"No, maybe not, because rarely do we choose our friends. They happen to us. Some we've known since childhood, and then it's not friendship, it's habit. When we meet someone we'd like to be friends with, we seldom have the opportunity. And so we go along with chance friends. But what were we saying? Oh! That you should do something. Know the satisfaction of constructing your own path, day by day. Feeling tired at night, and not tired from having lived another day as well as you could but from having fashioned it with your own hands."

"Words," said Emanuela, "textbook words and concepts. In reality what pushes you to wear your eyes out over papers is ambition."

"Ambition?" Silvia repeated and then agreed. "Maybe so. But not the ambition to be thought superior by others; rather, it's to be able to acknowledge in myself an inner superiority. Everything I do is an effort to gain that consciousness for myself. You don't even have that."

"My life is so complicated . . ."

"There, exactly: what complicates existence is boredom. People who have a busy life don't think living it is complicated. For example, you could take a course to become a Red Cross nurse."

"Me?!" exclaimed Emanuela. "I have a horror of blood, the dead scare me, I dream of them for a whole month. Then I'd need a nurse to treat me."

"Then . . ."

"Then all this talk is pointless: in June I'm getting married."

"Yes, it's true, there's also marriage. I always forget about that," said Silvia, smiling. She put an arm around Emanuela's shoulders affectionately. "Forgive me. I'm the one who's mistaken. I don't consider that there are other interests in the world, different from mine. That here—how many times have I said it?—we're on a bridge: when we've crossed the bridge some take one path, some another."

"Soon," Anna observed, "the bridge will be deserted."

"No, never deserted. We go down, others come up," Silvia said thoughtfully. Then she resumed, changing her tone: "Let's study now."

· · · ·

Returning to her room at midnight, Valentina put her books down on the desk and drew a sigh of relief, like a woman taking off her corset. She looked at herself in the mirror, combed her hair, undressed quickly, and got into bed.

She lay on her back in the bed, arms along her side, the sheet grazing her chin, luxuriating in the warmth that the covers contained around her body. Then she turned off the light and waited, eyes closed.

The window opened slowly, like the curtain in a theater. The air that penetrated the room was sweet, smelling of magnolias. Outside everything was illuminated by the moon, and an infinity of stars sparkled in the sky above the garden: a fabulous garden where peacocks walked on white gravel, swans glided in a silver fountain. On the other side of the wall the domes and minarets of oriental temples were visible.

Valentina settled herself more comfortably, saying to herself: "All right, now it's starting." The door opened and he entered, cautiously. The carpet muffled his footsteps, but the silk of his wide pants rustled; his hands were loaded with rings, his shiny black hair waved over his temples.

"Are you sleeping?" he asked.

"Yes, my lord, I was sleeping."

It was a warm evening; the girl's body was lightly veiled in blue, and under the diaphanous gauze her flesh quivered at every breath. Her slender wrists, where you could see the delicate branching of the veins, were weighed down by heavy bracelets.

"Are the women still singing?"

"Yes," he said. "Don't you hear them?"

In the silence she heard the distant sound of a harp. And a voice, also distant.

"They're singing," he repeated, "but I was tired of listening to them, I abandoned them. Their eyes are restless, greedy: yours are dewy violets."

The perfume of the flowers rose more sharply from the garden. He sat on the bed, and with a start she retreated. "Why do you rebel?" the prince said tenderly, caressing her. The tone of his voice was irresistible; his hands were soft as magnolia petals.

It was sweet to let go in his arms; and, soon, yield to sleep.

. . . .

"A first-class woman," Dino's friends said, talking about Xenia. They didn't call her by her first name, as they did the others: she was Signorina Costantini. Dino listened, nodded slightly, at most acknowledged, indulgently:

"For a woman, yes, she's intelligent."

Often at night, instead of going to bars, the group gathered at Xenia's. And when important friends (connected with the "deal") came to Milan from abroad he invited them to Signorina Costantini's. There were only three rooms, but they were furnished with confident, sober taste: antique furniture, low, muted lighting, two or three modern paintings, and a lot of books. Old friends, showing new friends around, said: "Charming, don't you think?"; and, with a glance, made it clear that they were alluding to the woman.

Xenia had become more beautiful. Her body acquired slenderness in her new, stylish clothes; the greedy look that hardened her eyes had disappeared, or at least was more deeply hidden. Furnishing the house had been a pleasant occupation that had both revealed and refined her natural good taste.

"Wouldn't you like to do interior design?" people sometimes asked. "It's an idea." Pretending to be interested, she answered, "Why not?," and meanwhile thought: "What an idea, working!"

Vandina had understood that she had to keep her distance now, and visited in the afternoon. Other women didn't come to her house, apart from Barchi's Mary: their friends had common interests, Mary tried to make herself likable, and Xenia recognized that she was; yet despite mutual good intentions they couldn't establish a real friendship.

At night, the men played poker: a cloud of gray smoke formed around the table, and the players often got irritated. Only Horsch remained calm. Dino said: "Xenia, give us something more to drink." The next day she said to him, "Whiskey's expensive, give me some more money," and Dino always gave it to her happily. "When one has a house business gets going better. Besides, soon there will be the earnings from the big trailer truck deal." At the end of the summer, Xenia said: "So that position at the cement company?" But Dino replied: "Why, you want to go back to work now? We'll think about it." So the money he gave her seemed her due: compensation for the salary she wasn't getting.

During the day, Xenia moved from one couch to the other, with cigarettes, a pillow, a book: books had resumed an important role in her life; she appreciated the studying she'd done, the university, the discussions with her friends at the Grimaldi. Yet she considered that she had wasted those years pursuing vain illusions. "I wonder what happened to Vinca and that penniless Spanish guy who took her to cheap movies." Now, thinking of the emerald, she said to herself: "Too bad, I should have kept that, it was such a beautiful stone." She pictured the hotel where she'd slept the first night, the third-class journey with her bundle, the glove store . . . How far away it all was, even though only a few months had passed! She seemed to have undertaken that journey not out of necessity but out of a love of adventure. If the Grimaldi had been in Milan, she would have liked to call her old friends, invite them over—"Come and see me. I'm in such and such a street, such and such a number"—and offer them whiskey, *marrons glacés*. She imagined them arriving, in their shabby dresses, talking in loud voices with their strong regional accents. What impression would she have made on Dino, on the maid? With Horsch? If she had met them on the street, she would have had to pretend not to see them.

Dino mostly left her alone: he was out, looking up people, meeting them, he made phone calls, visited offices, restaurants, casual in his loose-fitting sport coat. He went to Xenia's after lunch to have coffee: he talked about business, but vaguely, without specifics; sometimes Tom Barchi was with him and both were irritated with Horsch.

"He keeps our hands tied," they said. "He won't let us move."

One day Dino, coming in, said to Xenia: "You know what? The old thug . . ."

"Which one?"

"The one where you worked, the one at the X&X Company . . ."

"Yes, well?"

"He was fired. The company failed—someone will end up in jail. Someone who's not Horsch, naturally."

Raimondo Horsch became, in Xenia's eyes, an increasingly mysterious character. He was tall and bald, a man of measured gestures, with an elegant bearing, a manner that set him apart, and pleasant, varied conversation. He went to art exhibits and the theater; he read the books that were in fashion. You had to listen to him carefully when he spoke, partly because he spoke softly. Xenia was flattered that he addressed her the way men of his age and class addressed women who were in some way remarkable; it reawakened in her the memory of some lines of D'Annunzio, studied at school, and the image of a world that she had never even hoped to belong to. Horsch often sent her flowers, but not without a pretext: after an invitation to lunch, for example. Always orchids. From the couch where she liked to stretch out, Xenia contemplated with satisfaction those costly monsters, their petals panting like animal tongues. Then, seeing Horsch, she said to him, with offhand politeness, "Thank you for the flowers," as if he had sent a bunch of daisies.

Every month, Xenia sent some money to her parents and, every time, waited for her father to ask: "What sort of job do you have? Keep your money and don't come home again." Instead, by return of post, her father thanked her. Did they suspect nothing or, Xenia wondered, did they find it more convenient to be aware of nothing? She didn't know that in the village people talked, though they knew nothing about her, or about her life; in fact, precisely those who attributed her earnings to a job circulated slanderous rumors about her, unable to tolerate the idea that she had created a position for herself honestly. If they had known that she was a kept woman they wouldn't have cared: it was Xenia's intelligence, her merit they wanted to diminish. Besides, what could her parents do? Go and see where Xenia was, what her job was? They had no money, they were old: they found it easier to accept the facts without asking questions, searching for causes.

Xenia rebelled against this blindness of theirs; she fully condoned her own life, but she couldn't admit that her parents would. In fact, it grieved her so much that, in the end, she convinced herself: "No, certainly they don't know, they don't suspect." She needed to carry the weight of her own conduct herself, as an act of rebellion, and not as a means accepted by all three of them to live more comfortably.

She judged her life mainly when she thought of Silvia: with her squinting eyes, the black dress of her long periods of mourning. If Silvia lived in Milan, she would come to see her and ask: "Why are you doing this, Xenia?" And Xenia wouldn't find the strength to joke, as she did with Vandina, "These honest women . . ." trying to brush the dust off, lightly, with her hand. Yet she couldn't consider herself dishonest, since she had never betrayed Dino. What did it matter if they weren't married? Her other friends would have been more indulgent: Vinca would have understood out of love, Valentina would have asked what you felt with men, Emanuela would have admired the house, Horsch's orchids. Silvia, staring at her, would have said: "Why are you doing this, Xenia?" Xenia, imagining that question, settled herself more comfortably on the sofa, put a candy in her mouth, opened a book, and answered aloud: "Why am I doing this? Well, because it suits me, and because I like it."

. . . .

It was thus that Horsch surprised her, coming in. It was dusk, and Xenia hadn't yet turned on the lamp. In the early afternoon she had gone for a walk, seeking the pallid sun of Milan, and feeling a great impatience with that climate, that gray, foggy sky. She wanted to suggest to Dino that they go to the Riviera for a few days.

"Oh, I'm sorry, it's dark," she said, as Horsch came in, and she started to turn on the lights.

"Why?" he asked, restraining her. "Isn't this twilight preferable?"

"I prefer it," Xenia admitted, embarrassed. "Dino's not here yet, but he won't be long. I haven't seen him since yesterday, he didn't even call. Then he'll show up and say: 'We're going out, are you ready?' He's always unpredictable, Dino."

Horsch said nothing. It was hard to carry on the conversation: gripped by an unusual uneasiness, Xenia didn't know what to say. Looking out the window, she observed: "What a leaden sky! I'd like to go to the Riviera for a few days, get free of this oppressive autumn melancholy. I'm going to ask Dino."

The Riviera, evidently, didn't interest Horsch, who continued to say nothing, staring at Xenia in the shadowy light.

"Where shall we go tonight?" she resumed. "Let's see if we can find something new. Maybe Dino will have some ideas, Dino always has so many ideas, right? If you have an appointment, he can't be long."

"I don't have an appointment with Dino."

"Oh no?" Xenia didn't know what to think; his behavior, his tone of voice were making her nervous. "Then when he comes he'll be happily surprised."

But Horsch said: "Dino's not coming: he's been arrested."

. . . .

When Horsch left, much later, Xenia stood listening to the sound of his footsteps as they grew distant, vanished on the stairs. Then she heard the dull thud of the front door and silence returned.

"Dino," she called softly. "Dino . . ."

She called him as if he were dead, knowing that he couldn't answer. "They went to his house early this morning," Horsch had said. She had been asleep at the time. Even two lovers are two alien, different worlds. What would prison be like? She couldn't imagine and so she helped her imagination with the memory of the prisons she'd seen in American films. It was impossible that Dino was locked in one of those cages. At first she had said: "Arrested?! That's absurd. Dino will explain everything and get out. Let's go pick him up." Horsch shook his head. "It's pointless to go," he said. "I'm afraid it won't be so easy to manage." And Xenia had felt the weight of her own life falling on her shoulders. Even before asking the reason for the arrest, and fearing for Dino, material details crowded her mind: the rent, the installments on the furniture. Food. Only six hundred lire in her pocket. And she began to cry.

For days, Dino had been nervous. "The trailer trucks," he said. Nothing else. But, naming Horsch, he always added, "That pig." And now Horsch was sitting across from her, in the chair, free, tranquil—his forehead barely furrowed to save appearances—and Dino was in jail. She had questioned him harshly:

"But you?"

Horsch had responded, coldly: "I don't know anything about it."

Xenia should have replied that, on the contrary, he knew everything, that he was the one responsible, as he'd been for the old director of the X&X Company, but something kept her from opening her mouth; in fact, something told her that only Horsch would be able to help her. She should have sent him away and instead she begged him: "Don't leave me alone."

After Horsch had gone, Xenia began pacing, beating her fists against one another and murmuring: "I must, I must find a solution." She understood that Dino's situation was serious. "I want to go see him," she had said to Horsch. But his response was: "You can't yet, maybe after the interrogation, I'll talk to the lawyer." "There's already a lawyer." "Yes, I took care of it today."

Xenia's pacing became more and more restless; sometimes she stopped to listen, thinking she heard a key in the lock. Then she resumed walking, always more nervously, her fists tighter and tighter. She'd been walking like this at the Grimaldi the night she decided to steal so she could escape. That resolution, at the time, had restored her tranquility; she had gone to bed, had even read a few pages before going to sleep. "I'll run away from here, too, but immediately. I'll go to Genoa. I'll find work there, I have the reference from the X&X Company (it failed, Dino said, someone will end up in jail), Genoa is a business city . . ." She remembered her first days in Milan, going from one office to another, often not even given the time to explain herself: we have no openings, they said, and she went down the stairs discouraged. The street noise muffled her vain steps, stunned her, what should I do, what should I do? The nights were interminable, at night you can't go knocking on office doors, and finally, one day, there's Vandina. She owed everything to Vandina. A chance. Otherwise where would she be now? She had to talk to Vandina. But she had come by a few days earlier to ask for a loan of fifty lire: Vandina could only ask for help now, not give it. Why had Horsch left so soon? The night grants no distractions; it's long, inexorable.

She thought of going back to the man at the bank. She had run into him one day in a pastry shop: recognizing her, he had greeted her respectfully and she had blushed, ashamed of no longer being so poor. Now, to the references of the X&X Company, Horsch could add his. Who in Milan didn't know Horsch?

Yes, but how to get free of the apartment? The monthly installments for the furniture? Everything was in her name. In a bank she would earn five hundred lire, at most. Early mornings, in winter, at the typewriter. This last year, waking, she'd find icicles on the windowpanes. She barely washed, ran for the bus, arrived breathless, signed in under the clock, entrance bell, exit bell. And at night, wherever she went, she seemed to still be wearing the black smock.

Better to return to Rome. Sell the furniture, collect a little money, and show up before Sister Lorenza. "Forgive me, Sister, have the Mother forgive me." Then she would enter her friends' rooms by surprise, while they were studying around the oil lamp, saying: "Make room for me next to you." What a moment it would be, how moving!

She had always felt nostalgia for their endless conversations, the evening talks, when they sketched by candlelight ambitious plans for the future. But, remembering that time, Xenia suddenly saw that returning among her friends was impossible, because she lacked precisely what animated the others: faith in the future.

Silvia was deluded: if you want to become a professor you'll first have to be recommended by some disgusting old man or other. Valentina's also deluded: she won't find a husband, because she doesn't have money, even if she's honest; honesty gives you just what you need to die of hunger. How could she return to them knowing all this? Not to them or to the village. She could no longer believe in certain values, since she'd learned that you live better by ignoring them. Sin no longer frightened her. It's not true that the soul is weighed down after sin: it's weighed down by the uncertainty of being able to commit it; then it becomes a habit of life. Certain principles endure until we understand we can do without them. The only trouble—when you gamble your life on all or nothing—is that, if it goes badly, you have to manage alone.

She was alone, and Dino was in prison: Dino, with his yearning for greatness, for distinction. With his silk shirts. He had ruined himself for her, had pursued the trailer truck affair to earn more, letting himself be trapped by Horsch.

"Horsch," she repeated aloud. She saw him as he'd been shortly before, in the armchair, calm, tapping his fingertips lightly, hand against hand. Meanwhile he was looking at her. "Horsch looks at you," Dino often said to her. And from then on she, too, had noticed: he looked at her.

She shook herself, went to the bedroom, and stopped at the mirror: her eyes were shining, her lips tight, her reddened skin tearstained. She clenched her fists, one against the other, talking to her image to give herself courage: "I have to get through this first night. Tomorrow everything will sort itself out, I know from experience, everything always sorts itself out." She ran a hand over her forehead as if to chase away the thoughts; and, looking at herself in the mirror, murmured, "Horsch has to . . . Horsch has to . . . Horsch has to . . ."

. . . .

The defense of Silvia's thesis was set for November 28, Anna's for December 3. The two girls, locked in a rigid schedule, kept apart from the others. Anna was tired but resigned; sometimes her friends came to distract her, sure she would welcome them. With Silvia, on the other hand, they wouldn't have dared: she came down to eat, went right back up, and didn't exchange even a casual word with anyone. Under the door of her room the light could be seen far into the night.

Every day, after lunch, she went to Belluzzi's. At that hour, feeling heavy from the meal, she was overcome by drowsiness; then, mastering it, she left. In the street, she walked quickly; gradually the drowsiness dissipated, but like pain that lies in ambush beneath the means used to fight it. "I won't make it," she thought. At the old entrance to the Belluzzi house a gust of cold air awakened her fully.

She had grown even thinner, and her small eyes, with their graceful squint, burned in her gaunt face. Yet she emanated a sort of light, a new force; now she was sure she was essential to the professor, and that gave her confidence.

One afternoon, while she was answering the mail, the door opened softly, and the maid looked in cautiously, peering around.

"Is he there?" she asked, pointing with a mysterious expression to the door of the study.

"No," Silvia answered. "He's not back yet."

Then the girl changed her tone: "Signorina, help me!" she said, in great agitation. "The signora has taken Veronal!" Collapsed on the chair in her room, Signora Belluzzi was struggling to breathe. Hearing the door open, she started, widened her eyes, and, seeing Silvia, appeared dubious. Then, looking upward toward the ceiling until the whites of her eyes showed, she fell back again, inert.

"When did she take it?" Silvia asked.

"Just now: the package's still there on the night table. I came in and, seeing she'd swallowed something, I understood what it was about because since that letter arrived she hasn't stopped crying. 'What are you doing, signora?' I said, and she said she wanted to die."

The package was half full; only five or six pills were missing. Silvia was bewildered for a moment, then she said to the girl: "Bring me a glass of warm water," and ordered the woman: "Come with me. You have to recover immediately, do you understand?"

Dora rebelled, crying; the tears fell down her made-up face; the open bathrobe revealed her soft, swelling bosom rising as she struggled to breathe.

"Leave me, signorina, I can't go on, I want to end it, let me die . . ."

Silvia, overcoming an instinctive repugnance, took her by the arm: "You won't die, you haven't taken enough. You have to recover, otherwise you'll only feel bad and cause a scandal, think of the scandal. Come on, get up." When the woman resisted, Silvia said to her harshly: "The professor will be back soon. Do you want him to find you like this?"

Dora began crying harder. "No, no, poor Guido, you're right, you're good . . . But if I die I'll end my suffering . . ." Still, she followed her into the bathroom. Then she froze, saying: "My head is spinning," and, leaning backward, pretended to faint, without success. She waved her arms, brought her hands to her throat. "God, oh God!" she cried in a tragic tone. Silvia put the glass of hot water in her hand and she looked at it, puzzled:

"What should I do?"

"Drink it right away. Try, you have to throw up, you understand? Touch the trachea, here, here," said Silvia, indicating the indentation in her throat. Dora swallowed some water and then, as if having repented, resumed: "I want to die." But Silvia pushed the glass between her teeth, ordering her: "Drink and then cough, stick a finger in your throat." She took her hand and forced her to obey: "Let's go, head down now, down!"

And she threw up. She threw up weeping, without restraining herself when a new surge rose to her mouth. On her face, purple with effort, the tears, dissolving the mascara caked on her lashes, formed black bruises around her eyes. Silvia pictured that face, so devastated, topped by the hat with the green feather, as on the day of the talk, while Dora stared with painful intensity at the mirror opposite. Now she'll see, Silvia thought. She'll see and return to herself, of course. Instead the image of her suffering moved the woman to pity and she wiped away the sweat, murmuring, "Poor me, why didn't you let me die?" Playacting, thought Silvia. "Maybe the package had already been started, maybe she took only one pill, waiting for the maid to come in before she swallowed it. A role she plays to dramatize her disappointment. She has no reticence even in front of the maid, who will report the event to the whole neighborhood."

In a feeble voice Signora Dora implored: "Take me to bed, I think I'm fainting . . ."

They accompanied her, supporting her. The maid hurried to pull down the silk coverlet, plump the pillow. When the signora had managed to get on the bed and lie down, she covered her with a quilt.

Dora groaned, "Help me, I'm fainting," fearing that death might take her naturally. "You don't know, dear signorina . . . you don't know," and she reached for her hand. "You're young, you can't understand . . . you can't imagine what a tragedy it is, what ruin. You're good, poor signorina . . ." Suddenly she was silent, holding her breath to make them think she was dead. Silvia felt her pulse with distrust. "An old woman," she thought, observing the flabby body piled on the bed, the large legs with ankles too thin, the mahogany-colored hair, the face pasty with powder, tears, and mascara.

Signora Dora, seeing that holding her breath wasn't enough to make her die, started up again, panting: "You're good, signorina, Guido's good, too," and every time she said it the name provoked in her a wave of emotion: "Very good, poor Guido, but the two of you don't understand . . . You're shut up with your books, you don't know the world, passions . . . Yours is an egotism, ultimately . . . But you're young, very young, and one day, perhaps, you'll understand me." She went on complaining, "I have a headache, a bitter taste in my mouth," but wearily, until she closed her eyes.

Silvia gestured to the maid to pull the curtains and darken the room. At the sound of the curtain rings moving, Signora Belluzzi gave a start.

"How can you think I'm sleeping?" she said, with an angelic and distant smile. "There's no more rest for me." Large tears welled up below her lowered eyelids, lining her face. "But close them, close them and go, you poor things. Thank you ..."

Silvia sat near the bed. A moment later she saw that Signora Dora was no longer crying; rather, from her half-closed mouth escaped a noisy and even breath. Then she got up, put the package of Veronal in her pocket, and, making a sign to the maid to leave with her, returned to her work.

The professor arrived shortly afterward, with a satisfied smile; he was coming from a department meeting where his arguments had prevailed. "Then, on the way home, I prepared the class for tomorrow: it's all here," he said, tapping a finger on his forehead. "But I need to compare that sonnet of Chiaro Davanzati we talked about yesterday. "You can find it ..."

She interrupted. "I know where it is, thanks."

"Then I'll go and ask Dora to bring us a cup of tea, what do you say?"

"The signora isn't well," said Silvia, detaining him. "She had a little upset, maybe indigestion ..."

"Not well?" Belluzzi repeated. "I'll go right away."

"No, don't, no. She's resting now, sleeping."

"Oh, she's sleeping," he said, reassured: "Then let's ring for the maid for tea, a nice hot tea ..." And he went to the desk with the delicate steps that were particular to him, almost on tiptoe.

Silvia, taking a book from the shelf, leafed through it looking for the sonnet. Every so often she glanced at Belluzzi moving serenely, in the air of his thoughts, as on an unreachable island. "You people don't understand," Dora had repeated many times: and certainly she meant to say: "You don't understand love." She had also said: "Yours is an egotism." Those words, although uttered by a person and for a reason she despised, had sent a shiver down her back. Forever—since she was born, perhaps—everything had driven her toward those who live among books, and are accused of using them as protection. But were they protection after all?

She wondered, looking at Belluzzi: don't the strongest passions have their root in the mind?

"*Io son cierta messer che voi m'amaste . . .*" she read slowly. "I'm certain, sir, that you loved me."

"This one, professor?"

"Yes, yes, good, give it here, please," said Belluzzi and, holding the book, smoothed the page carefully: "*Ed io amai voi, e del mio amor pigliaste . . .*" he continued. "And I loved you, and you took of my love." At the end he looked up: "This sonnet is a jewel, isn't it, Custo?"

"Yes, professor," Silvia answered sweetly. And she smiled at him like a woman. But he, making notes on those lines on a piece of paper, didn't notice.

• • • •

Returning to the residence, Silvia shut herself in her room, waiting for dinner. She was distraught: she couldn't forget the ravaged face of Signora Belluzzi, and the performance she had put on to try to avoid her suffering. But soon Anna and Valentina came and knocked on her door.

"Oh, you're here, finally! I've been looking for you for two hours!"

"I just got back, what is it?"

"Pilar called today saying that Vinca was asking for you or Emanuela, to go and see her right away. You weren't here, neither was Emanuela. Valentina went: Luis is wounded."

"Wounded?!" Silvia repeated, and she thought it was a day of extraordinary events. "Is it serious?"

"I don't think so, but they don't know anything specific yet. Pepe, Pilar's fiancé, wrote to them," said Valentina. "Vinca is in a state!"

"And I can't go tomorrow . . . Emanuela has to go, we shouldn't leave her alone. Remember how agitated she was when she found out Luis was leaving?"

Valentina, shaking her head, said: "Vinca always exaggerates, it's her character."

"I think it's love. As you know, I smile when I hear talk of love. I don't think it can serve as a basis for life; but maybe what's essential is to give all of yourself to one thing, not a small part to many different things. And then love, family, work . . . all assume the same value." Then she returned to Vinca: "We have to do something for her. Emanuela's not back?"

"No, at least she wasn't a little while ago."

They met her in the dark hall that led to the refectory and called to her, speaking all together, excitedly: "Luis is wounded . . . Vinca's looking for you . . . you have to go to her tomorrow."

"Wounded?" Emanuela repeated suspiciously. In her memory emerged the face of the officer who had greeted her at the airfield, many years before. "It's a long flight, we don't have any news yet, maybe the radio is broken." He talked, he explained, he piled on useless details. And already since that morning Stefano had no longer existed, his eyes no longer existed. "Might he not be dead, rather? Maybe they've told her he's only wounded to prepare her."

They were all stricken. "We hadn't thought of that," they said. "It's true, such news is always given cautiously."

"If he were dead, the other two would have told me," Valentina replied. "But we were never alone. And their faces were devastated. Or maybe Donna Inés and Pilar don't know anything, either. My God, if he were dead, Vinca would kill herself as soon as she found out."

All they did was talk about it, at the table; they were so agitated they left nearly everything on their plates. When the sharp crack of Sister Luisa's hands ended the meal, Anna said, "Let's pray it's not so." In chapel, they mingled with the others as usual. But it was November, and the prayer for the dead was said before the evening service ended: when Sister Lorenza chanted the De Profundis Vinca's friends shivered.

Luis had been wounded in the right arm; it wasn't a serious wound and he was sent home on leave, for a month. Vinca had received a letter from Ignacio: Luis couldn't write, but he urged her not to be upset. He was fine, he was happy to see his parents, and maybe, before his leave was up, the war would be over.

Since Luis ordered it, Vinca tried to be serene, to smile: all the more now that she could imagine him in the city, on the streets, where she, too, had always lived.

"Until now it didn't seem to me that he had returned to Spain—war's the same everywhere. Now I dream I'm in Cordova every night: Luis is there, we walk, the streets smell like oranges. What beauty, I think, and finally I feel at peace. But when I wake up I hear different sounds coming from the street; every place has its sounds, its cries. What? I say to myself, what? It wasn't true?" And she put a hand over her eyes to hide her tears.

Donna Inés scolded her: "*Vamos!* Why talk about these things today? Remember Luis *no* is serious, that he could have . . ."

"I know, I know, I won't say any more. The rest, all the rest, has no importance."

* * * *

Despite the good news, the atmosphere in that house was dispiriting. Leaving it, Emanuela felt she'd returned to life. She didn't want to let herself be overwhelmed by others' troubles. She had done a good deed, going to see Vinca: a duty, rather, since it was a friend. But, after all, who had ever suffered for her? Who had ever helped her?

It was a beautiful evening, and the shop windows were all lit up. "If I see something I like, I'll go in and buy it." She had a confident, happy expression: people looked at her, and, noticing that a man was following her, she held herself more erect. A tall young man: every so often he approached and whispered a few words. She remained impassive but found it all very amusing.

She thought of Andrea, of Stefania: the fresh wind, brushing her face, swept away their images. She was glad that Andrea had stayed home to study. She had told him that she would stay with Vinca until late and so couldn't see him that evening. "One needs a little freedom every so often." She wasn't doing anything bad, but it was pleasant to wander alone, stop to look in a window, not be constrained to talk and respond. When there are two of you it's easy to forget that it's also nice to be alone.

In recent days, instead of meeting Andrea on the street, she'd gone to his house; while he studied for an exam, she sat with his mother amid the dark furniture in a dimly lit, not very comfortable living room. The old woman was knitting. "Why don't you bring some work?" she said to her. Every quarter of an hour the grandfather clock chimed with a clamor of bells, then everything fell silent again.

If the weather was good, they went out. Andrea took her to visit museums, small churches where tapestries were conserved, often invisible in the shadows; but these meetings, now that they were no longer secret, seemed to have lost their charm. Emanuela was bored; she would have preferred to go occasionally where there were people, to some fashionable gathering place. "What?!" said Andrea. "I don't care about that. But if you want to . . ." Emanuela gave it up with a readiness that he took for agreement.

"There's nothing about you that irritates me," he said, "and yet sometimes I'd like to discover an attitude, a gesture—something, in other words, that I don't like, to feel that I'm free. I can't endure the company of other women; they were boring before, now they would be unbearable."

Maybe that would have been the moment to tell him: "Well, I'll tell you, I have a child; I had her with a lover who's dead, but whom I liked. Is that enough for you to feel free? What do you say?"

The evening before they had walked along the river. By seven, in the month of November, the stars have already come out. Emanuela said with a sigh: "How long since I've seen the night anywhere but through the barred windows of the Grimaldi!"

"Soon we'll have all the nights for ourselves. Do you think about it? I think about it all the time," Andrea confessed. "That's why sometimes I don't even kiss you. I desire you too much, a kiss wouldn't satisfy me. If I act like that it's not out of foolish morality—we could do without waiting for our wedding day, you're already my wife now—but to take you where I've been with other women, undress you, dress you, and then you go to the residence, I home . . . No, it may seem nice at first, but afterward it's depressing. And, after all, this wait, which burdens me so, is another way of deserving you. I prefer you to remain unknown. You know, sometimes, when you're absent in thought, or when I watch you go off at night, it seems to me that there's a mystery in you, something I don't know, that I don't understand, as if I didn't know you completely. I think I'll have that impression until you're mine. But also the secret you carry in you, to be revealed, attracts me."

Emanuela was afraid that at this point it would be impossible to speak: maybe the only solution would be to depart, leaving him a letter ("Don't look for me, don't try to learn anything"), as in a nineteenth-century novel. Better to remain unknown, in his eyes, than to destroy herself by telling him everything.

Then she considered that Andrea—seen from close up—was bourgeois. Stefano, maybe because he traveled, because he had always been away from home, had a different mentality. Or maybe because he was from Trieste and people from Trieste say it's very free. "One day I'll have to go to Trieste, with Stefania; but putting flowers on a grave isn't the best way to know a city."

In Piazza di Spagna she glanced back out of the corner of her eye to see if the man who was following her was still there; and, glimpsing his tall shadow, she felt a spark of joy. Amusing, she thought, very amusing.

The man had noticed that glance; and, seeing Emanuela head toward the darkest corner of the square, he quickened his pace, full of hope. But she had already rung the bell: "Twenty-eight," she said, like a password, to the porter nun through the spy hole. He reached her the moment the door opened: Emanuela entered quickly, laughing to herself, while the sister bolted it behind her.

She was happy for no reason: maybe because that dress looked good on her, maybe because it was a beautiful fall evening. She didn't have the usual impression of melancholy on seeing the identical doors along the halls, the barred windows. She went up lightly, almost dancing; halfway up she blew a kiss on her fingertips at a Madonna who appeared to be made of sugar among the paper flowers of an altar, and entered Silvia's room without knocking. She found her writing, bent over in the circle of light made by the lamp placed on the desk. "Enough!" she ordered cheerfully. She turned on the overhead light, then sat on the bed, making it bounce. "What a lovely evening!" she said.

Silvia turned as if asleep, her eyes puffy with studying. "And so, Luis?"

Emanuela had forgotten both Luis and Vinca and the sighs and tears of the apartment on Via Sistina.

"It's nothing. A scratch on the arm and he goes on leave. Last night we created a tragedy. Now I understand why I'm in a good mood tonight; the nightmare of Luis's death is over. Vinca was calm, she talked about Spain and made me feel a great desire to go there. And I will. When the shooting's over, naturally."

. . . .

At the table they were all happy for Luis. Valentina said she imagined him: "Haven't you seen Luis? He has the face of a sly horse. Now, with the excuse of a glorious wound, he'll manage to get out of the army." They also laughed at Vinca, who, since she couldn't weep for Luis, wept with homesickness for Spain. Augusta observed: "There are places that don't abandon us, not even if we abandon them. But you," she said, turning to Emanuela, "you never talk about Florence."

After a moment of reflection, she admitted it was true. She had adapted easily to Rome; but then she adapted easily to wherever she was.

As they left the refectory Augusta proposed: "Come and see me later? But don't tell the others. Just you."

"Tonight?" Emanuela repeated uncertainly. "No, I can't. I have to write."

"Are you writing, too, now?" Augusta observed, smiling.

"No, what are you thinking? I don't know how to write. It's a letter to my father." Meanwhile she had resolved: "I'm not going, and not just tonight: never again."

She already knew how the evening would unfold: the cigarettes, the liqueur that, as she talked, Augusta poured generously; and finally the novel. Rather, men. Augusta had decided to tell the others about the novel, but vaguely.

"They'll read it in print. Silvia will be sarcastic. Valentina will understand, maybe," she said uncertainly, examining from a distance the youngest of her friends. "They don't know what it costs to write. No one knows, anyway," she added, with a note of contempt.

The curiosity that, at first, drove Emanuela to go up to Augusta's had changed to a sort of repugnance: now, when she entered the room, she had the impression of setting foot in a trap.

"The problem is one," Augusta had said the last time. "To free herself from the tyranny of the man, the woman has to take his place, creating an autonomous life, freed even from the slavery of the senses: she has to gain independence of the spirit and the flesh." She spoke in a low voice, breaking off every so often to drink. "No longer will any woman fear the advancing years. It's terrible to see our body wither little by little, the once slender figure become a graceless mass, the skin sag, lose its youthful glow. And yet going forward we improve ourselves: we are born female and become women, over time. Time frightens us because of men. When each of us has her own independent life, in every field, we'll be safe from fear:

safe from old age, from death, you understand? Those are the disturbers of the order that the woman establishes in the world."

Emanuela had, yet again, been overpowered by Augusta's person. She had gone back over her life, the secret meetings with Stefano—and all the secrets those had produced—then the fear of speaking to Andrea. She had a transparent, frank character; besides, she was too lazy to lie. But, she considered, in relations with men there are always facts that are unspoken, concealed, even if they're innocent. Really, the only time she had been happy since she was born was at the Grimaldi; at home between her and her mother her father's presence, her father's will, was a thorn. If she had had to lie here, it was, again, because of a man. And yet only here did she feel a sense of comfort, of peace when she returned.

She said to herself that perhaps Augusta was preaching a new religion; she imagined her going through the woods, the countryside, like a missionary, traveling the provincial roads in a cart, stopping in the town squares, summoning the women, and speaking. Maybe, gradually, all the women would leave their homes to follow her, they would go and camp in a great plain, protected by mountains and rivers, they would found a happy city, where the lie would be unknown forever, along with the pain of giving birth.

"You know, Augusta," she started to say, but Augusta was no longer listening. She talked to hear the sound of her own words; to invent as she spoke, and thus test her power of invention. Everything in her had become solitary: the taste for drinking and smoking, the pleasure she got from literature and music. In the end Emanuela's presence irritated her and she rose to say goodbye distractedly, putting the pages of the manuscript in order. Emanuela didn't want to go back there.

"Tomorrow night, then?" Augusta insisted, trying to force her with her gaze.

Luckily Silvia arrived to spare her the awkwardness of refusing again: she said that Sister Lorenza had sent Sister Prudenzina to call her, and, with a sigh, had warned her: "The Mother isn't well, it's nervous exhaustion."

"It's strange," Silvia said. "There's still the shadow of the old Mother in those rooms, her smell still saturates them: Sister Lorenza has the air of being shut up alive with her dead predecessor. She sat me down and asked me to answer her sincerely. 'You've always been devoted to me,' she said. Then she asked me if Sister Luisa gives us orders in her name. She wanted to warn us that she, on the contrary, is in the dark about what goes on here. I assured her that that never happened—and I don't even know if it's true, I've never noticed—but I'd never seen her in that state: she who was always in control, master of herself. She didn't believe me: I talked and she shook her head. In the end she said she'll write to Genoa to ask the Mother General to intervene. That's the peace of the cloister," Silvia observed, smiling.

They went up together. Augusta had preceded them. (She understood, Emanuela thought. And anyway she'll have to understand.) "Well, bye, see you tomorrow," Silvia said, without stopping.

Emanuela reached her room and instinctively would have liked to go on to the door of the room that had been Milly's. It hadn't been occupied since then; how was it that she didn't feel that void? Her friends were right to wonder if Milly had ever existed. Maybe she represented only an ideal that often remains behind a closed door.

Now everything that happened within the walls of the Grimaldi seemed to her in some way threatening, abnormal. In the silence she seemed to hear the anguished steps of Sister Lorenza, pacing up and down to escape death. Similarly Augusta wrote to forget her own uselessness, the breakdown of her body, to vanquish time: but they were all alone in their own rooms, and time went by equally.

The harm lay in the comfort one learned to draw from solitude, Emanuela thought, entering her room. The joy she had brought with her that evening had turned to ice in the damp cold of the entrance hall as the porter nun closed the door behind her. "Twenty-eight," she had said, taking the key from the panel and handing it to her. "She's come back, too," she might have been thinking. "Maybe she'll stay with us forever."

. . . .

Right after Dino's arrest, Tom Barchi left. Mary, coming to see Xenia, kept looking around, afraid she was being followed. A document had arrived summoning Tom to police headquarters, but the lawyer said there was nothing to worry about. All the signatures were Dino's, everything was on Dino's shoulders, and he, certainly, wouldn't drag his friends down with him. So Tom would be back soon. Mary, paler than usual, coughed frequently. For the first time she talked bitterly about Horsch.

"You know how things went, you know the deal was Horsch's. But Horsch always put Dino in front, and Dino was a little careless in business, he believed in everything because, after all, he was honest: but he was seduced by the charms of the easy life."

"It's hard to reject the easy life," Xenia objected.

Mary nodded, sighing; then she said that Dino's situation was complicated. "Years ago, maybe you know this, he had some trouble, and he got out of it. Now he's ... what's the word? The lawyer said it: recidivist."

"I didn't know, but I understand."

"And does it seem fair that Horsch ...?"

"No, it's not fair. But to live, you have to learn to endure a lot of things that are unfair. Does it seem fair to you, for example, that the two of us, you and I, only because a man supports us, aren't respected like women who are supported by a husband and go to bed with someone else? The truth is that in the world there aren't the honest and the dishonest. There are the rich and the poor; and it's pointless for the poor to go and storm the Bastille. The only power is money. With that you can even buy yourself honesty."

Xenia had been thinking in those terms for a while, because, in her life, what at first seemed irreparable had then helped to settle things for the better. Where would she be now if she had gotten her degree? If she had been able to provide good references, she would have been hired by that bank for a poorly paid and anonymous job. Ultimately, she owed everything to Vandina, who hadn't even realized she was doing her a good turn. Our fate is ruled by unforeseen encounters. She had always intuited that something was waiting for her, that she shouldn't give in, resign herself. She had waited, and, in fact, Raimondo Horsch had arrived.

Horsch came to see her every day so that she wouldn't be discouraged; one day, he didn't show up, and she telephoned. They said he was out: on Saturday he always went to Menaggio.

In Menaggio, Dino had said, lived his wife and daughter; Xenia tried to imagine the house where these two women lived, he said, very modestly, but her thoughts retreated with a sort of uneasiness. Unjustified, besides: Horsch was only a friend. Yet she doubted that he talked to his family about their friendship.

On Monday she asked him: "How did you spend Sunday?"

He answered with another question: "And you?"

Xenia understood that in the life of Raimondo Horsch Saturday and Sunday had to be, for her, a dark area. She was wounded by it at first; then that, too, became natural. Gradually everything became natural in their relations.

Horsch said very little about Dino. Every day Xenia asked: "When can I see him?" He answered, "Soon, very soon," and deliberately changed the subject.

Xenia recalled Dino with some condescension, as she did her friends at the Grimaldi; if he had been released she wouldn't have known how to act.

Now, used to Horsch's refined ways, to his conversation, she recognized that Dino was a little vulgar. In Horsch's presence she was always watching herself, marveling that such a man could be interested in her.

Horsch had said: "Leave, why don't you want to go anymore now? Go to the Riviera."

She had objected: "And the apartment?"

"I'll take care of everything, I'll arrange everything. Besides, we'll have to get rid of this apartment, it would be sad for you to come back and live here."

The next day, for the first time, he gave her a sum of money; without looking at it, she put it between the pages of a book and went on talking about something else. What did money matter to a woman like her?

Once, when she was talking about the residence and her escape, Horsch interrupted her on some pretext. And she understood that she shouldn't refer to the past; in fact, why not invent another, a different one? It was enough to hear the tone in which Horsch, as he left, said, "Good night, my friend," to understand that that poor, mediocre past couldn't be hers. Now, when Mary called, offering to visit, she always said she had to go out on some important errand. Otherwise, she thought, she'll start again with her talk about justice.

The night Horsch brought her a ruby pin, Xenia, even before thanking him, exclaimed, "Oh! I love rubies so much!" She said it as if she were used to choosing among various stones. She poured him a whiskey, curled up on the couch, and, talking, tried not to notice that red flame on her chest: but when he left she hurried to look at herself. She thought of Emanuela, of the remorse that modest emerald had cost her. Then she understood that the marvel roused in her by that gift proved the extraordinary nature of her good fortune. "I pretend not to be surprised by anything. But in fact I shouldn't be surprised by anything."

Finally, Horsch let her know that the following Thursday she would be able to visit Dino: the lawyer had obtained a special permission. She said only: "Oh, good." But her heart began pounding as it had the night of the arrest, when everything around her seemed to collapse, overwhelming her. On Wednesday Horsch wanted to take her out to dinner, but she said, "Not yet," as if asking him to respect a mourning too recent.

They decided to have dinner at her house, and when she said to the maid, "The gentleman will stay for dinner," she understood that something really was starting. And the maid's silent indifference confirmed that this, too, was natural. They sat at the table without speaking, almost embarrassed. Xenia examined Horsch carefully in the light that fell on him from above. He must be at least fifty-six, she thought, and while he served himself she observed his hands, the twisted violet wrinkles that made their whiteness vivid. Hands already old. Yes, certainly, he must be more than fifty-six.

· · · ·

On Thursday afternoon the sky was rainy and low, the streets, covered by a film of water, were like mirrors. Xenia put on her raincoat, pulled a hat down low over her forehead. She left early and went to get the tram: it didn't seem fitting to appear at San Vittore in a taxi. The tram took forever to arrive: when it did her shoes were soaked, her feet numb, and dripping umbrellas formed puddles on the muddy linoleum floor. She got off, got on another: San Vittore was very far away. But, as she passed through the entrance, weariness and bewilderment gave her an air of suffering.

The visitors' area, a large dust-colored room lit by a skylight, was divided in half by two parallel grates between which a guard walked up and down, looking at the floor. On the visitors' side, as on the other, wooden stools were placed in front of openings that were scarcely the size of a face.

A woman was already there, talking to an old man who was so fat he had to sit with his legs spread; the old man smiled and, listening to his wife, nodded his head yes yes while he peeled an orange that gave off the odor of a hospital. The woman wore a small hat and a plush coat. "Don't worry, the lawyer said it's a matter of days," she said in the sort of tone one uses with children. He continued to nod, putting sections of orange in his mouth.

When Dino came in, Xenia jumped up, pale. She called him and would have liked to embrace him, but the grate divided them. He approached the grate and said in a voice intended to sound confident:

"It can't always go well, right, little girl?"

He smiled, trying to recover his bravado; instead, embarrassed, he put a hand in his pocket and rummaged as if looking for something. Without a collar, his clothes creased, a two days' beard, he appeared thinner.

Xenia looked at him and didn't know what to say; finally, she asked gently: "How are you?" They talked about insignificant things, even the weather, and the minutes passed in that empty discourse.

"Are you eating?" Xenia asked.

"Oh yes," he answered. "If you pay you can have what you want, and the food is good; but often you don't feel like eating. Then I send my dinner to a poor fellow who, when he passes my cell on the way to the courtyard for a little air, puts his eyes against my grate—three inches of perforated tin, the grate, no more—and says to me: 'Courage, eh?' The first days are very hard. Not the first, maybe. The first you expect at any moment the door will open and they'll let you out; you don't even sit down—it's pointless, since I'll be going out. You think every footstep in the corridor belongs to the person who's coming to free you. The second, you're still sure you're getting out: there are friends outside who, thank goodness, are taking care of it. The third ... The fourth is desperate: the hours pass, you hear the bell of a nearby church chiming, the light fades, another interminable night is about to begin, and no one comes: you're alone, really alone, you don't know who to vent to and the people outside aren't doing a thing. Maybe they don't even remember you're in here." He paused. "Then you get used to it."

Xenia comforted him: "You know it's in the hands of Ranieri, and you know what sort of lawyer he is; so you don't have to worry, it's a matter of days." And she realized that her words were the same as those of the woman who, chilled, huddled in the plush coat; her husband looked at her, hands dangling between his legs, and they were both silent, waiting for the moment to return: she outside, he inside.

Dino's gaze was vacant, like that of the other prisoner; he, too, said, "Yes, I know, it's a matter of days." Xenia observed him: a man who was finished, finished. It didn't seem possible that he was the same man with whom she'd had dinner that evening in the hotel in San Remo, when they were drinking and the orchestra played Mozart; those were happy hours. Dino never talked to her about love; but he had done all he could for her, and even ended up in jail. Maybe he didn't understand that his case was serious, that the others cared only about staying out of trouble, and that it was all falling on him. Xenia stared at him with desperate tenderness, as at an image that we try to hold on to for another moment, before it disappears forever.

"Dino," she called affectionately.

"Yes. And how are you doing?"

"Don't worry about me."

She let him understand that he shouldn't be concerned, should think of himself: it was the most important thing at the moment.

And Dino agreed, creating in himself the belief: "Anyway, you know, I'll be out soon," he added confidently.

"Maybe, with that phrase Dino wanted to avoid explanations," Xenia thought; "and, given that he can't take care of me, he accepts that in some way I have to take care of myself. He knows it's all over now, I'm free." Or so she thought she understood. But maybe he had said that only because he was inside, with the thoughts of a man locked up, and she was free. And just as outside no one thinks about prison, about the incarcerated, inside they don't remember that outside there's the need for money, there are debts, rent.

Dino asked: "And Tom? He's a friend, Tom."

"They love you, Mary, too. She comes to see me often, Tom was traveling for a few days, you know? . . . but now he's back."

"Oh, he's back."

"Yes, yesterday."

"Yesterday," Dino observed, "yesterday it was fifteen days from the morning when I was taken. Sixteen, today."

Xenia waited for the other question. "And Horsch?" She couldn't have
lied to him: "Yes, Horsch has also come often," she would have said. And
Dino would have understood. What were you supposed to do, poor Xenia?
Yes, like you, in fact—you couldn't do otherwise, either, poor Dino. But
Dino didn't ask.

The guard came in, announced that the visiting hour was over, and
stood at the door, waiting. The prisoners got up obediently. Dino held his
arm out between the bars, to give her his hand. Xenia reached hers out.
The tips of their fingers barely touched, but they stayed like that for a long
moment, looking at each other. "Courage, kid," Dino said. He seemed to
have returned to what he'd been before: but it was only a moment. Then
he turned to the guard to reassure him that he was going immediately and
said to Xenia: "Come again, okay?," waving his hand in a sign of farewell.

Xenia nodded, smiling, and, poor Dino, she saw him only dimly, because her eyes were blurred by tears. The little woman, standing beside
Xenia, looked at her: "Is he getting out soon?" she asked, pointing to the
door where the two men had disappeared.

"Yes, soon."

They headed off together, familiarly. In the corridor a prisoner wearing
stripes, light brown alternating with dark brown, was repairing some elec-
trical wires. Xenia stared at him, imagining Dino wearing those stripes,
with those shoes. The old woman continued her conversation.

"Mine won't be out soon. Who knows when he'll go to trial. He thinks
he'll get temporary freedom, but no one's talking about it. Yours, what's
it about?"

"What? ... Business."

"Fraud," the old woman corrected her.

Xenia, without protesting, asked: "You too?"

She shook her head. "Attempted murder. But always because of
this ..." and she slapped her mouth with her hand. "Hunger. Someone
who worked with him and wouldn't grant him his share. He took advan-

tage of him for years. But he didn't get him," she added regretfully. And it was clear that she was regretful. Then, in a confidential tone, she asked: "Is he your husband?"

Xenia assented. And she tried to recall the face of the old man: a plump, good-humored face.

The woman swayed as she walked. At the entrance she stopped and said: "It's still raining. Excuse me, I'm in a hurry, I have to make dinner." And with a nod of farewell she went off, bent, in the rain.

. . . .

Horsch didn't show up all day. Xenia didn't look for him; she was irritated by the submissiveness she had heard in Dino's voice. Maybe Dino knew that Horsch was taking away his woman the way he had taken away his freedom: out of hunger. But Xenia couldn't accept that excuse, which came only from self-pity; it wasn't hunger, it was ambition. The next day Horsch called to say he would be there around eight. And when he came in, he suggested: "Shall we go out?"

They went out. In the street he began: "Yesterday? . . ." But Xenia interrupted: "Why talk about yesterday? Let's talk about tonight: where shall we go?" Not that, she thought: the satisfaction of describing Dino behind bars, discouraged, unshaven, shattered, she wouldn't give him that. "I'm coming with you, I'm happy to come, but enough." Of Dino not a word: the prison, their conversations would remain obscure to him, as his trips to Menaggio were to her.

Horsch thought for a moment: "Shall we go to dinner at the club?" The most exclusive club in the city. Horsch had never allowed anyone involved in the "deal" to set foot there; if they had something to tell him, they would call, and even that he didn't much like because—he said—at the switchboard the operators were always listening in. At the club, at night, he met his friends, the most important ones. She agreed with indifference: "Fine, the club."

The dining room of an exclusive club is rather boring, Xenia thought. The waiters moved silently, the few diners greeted one another with their eyes, as if they were members of a brotherhood. They were, mostly, old bachelors who had their little manias: one complained that they had salted his vegetables, which according to his diet should be bland; another, tired of waiting, fidgeted nervously with his hands on the tablecloth. Later, others arrived, whom Horsch invited to have coffee: robust northern men who laughed easily. They were the big names of industry: Rubber, Textiles, another Textiles, Cement. Introducing Xenia, Horsch said: "Signora Costantini." The men leaned over to kiss her hand.

Unlike what happened with Dino's friends, she was the center of conversation; the men, speaking, turned to her, and Horsch encouraged her to talk. Xenia was intelligent, she expressed herself in precise and clever language. Rubber, who seemed very interested in her, asked:

"You live in Milan?"

Before Xenia could respond, Horsch explained:

"Signora Costantini lives in Rome; but she'd like to have a pied-à-terre in Milan and has come with the intention of finding one." Rubber, Cement, Textiles smiled with satisfaction.

Horsch and Xenia understood each other without a glance, already complicit: so no more Dino, no escape from the Grimaldi, and how could she have worked at the glovemaker's? She had never lived in Milan. Horsch, without even asking her consent, took possession of her past, reformed it according to his own desires. Vandina, Tom, Mary: disappeared. Now, perhaps, Horsch would create an imaginary husband, a baron, maybe, a cavalry officer. The baron is dead. Died, let's say, in the war in Ethiopia. Too recent. Died in a car accident, then. Very good. The baroness, seeking distraction, leaves Rome and settles in Milan. Where, she doesn't yet know, she knows nothing: her past and future life depends on the bald man who sits next to her, Automobile Transports. Nothing has changed between them and yet from tonight he is no longer a stranger (maybe because of the tacit understanding not to mention poor Dino anymore). There is already something between them, as a result of which Xenia intuits that Rubber has to be treated with the greatest regard; Horsch introduced him with a special smile, gave up his seat next to her and let them talk. He smokes, seems absent, and yet looks at her and listens, approves everything she says.

Two others arrive: Cellulose and a small round provincial man, who speaks with a Pugliese accent and is called, simply, Alfonso Bortone. Signor Alfonso Bortone is coming to the club for the first time: he peers around, sits on the edge of his chair, looks at Xenia and smiles. Evidently Signor Alfonso Bortone likes women. But he is neither Rubber nor Asphalt: from Horsch's cordially indifferent eye, Xenia has understood that the new arrival is negligible.

Xenia drinks: a chilled wine, almost colorless, a French wine that goes down easily and leaves a dry, bitter taste in the mouth. Meanwhile she's thinking: "Bortone . . . A name that's not new to me. I've heard it, many years ago, but where, where?" Suddenly she finds it: at the Grimaldi, Anna Bortone, blond, good-natured Anna Bortone, who ate roasted chestnuts and wanted to return to the countryside. Yes, yes, Anna, friend of that Valentina whose nostrils quivered when there was talk of men. Maybe this man is a relative of Anna's.

They're all talking about Christmas vacations, making plans, they mention luxury hotels, in the mountains, on the Riviera, the lakes. The Pugliese sighs: "I'm in mourning, you see?" and displays the band on his sleeve: "I lost my mother." (Xenia laughs to herself: maybe it's the wine, but Bortone's mother could hardly have been young! Orphan, poor man, how can you not laugh?) "And then," he adds, "we usually spend Christmas at home." (Yes, yes, just as in Veroli, traditions handed down from generation to generation, capon, grapes stored in the cellar, toasts and the lottery.) "I'll go back for the administrative council, if possible. But just then, at the end of January, my daughter's getting married. She's in Rome, studying, she should get her degree in the next few days, and then"—he spread his arms as if to demonstrate the impotence of his will—"as soon as she comes home she's getting married." Xenia would have liked to ask, "Anna? Anna's getting married?" But she held back: she couldn't have been at the university this past year: she was in mourning in her villa in Lazio. So Horsch would have decided.

At the Grimaldi, then, everything went on in the same way. Anna gets her degree, leaves, marries (who in the world is she marrying?). Xenia, on the other hand, ran away and is a kept woman. Yes, kept, why not have the courage to say the word? In her mental picture, the friends were arrested in time, they remained as they were on the day of her escape. How could she say to Bortone: "You know? I know your daughter." "Impossible!" he would exclaim. "Yes, at the Grimaldi." Signor Bortone perhaps would think that the environment at the Grimaldi was a little mixed. What a small world! Anna, having graduated, returns to her village and gets married; and Xenia would continue to imagine her at the Grimaldi. If Anna leaves, Silvia, too, will leave, they were in the same year. And how's Milly? One by one they leave, they scatter. Who knows if they still remember that also among them there was a Xenia Costantini? They must have talked about her, sometimes? When they've all left, those four years of her life will vanish into thin air. She'd like to ask: "Signor Bortone, when is your daughter getting married?" She'd like it if, on that day, Anna—who at the Grimaldi slept on the other side of the wall from her—received a nice present from Xenia, the one who ran away. Or, rather, not even a card, anonymous. But the tall bald man who is sitting opposite has decided that all of that never was: Baronessa Costantini has never met Signorina Bortone. That's how it is now; and it's fortunate that it is so.

· · · ·

In the night silence, Sister Lorenza listened to the ceaselessly pelting rain; the bed's white curtains separated her from the world, confining her at an unreachable distance. Before, her sisters' tents had been next to hers. From the day she was named Mother Superior she had understood what it meant to be a nun; until then she had felt united with other women—the only difference was the black coif on her head. She had never regretted her freedom, and now, instead, thinking of the Ligurian village where she was born, she felt an acute desire to run barefoot on the beach, gather the beautiful rainbow-colored shells, swim with the sun in her face. It was a hardworking, peaceful village that echoed with the crashing of the waves against the cliff; on stormy nights the women went down to the port to wait for the boats returning, the great fan of their sails tossed by the southwest wind. She studied in a convent above the sea. During recess she sat with the other girls on long benches in the garden, warmed by the sun and the sweetness of a female community. Her younger schoolmates loved to gather around, listen to her talk. She didn't know why, but one day, naturally, as if it couldn't be otherwise, she found herself on the bench in a nun's habit.

Now she was tormented by the idea that she no longer knew those who surrounded her. When she passes by, there are smiles, bows; when she enters the refectory the girls jump to their feet and are silent. They no longer rebel against her, or ask to go out, like Costantini or Ortiz, they don't even say anymore that the food is terrible; they wait for her to leave. But what are the sisters plotting, unbeknownst to her. She always seemed to be hearing mysterious comments, whispers. Harassed by these suspicions, she paced for hours in her study.

Sister Prudenzina surprised her like that one day. Sister Prudenzina comes from the desolate Pugliese plain, where there are no mountains on the horizon, no trees: in her round eyeglasses only the image of God is reflected.

"Mother," she said to her, "you've lost the peace in your heart." Who speaks like that to the Mother? Who dares? The sister looks at her confidently: she will bow, beg her pardon, if the Mother accuses her of lacking respect, but will stick to her opinion.

The Mother doesn't protest. "The girls . . ." she confesses.

That word echoes continuously in her mind; if she shakes her head, if she stops up her ears, she's not free of it. At night she wakes with a start, murmuring: "The girls . . ." She doesn't know the new arrivals; the old ones, gradually, leave. For a while the Mother's lips have had a tremor, she wrings her hands nervously.

"You have to pray," says Sister Prudenzina.

But Sister Lorenza loves God in life: in the sea as in the girls. For Sister Prudenzina, on the other hand, the girls are only tools that test her patience and assure her eternity. She carries God in herself, blue and white, like the statue of Jesus in the chapel: her faith is consumed in adoration.

"You have to pray a great deal, for the girls, too," she adds.

How to pray for them? They are so mysterious, you never know what they're thinking, what they want; even by force, you can't ever penetrate the secret that envelops them. You have to intuit it by means of imagination, invention: love. No sister ever tells anything about herself, no one explains why at a certain point she shut herself in a convent. Sister Lorenza finally understands she's done it because of something she's compelled to give up.

The bed's white curtains enclosed her in an oppressive solitude. She listened to her heart beating with disorderly violence, like the rain on the windowpanes. She would have liked to say goodbye to the girls who were leaving and wait for them at the end of the summer, trusting in their return, as in her village the women who have men at sea wait, huddled on the rocks at the port. For her no one would return. Lost, she looked for the switch, turned on the light.

On the wall of the courtyard, her window shone like an eye that suddenly opens.

• • • •

Another eye was awake in the dark, another window stayed lighted all night: Silvia was to defend her thesis the next morning. Her friends had embraced her before going up to their rooms, and she would have liked to implore them: "Why are you leaving me alone?" She had only a few hours before her, superfluous now.

"Go to bed instead," Anna advised.

Go to bed to what purpose? If, in recent days, she allowed herself some rest, she dreamed of the big hall, wallpapered in green, where she had gone occasionally to watch a friend's thesis defense. She saw herself before the committee's table. Belluzzi should speak first. But it was always Trecca, with his insidious objections. "Why don't you respond, Signorina Custo?" and she would have been able to respond convincingly, but she couldn't open her mouth. "Why don't you answer?" the other insisted. Finally, with a superhuman effort, she unlocked her lips and began to speak, but her voice had no sound. Trecca, with an ironic smile, turned to Belluzzi, who said nothing, pretending not to know her, and she woke up in a sweat.

In reality, the professor had reassured her: "Yours is much more than a thesis, you know that," adding: "It will certainly be published." But he seemed distracted. For a while Silvia had felt something new in him, which escaped her.

At nine her friends came to get her. She was ready, smelling of soap, her hair pulled back tighter than usual; she wore a black silk dress that gave her a celebratory air, and her friends didn't dare speak to her the way they did on other days. They said to her, "Be strong," as if to the relatives of a dead person before the funeral. Silvia placed the manuscript of the thesis in the folder. Emanuela wanted to take the folder, but she hugged it to herself: "Thanks, I'll carry it." Then Augusta decided: "It's time to go," and Anna took her arm. As she closed the door of her room she said to herself: "When I come back here, it will all be over."

They went down the stairs in silence; the nuns and the other girls, meeting her, gave her a smile. In the street, Silvia considered that for others it was an ordinary day. "They go in and out of shops, go for a walk, take the tram: nothing alters the normal pace of their day. Life can't be shared with anyone," she concluded bitterly, seeing that her friends, too, got distracted. "No one can be close to us, except fleetingly. We have to bear, alone, the weight and difficulties of it." But when Anna said to her in a low voice, "It's a terrible moment, isn't it?" she answered in her usual ironic tone: "In the end, it's only a thesis."

They arrived early at the university and had to wait, as if outside an operating room. Their stomachs were empty, and they yawned. Finally they heard the slide of curtain rings and a porter nodded to Silvia, who separated from her friends without even a glance and disappeared. The others followed, holding their breath, and in a group sat down on some stools at the back of the room.

Intimidated by her role as protagonist, Silvia sat down, smoothed her skirt, and opened the manuscript; for the first time it didn't belong to her alone, and, skimming the first paragraph, she judged it mediocre. She felt the gazes of her friends on her neck, and instead of instilling courage they doubled her fear. Opposite her sat the professors, but, because of the sun coming through a window behind them, she couldn't distinguish their faces: they were all strangers.

Even the voice of Belluzzi, who spoke first, seemed unfamiliar. At that moment, nothing could help her, not even their daily intimacy: she was alone with that stack of pages marked with black symbols and her voice, which under the vault of the big room also acquired unheard intonations and resonances. The dialogue unfolded between those men whom she couldn't distinguish and a girl sure of herself—as she had never been—who easily exploited the knowledge gained over years of study. At the end she closed the file calmly and left. Her friends followed her immediately and as soon as they were outside embraced her, touched her, shook hands, saying all together: "Great, you were extraordinary, fabulous!" Vinca, too, had come, and Andrea and some others. Silvia said nothing: she was laughing.

When she was summoned again, she looked in hesitantly from the threshold, leaning with her hand on the doorpost. She thought of her mother, her father, while the professors asked her to come forward and she advanced, uncertain, as if she didn't dare confront what awaited her. Belluzzi rose to his feet; now she could distinguish his fine white hair, his fine face, and also his intense, deep eyes, since he had taken off his glasses to announce to her that she had graduated in literature with the highest marks cum laude of the college.

Silvia barely smiled, bowed her head, then, walking on clouds, headed for the door.

· · · ·

Andrea soon left them; he understood that the girls had to be together, as they were at the Grimaldi. They laughed and joked, relieved. Vinca seemed to have become one of them again.

Passing through the entrance hall of the university, Silvia stopped for a moment, with an affectionate gaze. It was all over now: highest marks. She would get a parchment with her name in gothic letters surrounded by red and gold flourishes. She had to send a telegram home, putting an end to the novenas they'd been saying for months for her success. It hadn't been difficult: it's always more difficult to imagine actions than to live them. Her mind was pervaded by a vague melancholy, as at the end of a party. The degree had consumed a big slice of life; rather, Augusta was saying, a big slice of youth. For four years, youth for her had been only classes, libraries, books, the smell of dust, the light of an oil lamp: until last night, with the rain hammering the windowpanes.

She remembered when she had left her village to come to Rome to enroll at the university. It was evening, and the stars were beginning to come out. On the train she hadn't closed her eyes, afraid of wasting precious hours in sleep. Later, at the Grimaldi, she had realized that the students led a carefree life: they studied, yes, but they went out with boys, too, they went to the movies, for walks, they danced, fell in love. Almost immediately she had become friends with Xenia, who, like her, was in a hurry to become someone.

Absorbed by memories, she walked slowly: her friends rushed her, since it was customary for her to invite them for a glass of vermouth. They entered an old café on Via dei Condotti where writers and artists once met. It was deserted. They sat on red velvet couches, trying to conceal the awkwardness of finding themselves all together in a public place: an unusual situation for them.

Silvia asked: "What's the matter? Are you all overwhelmed?"

"It must be the emotion," said Augusta, smiling.

"No. Something is over between us." The others protested.

"Let me speak. It took an hour to separate my life from yours. I'm the same, the degree can't have changed me, and yet . . ."

"And yet what?" asked Anna.

"Don't you feel it? Well, I've finished and you go on. It would be better if I left right away. Why return to the Grimaldi now? In a few days, when the paperwork is completed, I'll have to pack my bags."

"I can't think of it," said Emanuela sincerely.

Silvia shrugged. "When Vinca left, the next day we forgot her. Just like that," she said, turning to Vinca. "We didn't even miss you. Why should you miss me?"

Vinca confessed: "I also remembered you vaguely during the day. If something serious happened to me, I would call you, as if to reproach you for the privilege of being still in there: protected from love, from war. From life. It's all disheartening: it proves there's no feeling, or alliance, or condition that lasts."

"No, it's natural," said Emanuela. "To me life seems made up of many successive brief lives. In each one we begin again; and we can appear and be completely new. Otherwise we'd end up getting bored, don't you think?"

Silvia said uncertainly: "Maybe it's a matter of character. But taking pleasure in separations, in change, seems to me a tendency to superficiality or a vocation for suffering."

"You're always so dramatic!" Emanuela concluded.

"Yes, that's true. It's one of the flaws of my race. You're Tuscan . . ."

"And rich!" Valentina added with one of her neurotic laughs.

"What does money have to do with it?" Emanuela objected.

"It does, it always does . . ."

"And Tuscany?" Emanuela insisted. "We're never going to be a serious, coordinated people with this mania for regions."

"In fact I don't think we will be," said Silvia. "I wouldn't want to start practicing today, inflicting on you a history lesson. Or, rather, economics. See chapter: 'On the consequences of the historic conditions in the underdeveloped regions.' Better psychoanalysis . . . So, have you ever been afraid crossing a busy street or a big square, let's say Piazza di Spagna near the Barcaccia Fountain?" Emanuela's surprise was equivalent to a denial. "I have," Silvia continued.

"Because you're nearsighted."

"Or because I'm not used to the traffic in a big city. Those are the excuses I give others. But actually I'm afraid that a sudden, unstoppable danger will strike me, alone and defenseless. We've been defenseless for centuries: for centuries someone stronger has come up on us, overwhelmed us, if we abandon the bit of land, or sidewalk, that, good or bad, shelters us. Separating from what we possess—a friendship, a place to live, even the tiny space of a room—is a bold, unnerving act."

"Does this seem like a conversation to have on the very day you get your degree?" Vinca reproached her.

"You're right: I'm pedantic, boring, dissatisfied . . . Dramatic!" Silvia said, smiling, and put an arm around Emanuela's shoulders. ("Precisely today, she thought. "Because today I see how daring it is to face the future protected only by a piece of paper.")

. . . .

The porter nun said to Emanuela as she returned with Silvia and the others: "Go up to Sister Luisa."

"What is it?"

"She has to talk to you."

Emanuela delayed a moment to examine the face of the old nun: it was serious and not only gruff as usual. So why go up to Sister Luisa? They had found out everything about Stefania, it was clear; they would throw her out. Instinctively she turned to flee, like a thief caught in the act; but the door had closed and the key was hanging at the porter nun's waist. There was no escape.

Sister Luisa, warned by the bell, was waiting for her on the landing, in front of the altar of the Virgin crushing the serpent with her foot; her gaze was so kind that Emanuela thought, "She doesn't know anything."

"A telegram arrived for you, Emanuela. You have to go right away, your father is ill."

In a choked voice Emanuela repeated: "Papa?"

"There's a train at two fifteen, an express."

Emanuela returned to her friends saying only: "Papa . . ." All together they packed her bag for her. Vinca and Valentina telephoned Andrea, and Andrea took her to the station.

During the journey, the huffing of the train, the sound of the pistons seemed to repeat two childish syllables that shook her breast like a sob: "Papa . . . Papa . . ." and the hurry to reach him, Papa, and regret that she had given him no satisfaction, had remained a stranger to him, deliberately appearing hostile, cold, or, worse, indifferent. She didn't walk with him, didn't stay to read with him, though he was now an old man. Thinking of him she remembered only the rare punishments, the harshness, and the few times he had reproached her, opposed her. Of his forgiveness she had no memory; she treated him like a stranger but accepted everything he did for her, as her due; in exchange she had never brought him joy, had never said to him, "Papa, I'm happy." She was always unhappy, good morning, good evening, and that was all, judging him and criticizing him—with what possible right?—for being what he was. Only now that she feared losing him did she understand him: she would have liked the train to go faster, to fly, because she was yearning to be close to him, to do for him what in twenty-five years she had never done, to tell him everything she had never said and now, finally, would say.

She didn't say it. Papa had died suddenly, in the night. He had departed taking with him his silence, his indifference. She would never know anything else.

While the notary read the will, Emanuela every so often turned to her mother, who seemed smaller in her black veils, and saw that she hadn't known she was so wealthy, either. On their last trip Papa had tried to save on hotels, on gas. He wasn't miserly, or worried about leaving a solid inheritance, but spending more didn't bring him greater satisfaction. So the money had accumulated, and Emanuela found that she possessed great wealth. At the end of the will there was a large bequest for his granddaughter Stefania. The notary knew all about the child, evidently.

Her mother spoke of her husband without emotion, as if he were still alive: referring to him as "poor Bepi." She went on as before: the same schedule, the usual habits. One day she said to her daughter: "Poor Bepi was always saying: 'I'm afraid Emanuela hasn't talked to that young man. She has to talk to him.' And even the last night, when he could no longer speak, poor Bepi, he seemed to be urging it, indicating the photograph with his eyes."

Emanuela wished she had been in time to tell him that she had tried just a few days earlier: Stefania, recovered, had asked if they could go for a walk, and, fearing that they might meet Andrea, she had resolved to talk to him that day, to put an end to the anxieties caused by the secret. But Andrea had come to meet her saying: "Guess what I bought? A refrigerator! It's not the most necessary item, you'll tell me—and you'd be right—better the bedroom furniture or the kitchen equipment. But it was suggested by an old classmate who's starving, along with his wife and two children, twins, incredible . . . But it's lovely, I assure you. It makes ice cubes." He laughed, he was cheerful, he talked enthusiastically about the house: and she, yet again, was silent.

Now, before speaking, she had to let him know how large her father's inheritance was. She was afraid that Andrea wouldn't want to marry a woman with a past; as a child, hearing reference to "a woman with a past," she had pictured a shapely mature woman, with a large hat and a feather boa. The woman with a past couldn't be her: twenty-five years old, low-heeled shoes, boarder at the Grimaldi institute. Yet she realized that nothing can destroy the past: you conceal it, you hide it, no one knows it apart from you, and you'll never talk about it. But one day you will talk about it: you yourself will dig it up, you'll realize that it's still alive, that you've been constructing your life around it, like a butterfly its chrysalis.

She felt pursued by a hostile fate: so many girls act as she had, without consequences. "Why did I do it?" she wondered. After all, she hadn't been very much in love, and the senses can be mastered: or at least so it seems at a distance of time, when the past, having already been lived, seems simple and smooth. But what we live today will be the past tomorrow. We have to be sure we won't find it, magnified and threatening, cutting off our future.

Suddenly she thought it might be easier to write to Andrea than to talk to him. But then she said to herself that on paper the facts can assume other dimensions. "I have to tell him as if it were something unimportant. It's all in the way I begin. 'You're an intelligent man,' I'll say, 'a man who understands . . .' and then, however badly it goes, what's the worst that can happen? He'll leave me."

. . . .

But she didn't want him to leave her. She harbored an undefined feeling that at times made her wish for peace, at times drove her to flee from it, fearing its monotony. She deplored the emptiness of her life without aspirations: but nothing, until now, had satisfied her. She had an innate discontent, along with a solid capacity to adapt, not to mention a vague longing for sacrifice, for altruism.

Florence seemed to her unbearable, the house oppressive: her mother kept the shutters closed and often talked to herself. Maybe she should stay with her; but there was an unbridgeable distance between them, which she had always attributed to the fact that her mother was already old when she was born. Or perhaps she judged her old because she was her mother. Once Stefania had asked her: "What were you like when you were young?" Emanuela had laughed while the child, not understanding the reason for that sudden hilarity, stared at her, serious and as if offended.

"Mamma, do you want me to stay with you?" she said, breaking the silence of their meals.

Her mother shook her head. "No, thank you, my dear."

"But what will you do, alone?"

"I've always been alone," the other corrected her. "You went to your father when anything happened to you, from the least to the most important."

"It's not true," Emanuela replied. "When I realized that I was expecting a baby . . ."

"Only then you confided in me: because you were afraid," the mother made clear. "Your silence has made my life bitter. When you went to Rome, for me it was the dress rehearsal for death; I suffered a great deal, to get used to being alone, and now I wish to remain so."

Emanuela had always believed that her mother's attention was concentrated on taking care of the house, on her endless knitting. She hadn't suspected that, on the contrary, she understood everything and was secretly resentful.

Emanuela considered her in this new aspect, but her mother had low-ered her gaze to her plate: all Emanuela could see was the gray head with the part in the thinning hair.

. . . .

Xenia arrived in Nice at night, driving the car herself. The journey had been tiring, her attention always alert on the winding road, then the stop at the border, where she crossed the San Luigi bridge over the gorge, and, on the other side, was no longer in Italy. Closing the door behind the porters who had brought up her suitcases, Xenia looked around, happy: she heard footsteps in the hall, but no one could knock or enter, no one knew her.

She turned on the water in the bathtub. She threw in a handful of green salts that spread a pleasant odor of lavender as they dissolved. Then she put her feet in the water and sat, naked, on the edge of the tub, mov-ing her legs lazily, expressing with that gesture a childish happiness. Years ago, in the same way, she'd gone into a stream that ran along the edge of the olive grove: at the bottom of the stream you could see clean white pebbles; but the water was cold and after a short time she had to get out because her ankles turned red and hurt.

She'd been thinking of her childhood a lot lately. In those years, she sometimes doubted she was alive. "Am I alive?" she'd ask herself. "Am I really alive?" And she caressed her arms to be sure of possessing the sense of touch, said her name aloud to hear herself: "Xenia . . ." She didn't want merely to live and be aware of it, as now. Was it really her, Xenia, immersed in that perfumed bath in the best hotel in Nice? Was that her car in the garage, the most beautiful car in Milan? Was it really to her that the most renowned dressmakers sent boxes containing expensive dresses?

When she was still at home, she would often grow sad, imagining that she would never have any extraordinary adventures. Yet she'd had a sense that her future would be different from that of the other girls she knew.

Everything was easy for her; she hardly studied and was first in her class, without effort. As soon as she was an adolescent she noticed that men looked at her, even if she was in the company of more conventionally beautiful friends. But her family didn't even have the money to buy shoes. When she finished high school, she herself had decided: "Like this you don't get ahead. I'm going to Rome, to the university; and once I've graduated, I'll work." Her parents had mortgaged the vineyard and Xenia had left.

Now, closing her eyes, she thought of how many of her childhood friends had married local men who went to the tavern at night, got drunk, and, coming home, took them, sleepy as they were: and every nine months a child. She opened her eyes to look at her smooth white belly. The water, motionless around her, kept her in a pleasurable lethargy. As a child she'd washed with cold water in a zinc basin; sometimes, because of the cold, maybe she was still a little dirty. "Yes, a little dirty." She laughed at the idea, splashed water with her feet, then got up and, dripping, wrapped herself in the bathrobe.

"This is the most wonderful night of my life," she thought, stretching out in the bed; if a man had entered, even if he was the best in the world, she would have shown him the door. Of all pleasures, being alone was incomparable: enjoying herself, her company, her image.

Women think happiness comes only from love. She was perfectly happy and yet she had never been in love. Dino yes, my Lord, poor Dino, in a month he'll be on trial! Unlike Dino and Horsch, she didn't have a taste for risk, for adventure; she had had it as long as it was necessary to gain the opportunity to sleep in a soft bed, under a feather comforter, watched over by a lamp that illumines the open book.

But she couldn't read: her physical well-being made her lazy, without even the strength to raise an arm to turn out the light; it made her forget everything.

No, everything no: every so often, the memory of Horsch dragged her out of that state of happiness. To him Xenia owed the luxurious apartment where she lived, the maids, the car, the bank account, the jewels, the clothes; and also the past, the title, and that aura of a respectable woman that he had been able to spread around her. Horsch was an exceptionally intelligent, courteous, pleasant man.

They went out together every night; often they had dinner at the club, and their bond was known to all those they spent time with. Now people said, "Horsch and the Baroness," as if they were a single person. Xenia knew all his business, he never acted without asking her advice. But two nights a week Horsch stayed with her; and from the moment she closed the bedroom door behind them, the affectionate friendship that Xenia felt for him was transformed. The refined manners, the submissive adoration that oozed from his words, his gestures, and even from his embraces, didn't soften her repugnance. In the dark, eyes wide with horror, she would have liked to cry out: rather, she did cry out, she rebelled, but in silence. She stayed awake while he slept, afraid that if she slept that disgust would grip her again in a nightmare. Horsch left at dawn, kissing her chastely on the head. She smiled at him weakly, as after an illness. "Bye, Raimondo," she said fondly; and, in the ineffable pleasure of solitude regained, she slept peacefully.

. . . .

After the foggy Milanese winter, the spring in Nice, bursting with mimosas, sun, sea, fresh air, threw her into a happy daze. She woke early and enthusiastically decided on a program, and the days were always too short for what she intended to do. At night she went to the theater or a concert; returning she gazed at the sea from her balcony, intoxicated by the awareness of living as she had as a child.

A week later, in the hotel, she met an older but still beautiful Dutch woman, who spent several months a year in Nice; her daughters, twenty-year-old twins, had beautiful figures, beautiful hair, and beautiful teeth, but their gazes held the unhappy disorientation of the cross-eyed. The mother, almost out of shame, hid her big blue eyes behind dark glasses. She walked resolutely, one step ahead of the girls—who followed her, looking in what direction you couldn't tell—and at night she invited some young people to a dance at the hotel, hoping to snare a future son-in-law. The twins overwhelmed Xenia with kindness and affection—she was only a little older than them, and already a widow, poor baroness!—since their imperfection, instead of making them bitter, made them angelic. With them Xenia met Maurice de Langes.

They introduced him to her excitedly, saying he had won a lot of tennis matches and if he wanted could become the French champion. He protested: "Apart from anything else, it's too late—I'm too old." Xenia looked at him disdainfully, imagining that he was vain and had limited interests, and began talking to him out of mere courtesy.

Maurice was twenty-seven: he wasn't very tall, but he was nimble, quick. His lively black eyes seemed carved into his lean face. Unlike many young men of his age, he didn't dance, and he spoke with moderation, trying to hide, at the same time, his gifts and his timidity. He said that, outside of tennis, "excellent for one's health," he did nothing. In the summer he traveled, often by impromptu means. But those journeys represented for him a true intellectual activity: he described them wittily, giving color to the landscapes, life to the customs. Naturally he had been to Italy many times, but he didn't know the fashionable cafés or the worldly spas: for him Italy was an immense art gallery surrounded by marvelous deserted beaches. At the end he explained: "I paint." He said it with irony, implying that it was merely a pastime. And precisely from that self-mocking tone Xenia understood that painting was the only thing he was truly passionate about.

He came back the next night: the seat next to Xenia was occupied, and he secured it little by little, with stubborn tenacity. Finally the girls went to bed, their mother took her place at a bridge table, the others scattered, and the two of them, as if by agreement, moved away from the crowd and the noise. The night after that Xenia went to the theater: returning, she found Maurice waiting for her at the door of the hotel. "I was afraid you'd left," he said with a lost expression.

Later, in her room, Xenia went on thinking about Maurice, talking to him in her mind; she moved as if he could see her. "A boy," she thought, shaking her head; but she softened, remembering his sharp, nervous way of laughing, a sudden explosion that left a sparkle in his eyes, like the foam of a wave on the shore. "A boy like so many others, maybe more sensitive, more intelligent." Yet the next day seemed to her endless, and she invited the twins to go for a drive, hoping to run into Maurice, who never appeared during the day: "He must have a lover. It's natural, at his age." At night he explained to her that during the daylight hours he painted.

The orchestra played without interruption: couples whirled on the dance floor like figures on a carousel: they moved away, came back, smiling. Xenia and Maurice sat apart, followed by the sympathies and vague looks of the two cross-eyed girls. They went on talking until the music stopped and in the hotel garden only the sound of the sea could be heard, the rustling of the trees while the sky lightened.

They could no longer be separated; for three days now Maurice had come to get her in his little old French car; they drove around, stopped to eat in inns, talked, enjoyed themselves, laughed.

He called to her at every moment, for no reason. "Why did they give you that name?" he asked. "Do you have a Russian relative?"

"Oh, no," she said, laughing. "I'm called that after the protagonist of a novel my mother was reading while she waited for me to be born." And she considered that many things in her life had depended on the fact of having that uncommon name. In Veroli everyone was surprised by it. "Xenia! What kind of name is that?" Then they said "Pretty" or "Ugly," but, in the end, they said something.

"Xenia," Maurice observed, "means foreigner."

"Maybe that's why I never form friendships with anyone."

"As a child, I always complained that being alone gave me a headache," said Maurice. "Then I felt that I was split, as if someone else were living in me: a real live boy, with a name: René. That boy did everything I couldn't do: he was what I would have liked to be. Free, naturally, and a painter," he added with a smile. "I'd go for a walk with my mother, for example, and René would walk next to me. Sometimes I saw a place I liked and I would have wanted to stop there, but my mother pulled me by the arm. Then I said to René: 'You stay.' He'd leave me, open the paintbox, begin to paint. And I went off, feeling as if I'd gotten some revenge. It's nonsense. You're the first person I've told that to."

Often Maurice broke off, apologizing: "I talk and talk . . . instead I'd like to know about you, about your life as a girl."

"The life of a provincial girl resembles that of all other provincial girls," Xenia observed. She didn't want to tell him the usual story invented by Horsch. She talked about Veroli and the poplars that grew around the house.

"Is it still there, the house?"

Xenia said: "Yes, my parents live there," but she didn't say how it was.

"We once had a castle in the Vendée. Now this castle belongs to someone else; Saturday and Sunday you can visit it. I went to the castle and paid the entrance fee. There were some tourists, and the old caretaker who took us around had worked for us. He didn't recognize me—the castle was sold when I was scarcely ten—but they asked him if there was still anyone in the family left and he said, 'Count Maurice.' I lingered in the rooms I'd lived in, I went up to the tower. From the height of the tower you overlook the woods where I had often walked, talking to René: and when the bell forced me to return, he stayed to paint. The lawn below the tower was of a green so intense that, suddenly, I had the impulse to throw myself down . . . I don't know how I managed not to."

Xenia, seeing that he was disturbed by the memory, asked: "But why?"

"I don't know. Maybe because my life, faced with the majesty of those walls where the people of my blood had lived, seemed to me vain, empty. Or maybe . . . but I don't think it's worth the trouble to tell."

"Tell me, please."

"Maybe because the tourists, at a certain point, seeing on the walls the portraits of my ancestors, in armor or in skirts and ruff—one, an architect, with the compass in hand, another with a book of poetry he had written—asked: 'What does Count Maurice do?' and the caretaker, shrugging his shoulders, answered: 'Nothing . . .' Nothing in fact. I did something only through René: in fact, I'm afraid of being a mediocre painter, and mediocrity in art is intolerable. It's true that I play tennis well," he said with a smile. Then he added: "I think that to succeed you have to be poor. You do something, in one field or another, believing you're working night and day just to make some money, to survive. I have modest means. Very modest. But this modest security is my ruin. When you're not poor enough to make something of yourself, you should at least be rich enough to do something with your money . . . But what do I do? I'd like to live in seclusion and paint; and instead I go out, I see people, I'm always unsatisfied, always disdainful. But if I lead this life it's a sign that after all it satisfies me; or at least it amuses me."

"Don't you think it's like that for everyone?" Xenia replied. "The life we lead is formed on our character, unknown to us. The other, the dreamed-of life, is only an aesthetic aspiration."

He had stopped the car on the edge of a pinewood that looked onto the sea, dazzling in the afternoon.

"And then, what is the dreamed-of life?" Maurice resumed. "You'd have to not have so many contradictions in yourself. While I paint, I dream of the air, the sun; while I play tennis I think of the incomplete paintings, of the works that are in museums, and I wonder what I'm doing there, sending a ball over a net for hours. There's never been anything serious in me until today," he confessed, caressing her face. "They say that love inspires great works. From the pictures I'm painting, you wouldn't say so: in fact, I'm afraid that a person in love does nothing good. Nothing, except love. But what does the rest matter?"

In fact the idea of leaving Nice frightened Xenia.

The two weeks that remained would pass like the last three days: in a breath.

Maurice wasn't sad. "You'll come to Nice every winter, right? You'll be able to do that?"

"Yes, of course . . . But it's far away, winter."

"Winter!" he repeated and burst into laughter. "You leave at the end of the month, and a couple of weeks later I arrive in Milan. May and June are the most beautiful months in Italy: we'll take a long tour of the minor cities, the provincial museums . . . we'll also go to Veroli because I want to know your old house, your poplars. Then we come back up. I'd thought of taking a cargo ship and going to Argentina this year: to a peninsula called Llao Llao, where there are some long narrow lakes like fjords. Instead I'll come to Milan: if I find a studio that's not expensive, I can stay in Milan two, three months."

Maurice didn't know that in Milan there was Horsch. Horsch had the key to the apartment and now was coming every night. Without him, Xenia would never have set foot in Nice. In those few days, she had discovered something that poverty had kept her from enjoying: youth. She was only twenty-three, but she wasn't supposed to get used to the taste of youth. Only by being the friend of Horsch could she be the lover of Maurice; but if Maurice knew the truth he would abandon her with the pitiless intransigence of the young. "I can't bear that a single one of your thoughts doesn't belong to me," he had said to her. And Xenia couldn't give him anything because nothing belonged to her: not even the past.

That night, Maurice waited anxiously to be alone with her. Finally the girls went up, and their mother joined the bridge players. "Let's go," Maurice said to her: "Let's go to my house. I'll bring you back here tomorrow morning early, when the fishermen go out and the sea is white."

Xenia hesitated. "I don't like coming back here in the morning in my evening dress," she objected, lifting the hem of her skirt. "Why don't you go up and change?" "Because then they'd see me leave. You know they play until late . . ." "You're right. Tomorrow I'll come get you in the afternoon, we'll have lunch out. And the next day you know what you should do? Say you were suddenly called back to Milan, say goodbye to everyone, pretend to leave, and come and live with me." He laughed, with that harsh sharp laugh. "All right?"

She nodded.

But she had to give it up. Otherwise, she could never again spend evenings in the public room of the club, listening to the conversations of Horsch's friends, she would no longer endure feeling Raimondo's hands on her. All the revulsion that filled her at those moments would explode in a cry. "No!" she would say: "Go!" Horsch, without responding, would say goodbye with a bow, would leave, closing the door behind him, and Xenia's life would roll into the darkness. Besides, Raimondo wasn't only generous: he was sensitive, refined, he had learned to live in the world in a respectable way, apparently. She had accepted the role he offered her: loyalty was the trade-off, the only honor that remained to her. Besides, to him alone could she show herself as she was. Between them was a deep affinity, a secret resemblance: for her, as for Horsch, the dreamed-of life was only the possibility of arriving where they wanted, by any means.

She spent the night dozing; at dawn she fell into a restless sleep. In sleep Maurice appeared to her: they were in Argentina, on the Llao Llao peninsula, she was swimming and Maurice was painting in the sun, with a big straw hat on his head. But from the sea she suddenly saw the castle tower: Maurice was standing on the parapet, leaning out into emptiness.

She woke with a start: her heart was pounding furiously. It must be late: the morning was already heavy with sun and the smells of spring.

Xenia said to herself that a painful break has to be carried out coura-
geously: she picked up the phone and called Horsch. She told him she'd
had enough of Nice; the next day carnival would begin, too much noise,
too many people. She was returning to Milan.

"Will you meet me in Genoa tonight?"

"If you like," Horsch answered, and the unexpected joy kept him
from noticing Xenia's lifeless tone. "Then, see you soon. Thank you,"
he added devotedly. He didn't expect that suggestion, he wouldn't have
dared hope for it. But otherwise Xenia—before embarking on the gray
highway that goes from Genoa to Milan—would have turned back in
an instant.

Sitting on the bed, hands intertwined in her lap, she waited to feel the
relief of the decision made. "In Milan I'll buy a lot of clothes, there's nothing more fun," and she tried to imagine what they might be like. Instead
she imagined Maurice coming to get her at the hotel in the afternoon, as
they had agreed. "Left? What do you mean left? When?"

Yes, left, ran away, another flight. If she'd stayed there she would have
done something stupid. In Milan she had to speak right away to the architect for the villa in Cortina: Horsch had told her to choose, decide, as she
thought best. Always perfect, Raimondo. But with Raimondo she would
never be able to run a race on the beach: it would be ridiculous. Maurice's legs, when he played tennis, were tan and young against the white
shorts . . . "You can't eat youth!" she thought. "And what's so important
about running on a beach?"

Yet she couldn't picture without anguish Maurice's face in front of
the hotel doorman: "Left?" The same face she had found waiting for her
the night she returned from the theater. Maybe Maurice would remember
that he himself had suggested that fake departure. He would rush home,
driving the car as if he were spurring a horse. "Xenia!" he would call,
entering his studio. Xenia wasn't there. The hours would pass and Xenia
wouldn't come: she really had left.

"And if I go," she wondered, tempted. "Then I leave immediately, I leave tomorrow. Maurice can't find me: he doesn't know the address in Milan, the phone number isn't in the book ... I could even leave tonight. Go to Maurice and afterward—with the pretext of getting the suitcases at the hotel—take the car and leave."

But afterward she wouldn't leave; since, leaving, she would give up not only youth and love but also that happy satisfaction of the senses that had always been for her behind a locked door. She was already horrified at the thought that Raimondo was waiting for her in Genoa. "You're not tired, are you, darling?" Raimondo loved her. So he could get from the act of love what she hadn't yet experienced. "Luxuries of old age," she thought, beginning to pack the suitcases.

"Prepare my bill, please."

"Will you help me close the suitcases, please?"

"Take my luggage down, please."

Sitting in the car, she looked around for a moment. There was sun, but the breeze gently stirred the leaves of the palm trees: and she was leaving. She had acted hastily, it was absurd, foolish. "I should at least see Maurice again, talk to him ..." On the contrary: she had to leave right away, without hesitating. This flight was more painful than the first because, this time, she was fleeing from herself as well, and forever.

At the hotel entrance, the doorman, the porters, waited for the car to move. Certainly they were wondering, What is she waiting for? Seeing her still there, unmoving, at the wheel. But it was hard to leave. Hard to drive with blurred vision, not seeing clearly in front of her. Then she started the engine, released the brake, shifted into gear, pressed the accelerator.

. . . .

In the house on Via Sistina, waiting had become a way of life. On the street, in the stores, Donna Inés talked about the civil war to anyone, and many thought of it as a sort of senile mania.

Yet she alone kept up her spirits, although she had a son far away and, in her heart, a constant premonition of disaster. The girls were exhausted. Until late at night all three of them sat around the stove, in a corner of the dining room where they had gathered together the photos of the absent ones. Pilar was knitting a scarf for Pepe, Vinca was correcting her students' homework. From the street rose the voices of passersby, car headlights fleetingly illumined the windows. For more than a month there had been no news of Luis.

When the girls were most depressed, Donna Inés read the cards; so as not to move away from the stove, she arranged them on a board placed on her knees. She always said the same things: return, joy, a man who knocks at the door. Anyway, the cards had become guardians of hope.

"What is there for me?" Vinca asked, and Donna Inés, showing her the two of hearts and the three of clubs joined, promised: mail in three days.

Three days passed, then another three: Luis didn't write, and Pepe didn't mention him in his letters, since one was at the front and the other in Cordova. Vinca said, to reassure herself: "I know what Luis is like: he doesn't write and then one fine day he'll just show up."

The other two agreed that's what would happen, it was in his character.

But one day, exasperated, Vinca burst out: "It's not true, you're saying it out of pity! You know very well that something serious has happened."

That same night, assuming a natural tone, Donna Inés proposed: "What about going to the movies?" She wanted the girls to go back to loving life, at whatever cost: even at the cost of leaving their fiancés. "Shall we go?" she repeated with an inviting smile.

Pilar and Vinca didn't even answer her. She muttered, mortified, "Forget it, then. We won't talk about it anymore. Never mind."

The next day a letter arrived from Pepe. Vinca thought that if something had happened to Luis, Pepe would know. She was so impatient that while Pilar was still reading she asked: "What does he say?"

"The usual."

"That is?"

"Nothing new."

"And about Luis?"

"About Luis? . . . No. Nothing."

But Vinca had caught a hesitation in her. Turning pale, she said: "It's not true."

Donna Inés, too, was suspicious, because Pilar had folded the letter in a hurry, and she came to her daughter's aid:

"But if she says so why shouldn't it be true?"

Vinca, paying no attention to her, insisted: "Let me read it."

"No."

"What does he say about Luis?"

"Nothing."

"Swear."

"What?"

"That he doesn't say anything about Luis."

"But of course," Donna Inés interrupted, "it must be intimate things, things fiancés say."

Vinca repeated harshly: "Swear."

"It's not necessary."

"Let me read it!" she ordered her, threatening; then, changing her tone, she entreated her: "Please, Pilar."

"I can't."

Vinca, bringing her hands to her face, asked with a cry: "Is he dead?"

Donna Inés thought Vinca would collapse and went over to support her. But Pilar, pale, shook her head:

"No, don't worry, no."

"Swear!" Vinca insisted. "Swear on Pepe's life!"

"I swear."

Vinca, still disbelieving, couldn't stop staring at her, fearing a glance of understanding with her mother. Donna Inés said impatiently: "What's wrong, then, what happened?" Confronted by her daughter's expression, it seemed to her impossible that Luis wasn't dead.

"He's fine," said Pilar. "Only, there's one thing."

"It doesn't matter," Vinca raved, "whatever it is, as long as he's alive. But maybe you swore falsely: in this case it's not a sin." And, entreating her with her gaze, she repeated: "Pilar, I beg you, tell me the truth."

Pilar waited for the strength necessary to speak. A peddler raised his singing cry from the street. Finally, Pilar murmured:

"He's married."

• • • •

"At first I didn't believe it was true: how could I believe it? It's a compassionate invention, to get me used to knowing he's gone, I said to myself. I asked: 'Who is she?' Pilar answered, 'Her name is Soledad Montalvo, that's all Pepe says.' And then I understood that it was true. Sol was the only one who counted in his life. There she was, before me, and remained. Ours was an episode that didn't touch her."

She was sitting on the floor, in her housedress, in front of a cabinet from which she was taking Luis's letters to reread them, and Silvia didn't know how to comfort her. If Luis had died it would have been easier: their love would remain intact, it would still exist, in memory and in itself. Like this Vinca had lost not only Luis but everything she had given, day after day, to love. "Vinca is too calm, we're afraid," Pilar had told her on the phone, begging her to come right away.

"They're very kind to me," Vinca resumed. "They bring me a cup of chamomile, hot broth. It's strange: when we're stricken in our heart the physical acquires great importance for others. They try to heal the only thing that can be healed . . ." Then she pointed to the letters: "This is the last. Ten days before he got married. I'll translate it for you. So . . ." And she ran her eyes over the lines: "'Vinca, my love, wait for me, wait for me forever. When I return everything will be as before.' And farther on . . . Here, listen: 'Whatever happens, believe that I love you.' Now I understand what he meant to say. After that he didn't write again." She was trembling, blue with cold, her face ravaged by tears. She leaned her forehead against Silvia's knees. "It would be better for me to die: What am I living for?" she wondered, in a broken voice. "It's unbearable. You don't know . . . you can't understand . . ."

Silvia considered that the same words could serve for Vinca and for Belluzzi's wife, the day of that disgusting scene. "You still love him," she said, shaking her head.

"What's strange about that? Don't we love life even if it abandons us unexpectedly? In fact we love it more at those moments. How could I forget everything that was? And who said he doesn't love me anymore? You heard what he says in the last letter? 'Whatever happens . . .' Maybe he married Sol because she's rich."

"And you approve of that?"

"No, I say love is one thing, money another. I can't even condemn him because each of us knows, about ourself, what others don't. The important thing is to love. Therefore I was the privileged one. Now I'll try to get used to the idea that another woman lives with him, sleeps with him . . ." She broke off, eyes wide, a sort of madness wandering in them. "But maybe it's a story. I don't know this woman, I don't know if she exists. Ours was something so beautiful, how is it possible that it's over? Luis knew I have nothing else."

"People always say that, in good faith," Silvia objected.

"I have nothing," Vinca repeated. "As a child I was always alone, no one worried about me. One day, the aunts, the relatives, all surrounded me, caressed me, picked me up, and I burst into tears. I distrusted that unusual attention: something serious must have happened. In fact,

Mamma had died. Since then, whenever people gather around me, I get scared. I was always afraid of life, before coming to the Grimaldi. And now, again ... I'm afraid fear is in my fate."

Silvia objected: "You can't believe in fate. It's an excuse for giving up, for not fighting."

Vinca shook her head: "Maybe fate is nothing but laziness, in fact we Spanish always say '*Mañana*, tomorrow.' We delay, hoping something will intervene in our favor. I would like only to sleep now. I thought of killing myself. I would kill myself, but I can't because there's God. You're not a believer, you could prove to me that the Earth formed by itself, explain everything according to science: you can prove it, data and facts at hand ... Just the same, I would believe that God exists, God is there. And the proof is this: if God didn't exist, at the first moment I would have jumped out the window."

The room darkened, Silvia got up to turn on the light, and Vinca followed her with her gaze, murmuring: "What shall I do?" as if she were alone, but in her eyes a request for help was visible.

"You wouldn't think of returning to Cordova?"

"When I left, my father's wife said to me: 'Remember, this is always your home,' but that assurance proved to me that it no longer was ... And then in Cordova there's Luis."

"You're afraid of meeting him?"

"I would go and look for him myself," Vinca confessed. "I would beg him: 'Take me with you, in whatever way, whatever happens, even like this ...'"

They heard the sound of the bell. Vinca started. "It's the mail," she said, while someone hurried to open the door.

"Why don't you come back to the Grimaldi?" Silvia asked.

"No, there you're not free even to suffer. But here I won't stand it. Pilar and I were bound occasionally by something more than friendship. Which in me could now become resentment. Hatred, even ... It's better for me to go."

"You're the wisest of us all," Silvia observed.

Vinca answered bitterly: "No ... don't you remember what it was like at the Grimaldi?"

Silvia remembers: sees again, rather. Vinca laughs, Vinca comes home late, Vinca makes up her lips and eyes as soon as she's out on the street, Vinca never pays attention in class. Vinca dances the fandango standing on the desk, the nuns come in and make the sign of the cross ... One day Vinca says: "I met a Spanish guy, Andalusian like me, his name is Luis."

Outside, Silvia walked slowly, indifferent to the sharp cold air. If she had had money, she would have helped Vinca. But Vinca wasn't worried: "I'll work. I'll go on giving lessons. I'd like to find something to translate for the movies. Apparently that pays well ... And I'll rent a furnished room, a modest one, in an old neighborhood. Luis liked the old neighborhoods ... You never know, he might return," she murmured. "His plans, his papers are still here. Do you think he might abandon his studies? In that letter, you heard? He says: 'Wait for me.'" "And you?" Silvia asked. Vinca didn't answer; besides, they were in the hall, because Silvia was leaving. When they were facing one another, on the threshold, Silvia insisted: "And God?" Vinca looked at the floor. After a silence, she looked up and answered: "God is love."

But what was love? Silvia wondered. Luis, in the end, was worthless: he had proved false with Vinca, and his fellow students considered his intelligence mediocre. And yet in Vinca's heart Luis was the only rival of the God she believed in.

· · · ·

At the Grimaldi on Saturday nights, before dinner, the girls took turns at the confessional. The chapel was near the front entrance: Sister Pruden-zina waited for them in the doorway to urge them to confess, distrustful of those who preferred to avoid it. "You, Ortiz, you're not going to confess?" she asked Vinca, stopping her by the arm. "I have a headache," she often responded. But the sister pressed her: "Go, go. What, you don't want to have communion tomorrow morning? You haven't been well lately: these constant headaches . . . Communion will help you get better." Vinca left the confessional looking drained and afterward had a crisis. She charged Valentina with calling Luis: "Tell him I can't today, I'm not well." She spent hours on her knees in the chapel, reciting the rosary. But Luis always won in the end.

On Sunday, the girls flew off like swallows from the old walls of the institute. Those who had a romantic appointment could be recognized by the footsteps that came down the stairs like a hailstorm. They stared impatiently at the hands of the porter nun as she searched for the key, slowly opened the door. "Quick, Sister," they said, eager to go. "I'm in a hurry." Silvia saw that the lives of women rotated like satellites around a planet: love.

She looked at her watch: it was two. She couldn't go back to the Grimaldi for lunch. Besides, she was too nervous. The evening before, Belluzzi had said: "Come tomorrow at three, I have to talk to you." Silvia went every day at three; why that special invitation? What would he say? she wondered, descending the stairs of Trinità dei Monti, covered with flowers. There, the day before, she had bought a branch of mimosa and put it on the professor's desk. She was afraid he had summoned her to ask, severely: "What does it mean?" She might have answered: "It's love." But she wasn't sure that it was.

Recently she had tried to define what love was, relying on texts of literature, poetry. It had seemed to her a feeling that was always different, although everyone called it by the same name. She thought the same was true of the idea of God. "God is love," Vinca had said; and she had a confident expression, uttering those words: and, after all, no one knew to what they corresponded, or what, exactly, they meant. It was all confusing. And in essence everyone preferred it that way.

She sat on a stone bench in Piazza Navona. She was tired: she felt the effects of nights spent at her desk, of little sleep. During the vacation she had been surprised to find that she envied her sister Immacolata, who, that summer, was placidly expecting a child, doing nothing. Silvia had wondered about the thoughts of someone who feels another life growing in her own body. "What are you thinking about?" she had asked her. Immacolata, surprised, answered: "Me?! I never think."

Silvia would have liked not to think, like Immacolata, and wait for what her future life offered, ready, without the intervention of the will. Instead she wore herself out reflecting, eliminating, choosing, before taking one path or another. Emanuela had said to her: "It's pointless to make so many plans. At a certain point, you'll see, life decides for us, even if we've racked our brains trying to decide, to prepare. And maybe it makes the very decision that seems to us unreasonable."

In fact, Silvia considered, it was unreasonable to stay in Rome: and yet she had decided to stay in order not to abandon Belluzzi.

For some time the professor had seemed different: now she was sure of it. He no longer appeared absent, detached from life. The day before he had opened the window and looked out, observing the passersby. "This month of January is very mild," he had said, brushing the windowsill with his hand, as if to caress it. He turned away from the papers, to the things of nature, to what comforted his soul, and she thought she had guessed the reason.

Two weeks earlier, hearing the doorbell, Silvia—in the maid's absence—had gone to the door. It was a special delivery letter for Signora Belluzzi, and she had rushed to take it away from her. Dora had recovered: a new brightness illuminated her, she seemed rejuvenated. The next day, entering the study, she had said in a whisper: "Signorina . . . since with you I can speak frankly . . . You know, now, you understand . . . If a telegram arrives for me, please give it to me when my husband isn't around."

Then the telegram arrived, and Dora had resumed going out every afternoon, ostentatiously dressed and excessively made-up. Before she left, she came to say goodbye to her husband, she kissed him on the head. "Nice, that perfume," the professor said one day as she embraced him. "French, *Amour amour!*" Dora exclaimed with a radiant smile and went out, leaving behind that penetrating scent. But for the first time the professor seemed annoyed. "She's going out today, too," he had said; and then with a sigh: "Who knows when she'll be back!"

Suddenly Silvia had a presentiment of what Belluzzi wanted to say. He wouldn't say it directly, of course: the two of them were used to understanding one another with brief references and even with silence. He would say to her: "Don't leave me alone." Now he knew that he could count on her devotion and knew also, if in a vague way, that she alone could protect him. She protected him, in fact, even at the cost of the horrible complicity with that woman; she would hide the truth behind work, behind books. Maybe that branch of mimosa had also told him something she didn't dare define.

She got up from the bench, numb. In the Fountain of the Four Rivers, the water flowed out so violently it deafened her; the wind sprayed water on her face, her coat. That water, Silvia thought, that sound, roaring or quiet, which she found in every square, in every corner, was the secret voice of a city that, from the start, had seemed to her mute and indifferent; instead, you had to know how to interpret its language. Maybe she would have to interpret the professor's as well.

She started off, skirting the fountain: on the Baroque rocks one of the statues was caught in a gesture of fear and surprise, in an attitude that resembled hers in the face of life, and which, perhaps, should have been the attitude of all men. But they went around confidently—alone or with a woman on their arm—as if they feared nothing. As if it were very simple to understand, to love. And yet, Silvia thought, the only time anyone had talked to her about love she had been unable to understand it.

She was nine years old: although she was small and thin, she played with the boys, because one of them had insisted that she ran like a boy. His name was Bruno: he was tall and disheveled, and must have been at least twelve. On Sunday, meeting at Mass or along the Corso, trapped in their own families, they barely exchanged a glance of understanding, like prisoners closely watched by their guards. But the other days, in an open space that served as a playing field, they ran toward each other so fast they were out of breath and couldn't speak. Hot, panting, they joined the others and played capture the flag: one team on this side, one on the other, divided by a line drawn in the dust with a stick. Silvia was always on Bruno's team.

Once, Bruno was imprisoned by the enemy; to save the leader you had to go outside the line, cross the opposite field, and capture the flag. Silvia set off, head down, running fast; she grabbed the flag with a cry of joy, but returning to her side she fell down. Still on the ground, with a sharp pain in her knee, she shouted to Bruno: "I was already across the line! You're safe!" The game stopped, because Silvia's knee was bleeding: Bruno took her to a nearby fountain, wet his handkerchief, and delicately washed the wound. Then they sat on the steps of the fountain and, with that icy rag on her knees, she was happy. "You're brave," Bruno had said, "you're smart and brave like Clorinda." Silvia didn't know who this Clorinda was: jealous, she suffered because Bruno was comparing her to someone else. "In fact," he added, "the two of us now are just like Tancredi and Clorinda, right?" Then he looked down, his face red, and started nervously tearing up the grass between the stones. "Don't you feel it, too?" She shrugged.

Two years later, in class, while the teacher was commenting on *Jerusalem Delivered*, Silvia had understood. Even now, at such a distance in time, she remembered the green, light air outside the window, the monotonous voice of the teacher who went on explaining, while she, stunned and moved, eyes dazzled by the light outside, yearned to find Bruno and answer him. But Bruno's father, a police marshal, had been transferred. Silvia didn't know where Bruno was, she hadn't seen him again.

Slowly, lost in these thoughts, she reached Belluzzi's front door. The sun had come out and lighted up the grand hall with its statues. Silvia went straight to the professor's study without taking off her coat; then she said, "Oh, sorry . . ." Helping her take it off, he observed in surprise: "It's raining!"

"No," Silvia answered, smiling, "I sat for a moment in Piazza Navona— it's the water of the Rivers."

"In Rome even the fountains are impertinent!" said Belluzzi.

"It's not true," Silvia protested. "They're joyful!"

"Do you like Rome?" She nodded with a smile. "Do you want to stay in Rome? Reflect before you answer."

Silvia's heart was in a tumult. Further, she had glimpsed the mimosa branch, withered, in the glass where the professor kept his pencils.

She answered, serious: "Yes, very much."

"Have you reflected carefully? Fountains apart, Rome is a hostile, disdainful city. Have you thought of the difficulties, the struggles . . . of everything?" he asked, looking her in the eyes.

"Of everything," she answered in a whisper.

"When do you take the state exam?"

"In a few days, around the first of the month."

"First of the month," he repeated. "Very well. From the fifteenth you'll have a chair at Pisa."

Silvia didn't answer immediately: she studied him. "And the competition?"

"No need: a teacher is leaving her post for health reasons. You'll replace her. I'm so happy to be able to do something for you," Belluzzi added, affectionately. "What's wrong?" he asked. "You don't seem happy."

"I won't be able to come to you anymore, professor," Silvia explained in a whisper.

Belluzzi went over to her: "Remember what I told you one day, in the department? I remember because I've often repeated it to myself in these months of shared work: you'll go far. I've been among young people for years, and when I imagine what they'll do, I'm seldom mistaken. You'll go very far. I've appreciated having you with me, initiating you into our work. But your future isn't here."

("Young people." So for him she was nothing but one of those young people from whom—despite what he said at his desk, in papers, and at conferences—he was, and kept himself, distant.)

"Let me stay here with you. Let me stay in some way," she begged him, recognizing Vinca's words.

He shook his head: "It wouldn't be right."

"What does 'right' mean, professor?" Silvia protested. "Words can create such confusion . . ."

"Well, for me 'right' . . . 'right' is what I'm sure I won't reproach myself for, sooner or later. If I agreed, I would reproach myself for it. You yourself would reproach me one day." Then he asked her jokingly: "You're not afraid of teaching, are you?" Silvia made a vague gesture. "Also, it's time for you to prepare the book we were talking about before your degree. It will be helpful for your career. In fact," he added, "I'd like to write the preface." Silvia couldn't insist further. She murmured a weak "Thank you, I'm pleased," telling herself that maybe she really was, but, as on the day of the degree, her joy was veiled by bitterness. Maybe that was the taste of goals achieved.

"Besides," Belluzzi began in a very different tone, "besides, my life is changing, too." It was the hesitant voice in which he thanked his wife when she handed him the tea. "I didn't tell you before because I was afraid of seeming ridiculous to you in my youthful joy." Timidly he explained: "We're expecting a child."

He was silent for a moment, looking at his nails; thus—Silvia knew by now—he revealed his embarrassment.

"For that reason," Belluzzi continued, "many things that seemed to me essential are becoming less important. I don't even know if I'll feel like teaching anymore, in the few years remaining before retirement."

Then he recovered himself. "But of course I'll teach, I'll work, in fact I want to work more, to succeed finally, to succeed in . . ."

He was looking into the void, following those dreams. Again Silvia saw Dora vomiting, the tears running black from her made-up eyes; again she heard her gasping voice: "You can't understand, signorina . . ."

"I understand," said Silvia, and placed a hand on his arm, "dear, dear professor."

Later Signora Belluzzi also came to greet her: maternity gave her an aspect of expansive well-being. She went up to Silvia and said to her deliberately: "Thank you . . . you've been very kind, very . . . To me as well."

And Silvia responded: "I've done nothing for you."

It was true. For her, nothing. That house had become insupportable to her. She couldn't stay there even for another hour.

They were near the door: the professor and his wife close, Silvia facing them. A curtain seemed to have descended between the two who had worked together for months: "Maybe he never really believed in the work, or even in literature, and not even in love," Silvia said to herself. She murmured "Good evening," and hurried out.

. . . .

Anna's thesis defense took place in the afternoon. She was the last, and finished so late that she and her friends had to run to the Grimaldi if they didn't want to miss dinner. She entered the refectory announcing: "Ninety!" Everyone applauded, rushing to embrace her, and she repeated: "Ninety! Ninety!" dragging Sister Prudenzina into a dance: "You bad girls, naughty children," she said, but she was laughing.

Anna was so excited and happy that Sister Luisa allowed her to go all the way to the corner store, accompanied by a maid, to buy some pastries to offer her friends.

"Come up when the lights go off," she cried as she went out. "And knock before you enter!"

They knocked. Anna opened the door, and the others, after exclaiming in wonder, clapped their hands.

The room was as bright as day, lighted by some thirty candles, placed here and there: on the dresser, on the night table, on the shelves, which had been cleared of books and other objects. A bottle of spumante towered at the center of the table, which had also been cleared; two plates overflowing with pastries were on either side of it, and the colored tinfoil of tiny chocolates scattered about sparkled in the candlelight.

"Welcome! Come in! This way, please! Do me the honor!" said Anna, as if she were playing ladies.

The others, in response, bowed, curtsied, took turns paying compliments: "Doctor! Your Excellency! Most Esteemed! I prostrate myself, I genuflect, I'm your porter, what am I saying? your servant," and, parodying the southern custom, they competed: "the platform your desk stands on, the laces of your shoes, the carpet where Your Excellency cleans your feet . . ." until Anna, laughing so hard she couldn't take any more, interrupted, saying: "Clowns!"

Then they devoured the pastries, while Anna prepared to uncork the spumante, handling the bottle like an explosive device.

"Here's an occasion when men are indispensable!" said Augusta. "There's also another, come on!" Emanuela pointed out, laughing.

Finally the cork took off with a loud *pop*, knocking over a candle.

"Bull's-eye! You've hit the bull's-eye! It brings good luck!" Anna smiled, embarrassed, pouring the spumante: in the glasses, on the floor, on their clothes. The others gathered around to toast with her: "Fortune! Wealth! Honors! Love!"

"Love?! What is it?" Silvia repeated, scowling and pretending outrage.

"'It's the shadow of a fleeting dream!'" Valentina declaimed.

"My goodness!" said Silvia, covering her ears. "You're always coming up with an inappropriate quotation."

From the next room someone pounded on the wall: "Keep it down!"

Anna ran to the wall and answered: "I'm finished! Be patient! It's my last night!" Suddenly she turned serious: "My last . . ." she repeated, embracing the room and her friends with her gaze.

"Really!" Silvia exclaimed. "What about the state exams?"

"I'll take them later. Or maybe I'll never take them. Since I don't intend to teach," said Anna. "See—my room's already empty? I'm leaving tomorrow and in three weeks I'm getting married."

They were stunned. Valentina asked, sneering, "And to whom?"

"To Trecca," said Silvia. "That's why he was so generous."

Anna laughed, then she said simply: "His name is Mario. Mario Aponte. From my village."

"Why did you keep it secret? It's not nice to keep secrets from us," Augusta observed.

"You have to forgive me, understand me. For me love is a possessive feeling, I don't know how to talk about it with others. In fact, I haven't even talked about it with Mario. I don't know if we'll ever be able to talk about it . . . But is there a need to?"

"Let's drink," Augusta proposed, draining the bottle.

Valentina got up suddenly. "Ah, love, love, love!" she exclaimed sarcastically, with a loud, nervous laugh. Then she said, "I'm tired, I'm leaving," and she left without even saying good night.

. . . .

Slamming the door of Anna's room behind her, Valentina stood outside listening, sure they would talk about her. But no: Anna went back to telling them about the countryside, about Mario. Evidently they didn't take her into account.

She groped her way along the hall, disoriented by her anguish. This was too much: Anna had been silent until today, like a peasant. "Mario must be very in love not to see her as she is—it's like she's made from the white part of the bread, she'll lose her shape with her first child. The land, the poetry of the land: nonsense. What she wanted was a husband. She managed it."

In her room, she lighted the candle. "Damn miserly nuns!" She saw her shadow monstrous on the white wall; her head, enlarged by the mass of her hair, appeared on the ceiling. She felt mocked by Anna: "I'm getting married," she'd said, without even looking at her. Surely Mario had told her about the letter she had written from Rome, after the vacation. He had answered with a few words on a postcard: he, too, was a peasant. She had been a decoy. In her presence, the two of them barely spoke, and then, at night, Anna sneaked through the fields to Mario's house. Mario lives alone: very convenient. "Maybe she's pregnant." She couldn't find any other explanation for that hasty, mysterious marriage.

She began to undress, hiding her more intimate garments under the dress lying on the chair, sleeves dangling, like a dead person. "I'm going to bed to think," she said to console herself. But she couldn't get rid of that obsession: Anna with Mario.

On the wall, her shadow undressed with disproportionate gestures, enormous hands that held nothing. "I'm only twenty," Valentina was considering; but already she could predict what her life would be. She would always live alone, in a room like this: cold, impersonal, full of books. In the morning, school: ignorant, insolent, sullen children, who come, go, start, finish, pass by, and—all of them, from year to year, class to class— make fun of the *signorina*. At the end of every month she would send some money to her mother, so that the brothers wouldn't treat her like a beast of burden.

What did the others have? In her slip, she approached the mirror, and, to observe herself more clearly, held up the candle. Illuminated by that warm, quivering light, her face flushed; the eyes, usually dead, sparkled. "Beautiful," she thought, "just a little too plump." But her mother said it was a misfortune to be born thin, in the South. "For the men here, there is no union of flesh without flesh," she sighed.

She straightened up, thrusting her bosom forward. Then she put
down the candle, took out the hairpins, and her long hair sumptuously
mantled her shoulders. "Beautiful. If Mario saw me like this he would
leave Anna!"

Nonsense. It takes something else for Mario! Beauty fades, the years
pass, they slide like sand between the fingers: the land remains. She took
the belt from her dress, wrapped it around her throat, and began to
squeeze hard, harder and harder, until her face was swollen. She would
have liked to drop dead in the middle of her hair. Be found like that in
the morning. Dead: at twenty, with that smooth white flesh, not Anna's
spongy flesh. Why dead?

Slowly she began to caress her shoulders, her arms, she ran her lips
over her wrists: the skin was salty. The candle, behind her, illuminated
her hair, making a golden halo around it. "Beautiful," she repeated, and
brought her lips to the mirror to kiss herself: on the cold glass, her breath
formed a damp, opaque circle.

Did the others do this, in their rooms? She had never received such
confidences, no one had ever wanted to be intimate with her. She perceived herself, among her friends, as a secondary figure. Always that, a
secondary figure. But certainly no one had sweet, stupefying dreams like
hers. No one had such delicate skin: too delicate, for the rough cotton slip.

She pulled down one strap, then the other; the slip fell in a heap at
her feet: she saw herself, naked, as a big white stain in the shadowy light,
and immediately, ashamed of her boldness, tossed her hair to the front
to cover herself. From the golden mantel that reached her hips her legs
emerged, white, shapely.

She remembered that queen who rode through the city on a horse,
dressed only in her hair. Queen Isabeau. She imagined passing between
two groups of people: naked but not ashamed like Isabeau; rather, proud,
dominating the crowd from the height of her steed. Everyone admired
her, acclaimed her. In the crowd was Anna. Valentina, seeing her, pointed

her out to her squires, and ordered her to strip in front of everyone. "Whip her," she commanded. "Whip her till she bleeds."

At that moment the door opened and the Indian prince appeared. He was dressed in blue, a pearl quivered on his forehead. She saw him in the mirror, staring at her with eyes made cruel by desire, and she was afraid. "No!" she said. "No!" That night the prince horrified her. The insidious image, in its oriental dress, had accompanied her since childhood: for thousands and thousands of nights he had come to visit her. At home, while her mother slept, he entered just the same; invisible, he arranged his props around her—fountains, couches, pillows—and every night she belonged to him. Then he disappeared, eliminated by sleep. When she awoke he was no longer there.

She would have liked to shout "Leave me!" but her cry—like the prince, like the words he said to her—was born from her flesh and died in it. "No, tonight no," she begged, retreating, moving back toward the wall. Inexorable, he followed her and approached, with a glassy smile. When Valentina took refuge in the bed, he lay down beside her: leaning on one elbow he looked at her, tempting her with fanciful words, caressing her to tame her. "Leave me!" she whispered, weakly, knowing she had no escape.

If a man of flesh and blood had entered her life, the prince would have vanished into thin air. Instead, he returned every night, with his gardens, his carpets, his persuasive voice, his hands. She was at his mercy: all her life, since childhood, married to a dream. Exhausted, Valentina gave in, closing her eyes. But from under the eyelids two tears fell down her face.

Chilled by that weeping, the prince disappeared.

· · · ·

Anna left the Grimaldi early in the morning, when the stairs were pervaded by the smell of *caffellatte*. Silvia, on the other hand, left in the evening.

The day after Anna got her degree, she was the first to wake: her friends were still sleeping, stunned by the spumante, while Silvia ran barefoot into the hall, in her pajamas, hoping to be in time to hug her friend.

The room was deserted, the mattress already rolled up on the metal frame, and the air, coming through the open window, still chilly. A maid who arrived with a bucket told her: "She left a while ago." She overturned the bucket onto the floor tiles: the pervasive odor of creosote, the candle stubs sitting on the furniture, the wax that had dripped on every surface gave the impression that a dead man had just been carried off. "It takes a mere hour and we've disappeared," Silvia thought. Anna had lived in that room for four years, she had jealously guarded her privacy, her secrets; and now the door was wide open, shamelessly, and every trace of her was erased. At the Grimaldi, on the day that was beginning, Anna seemed never to have existed.

Silvia preferred to leave at night. Sister Prudenzina's cry with that prolonged "i" gave the signal for departure. "What are you doing? You're still here?" the sister asked, finding her sitting in her room, among her silent friends. "The carriage is at the front door waiting for you." The others rose. "It's early," Silvia said. "That's why I took the carriage: so as not to be too early."

Sister Luisa, who was waiting near the door, went toward her with an ineffable smile.

"Here we are, then, at the moment of farewell. The Mother charges me to say goodbye and wish you a good journey. She can't receive you because . . ."

"I know," said Silvia, interrupting her. "I went to say goodbye to her."

"Oh," said the other. "She was sleeping, I imagine. The Mother works too much and at night she's very tired."

"No, she wasn't sleeping," she answered, staring at her. "She was watering the flowers in her window."

"Excellent," said Sister Luisa. And then, taking her by the arm: "Now hurry up. I hope you'll have a good memory of the Grimaldi."

"Very good. Anyway, I'm intending to write to the Mother General to praise the institution," she said in an ambiguous tone. ("What's got into her?" her friends thought.) "It would be unnecessary," Sister Luisa objected. "When you, too, have responsibilities, you'll realize that we are only doing our duty here. What we consider the good of each one. Even though it's often the case that neither the person concerned nor the others understand it." She went with her to the door and added: "God bless you and good luck."

"Two concepts that don't go together, wouldn't you think, Sister Luisa? God and luck. Anyway, thank you," Silvia said, getting in the carriage.

Her friends cried: "Bye, Silvia! . . . Hey, Silvia," and they wanted to go up to her; but Sister Luisa ordered: "Inside, girls. What have you still to say to each other? Haven't you talked enough in these four years?"

No, maybe not, Silvia thought, as the carriage left the Grimaldi. In any event, they had understood nothing. "I have to write immediately to Genoa, to the Mother General." She hadn't understood anything about her friends. As she turned to look at them—as she had looked at her parents, sisters, relatives, leaving the village for the first time—they seemed to her equally unknown. The city, on the other hand, the streets, the houses she hadn't entered seemed to her friends. And likewise the statues, motionless in the essential position that in faces is blurred.

Of the four years spent in Rome she carried with her as a guide only the image of the city at night—so different from that of the noisy, insolently sunny day, which had dazed her at first—the glow of the street lights, of the lamp on the table. All the rest disappeared: even Belluzzi. He had sent her the proofs of her thesis, which was being printed, and she had put them in her travel bag almost without glancing through them, before going to the Mother Superior.

No one went to say goodbye to her now. You had to overcome the obstacles presented by Sister Luisa: "The Mother is busy, the Mother is resting." Besides, it wasn't important to those who hadn't known her during the time when she was only Sister Lorenza. From the courtyard they looked up at the window of that room which issued strict orders, and, although it was softened by climbing plants, it instilled some fear.

Silvia had knocked on the door without being announced. Then she opened it slowly.

"May I, Mother?" The Mother was at the writing desk, before an open register, and looked at her, for a moment, as if she didn't know her. "I came to say goodbye."

After a further hesitation, the Mother rose, bracing her hands on the table: her height gave her a certain solemnity. "Come, come in, my child. Welcome." Then, pointing to the chair on the other side of the desk: "I'm working, as you see. I'm always in here because I have a lot of important decisions to make, a lot of correspondence, and a lot to reflect on. But the door of this room is always open to the girls. I'm sorry not to have been downstairs, to greet you on your arrival. You've done well to come; come when you like and together we'll see about resolving all your difficulties. The first days are hard, I know, far from your family. But soon you'll see that this is only a larger family, where we all love one another and work together in the joy of the Lord. When we're young, we think our house is the whole world; but the world is wherever we can love others and carry out our work in harmony . . ." In a different tone, she added, "If you don't mind, I'll take some notes to add to the form you filled out when you asked to enter our family."

At first Silvia froze: she would have liked to escape. Instead she reminded her gently: "Sister Lorenza, I'm Silvia Custo."

"Silvia Custo," the Mother repeated with the same vague gaze. She leafed through an index, looking for the location of a register that she then took down from the shelf behind her. "Here we are. A nice page all for you. When you leave, in four years—which will go by in a flash," she sighed—"your history will be here. Rather, ours: that which unfolds between you and the Grimaldi. The girls leave, but they all remain in here," she said, placing a hand on the books. "It's an innovation I made—following a suggestion of the Mother's, naturally—in the rules of the institute. On these shelves are all the girls who left before you arrived and the girls of this year. Hundreds of them. They think they've abandoned us, without leaving a trace, but really they've remained here." She turned to the shelves filled with registers and ran her hand over them; on her ring finger a ring with a cross sealed her heavenly marriage. "So it seems to me that I hold on to them. Safeguard them. Freedom, sometimes, loses them."

She opened the register and, after some alphabetical searching, pulled out a sheet of paper. "Here's the form you filled out. Would you tell me if, in these three months, anything has changed? We, in here, can't change, but you ..."

In the photograph pasted on the form, Silvia saw herself in the photo booth: motionless, eyes wide to keep them open while the camera flashed; her face—how young she was!—alight at the idea of leaving soon.

She reread: Custo Silvia, 18. Academic achievements: high school diploma with the top grade average. Father: small landowner. Financial situation: precarious, has a scholarship. Brothers and sisters? How many? Nine. Is she engaged? No.

"I must remind you," Sister Lorenza added, "that if you become engaged during your stay here, you have an obligation to tell us. We would then require the authorization of your parents to let you go out with your fiancé. At night never, in no case. The Mother, who has more experience than I do, is rather strict about this rule. In fact, very strict, as is right, given the great variety of the flocks she shepherds. But I, I confess, don't know how to be so strict when it comes to love or other problems of youth. That means that often I do my duty imperfectly; in compensation, it makes me feel close to the girls. I understand them. They don't all know how comfortable it is to live here: serene, protected from worldly passions ... By the way," she said, pointing to the piece of paper. "I don't

recall how you answered the last question, regarding a possible inclina-
tion toward the monastic life."

"I answered: no."

"Oh . . . Anyway, you'll like the institute. But you must get used to
thinking that God is always watching you here, through the eye of his
servant Lorenza. It's as if from this room, with an eye that looks into all
the rooms—an eye that only God could possess—I saw everything you do,
without your realizing it."

She became animated, speaking; she seemed the same person who
had welcomed her, four years earlier. So beautiful, still. As she put the
form back, she adjusted her veil, looking at herself furtively in the glass of
the bookcase. Silvia, meanwhile, glanced at the page where Sister Lorenza
had written her history. After a densely written series of observations,
which she couldn't decipher, she read: "In conclusion, Silvia Custo is a
girl who . . ." At that point she stopped looking. She didn't want to know
how others judged her. She wanted to preserve intact the illusion offered
by Belluzzi when he asked her to work with him, knowing only what she
wanted to be. Knowing how others saw her—and perhaps how she was—
might eliminate the possibility of conforming to the illusion.

"The place is pleasant," the Mother resumed. "The trees, the pines
that surround our house make the air aromatic. You haven't yet gone
walking on the avenue outside?" Silvia remained uncertain, but she paid
no attention: "We're an order of nuns . . . secular, as they say; therefore in
principle we could go out. But we never go out, no one goes out. For what
purpose? Here we're free, we love each other, sometimes we all sit together
in the courtyard and listen to the voice of the sea. The sea is right below
here. Have you seen it?" she asked, opening the window.

Silvia was horrified: the grate that, outside, was of wood painted a
beautiful green, inside was of iron. She remembered that Valentina, seeing
it for the first time from the courtyard, had said, laughing: "They've put
bars on the Mother's window!" "Bars?!" Sister Luisa had repeated, frown-

ing, indignant: "The Mother expressed a desire to have some flowers at her window: moonflowers, honeysuckle . . ." And she had explained modestly: "It's the gift we sisters offered her for her silver anniversary with Jesus."

Suddenly Silvia went over to the Mother, grabbed her by the arm: "Sister Lorenza, recognize me! I'm Silvia Custo . . . Make an effort. Do you recognize me? Silvia! I've graduated, I'm leaving now. Do you want me to do something for you, speak to someone? Tell me."

The Mother was stunned for a moment, as if pulled suddenly out of sleep; then she recovered her impassive serenity. Her gaze passed rapidly over Silvia's hand, placed disrespectfully on her habit.

"Of course I recognize you, Silvia Custo," she said. "For me a first glance is enough so that I don't forget any of our girls: I carry them always in my heart." She looked at her with the marvelous smile of the past; but Silvia, disturbed by different feelings, wanted to leave.

"Good night, Sister Lorenza," she murmured.

"Mother," the nun corrected her, caressing her hair. "I'm the Mother of everyone." And walking with her to the door, she added: "Happy night. I'm very happy here because I was born in a village on the sea and I like the sea. I hope that you, too, will be happy."

In the carriage, while the horse wheezed going up toward the station, and later, alone in the compartment on the train, Silvia thought only of Sister Lorenza: "I have to write to Genoa, inform the Mother General, report everything." Outside the window, in the dark, the nun's face was a luminous point that followed her, moving in the night sky like a star.

But then she began to doubt that writing to Genoa would really be for the good of the Mother. "What is the good? Maybe for each of us it assumes different aspects." During those years she had become passionate about etymology, convincing herself in the end that all words had a secret meaning—in addition to those known—that couldn't be defined. You had to know how to understand it. Maybe there was also one in the few words that Belluzzi had written to go with the proofs.

She took the envelope from her bag, opened it. "Two lines in a hurry," said the professor. "I will come myself to deliver these proofs so that they reach you before your departure. I've reread your thesis and I'm very pleased that here, for the first time, our names appear together."

No, Silvia concluded; there was nothing to understand. Yet her name, printed on a title page, assumed a new dimension. She closed her eyes, trying to sleep: behind the face of Belluzzi the face of Bruno emerged. She said to herself that the emotion of departure was mixing up, in the same backwash, all her memories. Besides, she observed, with irony, even if both Tancredi and Clorinda concealed, under their armor, the same courage, the same passions, he recognized her only when it was too late: when he had killed her.

She awakened to the voice of the conductor announcing: "Pisa . . . Pisa . . ." It was dawn: at that hour the first bell was sounding in the courtyard of the Grimaldi; but she no longer remembered it.

Opening the door, Silvia lingered a moment on the step. Beyond the station buildings, the city where she would live was still enveloped in fog. She had the impression of finding herself alone in the world, in a foreign country. "But maybe it's like this at every beginning," she said to herself, setting off with her heavy suitcase, full of books. Only then she began to understand what she intended to say when, on the form, she had answered the question "Why have you chosen to devote yourself to study?" with the words "To live."

• • • •

After Silvia's departure, the others returned to their own solitude, as in the time before they knew each other. Vinca called to tell them she had abandoned Donna Inés's house and was living in a sublet across the Tiber. She left her address, but no one went to see her.

The group crumbled. Everything was different from the year before or only a few days before. The others had departed, died, fled, got married, but only when Silvia left did it all collapse. Augusta isolated herself in her room, caring for the turtle and hating the world that paid no attention to her novels, and Valentina was a hysteric, Emanuela thought. Besides, she herself would stay no more than a couple of months, until her marriage.

She considered that, despite the familiarity produced by years of life in common, they had all remained fundamentally hidden in themselves, and, though believing they were open to the others, each kept something secret, which was, perhaps, the essential. Ephemeral, fortuitous living together wasn't enough to form a community. Silvia used to say, "It takes a mind, a thought, to support many lives together," and she concluded, sarcastically, "Even if that thought isn't enough to support one's own life."

A new intimacy had to be established, on a more profound basis, and, above all, with complete sincerity. For that reason, Emanuela was sometimes tempted to reveal to her friends Stefania's existence.

At night, out of habit, they met in Augusta's room: Valentina opened her books, lazily, then abandoned them to join the others. Augusta criticized Emanuela's coming marriage as a betrayal, and, hoping she would leave Andrea, tried to provoke in her something like remorse.

"You're deserting us. Just now when we would be so comfortable, the three of us alone . . ."

Instead, after those insinuating invitations, Emanuela felt more strongly the desire to abandon them: the Grimaldi for her was a season of youth. Augusta and Valentina, even if they left, would remain there: excluded from life.

"It doesn't change anything. I'll come and see you . . ."

Augusta shook her head: "No, you won't. Besides, it wouldn't be the same. You'd have on an unfamiliar dress, an expression we don't know, problems, friends different from ours. Even your language wouldn't be the jargon that we of literature use here at the Grimaldi. You couldn't wait to leave."

"We'll see each other at my house."

"Worse: we'd be out of place. When we went to see Clara—"

"A girl who left right after I got here and married immediately," Valentina explained, interrupting.

"We didn't know what to say," Augusta continued. "We clutched at memories as if to a life preserver. 'You remember?' we'd say, mentioning events that, at the distance of time, appeared insignificant or even foolish. Then the maid came in with a big silver tray and, in white gloves, served us tea. After all the cabbage soup we'd had together!"

"But we had our revenge," said Valentina, laughing. "We gorged ourselves. Clara was uncomfortable in front of the maid. 'What pigs, so rude!' she must have thought when we left."

"You think it would be the same in my house?" Emanuela asked, offended.

"Yes, apart from the tea. It can't be otherwise," Augusta replied. "Here we're not living in reality."

"We're on a bridge, Silvia said ..."

"Call it what you like. Here we're still looking: looking for our true way of being."

"You think we'll stop looking for it, once we're outside?"

"No, but here we have the illusion of not searching alone."

"The illusion ..." Emanuela emphasized.

"It's just enough. Sharing the same illusion is, in the end, the only solid bond."

Emanuela took her head in her hands. "I think that at a certain point you have to stop searching and accept yourself. Find the courage not to count on others anymore, to separate from childhood even at the cost of solitude."

"It's all a matter of courage, in life. If you have it, you do well to leave," Augusta murmured, tapping the ashes from her cigarette.

Her gestures became less feminine every day. She had puffy bags like a weight under her eyes, from lack of sleep. The new novel had also been rejected: she had put it back in the drawer without saying anything more about it and started another.

She drank to write; or maybe writing was nothing but an excuse to drink. She hid the wine behind the night table under which Margherita slept. The room was saturated with a stench that seemed to emanate from her skin. Her friends pretended not to notice; the nuns tolerated it because Augusta was reasonably well provided with money and sometimes hinted at staying at the institute forever. Sister Prudenzina, opening the door before turning out the lights, always said: "Good girls . . ." and looked into the other rooms with a severe expression. The new arrivals weren't noisy but were more difficult than the old. Especially a group that formed around a Swedish girl named Ingrid who was studying both law and philosophy.

One day, Ingrid said to Emanuela: "Why do you hang around with those two?" In fact, between Augusta and Valentina, Emanuela was beginning to feel uneasy. She reassured herself, thinking: "I won't end up like them." Getting away from those walls arm in arm with Andrea was a relief.

Now it had been decided that they would get married in a couple of months. The parents were pleased, everyone was pleased, there was no longer anything to overcome, no difficulty. Usually they met at five. As she came out, she'd see him standing at the corner and already knew what he would say. He didn't present risks or surprises, he never had an unpredictable comment, a small vein of madness. If, excited by the outside air, by the new season, she smiled, looking around, Andrea would ask: "Why are you smiling? What are you looking at?" He was a little boring, in other words.

In the morning, while he was studying, Emanuela went out alone; most of the time she took a taxi and went to Monte Mario to see Stefania for a moment, during her recess. That sullen, sour child was the only person she felt close to. And not because she had produced her; on the contrary, because their relationship was concealed, secret, because seeing her was a risk that rescued her from the monotony of the meetings with her fiancé.

Sometimes she wondered if she really intended to marry Andrea; or if, from the start, she hadn't thought about it at all. Stefano yes. But with Stefano she felt free. They were two free creatures: their love was a danger to confront together as he confronted, alone, the danger of the sky. Andrea had a mania for plans that excluded the pleasure of the unpredictable, of what might happen despite our wishes.

She was tempted to tell him about Stefania, to throw a stone into the pond. But that silence represented the only attraction she still found in their love. She was sure that, knowing the truth, Andrea would accept it and would start loving Stefania like a daughter. If not, there would be scenes, dramas, a series of unpleasant encounters. Emanuela was too lazy to face that. Besides, by waiting for the right moment to speak, she had seen that, after all, it could go on even like this. Now there was no longer her father to push her: she was free to decide; and she had decided to be silent.

She didn't know herself why, suddenly, she changed her mind. "I have to see you, yes, this morning. I have to talk to you," she said on the telephone. Afterward, she regretted it; to have waited so long, hidden everything so carefully, and then say on the phone one ordinary morning: "I have to talk to you. It's something serious." She couldn't retreat now. But, coming out of the Grimaldi, Emanuela said to herself: "Who can stop me from talking to him about something else, something inconsequential?"

The weather had changed: a threatening black cloud, driven by a stubborn wind, had vanished, and the sky was shining blue amid the trees, the cupolas, the old pink and yellow buildings, the blood-red walls.

There was no doubt: it was spring now. The season, advancing after a series of gray, uncertain days, had suddenly burst forth. Emanuela had called Andrea: "Let's go out this morning?" although she knew he always studied in the morning. In fact he answered: "Impossible." At five they were going to see an apartment whose address he had in his pocket.

"I should also study this afternoon, but it's an occasion." "An occasion more important than spring?" He answered, laughing: "I'm a practical man." Emanuela then changed her tone: "Andrea, spring was an excuse. I have to talk to you." At first it had been only a whim, a means of getting her way. She could tell him she'd used that stratagem to persuade him to go out. Andrea would be angry, he would say: "You're wasting my time." He was a born businessman, hardly a poet. Every hour, every day had its price, bore its tag.

Emanuela started walking up the street that led to the Pincio; she felt sure of herself, maybe it depended on moving one foot after the other, on the looseness of her limbs. She was wearing a new dress, but these days clothes no longer gave her confidence. "It looks good," Andrea said, and that was all. In the blink of an eye the new dress became an old dress.

The trees along the avenue were all illuminated by new leaves. The sun lay on the roofs of the buildings, on the streets, made the window-panes go phosphorescent. It took a lot of courage to talk to Andrea on a morning like this. Why today, she wondered. Maybe the idea of finding an apartment had decided her. She concluded finally that the new season had got her into this mess; she couldn't enjoy it, always having to return at the same time, depressed by the evening that awaited her with Valentina and Augusta. She wanted to leave the Grimaldi, otherwise she, too, would start drinking, out of desperation. Marriage was a way of leaving; she had only to be patient for two more months. But the life that Andrea promised her was another prison. He at the store, she at home with the maid, the mother-in-law who would come to visit, bringing her knitting. Christmas and Easter in the Lanziani house with the tolling of the pendulum. After dinner, father and son would play cards.

Andrea didn't like traveling. Theater, movies: not much. He didn't have friends. "Telling him, after so many months, would be a blow too strong. I don't have the heart to witness that. I'll run away, leaving him a letter: in these situations, letters are a great solution. As for this morning, I'll find an excuse."

Sitting on the bench she tried in vain to invent a story. Under that sky, that sun, Emanuela felt like a tree, a rock: without past and without memory.

· · · ·

Andrea sat down next to her, took her hand, and immediately asked, "What is it, Nuela?"

"What do you mean, what is it?"

"What did you want to tell me, what happened?"

Before answering, Emanuela looked at him: at the thought that she might not see him anymore, her heart contracted. Yet her fear seemed excessive: there would be a fight, then Andrea would give in.

"Do you love me?" she asked.

"I adore you," he said absently. "And so?"

Emanuela shrugged. "Distant things," she said. (At the same time she thought: "What a stupid way to start.")

"Tell me," Andrea insisted. "You're making me nervous . . ."

(Impossible to say that her mother was ill. How would she have been able to joke on the telephone? And why make a mystery of it? A matter of money, someone was blackmailing her. But who? Why? Everything was crumbling around her.)

"Tell me," Andrea repeated.

It was as if only then did she understand the seriousness of what she had been silent about. "It's something terrible," she said, moving away, frightened.

Andrea turned pale and took her arm.

"Tell me!"

(The sun, the people passing, the children playing: "If I could at least faint," she thought.)

"There's something I've never told you," she began in a near-whisper. Andrea was on the defensive. ("Now he'll hit me.") "Something huge." Her heart was racing, as if it would burst. "I've always concealed the fact that I have a child."

"What are you talking about?!"

She continued, staring: "Yes, a child . . . She's five. Don't go, Andrea, please, listen . . ."

. . . .

Andrea listened, impassive. "Tell me," he urged her, every time she stopped talking. "Go on."

"Something in the past, no one knows anything, I myself don't re-member anymore . . . Then he died. He was an officer pilot. Papa wanted me to hide everything, but I wanted to acknowledge the child. It was a drama. You understand, right? You're intelligent . . . Is it my fault? I was so young, a child myself. Listen to me, Andrea . . ."

And he listened, or, rather, he demanded, biting: "I want to know ev-erything."

"One day while I was waiting for him, he crashed, the plane went up in flames. He didn't know about the child, I didn't even know. Everything happened without my wanting it. Without realizing what I was doing . . ."

Andrea was pale: "But you loved him. Tell the truth." ("Now he'll kill me, throw me off the wall.")

"No, I didn't even love him. I've loved only you, I swear. I didn't love him."

Jumping to his feet, he said: "How disgusting!" He turned his back and walked away. Emanuela followed him whispering: "Andrea . . . Andrea . . ." But Andrea walked rapidly, without even turning to look at her.

. . . .

In the afternoon, at the Grimaldi, the girls go out, go to classes, or study in their rooms, getting cold. Every so often a bell rings, insistent, the

monotonous voice of a lay sister calls: "Thirty-five, telephone!" You hear
doors open, footsteps, voices in the corridor, on the stairs. Then again the
bell: "Eighty-four, intercity call!"

Emanuela, lying on her bed, in the dark, strains her ears. Twenty-eight
is never called. "What time is it? It must be late, it's already dark." Finally
the bell chimes three times, summoning the girls to dinner. They rush
down, they're always hungry.

In the refectory, after the hurried murmur of prayers, a hundred chairs
are shifted, two hundred forks and knives meet on the plates, water and
wine are poured in two hundred glasses. The voices would be raised but
the whispered shush of the sister is like a gag.

"What's wrong, Emanuela, you're not eating?"

"I have a headache."

"Eat, you'll see, it will pass."

"I'm not hungry."

The refectory smells of oranges: the girls rise, veil their heads, line up,
enter the chapel.

Outside people go to and fro in front of the great gray building: four
windows in a row on the ground floor let in a warm light and a low murmur that, gradually, fades, disappears. The Amen is a note held with the
pedal.

"I have a pill, you want it?" Valentina whispers to Emanuela.

"No, thanks. I'm going to bed."

The night is endless. Only the tolling of the bell, every quarter of an
hour, shakes the silence: "If I count, maybe I'll sleep. One two three four
five . . . a hundred and ninety-nine ninety-eight." Sleep doesn't come. She
hears again that voice, sees again the sneer of revulsion. The darkness
seems to swirl around her ("At last I'll faint") and instead she drops into
sleep.

Andrea enters and tears off her nightgown, shouting again: "How disgusting!" She entreats him: "Quiet, Andrea, for goodness' sake! They'll

wake up, they'll understand ..." Already steps can be heard in the hall: the nuns and her friends come running in their nightgowns, white as ghosts. She struggles, she wants to flee, but Andrea holds her by the arm, shows her, half-naked, to her companions: "Look at what she really is!" They all stare at her, indignant, all repeat: "How disgusting!" A deafening noise, a din, that wakes her.

Emanuela starts again: "One two three ... a hundred and ninety-nine ninety-eight ..."

· · · ·

"I couldn't sleep, either," said Andrea, then he broke off, seeing the waiter approach, and ordered: "Two beers."

Emanuela stared at the red-and-blue checked tablecloth on the table, right at the spot where it was stained with rust. They had often come to this *birreria*: in the garden, in summer, groups of ruddy, playful priests gathered, talking loudly in German.

"It would be easier to forgive you," said Andrea, resuming the interrupted conversation. "I didn't sleep precisely in order to convince myself that to forgive you is impossible. I know that tomorrow, when I realize it's truly over, I'll go mad. Tonight I knew that I would see you again, to explain. It was as if it weren't completely over. But soon, in an hour ... No, just as you are I don't love you: the Emanuela I loved if she had gone to bed with someone would have done it out of love. But you didn't love him, you said. You did it to know what it was, no? A kind of woman I hate ... What's the child's name? Stefania? She's at a boarding school, right? I understand that you don't even love her. No one ... No, please, don't tell more lies. Why should I let you speak? To what purpose? I no longer believe you. And when did you go to see Stefania? ... Oh, Sundays. And where did I think you were? Every time a different excuse, very good. Maybe, later, you would do the same to go to a man ... But yes! To know the taste of betrayal, to resolve another curiosity. And yet, you see, today I had the absurd hope of hearing you say: 'It's not true, none of it's true,' I hoped to be able to see you still as I did yesterday morning, before you told me everything." He paused, then continued: "Why did you speak? I wouldn't have noticed, the wedding night: you're skillful enough and I'm very trusting. I would have been happy. I would have had a completely invented wife, completely different from reality: a complete lie. But I wouldn't have known."

Andrea continued like that, to wound himself. Emanuela took refuge in tears: things were always presented to her in a difficult and dramatic way. What could she do? Maybe she should have thrown herself into the Arno when the child was born inside her. Not even money was of any use. She would have liked this conversation to be over: Why was Andrea talking so much if he wanted to end it?

"You must have thought I was very naïve, with my wish not to touch you. I remember some absent looks you had, when I referred to our future: you smiled and nodded, as if to soothe a child. Tonight I wondered if I, too, in some way, had lied to you." He shook his head: "I was honest from the first moment, I didn't even pretend to be better, to please you, I showed that I was nervous, impatient, even harsh. The only thing I hid from you is that I've had, in passing, some women. Women never seen before, as one takes an aspirin for a headache. But, returning to my room and seeing your photograph—your childlike smile, your steady, confident expression—I was horrified. The men of today are the way women should be, they believe in feelings that you no longer believe in. You never understood how much I loved you ... What a fool I was!"

Emanuela could only repeat: "I was afraid of losing you," because every so often she had to say something; but in her heart she was alienated by what he was saying.

"It's not true. You couldn't be afraid of that, because you didn't love me," Andrea protested. "Maybe you loved me in your way: that is, a way that wasn't love but a game, something ordinary. Otherwise, you would have preferred to lose me rather than go on like this."

Now it was dark: through the windows of the *birreria*, which looked onto Piazza San Pietro, trams were visible, passing by with their head-lights on. Emanuela couldn't bear that implacable voice any longer; she would have liked to cry, "Enough, that's enough!," fold her arms on the table, put her head down, and sleep.

"You know what? In the end I was glad you didn't come to the first appointment, near the fountain of Moses," Andrea said. (And she thought: "Good Lord, now he's starting again, starting from the beginning!") "It was like the proof that you were different from the others, that you had a different way of behaving. ("Also moralist, conformist, but above all bor-ing.") "Then there was Milly's funeral ... Did Milly know?"

"No."

"No one," Andrea concluded with a smile. "You let me love someone else, Milly loved someone else, your friends put faith in someone else ... Why did you speak? That I can't forgive: you had been silent until now, you should have been silent to the end. I could have ..."

"Listen to me, Andrea: you could ..."

"No," Andrea interrupted her, shaking his head. "Neither you nor I can do anything now."

· · · ·

Emanuela stayed in bed for two days, in the dark. The nuns and her friends came to see her: "Do you have a fever? Headache? Sore throat?"

She always answered: "I'm tired."

The nuns urged her to sleep and entreated Augusta and Valentina not to disturb her.

"It's nervous exhaustion," they said. "The sudden death of her father, on the eve of her wedding ... Certain blows we feel only over time."

But Emanuela wasn't sleeping, she was thinking about Andrea: about the home they could have had, the security he would have offered her. All that had distanced her from him became desirable: she regretted even the afternoons when she sat knitting with Signora Lanziani. And hearing in her memory the pendulum striking, she felt a painful spasm in her chest.

Andrea couldn't forgive her for speaking. "You shouldn't say anything," her father had instructed her when the child was born. She would have liked to keep Stefania with her from the first day; but upon learning that that was her intention Papa—who at the time was still president of the bank—had said: "You have no sense of morality."

The sense of morality, therefore, consisted in silence: in keeping others from speaking; that is, in the fear concealed behind apparent strength. At a distance of years, Emanuela recognized in the silence that burdened the Lanzianis' apartment the silence of her house in Maiano; the home she would have had with Andrea would also have been pervaded by it. The security he offered was that: but perhaps it was rash to despise it.

After Stefano's death, every time a man had shown liking or interest—or had been in love with her—Emanuela immediately rejected him. Her father was pleased, thinking that that first confusion was due to inexperience, and that his daughter, although free, had not had other lovers. In truth, for Emanuela female honor wasn't dependent on sex—which, in any case, was fairly indifferent to her—but, wanting to be loyal to her father, who supported her and supported Stefania, she avoided every occasion, kept everyone away, in order not to be forced to lie. So, eventually, she had remained alone.

At the Grimaldi she had been betrayed by the illusion of a rebirth. She had felt young in a way that she never had been, as the only daughter of old parents who lived like old people. Andrea couldn't understand that she herself, pretending to be something else, believed she was that; she wanted to experience an age that her parents, because of their habits, had cheated her of. Besides, her friends possessed the innocence of those classes that can enjoy themselves with very little; and to her that—that, too—was unknown. Some Sundays they'd go ring the bells of all the villas on the Lungotevere and run away. At night they'd walk around the dark hallways wrapped in sheets, to frighten the nuns; they stuck handfuls of walnuts in Vinca's mattress so that, getting in bed, she cried, "Ow, ow!" while the others, behind the door, laughed and laughed. Andrea had written soon after he met her, making a date on the Pincio; and now he confessed that, when she didn't appear, instead of being disappointed he was glad. The same would have happened if he had asked insistently for the famous "proof of love" and she had resisted. Yet that way of acting, and the principles that determined it, weren't considered dishonorable, they weren't equivalent to a deception. Stefano, on the other hand, would never have brought her to the house on Viale dei Colli and then reproached her for going there.

Suddenly, Stefano's face, his footsteps, his gestures returned to mind: usually she drove out the memory because, in the depths of her heart, she felt bitter toward him. The tragedy of his death had been overshadowed by the fear and then the certainty of expecting a child. Now, though, she realized that she had been sincere only in the brief months of their love: with him she had been able to be herself; she hadn't had to hide her character or her ideas or her instincts, by lying (that is, violating morality) to fit in with a morality that had no basis other than the universal dissemination of similar lies, through a vast, entrenched system of personal lies. Stefano had asked her to marry him not to "protect her" but because they were happy together. The child had been born from a spontaneous, disinterested union, a harmonious understanding. Instead she was considered the fruit of sin. A bitter fruit, poisonous in itself. Certainly, the nuns judged it to be such. She had to get her away from the nuns.

"Where do you go, Mamma, when you go home?" Stefania had asked her a few days earlier. "Where's your house?"

She answered: "I don't have one." It was the truth; but, because of her mother's house, the one she would have had with Andrea, her room at the Grimaldi, it seemed to her she was lying. "I don't have one because I'm always traveling," she added.

"Why do you travel?"

"It's not my fault."

(She meant: "I'm not the one who invented this character of the mother without a fixed home, who crosses oceans, travels over continents, having no other shelter than the ship's cabin or the sleeping car.")

"Whose fault is it?"

("Silence is a desert of quicksand, it drags you to the bottom, swallows you, if you don't hold on to the lies.")

"No one's," she answered. "I work."

The child was astonished: "You work?! What work do you do?"

"I travel, just that. I travel for a cosmetics company."

"Then it's the fault of that company. Of that bad company," Stefania declared, frowning.

In her solitude, Emanuela meditated on those words of her daughter's; and on the truth they unconsciously contained. She would repeat them to her when she was grown; but maybe Stefania wouldn't really understand them. As for her, she no longer belonged to any society, from the moment she had spoken—if only to a government official—and, declaring her own name, had taken her daughter from among the innocent to situate her among the guilty. "Society doesn't speak, society is silent," she thought, wondering how she would be able to insert herself into it, where she would go, once she left here.

"Stefano . . ." she murmured, finally crying.

• • • •

"Why are you crying, Emanuela? What's wrong?"

"I don't know."

Valentina had brought her some flowers and was arranging them in a vase. "Why don't you talk, confide in us?"

"It's nothing, really."

"Leave her alone," said Augusta. "Sometimes we cry, like newborns, simply because we're alive."

Two or three dull days passed. Emanuela got up with her head empty; she was weak, she had no desire to live, to resume the habits, the programs she'd been used to for two years.

The new arrivals had invaded the Grimaldi. Timid at first, now they looked insolently at the old girls, imposing their rules. Every year they were more numerous than the preceding year, and therefore stronger, disposed, in the best case, to a condescension veined with sarcasm. Once, returning from the university, Valentina announced: "You know what? They call us 'the old ladies.'"

Although Valentina was nearly their age, the new girls approached only Emanuela. One day Ingrid said to her: "You've finally managed to shake off those two."

In fact Augusta and Valentina no longer sought her out so frequently. Ingrid gave her companions a questioning look, then offered: "You want to come with us?"

Only a few years separated them from the old group of the literature department and from those who had come together, at the same time, in the other departments. Yet it seemed that an entire generation divided them. The new girls all dressed the same way and—because of the similar way they wore their hair—their features appeared taken from the same mold.

Emanuela heard again in her head the invitation Xenia had addressed to her two years before: "Come with us from literature." It was a group held together precisely by the diversity of the girls who made it up: lively and, each in her own way, intelligent, with a marked tendency to argument, to discussion, which, among the "new girls," seemed to have disappeared under a blanket of distrustful indifference. But also among the "new girls" she would have had to construct a nest of lies, and one day, inevitably, cut off her fictitious bond with them.

"Thank you," she refused politely. "We wouldn't have time to get to know each other: I'm leaving in a few days."

But as she spoke, she understood that, on the contrary, she wouldn't leave. She would put it off from year to year and, by putting it off, would remain there. Like Augusta, like the one they all called "the employee," ignorant even of her name. She had gray hair and, introducing herself, said: "I'm a soloist," although all she managed was to accompany some amateur on the piano at charity concerts. (Cloe, on the other hand, had left the Grimaldi without saying goodbye to anyone; and the girls, in the street, cast a proud glance of understanding at the poster for the Teatro dell'Opera where her name appeared among the singers in *La Gioconda*.)

Yes, thought Emanuela, better that way: Stefania in Monte Mario and she at the Grimaldi, like two stateless sisters, without parents. She would have no other homeland than the convent, no other family outside the one where in four years young women become old. She had bought a record player that she played at low volume and locked in the closet when she went out, because the rules prohibited it. The nuns pretended not to see it, as with Augusta's wine.

For more than two weeks she didn't write to her mother; she managed to communicate with her only when their mutual presence awakened in them an ancient animal warmth, when, within the walls of the old house, they found the same words, without depth and without echo, they had used for years. They wouldn't live together now except during the last year: the one when, following customs handed down unrevised, the mother, rather than die under the eyes of the old servant who had always been with her—and who in fact was her only friend—would have to confront that tremendous, ultimate human experience before a young stranger who knew nothing about her, although she was her daughter.

One night, after dinner, Emanuela prepared to write to her about the break with Andrea and her intention to stay at the Grimaldi, when Valentina looked in at the door. Happy to avoid that obligation, she invited her: "Come in."

"No. You have to come up to us."

"Why?"

"Come up, I said," the other repeated and closed the door.

Recently, Valentina had lost her usual, slightly forced cheerfulness; she had become moralistic and her voice had a bitter edge. Her body, with its fleshy curves, had withered. Now she spent much of the day in Augusta's room. Emanuela found them at the table, sitting side by side and reading verses: Augusta's arm resting on the chair surrounded Valentina's shoulders.

"Hello, girls," she said, entering. "What is it?"

The others didn't answer. There was something, though, since they stared at her, frowning, contemptuous.

Emanuela repeated, aggressively: "Can I know what's wrong?"

"You should know," Augusta answered, calm; but her lips were contracted, her gaze sharp as a weapon. She went toward Emanuela slowly, as if she didn't want to dissipate too quickly the rancor that filled her.

Dismayed, Emanuela took a step back. Suddenly Augusta raised her arm and hit her in the face with the back of her hand, as if to whip her. "Thief!" she said in a choked, thick voice, and hit her again.

Emanuela brought her hand to her cheek, her eyes asking Valentina for help, but she didn't move. Her hair pasted by tears to her flushed face, she crumpled onto the bed, without asking for explanations, without even trying to rebel.

"We know everything: Andrea talked to Valentina."

"Fine gentleman, Andrea."

"He wouldn't have said anything," Valentina protested. "But today when he saw me in the department, he turned pale and his eyes were red, because I'm a friend of yours. I led him outside, comforted him, persuaded him to talk."

"You've been here for two years, you know everything about us," Augusta resumed. "We've said things we wouldn't have said if we'd known that you, in exchange, were telling us lies." And incapable of finding a worse insult, she repeated, "Thief! Thief and liar!"

That bleak, hostile voice saturated the air of the room. Emanuela felt that the past and its lies were suffocating her, would end up killing her. "Jump into the Arno," she thought, and not to come out safe and sound as she had imagined when she was expecting Stefania.

"What did you come here for? Silvia asked you that the first night, I remember very clearly. You calmly began to lie: your parents in America and so on."

"It wasn't my fault. Papa wrote to the nuns, arranged it all, and ordered me not to say anything."

"Stop it, Emanuela! You let other people order you only when you want to!"

"Today Andrea wondered why you didn't say anything before?" said Valentina, compassionately.

"To be sure of a way out, obviously!" Augusta answered with a laugh that made her vulgar. "When we did the séance you were about to lose control, but no. Today, after talking to Andrea, you could have been open with us, too. Instead, silence. We understood that between you two it was over and we were ready to welcome you. Right, Valentina?" ("They're only a single person," thought Emanuela.)

"What were you hoping, going on like that?"

"Nothing," Emanuela answered, bewildered. "That's the truth: I never hoped for anything."

"Maybe you had the illusion you'd change," Augusta replied, sarcastic.

"No, why? I've never wanted to change. Maybe, in some moments of emotion, feeling sorry for myself . . . I've never made plans. I wouldn't know how to arrange anything, certainly not a deception. I'm here because I don't want to go back to my mother, I wouldn't know where to settle down, why choose one place rather than another."

Augusta was silent for a moment, examining her. "Going home. It's not possible. But for you it's not possible to stay here, either," she said firmly. "You have to go now."

"Where?" Emanuela asked, bewildered. She continued, observing: "Besides, you have no authority to get rid of me, no authority, above all . . ."

"I think it would be sufficient to talk to the sisters, but I'll never do it, remember that. You have to go yourself. Xenia never came back to the Grimaldi, we have no idea where she ended up. One can't return here, nor can one remain here when . . ."

"When the others know the truth about us?" Emanuela burst out violently. "When, knowing it, they keep us from deluding ourselves on our own account, the way you delude yourself?"

Augusta confessed: "It may be. But the other night you were saying that it's necessary to leave the Grimaldi, where we lose the measure of reality. That, at a certain point, it's necessary to leave childhood. Leave it, then. Besides, why are you afraid? At least you've done something, even without wanting to: your daughter. Something will remain of you. I don't even have that certainty. Rather, to be honest, I know already that I will leave life as one leaves here: without depositing any trace of our passage but a name in the registry. A name that, as soon as we leave, someone crosses out with a stroke of the pen."

The usual voice announcing darkness tore the silence that followed Augusta's last words. Valentina clutched her friend's arm as if she'd received a sudden shock. Meanwhile the door opened: Sister Prudenzina, finding the three girls standing, silent—Emanuela head bowed before the other two as if before a court—was disconcerted and without a word, not even "good night," closed it softly.

The cry "Lights! . . . Lights! . . ." shook the hallways, faded, vanished, then the light went out, obliterating the girls' tense faces.

"The dark . . ." Emanuela murmured while Valentina groped for the lamp.

From the shadows Augusta answered her: "You go, leave. The world is all lit up. What do you care about the darkness that remains here?"

Emanuela covered her face with her hands. Her father was deluded that life could begin again, intact, at the price of a secret, a lie; life goes forward, the past accumulates behind us, the acts, the gestures carried out form a wall, make a dike. Although she was humiliated, shamed, expelled, that was what Emanuela feared. Being unable to halt, to go back, even if she were to do the same things again, as she would have, she who was neither disappointed nor penitent, because she had never hoped for anything, she who had never had the strength to hope. Being unable to stop the river that carries along the hours, the months, the years, and, with them, carries us to the mouth.

In the still tremulous light of the oil lamp, she looked up at her friends. At the Grimaldi one felt sheltered from the current, from floods. Maybe they would say to her "Stay."

But Augusta, already distracted, offered Valentina a cigarette, took one for herself, lighted them; then, filling her friend's glass, handed it to her, saying, "Here, dear." She filled her own to the brim, drank it in one swallow, and filled it again.

"All right, I'm going," Emanuela murmured, looking at them. The other two didn't try to stop her.

· · · ·

After the delayed spring, summer arrived with violence. In May the temperature was unusually high throughout the peninsula.

In the chapel at the Grimaldi it was suffocating at night, since during the month of the Madonna the nuns were lavish with candles. Not a breath of air entered the rooms through the curtains, beyond which the tops of the trees along the avenue leading to the Pincio were motionless. Next to the books on the desks of the girls who were preparing for exams, there was always a handkerchief to dry their sweat: the sound of the water running in the fountain and the scent of the honeysuckle flowering at the Superior's window brought some relief to those whose rooms faced the courtyard. The city was on fire; on the windowsills of Trastevere only basil and geraniums thrived; the Andalusian carnations that Vinca had planted on her balcony hadn't survived.

The highest averages were recorded in Puglia: Anna wrote that the grain was already golden and the harvest would come early; but for the other crops the drought was a disaster and also for her, since the heat increased the discomforts of pregnancy.

In the north, as usual, the sky was gray and the humidity oozed a tepid drizzle that lasted whole days; Milly's grave was mud, covered with weeds. Farther up, in Alto Adige, cloudbursts raged and the streams flooded because of the continuous rain. Xenia regretted building in the mountains: the work was taking forever—with the bad weather the walls never dried—and resolved to buy a house in Portofino the next year: given that there Horsch's friends stayed on their yachts, at anchor, the company was varied, and life amusing. Besides, by the sea there's always a breeze and, no matter how hot it is, you feel it less.

· · · ·

In fact in Naples a breeze was stirring sails and spars when Emanuela arrived at the port. The dusty red velvet of the train seats had been scorching, even though at Mademoiselle's insistence they had traveled early in the morning so that the heat wouldn't exhaust the child. For that reason, arriving ahead of time, they were the first to board: the decks were still deserted. On the gangplank where Emanuela stopped to cool off, a cheerful sparkling wind ruffled her hair and lifted Stefania's pleated skirt, and she laughed as Mademoiselle, hindered by the coat over her arm, struggled to hold on to her straw hat.

As soon as the trunks were settled, Emanuela went back up to the main deck and looked overboard. In the shadow of the ship at anchor, the mirrorlike water was a dense shiny black on which opalescent spots appeared, restless as eyes. Instead of the odor of salt there was the stink of gas.

Embarrassed at having arrived so long before the departure, Emanuela looked around with exaggerated interest, as if she had arrived early on purpose. Sailors and officers hurried back and forth, following unknown occupations and schedules. No one paid attention to her, and she felt uneasy in her solitude, as she had during the first days at the Grimaldi and, she now realized, even sometimes as a child. She turned her gaze to the landscape, to the city dwellings that sloped down to the port, burned and abandoned in their whiteness, and to the motionless trees at the top of the hill. Because of the heat, the air was as if veiled.

Stefania joined her, escaping the governess—who was standing in a shadowed corner with the child's sweater in her hand—and every so often asked: "When are we leaving, Mamma?" as if it were up to her mother to give the signal for departure.

Emanuela said, "Soon, you'll see."

Now other passengers were embarking along the gangplank, followed by baggage swaying on the bent backs of the porters. "My shipmates," thought Emanuela, examining them with benevolent curiosity.

It was one of those cruises organized to entertain people who, having everything, can no longer enjoy anything; but many were there simply to rub elbows with people famous for their wealth, the elegance of their attire, their name, their expensive worldly eccentricities, and the famous clinics where they ended lives packed with names and yet desolate. Almost all the women who boarded were encumbered with boxes of sweets and bouquets half withered by the heat, which gave them a funereal aspect.

Africa, America, Asia: five months of travel. They would leave at the start of summer and return with the first autumnal chill. Departing from Naples, the *Amazonia* would linger in the Mediterranean basin; move along the glamorous coasts of the Middle East; then very slowly cross the ocean, allowing the passengers to be distracted from their (perhaps nonexistent) cares, and, after the vast American bays, the colorful Asian ports, the endless, deserted green African beaches, it would sample winter on the cold shores of the Norwegian fjords before returning to the calm and reassuring waters from which it had sailed.

Emanuela was there by chance. The day after leaving the Grimaldi she had gone to see Vinca, and, walking from Trastevere to the hotel, felt an incurable fracture between herself and the city: she was like a shade returning to the places that had been dear to her in life and no longer roused in her any sensation. In those two years, Emanuela had lived not in Rome but at the Grimaldi. The institute was a city in itself, with its laws and its courts, she considered, remembering the last scene with Augusta and Valentina. She hadn't seen them again. She had left twenty-four hours later on the pretext of a trip to Florence for business having to do with the inheritance, resolving to write later and have them send her luggage. Sister Luisa, going down with her, had asked: "Why don't your friends come to say goodbye?" She said she had already said goodbye (which wasn't true), adding that she hated farewells. "Besides," the nun observed, "the word 'friends' here is only a locution."

On the way back, she remembered that at that very hour the girls were entering the refectory: her place was empty, in fact abolished, and Augusta would be satisfied. It seemed to her that the city, too, was chasing her out: the old cobblestones, hostile to the step, seemed to be shaking her off; the first shutters coming down, with a tug, seemed to deny her any possibility of refuge. These were streets of sumptuous architecture yet, at the same time, they were neglected; in the rigorous design of a palazzo stores overflowing with secondhand goods opened up, and the world of Walt Disney—invading the windows of the pastry shops with huge, shifty-eyed animals and hateful dolls—revealed the prevailing taste. Faced with the empty evening and the others like it that were ahead of her, Emanuela wondered yet again what to do, where to live. However alien—or perhaps because of that—Rome seemed to her the only city, the only world, in which she could find a place for herself.

She walked, worn down by discouragement; men looked at her in a way—typical of the Romans and all men of the South—that was intended to be charming and was, instead, insulting. To escape them, she had stopped in front of the display window of a travel agency where, in succession, gracious Japanese gardens, green shores of the Gold Coast, airy Greek temples shining against the blue, ambiguous faces of Egyptian statues were projected. She was seized by an overwhelming desire to get away from Rome, from that horrible Galleria Colonna, from the slimy looks, the obscene proposals; and, even more, from her life, all splintered by availability, by uncertainty. She leaned her forehead against the window and contemplated the model of the ship, glittering with lights in the portholes and on the decks. "Five months on the *Amazonia*: five months away from daily reality, five happy months," said the ad for the cruise. She felt excluded from all that, like a beggar, when, suddenly, the privileges she hadn't taken into account in the balance of her life came to mind: she was wealthy, free, she could go where she wanted. While she wondered, with anguish, "And Stefania?," she saw a clerk preparing to pull down the shutter.

"Just a moment! I urgently need information about that cruise," she said to the young woman, pointing to the window. "The *Amazonia*? It's pointless. It leaves Wednesday, fully booked," she answered. "There's nothing? Not a single place?" Emanuela insisted. The other shook her head and then, glancing at the simple student's dress Emanuela was wearing, said, "But do you know what it costs?" and threw in her face an exorbitant figure, to confuse her. Emanuela nodded: "All right. As long as there's a cabin." The saleswoman glanced at her watch: "It's seven twenty, and the Navigation Company closes in ten minutes and tomorrow is Saturday . . . I'll try to telephone."

Emanuela had followed the conversation with her heart stopped. "No singles," the saleswoman had said to her, staying on the phone: "Someone has withdrawn, but it's three places: two cabins. There's a client who wants two but in separate cabins. If you take all three . . ." "All three!" Emanuela had repeated. "Yes, otherwise they'll take the other offer." After a slight reflection she decided: "All right. I'll take them." The clerk reported to the receiver, with little conviction. "She says she'll take all three . . ." and then to Emanuela: "You have to pay a third of the figure before closing. That is, now. In five minutes." Glad to be able to satisfy the request, Emanuela dug nervously in her bag. "I think I have the checkbook with me . . . Here it is!" she exclaimed, radiant, like someone who has managed to get hired. Only one check was left: the others had been written to the Grimaldi or the nuns of Monte Mario. The one she wrote to the Navigation Company was much bigger than all the others together.

"Why don't we leave, Mamma?" Stefania repeated, petulant.

"I don't know, Stefania. How would I know?"

A gray-haired woman boarded with two daughters of marriageable age; a third, still adolescent, had a dog on a leash and looked around, intimidated; then she picked up the dog in her arms to find some familiar warmth. Stefania, on the contrary, was always sure of herself, thought Emanuela: in fact she was asking an officer about the departure, and he answered her kindly.

Friday night, coming out of the travel agency, Emanuela had hurried to a bar to telephone the school and had Stefania summoned, despite the rules: "Listen, Stefania, Wednesday we're leaving. I'm taking you with me." But the child said: "I don't want to leave. I have lots of friends here, it's fun." "You'll have more fun on the trip: we're taking a big ship and we'll see parrots, giraffes, and so many other animals." "Monkeys, too? Will you buy me one?" And having obtained the promise Stefania agreed: "Then I'll come." Nothing more. Emanuela, leaving the Grimaldi, was moved; she had said farewell to the stairs, the chapel, the courtyard; her daughter had calmly given her hand to a teacher she didn't know and left the school without turning back.

"That officer said we're leaving now," Stefania announced. "He said it to that sailor," she added, turning to greet the officer familiarly.

At that moment Lady Royl boarded, smiling, as if she were the ship's godmother. The captain went to meet her, kissed her hand, bowing, and thus confirming the reasons she had to be so self-assured. She was dark and tall, at least forty-five; she was dressed in black, and wore a big black hat, and pearls in her ears, pearls around her neck, pearls at her wrists.

Emanuela was annoyed to find herself there, on the side, alone with her child. "I don't know anyone, I'll be bored. Five months! ... Madness." Meanwhile she watched Lady Armilda Royl, who entered a cabin on the bridge.

Stefania asked: "Who is that lady?"

She answered impatiently: "How should I know?"

"Why is she here?" Stefania insisted: she wanted to know the reason for everything. "Does she work, like you?"

"I don't work. I don't work anymore." (Enough lying: she didn't want her daughter to grow up amid lies and silences, as she had.)

"Why are we going, then?"

Emanuela said brutally: "Because we're rich." As if the ship really had been awaiting the arrival of Lady Royl, the siren gave a lacerating shriek. That electric siren was the only thing that evoked the sea, like the secret voice of shells. Or like the nun shouting when, at the Grimaldi, the girls all left together, into the darkness. Emanuela felt her heart beating violently; she would have liked to run to the gangplank, crying, "A moment! Just a moment!," and rush down to the land, gasping, as if she'd escaped a danger. But she remained motionless; no one could have imagined that she had such thoughts. What did the others think, departing? Stefania, excited, was hopping up and down. Slowly the *Amazonia* left the dock. The passengers were all on the bridge, only Lady Royl was missing, too accustomed to departures and separations. No one was moved, even if relatives and friends who had come to see them off waved farewell from the dock. Some took photographs, others filmed the scene with movie cameras. The siren emitted two more grim cries, and the orchestra on board began to play a loud march of the type that in Spain are played at bullfights when the dead bull is carried off. Only the sailors' women and some servants sobbed, accompanying the steamer along the wharf; one girl went as far as the point, and it seemed that—in the desperate attempt to follow—she would throw herself into the sea. On board the passengers drank cocktails and made toasts, dazed by the band music played at full volume to drive out emotion.

Emanuela has no one to wave at her from land: "I wonder what Andrea is doing right now," she thinks, with a tug at her heart. "He doesn't know I'm on a ship, departing . . . nor do my friends . . ."

And yet she seems to see them, she sees them, in a group, on the dock: they've all come to say goodbye. There's Andrea, too, overcome as he was that morning on the Pincio, when she told him everything. There's also Vinca. Emanuela would like to cry: "Wait for me! I'll be back!"—precisely because now she's sure she won't see them again, won't know anything about their lives.

Hearing someone nearby blowing her nose repeatedly, she roused herself: it was the child's governess, who, with that, relieved her desire to cry. She said, apologetically, "A departure is always sad, Madame."

. . . .

The voyage was pleasant and peaceful. On the days when the ship didn't stop at some port, the passengers sat in the sun at the pool in the morning; after lunch rested; and at five had tea on the bridge.

In the best corner of the bridge, in the shelter of a tent, was Lady Royl's table; at that hour, she liked to gather her friends around her, like a small court, and pour the tea herself with the solemnity of a rite. The season was already advanced, and, because of the hot drink, the guests all had red faces. But she maintained: "Tea is thirst-quenching, tea is refreshing even in summer: in the hot countries, I drink only boiling-hot tea." And the others nodded, smiling.

Emanuela appreciated at its proper value the privilege of finding herself in Lady Royl's group. Not that it was fun, but the other passengers looked at them with a mixture of deference and envy, as if they were enjoying a true entertainment, and gradually she herself was convinced of it.

Lady Armilda Royl appeared on the bridge a few minutes before the second lunch seating, and sat at the captain's table. Her clothes were always elegant, rustling. Emanuela would have liked to move the way she did, speak in the same lazy and casual tone. In the first days, not knowing anyone, she walked sadly on the bridge with Stefania, thinking: "No one approaches a woman with a child." But it was precisely because of Stefania that she had met Lady Royl. "That unusual child is yours, right?" she asked, meeting her on the bridge: "I offered her a candy, but she refused very politely, saying: 'We don't know each other, signora, and I can't accept anything from someone I don't know.'" Like that, one word after another, they had begun to walk together; Lady Royl had taken her by the arm with the air of protection she had for everyone. Meanwhile she kept looking at Emanuela, certainly noticing that she was wearing a stylish, expensive dress. She introduced her to her friends, saying only: "She's the mother of that child."

Sybil made room for her on the rocking couch and gave her a toothy smile: she was American but had a Scottish mother; she was nineteen, with red hair, green eyes, and very white, blemished skin. Then, knowing that Emanuela was Italian, she said that once a man had said to her: "You look like Titian's women." "But at the time I didn't know who Titian was," she added, laughing. She was surprised that Emanuela didn't drink: "I had my first whiskey at twelve. I've gone on drinking ever since, to find out if I like it or not."

In the group were two young Englishmen, brothers, who always accompanied Sybil and Lady Armilda; they didn't talk much, but the older, who had bony hands, red at the knuckles, enjoyed telling jokes with an expression so serious and grave that the others were disconcerted for a moment and then collapsed in laughter. A Polish pianist, who didn't speak English, smiled without understanding a thing. Emanuela spoke English and French: for that, too, she was liked.

"Florentine: an adorable creature," Lady Royl explained in a low voice to her friends. Then she asked Emanuela to say her name. "Signora Andori," she repeated, without asking where her husband was. "Signora Andori is very interested in art history," she said to a decrepit Italian duke who had lived on the Côte d'Azur since the end of the First World War, but traveled all year with a lady companion who was a nurse: he got off one ship and a few days later left on another, because—the nurse explained—his parents had opposed his desire to be a sailor. Every so often the duke took a sheet of white paper out of his pocket, which he folded and refolded until it made a boat, and he contemplated it with satisfaction before setting it down wherever he was: on a table, on the floor. Soon he had assembled a real flotilla of white boats. The nurse had the job of following him, preparing the sheets of paper—all cut exactly the same— picking up the boats where he left them, and throwing them away.

Lady Armilda had also secured a tall, blond Anglican priest: Father O'Flynn. "Pastors are very fashionable," she said. "One can't open an English novel without finding one." Father O'Flynn was a handsome man, friendly in company, almost gallant: but he would suddenly leave, to go and sit in isolation on the deck, where he remained for hours staring at a point in space, Bible in hand, without ever opening it. "Who knows what he's thinking: these Irishmen are always a little mad," said Lady Royl.

At night they got together in a small, separate room: they didn't want to mix with the other passengers, considering that the café-society types were too noisy and the others too boring. Sometimes the Pole turned off the light and sat at the piano. Sybil didn't like classical music, but said that knowing was a duty, a must, so she listened seriously, sipping a whiskey. In the dim light from the big windows that were open onto the deck, you could see the white of the boats that the old duke placed delicately on the piano. Emanuela was comfortable, she was happy. Lady Royl had said to her: "Believe me, my dear, no pleasure is worth the pleasure of traveling, knowing countries, works of art, new people, new customs. Besides, it's the only one that endures," she added with a sigh. "In Egypt I'll introduce you to my great friend who lives a few kilometers from Cairo, in a strange, magnificent house. He's a romantic: I'm sure he'll fall in love with you."

Emanuela found that Lady Armilda was right: the world was worth knowing and she was glad she had enough money to know it. Her parents, anchored to provincial life, had been unable to take advantage of what they possessed: she and her daughter would. Wealth protected them. You had to accept the truth, without feeling guilty: some live on their labor, others on their mind, and the most fortunate on their money.

She had to be grateful to Stefania: without the child she would have married Andrea, out of laziness. She would have grown old beside him, among shopkeepers and middle-class professionals: an evening at the movies, then a pizza, and summer in Rimini or Riccione. She shuddered at the idea. And yet after leaving the Grimaldi she'd felt so lost she had even thought of calling him.

She had left the institute a little after sunset, with a suitcase. "To the station," she had said to the driver, since Sister Luisa was there at the door; but as soon as they turned the corner she said, as if to an accomplice: "Listen: I'm not going to the station. I'm going to a hotel." "I understand," he responded, in a tone that made her blush; then, turning, with a sarcastic and obscene smile: "Where to, then? The Excelsior?" Emanuela had stayed at that hotel with her parents when her father came to Rome for the bank and was forced to make those appearances that, in private, he disdained. "The Excelsior, precisely," she had said, getting her revenge. The desk clerk recognized her right away and, as she handed him her passport, asked: "Everything the same? . . . Then thank you: we already have it." Always the same. The same: unmarried, that is. Impossible

THERE'S NO TURNING BACK

to have Stefania at the hotel, Emanuela considered, as she followed the bellboy who was leading her deferentially to her room. It was a lovely, spacious room, the same she had occupied years earlier. After putting away the few things she had brought with her, she sat in an armchair, wondering how she would pass the hours, the days: life. The only person she knew in Rome now was Vinca; and, resolving to go and see her the next day, she had a *caffellatte* for dinner and went to bed.

The building where Vinca lived smelled of fried food; the girl who came to open the door stared on seeing Emanuela, and pointed to a gray door at the end of the hall. Vinca welcomed her with enthusiastic cries of surprise. "Come in, here's my room, it has character, no?"

The room didn't resemble the rest of the place. Luis's drawings were pinned to the walls among some views of Cordova; on the shelf were his books, the architecture treatises; on the table the squares, the rulers, the compasses. "I took everything that was left in the studio. Luis hasn't asked for it and so . . ." The trousers Vinca was wearing and the blue shirt with the sleeves rolled up also belonged to Luis. "I always dress like this—it's more comfortable," she explained; but those masculine garments couldn't destroy the graceful femininity of her appearance, her figure, her gestures. "Sorry, it's a mess in here," she said, confused by her friend's unexpected visit. On a table was a packet of salumi, a baguette, an apple: certainly her evening meal. "You know, I eat here, I work here, and the room is too small: but the owners are good people and I like the neighborhood, I like having so many houses opposite and being able to take part, from a distance, in the life of the people who live there."

Emanuela said: "It's picturesque."

"Yes, poverty is always picturesque," Vinca replied bitterly; then she confessed that at first she had been unable to orient herself. "Or find a job: those were difficult days—I didn't come by because when things are going like that we're afraid of everything, starting with ourselves. But now I can't complain, I have a lot of lessons, yesterday I refused another one.

It's hard when I come home at night. It costs me a lot to turn the switch, light the lamp in this room every evening, as if every evening I had to accept solitude all over again." She didn't mention Luis: but wearing his clothes, living among his things was a way of straining reality, to the point of not knowing whether Luis existed or not, outside of her. She didn't know that Emanuela had left the Grimaldi.

"Yes, you don't know any of it. Andrea . . . well, anyway, it's over. I'm not going to tell you the reason. They'll tell you." Vinca had murmured, "What does the reason matter: it's always something." Emanuela wondered why she'd contemplated this visit for so long, what she expected from Vinca. Their solitudes weren't similar: for example, Emanuela's pleasure, the night before, in falling asleep between pure linen sheets after so long made them totally different. In the morning, opening the window onto Via Veneto, all sunny and green, and, seeing from above the blooming flower beds drawn vividly on the asphalt of the sidewalk, she returned, suddenly, to what she had been before entering the Grimaldi: joyfully she resumed her old, comfortable habits, adapted immediately to a language she hadn't used for two years. At the Grimaldi, Emanuela and Vinca were equal; in a few hours the abyss had been dug between them that divides the solitude of the poor from that of the rich. "And Sister Lorenza?" Vinca wanted to know. "No one has seen her. She's always locked in her room, like the old Abbess, waiting for her turn to go to Genoa to die." "You don't think we're all, basically, waiting only for that?" Vinca suggested.

But she rebelled. "What do you mean? At our age? If I died today I would have the impression that I'd lived a few seconds. I'm afraid of death," she confessed.

Vinca said, "Not me. But luckily I'm not afraid now of life. That's important."

At the Grimaldi Emanuela hadn't felt sure of herself, either: it seemed to her that she was always last, because she hadn't finished her studies. On the *Amazonia*, among those people who a few days before had been strangers, in that continuous renewing of panoramas, Emanuela had found a way of life she liked. "The important thing is to know oneself: to know one's own character, tendencies, aspirations," Silvia said. Silvia didn't wash often, she wasn't pretty, but what she said was always true, even if it was often unpleasant.

After the last chord, the pianist sat with his eyes closed, hands abandoned on the keyboard, head fallen on his chest. ("The Poles are a little crazy, too," thought Emanuela. "But what does crazy mean?") A light breeze moved through the little fleet of perfect, identical white boats: they quivered, were pushed, advanced: some were shipwrecked, reflected in the shiny black of the piano.

· · · ·

"Sybil has gone too far," said Lady Royl, the day after they stopped in Istanbul, "but Americans are like that, you have to take them or leave them." And she took her because Sybil was the daughter of certain very important copper mines.

In Istanbul, Emanuela had disembarked with Lady Armilda, Sybil, the two young Englishmen, and the Pole. Sybil drained one glass after another and at the same time stuffed herself with sickly-sweet Turkish delight.

At the restaurant she had started singing, had continued in the street, and in the launch that carried them back on board. Emanuela had never seen a woman drunk: she was repulsed and at the same time attracted by that gaze lost in an expression of animal-like bliss.

"She went too far, yes, but it was very amusing. The Americans are young, they don't know how to control themselves—Sybil is a child—they drink out of bravado or to keep up their courage," Lady Royl continued. "Or, naturally, for other reasons that it's not appropriate to investigate."

They were walking on the bridge; Lady Armilda leaned on her, assuming, as if coquettishly, the rights of her age. Emanuela felt against her arm that too smooth skin, to which the pearls gave iridescence, and which always smelled of lemon.

"Take the two Morton brothers, for example. Each sees his own boredom reflected in the face of the other. They have a castle near mine, in England. Come and see me sometime: we'll organize a hunt, you ride, no? I thought so. Why don't you come this fall, for instance? When the cruise is over I'll go to England to rest: I like traveling, but it tires me. Afterward, I do my penance: I spend hours and hours lying down reading. Nowhere does one read better than in the English countryside. In Sweden, perhaps: there the days are shorter and even more boring ... Come: we'll have fun. I'll be there until it's too cold or too damp; then I begin to follow the sun. But at Christmas the Côte d'Azur is impossible, Sicily is full of Milanese. If you come, we can go and spend Christmas in Morocco. You won't want to make the child endure all that wind in Florence in December. Settled, then?"

Emanuela, tempted, said: "Why not?" Immediately Stefania came to mind: "And?" She would take her with her, she would have her learn English. Besides, now that she had told her the truth ("You're a big girl now, Stefania: you should know that your father is no longer here, he's dead") she didn't want to leave her in boarding school, like an orphan. Here no one asked questions about her private life: not if she was married or where she came from or where she would go once she got off the boat. In the same way no one would be able to say who precisely Lady Royl was or why the American girl, at the age of nineteen, was traveling alone and drinking to excess: and, even less, the reason the pastor was staying away from his flock for five months. He said he had undertaken the cruise to recover from a severe nervous breakdown; but maybe, once he left the *Amazonia*, he would go to the mountains and say the same thing. Maybe he wasn't a real pastor and used that disguise to keep people at a certain distance. But, even if true, no one would reproach him for it. He must have his reasons, Lady Royl would have said, thinking that each has his own and doesn't have to share them with anyone.

Changing the subject in her flighty way, Lady Armilda said: "I'd like to play a little bridge tonight. One of the Mortons plays quite well: naturally, he lacks boldness . . . Then you, me . . . To make the fourth we could invite that officer, what's his name? . . . Venier. He must be one of the Veniers of Venice, the line of the doge. He's likable, he's a gentleman—it's difficult to find a man like that in the navy these days. In the merchant marine, then . . . Let's say Venier. Venier will do very well. He's courting you, it seems to me . . ."

· · · ·

Only a little bridge tonight, Lady Royl had said. "Sometimes one has to go to bed early. Tomorrow we'll be in Alexandria and from there we go to Cairo: who knows what sort of welcome that friend of mine is preparing for us. I'm always in a good mood when I get off a boat in Egypt."

Sybil was at the bar with two American students; every night they played dice until dawn (very amusing, Sybil), and the four of them were in the small salon, with the light falling over the table. Every so often a passenger opened the door, to see what was going on in there, but a look from Lady Royl froze him.

The old duke sat beside a porthole with the other Morton and the pastor: they were discussing politics with long, silent pauses during which the old man took out a sheet of paper and began to fold it, looking at the ceiling, dubious about the fate of the world.

Shreds of their conversation reached the four players. "And China? What will old China do?" The Englishman shook his head, puzzled, and the duke, not knowing where to put the boat he had in his hands, slid it through the porthole into the sea. Then, relieved, he stared at the pastor, waiting for him to provide an illuminating interpretation of the future. But Father O'Flynn said nothing.

At the card table, Emanuela was sitting opposite Venier; every so often, pretending to look at the cards, she looked furtively at him: "He's courting you." Not exactly: he had only reproached her for disembarking in Istanbul with Lady Royl and the others even though he had offered to go with her. "Why didn't you come with me? I would have shown you an Istanbul that no one else knows. Besides, each has his own way of looking at a city: of interpreting it, I would say. To some, a city can deny itself, make itself indecipherable. We missed Greece, a pity, and also Turkey. Let's be sure not to miss Cairo," he had said with a long look. "Or the next one."

It was hot: the whirring blades of the fan disturbed the silence without providing any coolness. And although it was inaudible, the deep breathing of the engines could be perceived from some creaking of the wood, the sweaty air.

"Three hands, a hundred and fifty points under," said Lady Royl, noting: "Your deal, Venier." And then, carelessly: "The Veniers of Venice, right?"

He nodded, dealing the cards: "Yes"—one two three four—"my family is from Venice: as for me, in this career one leaves home at sixteen, enters the Academy, and from that moment no more home, no more family. After so many journeys, so many departures, so many landings, stops, passengers on board, friends in the ports, amid so many different languages . . . in the end one no longer belongs to any country. In reality"—one two three four—"our true homeland is the bridge."

Having dealt the cards, Venier took his and looked at them. ("Silvia always said something about a bridge, but what? I can't remember anymore.") He resumed: "Every time, there's the enthusiasm of leaving, of starting again. I've been traveling for so many years, and, every time, when I hear the siren, my heart pounds."

"You too?" Emanuela asked, surprised.

"Every time it's as if I were leaving for the first time. In fact I delude myself that it really is the first."

"And on your return?" Emanuela asked.

"Yes, well, on my return I feel I have one more journey behind me, and that the years are passing."

Lady Armilda, having finished her drink, lighted a cigarette and fanned open her cards. The others imitated her.

"Two hearts."

"Two spades."

The old duke continued to slide boats down through the porthole; and then he brought his head to the opening, as if to follow them on their journey. Dense spirals of smoke rose from young Morton's pipe, and Father O'Flynn stared into space, silently.

Lady Armilda is right: you have to sleep every so often, but it's fun to just sit here playing, with a glass of cognac at hand. Cognac with seltzer. Because she's been drinking it, she likes it.

"Four spades."

"Double."

"All right."

It's Venier who's playing: of the Veniers of Venice, of the doge. Lady Royl is right: hard to find a man like that today.

"They're in four spades, then."

ABOUT THE AUTHOR

Alba de Céspedes was born in Rome in 1911. Her father was a Cuban diplomat, her mother was Roman; her grandfather Carlos Manuel de Céspedes led the Cuban revolt for independence from Spain and was the first president of Cuba. She published her first story in 1934, which led to her contributing stories and articles to various publications. The following year she published her first book, a collection of stories, *L'anima degli altri* (The Soul of Others), and in 1938 her first full-length novel, *There's No Turning Back.* When the Germans occupied Rome in September 1943 she fled, and eventually reached Bari, where she broadcast for Partisan Radio Bari. She returned to Rome in 1944 and started a magazine, *Mercurio*, which published most of the great writers of the day, Italian and international. Her next novel, *Her Side of the Story*, came out in 1949, and was followed by *Forbidden Notebook* in 1952. She went on to publish other novels, and also wrote for the cinema, theater, radio, and television. In the late 1960s she moved to Paris, and died there in 1997.

ABOUT THE TRANSLATOR

Ann Goldstein is a former editor at *The New Yorker.* She has translated works by, among others, Elena Ferrante, Pier Paolo Pasolini, and Elsa Morante, and is the editor of the *Complete Works of Primo Levi* in English. She has been the recipient of a Guggenheim Fellowship and awards from the Italian Ministry of Foreign Affairs and the American Academy of Arts and Letters. She lives in New York.